GROUND LINES

Matthew J. Cooper

Lulu Publishing Services rev. date: 1/25/2016

To Ivy, and Mary, and Paulie

For Pop, and Mom

And for my students (most of them)

for EJM

But it is the same land.
And I begin to know the map
And to get my bearings.

Eric Van Der Meyer had just finished stapling another McDonald's application to the last page of one of his student's essays when he heard several muted, evenly paced knuckle-raps on the door leading to the English department core, capped by a louder, popping finale. Midway through a punishing pile of *Turn of the Screw* papers, he welcomed this unlooked-for opportunity to stray from his marking labors. Gazing upward and back over his left shoulder, he softly grumbled, "C'min!" and spun his seat in a slow arc in order to greet the knocker.

Lt. Gus Gurney leaned into the classroom, supporting himself on the oversized metal door handle as he peered in. Van Der Meyer could see only the profile of the man's head, held steady and uncertain, the rest of his body hidden by the angled, protruding door. Whoever he was, he appeared to be having difficulty adjusting his vision from the obscuring dimness of the core to the brightly illuminated confines of room 34.

Van Der Meyer took the lead.

"How can I help you?"

The police officer squinted to his left in the direction of the seated voice, smiled weakly, and nodded his head in greeting. Stepping further into the classroom, Gurney pivoted around the door's edge, and immediately began to push back on the handle, tilting once again. The industrial-grade door closer would have none of it. Indifferent to any sort of human persuasion, it flaunted yet again its obstinate resistant power, emitting, as it ever did, a barely audible hiss with each impertinent shove.

From his chair, Van Der Meyer, who had witnessed the door go through its implacable circuit innumerable times, made a fleeting attempt to intervene ("You don't have to push the . . . it'll clo—"), only to lean further back in patient expectation. Evidently, the visitor had a firm determination to see to it that the door did not remain ajar, and Van Der Meyer could think of no good reason to play the spoiler.

Task completed, Gurney turned once more and repeated his nod to the teacher. "Mr. Van Der Meyer?"

"Yes."

The newcomer produced a St. Louis Police badge. "I'm Lt. Gurney. May I ask you a few questions?"

The normally stolid English teacher hesitated, creaked forward in his chair to get a clearer glimpse of the badge, before eventually nodding his head. "Of course."

Pulling a red "Class Record Book" from his briefcase, Gurney turned to the single page that held any interest for him. Van Der Meyer instantly recognized the handwriting.

"Do you remember a student from last year named Ellis Mulnay?"

Van Der Meyer rocked lightly in his chair. "Yes."

"He was in your fifth-hour class last year?"

Van Der Meyer maintained a carefully modulated back and forth motion, peering up and down the class roster.

"You didn't mark him absent on May 5th?"

Van Der Meyer snorted and leaned back abruptly in his chair, whose aging workings obliged by emitting a grinding metallic squawk. "I don't know." Each syllable received an equal emphasis.

He eyed the lieutenant and smiled, spinning once again in a slow arc. "What's it say?"

"You didn't. And we think he was."

Applying the heel edges of his shoes to the tiled floor, the teacher gently put the brakes on his turning seat. He squinted pensively, looked up and down the line of the 5/5 column, and shook his head. He returned his attention to Gurney. "What d'you want me to do?" He smiled briefly, letting out a short, clicking exhalation and rocking back once more. "What *can* I do?" He lifted both of his thick hands from the chair's arms before returning them to the worn leather surfaces.

"We'd like to have Mulnay absent on that day. It's important."

"Why?" But now a sudden burst before Gurney had time to respond: "Wait. Did you check—"

"The Student Information System? Yes," he self-responded. "We did. We did." Gurney gazed about the room. "More than once." Tables were arranged in three jagged arcs, first three, then five, then seven. Chairs had been positioned for students entering from the opposite door. "And he's not marked absent for fifth hour." The squat detective continued to scan the classroom for a convenient place to sit down. Van Der Meyer, comfortably ensconced in his own seat, joined the search for another nearby chair. Just as the cop appeared to be giving up hope that he would be taking a load off anytime soon, the teacher swung back to his left, eyeing a dingy molded-plastic chair stationed in the corner, facing the rear wall and only inches from it. The seat of the chair balanced at a steep angle three lengthy lightwood broadswords, worn points down, hilts leaning against the wall. Regrettably, each one of the decidedly non-menacing weapons had long since surrendered whatever "Elizabethan" pretensions it may once have held. Taken as a whole, moreover, the peculiar combination of elements all but begged for a resolution to urgent aesthetic questions. *Contemporary art installation? Subversive Dadaist masterpiece? Or was it merely Van Der Meyer's sly modernist tribute to the dunce genre?* No matter. Not wasting a single moment on such rarefied speculations, Van Der Meyer seized one of the chair's legs, holding it aloft and steady as he spun back around, paying no heed whatsoever to the ensuing disarray. Scarred wooden blades clacked to the tile, like broken spokes to a wheel that had gone missing ages ago.

"Forgot this was back here," he explained as he skated the chair in the lieutenant's direction. "Never use it."

Gurney, whose eyes still seemed to be making adjustments, lowered himself gratefully. Index finger and thumb were engaged in gentle eye massage, interspersed by a couple of exaggerated eyelid stretches. He appeared to relent a bit. "Got a dead kid. Seventeen. Maybe sixteen. Killed last spring."

Van Der Meyer said nothing.

"Shot on May 5th. Just after one in the afternoon." Gurney leaned forward in his chair in order to withdraw a handkerchief from the rear right pocket of his pants. Van Der Meyer mutely observed that the crumpled cloth had long since passed even the most forgiving recommended due date for a Tide-job. The cop blew his nose repeatedly but lifelessly, re-crumpling the cloth twice in the process. Leaning forward once again, he returned the rag to its cell, never once looking at it. He leaned back in the plastic chair. "In the city."

Van Der Meyer waited for more.

"We know Mulnay shot him." Gurney breathed in deeply and exhaled slowly, his left elbow resting on a corner of the teacher's desk. He carefully positioned a finger next to an empty square.

Van Der Meyer gazed at the unmarked space. His eyes then wandered back to the edge of the Record Book's margin, raking the column of alphabetized names for some sort of assistance, some kind of explanation.

"You didn't mark him absent."

*   *   *

On a very cold January 1st, a date Morton Caper's grandmother still occasionally referred to as the "Feast of the Circumcision," a metallic green Buick Le Sabre drove north towards the heart of Pittsburgh. The car washes dotting the road into the city were closed for the holiday, a fact that would render absolutely certain something that was quite likely in any case—namely, that the sedan would continue to abide a quite visible layer of dried mud, as well as a somewhat thinner layer of road-salt residue. Morton, his grandmother, and his father were headed to Mass at St. Mary's at the Point, and thence to the Fulton Newsstand on Stanwix Street, where his father would purchase the New York edition of *The New York Times*. He did this regularly, and for one reason: to read (aloud, circumstances permitting) the Society page. The marriage announcements and their attendant articles filled him with great mirth, especially the fastidious care with which family partnerships were traced and celebrated, like an unusually ornate recipe. Somehow, laughing at a distant world of financial alliances made between the Von Such-and-suches and the de Moneyeds provided an outlet for something that

4

puzzled and intrigued and amused him. And you could only read the announcements in the actual New York paper.

On KDKA, the announcer interrupted whatever New Year's Day program was in progress to deliver the dreadful news that Roberto Clemente had perished in a plane crash the night before.

"Charles," his grandmother asked. "Is that true?"

"Must be. Wouldn't say so otherwise."

They continued to drive north on 19.

"Is it true?"

"Must be. It's on the radio."

They went to Mass downtown. Numbed, Morton submitted to the familiar regimen of standing and kneeling and sitting, not knowing what to think or how to feel. Nothing said or done in the course of the service could possibly hope to address the incomprehensible New Year's disappearance.

After picking up the *Times* (which, of course, had been printed far too early to carry any of the plane crash news), the Capers began the winding trip south, back towards Mt. Lebanon.

In the ensuing weeks and months, Morton would think a great deal about plane crashes, dwelling especially on the fact that they happened very suddenly. Quick life brought to a very quick end. But then again, the plane's occupants would also often be granted more than enough time to contemplate their impending ruin. Clemente would have. His plane had failed over the sea. In one discussion Mort had had with his father, the latter remarked how the water may as well have been concrete. That stuck with him. It was as if the speed of the rapidly falling object changed the substance of the patiently waiting sea. The plane had been received, violently, and had disappeared. It was now under ocean water, but would still be there. Scattered, but partly there. The food on board the plane (probably too much of it loaded onto the old DC7, it was later observed) as well as the occupants, would become in one fashion or another food for the ocean.

On the northern cusp of the city's snaky southern border, they ate brunch somberly at the Redwood Motel on that New Year's morning, listening to the urgent but hushed conversations of other diners, all of whom had heard but not yet read the appalling news.

Back in the Buick, whose exterior had a fresh spray of road salt behind all four wheels, they set out on the final leg of the circuit, black-tipped snow and ice attending them the whole way home.

* * *

Split lunch, Van Der Meyer thought. *Split fucking lunch.*

"The sixth and seventh hours are marked 'absent.' Kid was killed at 1:05 in the afternoon. We've checked. That's sixth." Gurney had the demeanor of a person who had done his homework, complacency and accusation equally apportioned.

"I know," Van Der Meyer said.

"He had to miss your fifth, too. North city's about 25 minutes."

"I know."

"What do you mean, you 'know'?"

"I know where north city is," the teacher explained to the cop. "And we've got split lunch."

"What's 'split lunch?'"

"Second."

"Second what?"

"Second lunch."

"Second lunch is . . . ?'"

"Between first and third."

"We can—"

"The hour is split in two. With lunch in between. The English department gets it every year. Sucks."

Gurney looked unimpressed. "So what? Who cares if—"

"Mulnay could've come to the first half of the hour, left campus, done what you think he did, and—"

"Never come back. And we *know* he did it."

Van Der Meyer furtively consulted the clock face suspended above the classroom's whiteboard.

"Don't you know if a kid doesn't—"

"I may not have noticed."

"'Noticed?'"

Van Der Meyer lowered his gaze. Uneven black and red smears betrayed imperfectly erased lecture notes.

"Any chance," the detective continued, "you could remember your way" –thumb and index finger now took the measure of beard stubble— "into an absence?"

"No." Van Der Meyer shook his head. "No. Definitely not." He was doing his level best to scour the events of the previous spring—anything that stood out as in any way suspect. A persistently underperforming Mulnay who inexplicably turned industrious. A Mulnay who may have suddenly disappeared for the latter half of a school week, only to return midday on Monday, talkative and confident. A shy Mulnay who, without warning, turned abrasive. Vice-versa. All of this without Gurney noticing that his mind was churning. "I can't even remember what I had for lunch yesterday."

"You can't?" Gurney's face assumed an exaggerated expression meant to convey an icy mixture of bewilderment and contempt. "Yesterday's *lunch*?" Still in his chair, he arched his back stiffly while holding his face in ice-mode, both nostrils emitting chiding streams of CO^2, a nasal stereo performance fine-tuned over decades of police work. Into the bargain, Van Der Meyer found himself ideally positioned to register the cop's affinity for Camel Lights. Or—wait just a minute— did the prolonged exhalation bear trace evidence of an L & M loyalist? Pugnacious Tareyton toker? Whatever his tobacco preferences, every single molecule of Lt. Gus Gurney conveyed the unmistakable message that he had never—not once in all his policing days—encountered such an inexcusably defective memory.

After a brief pause, the teacher appeared to have reconsidered. "You're right. I can," Van Der Meyer conceded. "I had bratwurst. I remember it very well, now that you mention it. It was left over," he added helpfully, "from the night before." He smiled.

Gurney, motionless and blinking at a metronomic tempo, blankly absorbed the recently revised lunch testimony.

Van Der Meyer continued to smile broadly. "I like bratwurst," he enthused. He paused once again and nodded his head faintly up and down, still grinning. "So I remember."

"That's interesting. What else do you 'like'?"

Van Der Meyer's eyes stared into a middle distance. "A 'dick' is a detective, isn't it?"

Gurney's face was stone. "Yeah, that's right. Used to be. Just so." Standing up slowly and with visible effort, the detective took two short, shuffling steps in the direction of the seated teacher, all the while nodding his head in the affirmative, as if to visually confirm his verbal response to Van Der Meyer's vocab inquiry. "But people don't use it that way in the present day and age," he said in a voice just this side of a whisper. The lieutenant tilted his head to his left and down in a dramatic manner. "Maybe you should follow their lead."

"Thanks for the advice."

"You're welcome, word-boy."

Gurney rotated a quarter turn, the heels of his charcoal wingtips producing distinctive rasping sounds on the institutional tile. He presented his profile to Van Der Meyer for the second time. Appearances suggested that he was attempting to extricate an enticing khaki-colored morsel of foodstuff from between his canine and left incisor, his tongue his tool. Additional auditory evidence tended to corroborate this conjecture, even as it put to bed any fears Van Der Meyer might have nursed that the law officer would prove to be unduly anxious about the unsettling noises likely to accompany such an undertaking. In the meantime, the unwilling and all too captive audience for this solo matinee performance placed his left hand back on the stack of Henry James essays, not making any effort to read them or even to pick up a marker.

Evidently satisfied, at last, that his upper dental mop-up operation had been successfully executed, Gurney now turned his back completely to Van Der Meyer and began to walk sluggishly towards the core door. "We'll be talking some more," he grunted to the wall.

"Yes, sir."

Alone, Van Der Meyer observed the heavy door repeat its slow, immutable round. His hand remained motionless on the essays. As the door clicked shut, he reached for a different and much smaller pile of quizzes lying on his desktop, not looking at them.

Exiting the core into a blinding hallway, Gurney raised his right forearm defensively against the sunlight. A custodian was standing on the other side of the floor-to-ceiling windows, expertly wielding a jumbo squeegee. "More light," he mumbled to himself. In the thick of a maelstrom of students darting in every direction for their next class, he spotted what he and his partner would often refer to as a "pander commander." Except this guy wasn't a pimp. White guy. White shoes. White belt. Another teacher, probably. The detective shook his head and grinned. How can they let him dress like that?

Red pants. No. Watermelon. Gurney smiled again. Satin green shirt. Green (or is that "teal"?) cardigan.

Color words. Funny.

Dude shooting color everywhere.

*   *   *

1. Lack of sunshine.
2. Dearth of sunshine.
3. Absence of sunshine.

This list—or something very like it—was the terse response of a newly arrived writer-in-residence at the University of Pittsburgh in the mid-to-late 80's. The question had been: "What three things do you like least about Pittsburgh?" Both the question and the responses were published in a Saturday edition of the *Pittsburgh Post-Gazette*, in the space reserved for "local culture." He was a good writer and left before two years were up.

These remarks were made, it bears repeating, in the 1980's. By that time, Pittsburgh was a galaxy away from what it had been in earlier decades. Of course, suburb-coddled, cake-eating Morton Caper had not grown up in anything like the steel city of lore, when men had had to change their white collars (if they wore white collars) at work halfway through the day. When the sun would be obscured at noon. "Hell with the lid off."

Those conditions had been significantly addressed in one way or another by some sort of "Renaissance" project in the 50's. Exactly how that worked he still didn't understand, given that the J & L steel and rolling mills on both sides of the Monongahela were still putting out loads of smoke deep into the 70's, let alone the less centrally located but much larger plants in Homestead, Braddock, Beaver Falls, and elsewhere. But if you definitely couldn't stare straight at the sun at noon, because the mills no longer provided that sort of dismal shield, Pittsburgh was nonetheless something of a mecca if you were an overcast-skies enthusiast. It was and it remains among the gloomiest places in the United States, never very far from Portland or Seattle.

Caper recalled, with genuine pleasure and affection, a very gray city. Buildings (especially churches, for some reason) were often caked and baked in black. A heavy snow would only exaggerate this dark hue, not least because the white blanket would immediately be absorbed by the native soot, often retaining it for weeks at a time. He thought he remembered reading somewhere that when the Oakland Raiders visited the city in 1972, for a game that would become legend because of an "Immaculate Reception," Al Davis, the wicked lord of the California team, remarked that it was like landing in East Germany. Caper, of course, didn't know if Davis really said this. But he thought it was pretty funny, and—at least with respect to chromatic distribution—not altogether off-base.

* * *

Arriving at the sprawling campus on the following day, this time with his partner Greiner, Gurney eyed the same technicolor teacher walking along the same hallway. Different get-up, equally loud.

He tapped Greiner's shoulder and pointed. "Watermelon pants."

"What?"

"Watermelon pants. Only he's changed into some new neon."

Gurney and Greiner were looking for Keith Luebbert, the English department principal. They were hopeful that he would help them get the fifth-hour absence they desired.

Luebbert agreed to meet the detectives back in Van Der Meyer's room.

"Who's the Tropicana man walking the hallways?" Gurney asked Luebbert the moment he entered the classroom.

"Excuse me?"

"The fruit salad. Looks like he's one of your teachers."

"Cape," Van Der Meyer offered, without looking up from a small pile of quizzes currently encumbering his conference hour.

"Cape?"

"Yeah," he answered, still not lifting his eyes from the pile. "Caper. He's an English teacher."

Gurney smiled and shook his head. "Is he fruity?"

Van Der Meyer studied the visiting cop, slowly puckering his lips so as to preempt any wayward smile that might be contemplating a brief visit to his visage. He blinked. "People don't use that word that way in the present day and age." The non-smile was still a go. "Maybe," he said confidentially, as would a man who had the best interests of his interlocutor at heart, "you should follow their lead." Then he stared down at the square, tiled floor in a disciplined manner, grinning gently. "And no, he's not."

Gurney responded by making, not for the first time, an ill-advised observation: "Sounds like a castrated rooster."

"That's a *capon*, Gurney," Van Der Meyer pounced. "A caper," he cast his eyes to the ceiling, as if to consult a hovering lexicon visible only to him, "is a trick, or a stunt, or"--the next three words received special emphasis--"a clever theft." The pleasure of saying this to a smartass cop lifted his spirits measurably.

Gurney chewed gum.

Just then Caper himself entered the classroom. Holding a pile of student essays and a weathered red copy of Dante, he looked quizzically at the four men gathered, waiting for an explanation.

"Know what a capon is, Cape?" Van Der Meyer asked cheerily.

"A very," Caper's voice conveyed all of the tragic pity he could reasonably muster at such short notice, "unhappy rooster." With solemn deliberation, he consulted the book's creased red cover.

Luebbert exhaled a laugh.

"'It's no life being a steer,'" Van Der Meyer said directly to Caper, still smiling.

"Amen, amen, dico vobis..."

"Fuck're you talking about?" Gurney asked, putting forth no discernible effort to conceal his irritation. Greiner, however, was suddenly brightly attentive, and made ready to join the conversation at the first opportunity.

Caper and Van Der Meyer, each believing the uncouth question had been directed specifically to him, began to respond at the same time.

After the two exchanged hasty, inquisitive glances, Caper graciously yielded to the younger, more lumberjack-like man.

"It's a line from a Hemingway novel," Van Der Meyer explained. "Capons and steers, steers and capons. Same thing."

Caper quietly hummed "When the Caissons Go Rolling Along."

Greiner leapt at his opportunity. "That's not even Latin, you know," he said enthusiastically.

Caper stared. "Half of it is."

"Are we going to get our fucking absence?" Gurney boomed.

No one witnessing Caper's reaction to Gurney's thundering question could harbor any doubt that he was sincerely baffled. "Wan' me to leave?"

"Yes!" Gurney responded emphatically, not bothering to look in Caper's direction.

The teacher nodded and spun around in one movement, exiting to the English department core.

With no opportunity to ask about the *Inferno* quizzes (his reason for entering Van Der Meyer's room in the first place), Caper nevertheless found himself quite intrigued by this urgent "absence" matter. Wait a sec. Maybe he said "absinthe." No. Couldn't've. Makes no sense. Good lunch conversation anyway. *Absinthe of malice.* Funny? Ask Iris. Might use it as a photo caption. *Absinthe-minded?* Yellowish-green number, maybe with the killer paisley shirt. Blows 'em away every time. *Absinthe makes the shirt grow fabu...*Subtitle? "This mean green ensemble's addictive!" There's that line, too, from *Twelfth Night,* or maybe *Midsummer* or *Much Ado* or one of those allegedly funny plays: "Melancholy's green and yellow cast." Probably something better than that. More haunting rhythm. Always is.

Caper shook his head yet again in doleful tribute to his memory's limitations—long term, short term, all terms. *All* of those characters in the comedies, he wearily recalled—hell, at least a dozen, often quite a few more—and each one sharing more or less equal stage time to boot. Toss in the fact that you've got to keep track of beaucoup plot twists, meddlesome imps, mistaken identities, gender swaps. Nor does it help that their names all end in an "a" or an "o" or an "i." "Io," too. "Atio" and "assio." No need to buy a vowel when the Italian influences are so pronounced. But somehow for Shakespeare all of this doesn't constitute quite enough dramatic intrigue, so He decides to exacerbate Cape's interpretive labor. The Bard has to have it that three-quarters of the characters go off and disguise themselves in order to win yon lover over there, or perhaps dupe cunning rival over here. Failing that, the poor lovesick suckers *get* disguised by a mischievous sprite or some other sort of comical demon. Can't keep the names straight to begin with, and now for more than half the cast Cape's got to keep track of *two.* "Oh yeah, Claudio's also 'Duke Something-o,' except nobody other than that other guy's twin brother knows about it. And remember, he can't change back to being just plain ol' Claudio without the pixie and the pixie dust, right?" Caper, not immune to conducting very precise calculations on the date when his pension would kick in, shook his head sternly once more. Too old to teach any of those plays ever again. Leave 'em to Roegner and all the other nimble, young instructors. These kids can *quote* the stuff from memory. It's all the C-man can do just to drop one of the titles now and again in casual conversation, hoping he hasn't mangled the job in the process.

Absinthe, baby. Ab-Romantic-sinthe. A beverage with a most colorful past. Green and yellow. Yellowish-green. Poe, they say. Not to mention quite a few others of the artistic persuasion. Kicked out of UVa, or so the story…Maybe just dropped out. University has a vested interest in keeping that sort of ambiguity going. Tourists love it. How many times had he been politely accosted on the way to class? "Excuse me, young man. But could you please tell us which room Edgar Allan Poe lived in?" Caper couldn't.

"Absintheur"? Words don't come any cooler. But just how could you wangle the thing into an actual convers—

Don't forget West Point, before that. Kicked out or went AWOL. Would be very difficult, come to think of it, to name any writer less likely to have been been cut out of officer cloth. "Second Lieutenant Poe, reporting for duty, sir."

Kidding me?

Duty. Honor.

Absinthe.

Trochees one and all. "Raven," too, most of the way through. *All* of the way. Bump-bah, bump-bah, bump-bah, bump-bah...Regular drumbeat of ghastliness.

Gurney. Greiner. Mulnay.

Absence.

Not everyone, you had to admit, is cut out for the full four, a whole course of studies capped by a slow, celebratory stroll across the stage for the diploma. Or an officer's insignia.

Lindbergh's colors, too. Close enough, anyway. That particular coincidence is unlikely to have been remarked before, now isn't it? LHS has absinthe colors. Should incorporate that happy fact into of some of our cheers. "Green and Yellow, Yellow and Green/Come on Flyers, let's get spirited!" Spirit of spirits. Drinking man's liquor. Parisian cafes. Would make your hair stand on end, and your body fall down in the street. Definitely would lend a whole new layer of meaning to "Flyers," too. The girls could rhyme with "green" about a thousand different ways. Not so much with "yellow." Not at all with "absinthe." Of course, there's "absence," but that's not really...

Don't think I should share any of these soaring flights of fancy with my tender young students.

E. A. Poe ends up in a Baltimore gutter, according to the story. Just where certain people would expect a dropout to drop. Face down. Absinthetown. Wonder if that's really true? Sounds like just the sort of tale Edgar A. would have orchestrated in one of his more lucid moments, eyes on the legacy prize. Untimely demise. Kicks influenza's ass. Consumption and rheumatism couldn't hope to buy anything like that sort of literary luster. Burnishes the green and yellow legend, doesn't it? Never forget, dead writers need to appeal to the young, over and over and over again. The black-clad teen demographic laps up that sort of thing, and always would. Move over Cobain Morrison & Hendrix LLC. Make room for E. Allan Poe, Esq. If the "father of the detective story" had a mind to keep those old heart-thumping tales beating, forever stoking a yearning in the pale bosoms of young readers, he couldn't have died a more fitting death. Maryland gutter. Prostrate. Louche.

Absinthe.

Cool.

Caper paused in the middle of the assembled eating tables, four or five set end to end, a semi-permanent banquet arrangement for English teachers. Something had captured his eye. Picking up a sturdy white plastic implement, he helped himself to two modest slices of chocolate cake.

Exiting the core, Caper approached two rather alienated-looking youths pressed against one another in the hallway, baggy garments commingling in deep sympathy. *Sucking face.* Wonder did kids still say that? Hmh. "Give it a rest," he barked. The two separated just a bit and looked blankly at Caper. "It's revolting."

* * *

Departing the building once again, an agitated Gurney released a loud and abrupt guttural noise. "Damn," he gasped. "Also a food seasoning. Midget-olives or something. Can't stand 'em."

"What the hell are you talking about?" Greiner asked.

Gurney shook his head. "Nothing. Should've said something else to Van Der Meyer." The cops continued to walk toward the parking space reserved for police. "Timing."

Greiner thumbed his key fob. The gray Caprice chirped, blinked its running lights.

* * *

Returning from Guidance, Caper entered the core once again, easing his pace as ever to allow his eyes to adjust to the three rows of bright blue fluorescent lights radiating from above, each line extending all the way back to the dead end of the tunnel-like corridor. As he did so, a ceiling air vent positioned only a few feet inside the door blasted chilling air directly onto the crown of his head, the combined effect producing a casual derangement of his eyes, one that he now took for granted. It did not help matters that for all their radiant power stretched along the ceiling, the triple line of lights seemed to be mysteriously impeded somewhere in the middle air, rendering them incapable of providing the dull linoleum floor tiles with the illumination they deserved. For this exact reason, a visitor to this passageway, sure to hear some sort of hum or clatter or muffled laughter behind each one of the nine classroom doors, or perhaps a silence signalling boredom or studiousness or a mixture thereof, was equally certain to walk with unsteady step, her head amply klieged even as her shoes trod on an entirely different, and far murkier, sphere.

Heavy metal shelving of the erector-set school stood tall on either side of the aisle, neatly stacked piles of *The Crucible, Lord of the Flies,* and *Fahrenheit 451* providing indisputable testimony, if any were needed, that at least a few things on this orb are genuinely indestructible. As if to accentuate this fact, a wide array of disconsolate orphans from decades past (*Darkness at Noon* over here; *The Naked and the Dead* over there) found themselves abandoned in nooks and oxidized crannies, each tobaccoing volume pining for that glorious day when it would be banned just *one* last time (whether this sublime deed were to be consummated by the Soviet State Committee for Publishing, or by vice-suppressing Boston clergy, was completely immaterial), and thereby vindicate all of these long, long years in the desiccating wilderness. Could reinstatement into high school curricula be far behind?

This same imagined visitor stepping uncertainly along the length of the core sanctuary would surely permit herself to soak up the stray teacherly voice probing, from behind one of the doors and for the millionth time, the significance of Atticus killing that mad dog out in the street with that single shot that one day, as well as (softly resonating through one of the other eight doors) a barely audible discussion of poor Lennie's star-crossed affinity for mice, and for little puppies, too. As these and other names and deeds woke up the dormant English class echoes (even if she'd much prefer they'd have stayed in bed), perhaps she would allow her squinting, blinking eyes to pan leisurely over the variegated parade of cracked paperback spines passing on either hand, hoary title fragments blending together in a mesmerizing montage: *Horses, Don't They?* dissolving into *In Cold* fading into *in the Afternoon.* Tolstoy's *War an—"*

That print! Caper brusquely severed his own lyrical musings. *That dirty French print! Whatever happened to...*

That smoky print we used to have of one of Napoleon's lieutenants, the one hanging next to the map of St. Louis? Ney. Ney's execution.

Face on the pavement, at once heroic and pathetic. "Execution of the Marshal"? Gérôme. Damn. Just when and where did that Ney go missing? It had to have been a most Pittsburgh-like Parisian day, if the painting could be believed, weak yellow light clotted with smoke or fog. Firing squad marching away in tight formation from the corpse of the Marshal ("most brave," he said), black hat knocked free from the fall. Refused a blindfold, didn't he? Pretty cool. Alsacian blood streaming into a Parisian street-level sluice. Face down on the stones of the Rue de something or other. Ney insisted that he be the one to give the order to shoot, or so the legend…"Soldats!" Self-possessed. He sternly bid them aim true, or something equally undismayed. The painting had it so that the departing uniformed killers were cloaked in the choked air, only one of them even bothering to look back at the prostrate corpse. Nice touch. Mourning? Mocking? Could be the marksman was simply mulling over the possibility of plundering the possessions of the courageous deceased. A most base consideration, mon ami. But then you couldn't say for sure. Gérôme was probably shooting for just that sort of bittersweet ambiguity. If so, would love to know where in the hell that little piece of framed bittersweet ambiguity has gone into hiding. Basement?

"Death must be so beautiful." Quotation's spot on, Cape. Just as Oscar wrote it. Once in a while, you remember the words just right. Wilde's syphilitic ear. Infected Parisian ear. Stringin' along some mighty taut turns of phrase, C. Should write some of this stuff down. Killed. Ghost of the king. Afternoon nap.

"Wormwood."

Absinthe.

Turning around sharply as he approached Van Der Meyer's door, Caper made a concentrated effort to abandon his morbid reveries at least until lunch. Attempting to administer a bracing dose of wholesome kitsch, he tried to recall the couple's names. Singing duo. Canadian Mounted Police. Horseback. MacDonald. Jeanette MacDonald. And *Nelson Eddy*. That's him! "The Singing Capon." Oy! Wonder how he handled *that* handle? "Ladies and gentlemen, please welcome tonight's featured attraction, 'The Singing Capon' himself, Mr. Nelson Eddy!" It would take a lotta bal…Not funny, Cape. Too obvious. Kind of thing Langwein would say.

He knew of the once-famous singing duo primarily because his old man was a devoted fan. In fact, Caper's father knew by heart several of their most popular songs. His mother, by contrast, had always taken a little pride in being more up-to-date. She and her Iowa high school chums had formed some sort of Sinatra club during the first wave of Frankie-mania in the early 40's. They'd listen to the latest records right there in the store, each one in her own booth. For her, Jeanette MacDonald and Nelson Eddy were for old people.

Flip, Caper suddenly found himself thinking. He couldn't say exactly why. Cowboys.

*   *   *

In the fall of '72, about two and a half months prior to Franco Harris' divinely ordained reception, and about those same two and half months + exactly eight more days prior to Roberto Clemente's mortal plunge off the coast of Puerto Rico, Caper, his father, and his oldest brother were idling in a yellow Chevy Biscayne at the intersection of Saw Mill Run and West Liberty Avenue, soon to enter downtown Pittsburgh. At that very moment, the Steelers were playing the Cowboys in Dallas, about to suffer a loss that would turn out to be one of only three in the regular season. What in the world? Myron Cope and Jack Fleming called the shots.

At present, their business was to purchase a small block of seats for an upcoming game with the Cleveland Browns at the ticket exchange at Three Rivers Stadium, a mundane task suddenly fraught with wild uncertainty. For the first time in recorded history, there was a real possibility that the tickets wouldn't be there for the asking. Waiting patiently for the green light, all three couldn't help but notice that the bumper of the vehicle directly in front of them featured a large-print sticker unambiguously proclaiming that "JESUS IS THE ANSWER." Caper, an adept young reader, took immediate solace in the knowledge that he was now satisfactorily prepared for at least one of the questions he would encounter on some as yet unspecified quiz.

Thus contented, he turned his attention to the rounded arches of the Tubes, their soft shape somehow managing to convey the fact that they were markedly older than the shinier, geometrically more concise Fort Pitt Tunnels burrowing under the same Mt. Washington dirt and rock only a short distance to the west. He preferred the Tubes solely because someone had bothered to rig up thick cable-lines just below the arched ceiling end to end, hefty antennae black in the dim yellow electric light of the underground, which would accompany your car's journey whether you sped toward the city or from it. As a result, you could continue to listen to your radio (AM stations, at any rate) far beneath the steeply sloping surfaces. That the signal would grow inevitably and notably weaker the closer you approached the midway point (even Myron's customary screech would be dirt-muted) dampened Caper's fascination not a whit. To the contrary, these diminished voices and subdued melodies only served to increase his appreciation for the mystical power of the radio—all the way through the mile-long stretch.

His attention evidently still held by the bumper sticker, Caper's older brother took the opportunity to ponder aloud: "I wonder what the question is?"

From the back seat, ten-year old Morton came to his aid. "Who is the youngest Alou brother?"

Caper remembered this episode all through the years. He couldn't say exactly why. Perhaps it was his hunch that both his father and his brother, laughing in the front seat, and looking back with slightly puzzled expressions, somehow suspected that little Mort had secretly stage-managed the whole thing.

*   *   *

At lunch, Caper worked on getting his elaborate and space-consuming midday meal out of his outsized cooler. Animated discussions triggered by the cop visits were already underway. He looked down the busy and lengthy table arrangement to Van Der Meyer, who promptly interrupted himself in mid-sentence, even as he raised an eyebrow inquisitively. Caper, in turn, suddenly recalled that he had a worn, curled copy of *Glengarry Glen Ross* nestled in the inside pocket of his black-and-white plaid blazer, reached for it, and softly frisbeed the profane play down the table to the besieged teacher.

"Thank you, kind teacher," Caper said as the spinning book gently nudged Van Der Meyer's Coke. "Still haven't managed to locate my own copy." He shook his head despairingly. "Just hope no one lifted it from my desk." Leaning back in his chair to glance inside his own classroom, Caper surveyed an unpardonably chaotic landscape, a doleful chamber littered with piles of paper of every description, consecrated, one would not be blamed for concluding, as a lasting tribute to disorder and mayhem. "That's probably not what happened," he said to no one in particular.

At the further end of the table, "May 5th," "absent," and someone or something named "Mulnay" were being bandied about with inordinate frequency. *Pinko de Mayo*, Caper reflected. *Sweeet pink pinstripe sport coat. Hold on, C. Could've been the Sears & Roebuck polyester shirt. Look it up.* He leaned forward again to attend to his still-burgeoning lunch arrangements, a jar of herring cheek by jowl with a serving of baked beans, leftover lamb abutting a cold pop. While engaged in these earnest and intricate food-arranging maneuvers, he repeated his request to Van Der Meyer: "Can I borrow yours again for tomorrow's classes?"

Even in the midst of two or three different discussions, Van Der Meyer still managed to signal that it wouldn't be a problem. *Borrow Mamet any time you like*, he indicated, mainly by reaching back with his left arm and placing the play in an uncluttered and conspicuously borrowable location in the center of his desk. Presently, to his relief, the bowels of Caper's blue cooler were beginning to show signs of diminishing returns. Satisfied at last that his own private smörgåsbord had been rendered ready for consumption, he gazed back down the table, opened and closed his hands as if to cue a follow-up clarification, and waited alertly to learn more about this distressing "absence" business.

"We can't help 'em," Van Der Meyer continued to explain to several of those gathered. "What can I say?" He was neither eating nor making any visible effort to satisfy his noon appetite. "I probably missed the kid."

Other English teachers in the core were in possession of varying amounts of knowledge concerning the murderous events of the previous spring, as well as of the more recent police visits. From zero to a whole lot. Caper waited to hear more.

"Luebbert back you?" asked Murry.

"Yeah, completely. He said right away that we can't retroactively change stuff like that."

"The cops've *got* to know that, too," said Schroll. "Can't believe they're wasting their time."

"This the 'absence' thing?" Caper discreetly cut in.

"They do, and I can't either," Van Der Meyer answered Schroll. "But they're pissed because of all the other evidence." He turned to Caper. "Ever have a student named Ellis Mulnay?"

"Never had the pleasure."

"Exactly." Van Der Meyer gazed disapprovingly at the ketchup packets nested inside the red plastic condiment holder directly in front of him. "I have. A whole year's worth. I think he got a D, maybe an F, maybe an NC."

"You weren't reaching him," Caper sagely purred.

Only muted laughter greeted the seasoned teacher's pedagogical assessment.

"Anyway," Van Der Meyer continued after a pause, "the police think—no, excuse me, they *know* they fucking know—that on May the fifth Mulnay did a drive-by somewhere in north city. And he did it right after lunch. *And*," he added after another pause, "neither the SIS system nor my little red book is cooperating."

Speaking as if he were mainly talking to himself, trying to make at least some sense of all this new information, Caper muttered tentatively, "So they want you to…?"

"Make him absent." Van Der Meyer uttered the words mechanically, looking at no one.

"Make him absent," Caper echoed, speaking at a notably slower pace. Elbows on the table surface, he held a bright black plastic fork horizontally between his index fingers, spinning the implement like a miniature, fast-food rotisserie spit. "They want you," he continued to deliberate in a very measured fashion, "to make him absent, a half-year after a young citizen was shot and killed on one of St. Louis' streets. During," he added, "the lunch hour."

"Yep."

"Because they want him present there." The fork continued its slow rotation. "Not here." Caper slumped back just a bit in his chair, his left forearm now flat on the eating surface. "And they definitely *know*," he said, hoping to confirm some recently acquired intelligence, "that they fucking know that your guy did it."

"That they do."

No one else present appeared to be eager to say anything.

"Why not," Caper leaned back into the void, his tone still tentative, "play it just as it lays? Put forth whatever they've got against the truant Lindbergh High School student, admit that there's a hiccup in the case—a bit of bureaucratic record-taking that doesn't completely square with all the other meticulously gathered evidence incriminating the accused—and go from there?"

Van Der Meyer was shaking his head long before Caper came to the end of his lengthy and eminently reasonable proposal. "Not gonna happen. Gurney called it an 'automatic case-dropper.'" Thick, curtly bouncing index fingers punctuated the not-present cop's unequivocal legal prognosis, one that Van Der Meyer evidently felt he had no choice but to accept.

"Bingo!" Schroll interjected. "Exactly what I think. What everyone should think, for that matter. So drop the case and solve a different one."

"They want the goddamn absence," Van Der Meyer responded wearily.

"I believe," Caper joined in once again, "that that would be just a wee bit illegal."

"No shit."

Caper gently clicked his teeth together in a side-to-side motion, watching the black fork continue its slow roll, searching for some angle that hadn't yet been considered. Everything's in the past tense. Difficult to shape things to your advantage to begin with, let alone…"Who," he began to ask, "taught Mulnay sixth and—"

"Absent," Van Der Meyer swiftly countered.

"Hell," Caper persisted. "That's just what I'm talking about. I mean, it makes a little bitty lunch-time miscue seem completely understandable. In fact," he added, now with growing ardor, "*you* could sing about our shameful split lunch schedule—sing about it to someone who just might listen, baby. Right up there on the stand, and under oath to boot." All signs indicated that Caper was rapidly becoming enchanted by these new and unexpected possibilities. "Sing it to the man in the black robe, sittin' on the bench!"

"Not in the cards," Van Der Meyer morosely countered the now visibly enthused advisor. "Lawyers can be very, very fussy about time and location." He worked a used napkin around on the table surface in front of him, although there didn't appear to be any sort of spillage in need of a sopping operation. "And in this instance, one can rest assured that they will most certainly wish to dwell on the fact that Ellis Mulnay could not possibly have been present in two very different places at the same time on a certain May afternoon."

That's just it, Caper thought. "That's just it," Caper said aloud, gazing down the table somewhere above the heads of all the gathered eaters.

"What's just it?" Van Der Meyer gave the napkin a rest.

"I'm pretty sure," he warned all those who were listening, "that I am on the brink of thinking a deep thought." He nodded his head confidently, as if to indicate that he had encountered these profound moments all too often in the course of his life, and had every reason to expect that the latest visitation was both authentic and imminent. "And I'm going to share it with all of you—with your permission, of course." He held his head bent and still in vibrant expectancy, hardly blinking, slowly chewing a bite of rye crispbread.

* * *

On a warm August Saturday evening in 1973, at least four—but perhaps as many as six—members of the Caper family attended a Saturday exhibition game between the Pittsburgh Steelers and Baltimore Colts. The Steelers prevailed, 34-7. It was a good start to the year.

This game marked the beginning of the first and only year the Capers had season tickets to watch the still Super Bowl-less team, and for reasons no one could pinpoint and few would have cared to try, their seats numbered between four and six, depending on the game. Rest assured, dear reader, the ticket plan was complex. And yet it proved to be a paragon of simplicity when compared to the normally unremarkable task of exiting Three Rivers Stadium. Pittsburgh police were present in force, stationed inside and outside every single gate. It was a billy-club festival, attendance mandatory. Owing to circumstances very few of them could have hoped to guess, all of the fans discovered that they would be obliged to pass single-file through tight revolving-door apparatuses at select points spread along the ground level, each one of which vaguely suggested an old-school bread-slicer set on end. Perhaps a guild of unusually svelte plumbers had designed the things, given that inch-and-a-half pipes provided the sole architectural feature. As "exits," they were unlikely to win any design awards; as crowd-cloggers, they had few peers. Impatient throngs soon discovered they really had only two things to do. They could watch as the police conducted a proportion of those who had preceded them in the painfully slow exodus to a second, thinner ring of officers, whose directive was to subject the lucky winners, it would appear, to further questioning and/or cursory pat-downs. They could also contemplate their bladders, with special emphasis on capacity and endurance.

Of the great many insights provided by social scientists down through the years, perhaps few are as impressive—but also as disturbing—as those which focus on the shocking alterations in human behavior one is liable to encounter when large gatherings of the species gather in close quarters. On this particular occasion, a few key considerations would have excited the vigilance of any capable anthropologist. Would there soon emerge a number of smaller groupings in the midst of these restive crowds, clumps of people neither particularly close to the maddeningly slow-spinning pipes, yet ahead of unknown masses behind them, who would decide to turn about and, against the tide as it were, conduct a tactical slog into one of the restrooms provided by the stadium's designers? If they made this fateful decision, would the people behind them be inclined to aid them in their quest? And if, in fact, they successfully completed their restroom journey, would the retreaters be setting themselves up to repeat that very same sequence, given that they would be placing themselves back at the rear once again, perilously far from the miserly exit spindles?

The four to six Capers managed to brave these trying circumstances, even as the question as to why all of this cop-business was happening yielded more or less completely to the far more urgent matter of how they would all find relief for their discomfort. After a very long wait, they were spit out of the stadium one at a time, and succeeded in not drawing the attention of the outer ring of cops, who continued to cherry-pick a percentage of recently escaped inmates for further questioning. Each one of hapless round-two lottery winners was engaged in brisk foot-and-toe calisthenics, left leg then right leg then back, for reasons all the Capers could well appreciate. Sparing not one second to make enquiry as to the cause of all their sorrow, they now relied upon their father, a 40,000 miles/year motorist, to work some magic with the Buick. He possessed an intimate—one might more accurately say, profoundly unorthodox—command of southwestern Pennsylvania's landscape, which, as any visitor can attest, is unusually tortuous to begin with. The old man knew back alleys the way lifelong residents knew the Boulevard of the Allies, and he even appeared to prefer them to the paved surface roads and parkways that all the other namby-pambies put their trust in. As a motorist, every fiber of his being was keyed into one eternal question: "Is there an even shorter shortcut?" The arcane knowledge he had acquired over the years must now do all of them yoeman's service.

Meanwhile, relaxing in the main bedroom of the three-story Caper house, whose every room on the second and third floors was replete with bedding arrangements for her expansive brood, Caper's mother was in the process of watching in a relatively late episode of *Mannix*, no doubt relieved to be rid of a sizable fraction of her offspring, at least for a few back-mollifying hours.

The telephone rang.

Happily, Mrs. McFarlin was on the line, her melodious speech the undiluted tincture of County O'this, situated dab in the middle of Province Mc'that. When residents of Pittsburgh had occasion to refer to U. S. Steel, the final syllable would invariably undergo a familiar vocal transformation, the long "e" migrating over into something very close to a short "i," the "l" swallowed into the neighborhood of a "w." Most people hearing this phrase would nonetheless be put in mind of a certain widely recognized corporate logo, or perhaps somebody or something named Bessemer, or open-hearth furnaces, or maybe even Andrew Carnegie himself. Some of a more imaginative bent might go so far as to envisage slag heaps glowing in the dark. When, on the other hand, Mrs. McFarlin said "United States Steel" (Mr. McFarlin having been a devoted employee of the Pittsburgh juggernaut for decades), an altogether different vocal metamorphosis would occur. The final word would be bent and stretched out just so, the long "e" would now find itself much closer to a long "a," and there was the unmistakable hint of an "h" puttering about. The word "steel" now had approximately 1.33 syllables. The overall effect was to transform the name of the world's first billion-dollar corporation into something that sounded like a pleasing flower, or, failing that, a flavor of ice cream you hadn't yet tried but would be happy to taste.

On this particular occasion, however, not even Mrs. McFarlin's beguiling accent could hope to work any of its long-established vocal magic. The mellifluous neighbor wished to know, in very blunt terms, whether or not Charles was attending the Steeler game that evening.

Yes, Kay, he was. However did you know? And, if you don't mind my asking, why are you interested in his whereabouts?

Well, Mrs. McFarlin politely but curtly explained. I think he's been shot.

Been shot?

Yes, Joan. Shot, she lilted. It was just on the television. Do you want a ride to the hospital? Jim can drive right over.

Been shot?! I've been watching *Mannix*. What tele—are you sure?

Yes, I'm sure. I'll bet you need a ride to the hospital.

Yes, please, his utterly confounded mother responded. Send Jim right over.

One can well imagine the robotic state of shock induced by this astonishing phone call, whether or not it were accompanied by an ambrosial Celtic breeze. Must get dressed; get picked up by Jim McFarlin; go to hospital; Chuck shot. Saw it on the television.

The telephone, meanwhile, rang and rang and rang. Where, everyone wanted to know, was Chuck? And do you need a ride to the hospital?

In the midst of this *Mannix*-interrupting mania, Caper's mother had the wherewithal to wonder to herself, "Which hospital would they take you to if you had been shot at a Steeler game?" She had no idea herself, but did manage to ask the next very concerned caller precisely that question. The caller suggested Mercy. Maybe she should ring, just to make sure. His mother did so.

Was there a Charles Caper who had been shot at that evening's Steeler game somewhere in your hospital? his mother asked the first person to answer the Mercy Hospital phone.

Yes, the woman answered.

I'm his wife and how is he and exactly where is he?

The woman responded that she would be happy to provide *all* of the unfortunate information if, to begin with, she could learn a few things about Mrs. Caper's husband. How old, she asked, is your husband, Mrs. Caper?

Forty-seven, Mrs. Caper replied.

Yes, the telephone operator responded in a neutral voice. How tall is Mr. Caper? was the next thing she wished to know.

Not sure, exactly. About six feet. Maybe five-eleven.

Longish pause. What . . . *race* is your husband, Mrs. Caper? Is he black?

No. Why do you ask?

Our Chuck Caper is black. And he's six-foot eleven.

When Caper finally returned home many hours later, together with his father and either two or four of his brothers, his mother hugged everyone with unusual fervor. Strangely, the cause of this outpouring of affection appeared to center on the fact that none of them had been shot while watching the Steelers defeat the Colts, 34 to 7.

Good thing, Caper thought. He went to bed. He had fat Sunday newspapers to stuff and pile and deliver in the morning.

Time sifted out some of the baffling elements of the football shooting, but not all of them. The man who had been taken to Mercy Hospital that late-summer night in 1973, and who would recover from his wounds, shared the very same name as his father. He was 6'5" or maybe 6'6" inches tall, according to statistical records gathered over an enduring and impressive basketball career. So the telephone operator had been wrong about at least one thing. He was, in addition, just four months younger than Caper's father. Quite understandably, newspaper accounts emphasized the fact that he was the first black player ever to be drafted in the NBA. He had also attended Westinghouse High School in the city—the 'House, baby!—an institution forever locked in a timeless deathmatch with Peabody. The two mighty Gilded-Age Georges lived on—in the city of Pittsburgh, at any rate—their blood struggles played out each year on both the gridiron and hardwood.

The 6' 6" basketball trailblazer had most certainly been attending the Steeler game on the evening in question, and had been shot at the half while sitting in his seat. But by whom? And for what reason? How had this confusing stuff made its way onto the local airwaves (*Mannix*-viewers excepted) long before the game itself had been concluded?

Not all of these questions would be answered, in the near or distant future. Police had been alerted, per Roy Blount's wonderfully jagged chronicle of that Steeler year, to look for a "man dressed in white and posing as a Liquor Control Board agent," or—more vaguely and, as it turned out, more forebodingly—"a man wearing a yellow shirt and khaki pants." The only thing missing was a grassy (Tartan Turf?) knoll. The figure posing as a Liquor Control Board agent turned out to be, in Blount's wry account, "a Liquor Control Board agent." The yellow and khaki guy, not quite as wryly, "never materialized." All sorts of sniper-talk ensued, resulting in nothing.

So a man had been badly wounded in the thigh with a .45 slug while watching the Steelers defeat the Baltimore Colts, but had survived. No one, evidently, would know who had done the wounding, or even if the bullet had entered the stadium from somewhere else. Two of the three local networks reported the deed as fast as they could, and had identified the victim, as best they could, by name and age but not yet by notable basketball past. In '73, it seems, there were still some distant echoes of the "we interrupt this broadcast to..." trope.

Concerned neighbors had seen and listened to these reports, pressed telephone buttons, or spun rotary wheels. They offered rides. Where the hell was Chuck?

Battalions of Pittsburgh police were dispatched to the still-new all-purpose stadium on the North Side, a brutal homage to the gods of concrete, but had not been able to identify who had pulled the trigger, or why.

* * *

"Well?" Two or perhaps three of the younger teachers revealed themselves to be so artless as to be snookered into posing the follow-up invitation—one that only appeared to be inevitable—in the process confirming their collective naïveté more or less at the same time.

Caper's mouth, still employed in an unhurried chewing motion, also bore faint traces of triumph.

"Do you *have* to, Cape?" Thus spake some far more experienced voice from the far end of the lunch tables. It was patently a last-ditch attempt to derail the fast-approaching wisdom train, and Caper instantly recognized it as such. It was doomed to fail.

"No, I don't," Caper politely conceded. "But that fact only renders my profound thoughts even profounder," he added, not neglecting to wag an index finger. "For when wisdom admits discourse with sty…"

Clamorous noises ensued, a percentage of which could be identified as words, but even these were foul with invective. Caper held both hands aloft, cupped, hoping to becalm the suddenly turbulent noon hour. "My friends, I beg you," he implored. "What I am about to say may well serve as a badly needed boon to our beleaguered colleague, Mr. Van Der Meyer." With or without the aid of this heartfelt plea, some measure of quiet eventually returned to the core area. "Thank you," Caper resumed. "We should all probably dwell with just a little bit more appreciation on the unfailing insight of this extremely capable English teacher, our beloved coworker, who, in the midst of a tumult the rest of us can only imagine, has succinctly identified the crux of this unparalleled act of truancy, an unexcused absence that also served as the occasion for a horrid act of violence last May." Caper paused to refresh his stressed lungs. "A body," he resumed, "we are compelled to agree, cannot be both present and not-present in a particular place at a particular time. Nor should we harbor any hope that the accused's lawyers will fail to make note of this fact, and to mention it as often as possible, quantum physics notwithstanding." He continued to gaze at the distant dead-end wall of the core, where the lights were dim enough to conceal the outlines of a faded paint-job only partly masking the cinderblock surface. "A murder," he repeated in a lower tone of voice, "in the afternoon. In," Caper further specified, after a discomfiting pause, "a garden."

He looked down at the food spread in front of him. With his eyes resting on a gently curving slice of bundt cake, something appeared to have clicked. His gaze quickly jumped back to the core's dim rear wall, but his face was now the very picture of calm perplexity. For their part, the faces of his English department colleagues failed to completely mask their own particular misgivings, whose overriding theme could be summarized in a single question: "Isn't it about time Cape adjusted his meds?"

"Okay, okay. I think I've decided to spare you my profound thoughts" (relieved noises were detected by a number of those present) "for the time being." Silence. "I hope you'll allow me to tell a little story instead.

"Once upon a time," he hurriedly launched before any significant opposition could organize itself, "a young man, probably about thirteen-years old, and possessing the unusual name of Manfred, was playing bumper pool with one of his friends."

"Manfred?"

"Yes, Manfred. Playing bumper pool. In fact," Caper volunteered, "he played bumper-pool quite often one summer in a neighbor's garage, a kind neighbor who was also a longstanding customer on Manfred's paper route. As it happened, the table was situated in a small room above the single-car parking area. A kind of garage attic, if you will."

"We will, Cape. We will. But what does this have to do with Van Der Meyer?"

"Plenty. Well," Caper briefly reconsidered. "There's definitely a connection to be made. A clear connection, in fact, for those of you who possess a modicum of insight." He moved an invisible cue back and forth as if readying to bank a particularly daring shot, his waist bent ever so slightly. "It was a fairly old house, as was the garage. Probably built in the '20's, if one had to say. No plumbing had ever been installed in the garage and, of course, no bathroom facilities were available."

"*Van Der Meyer*, Cape."

"Gettin' there, Langwein." Caper stood up straight, arched his spine, the pool cue summarily ditched. "No plumbing," he repeated, "but the room *did* have a window on the second floor, where we—*he*—would play bumper—"

"Cape, where's all of this—"

"Patience, people. Sometimes even the most ancient and edifying tales contain extremely unpleasant—even repellant—actions. Just open up an old copy of Grimm's to any page you please, and you will discover this truth once again."

"The bell, Cape. The bell." Two or three index fingers were pointing impatiently at wrists, though not one of them was saddled with an actual watch.

"I'm aware of the time, people. I, too, have got to go back to work in just a few minutes. But my thoughts happen to be directed toward a hard-working teacher, one who has been subjected to unkind treatment from a few detectives working a murder case." He stared soberly at Van Der Meyer. "Have they threatened you with saps? Blackjacks?" There could be no mistaking the fact that Caper was concerned for the safety of his colleague.

"No saps. Blackjacks not an issue."

Caper nodded his head in seeming relief, but couldn't entirely disguise his disappointment. "Good. But you'd better—bright light? night stick to the solar plex…?" (he could see that his interrogation leads were coming up snake eyes)— "you'd better watch your back." Returning his attention to the other members of the English department, Caper attempted to resume the bumper-pool saga.

"The room," he recommenced, "in which young Manfred played bumper-pool had, as I've said, a window. And in these circumstances, that win—"

"Saps and blackjacks and bright…nights? Cape, are we supposed to know what—"

"Look it up, Lang. Later. Let me try to finish this thriller before the bell rings. That window," Caper plodded on, "overlooked—sort of—a vegetable garden, neatly laid out on a steep slant about a story and a half below. Pittsburgh's a hilly place, you see, and what looks like the first or second floor from the front can easily turn out to be second or third floor from the back."

"'Sort of'?"

"Yes," Caper clarified. "The garden was off to the side just a bit."

"What was growing there, Cape? This is riveting."

"Tomatoes, Lang. Probably peppers, too. Squash, I'd wager."

"And?"

"And Manfred may have allowed himself to make a bad choice. He may have been playing bumper-pool one fine morning and drinking a lot of Tang, and somehow he failed to pay attention to things until it was too...and suddenly that window must have looked like a godsend. No doubt failing to consider the possible consequences, he proceeded to utilize the facilities, such as they..."

"'Gotcha, my man. No worries. We're just talkin' about waterin' the soil, Herr Manfred."

"Exactly, Lang. Exactly. Except," Caper paused and nodded, "it wasn't just tomatoes and peppers and squash down there in that garden."

Schroll: "No? Serpent, too?"

Van Der Meyer: "Someone napping?"

"No, my literary friends. But I do appreciate your mindful suggestions. There was..." Caper hesitated, perhaps owing to some lingering effects from an as yet unspecified trauma. "There was a gardener down in the garden, doing some gardening." He shook his head, as if he were reliving the entire horrible incident all over again. "Who knew?"

No member of the English department listening to Caper's cautionary tale could possibly have heard the concluding question. Hooting, laughter, clapping, and a host of other noises associated with grotesque entertainment ruled the core. Van Der Meyer was loudly muttering (one of the few people capable of pulling off such a feat) something about "porches" and "ears."

Langwein, always in the forefront of these sorts of discussions, now thirsted to hear more. "What'd he do?"

"She," Caper calmly replied to an even more raucous audience. "Lady of the house, in fact."

"What'd the lady of th—"

"Screamed. Screamed like they scream only in the movies. Except for this one time, which was not, unfortunately, a movie."

The din from the enclosed English core could now likely be heard in the cafeteria, a considerable distance.

"And?"

"And I don't remember a whole lot more, until the entire matter came to dramatic conclusion."

"Do tell," Langwein egged.

"Well, Manfred couldn't help but be extremely concerned about the consequences. Parents were bound to be contacted, and all sorts of hectoring about appropriate behavior would surely ensue." Eager faces awaited the impending catastrophe. "Thing is, there was an eerie silence on the parental front. Were adults simply toying with him like capricious Greek gods? Manfred cringed with every incoming phone call, anticipating the retributive bolt that would send him...he didn't know where it would send him. Surely, Manfred said to himself again and again, he hadn't been let off the hook? Impossible. Then again, maybe the long silence was part of the punishment?

"Then, some weeks after the ill-starred act, he and his bumper-pool buddy somehow whipped up the nerve to return to the upper floor of the garage, the very source of all the agonizing that had befallen the otherwise upstanding youth." Caper paused, reached down to the spread in front of him, and nimbly bit off a tasty bit of bundt.

"What happened?"

"Well," Caper continued, chewing slowly, "in the midst of what could only have been a skittishly played game, Manfred and his bumper-pool buddy heard heavy—I mean father-heavy—thuds on the wooden staircase leading to the garage's second floor. The man of the house was ascending to the scene of the crime. Justice for the garden deviance had certainly not been speedy, but was now at hand." Caper took a slow, deep breath, as if he were once again, forty years after the fact, on the verge of facing the Man. "Nowhere to go. No good excuse to offer. Nothing for it but to pay the piper. Young Manfred stared blankly at the still-open window with eyes Edward Hopper would have paid a ransom for. Vacant. Detached. Devoid of all hope."

"What'd the old guy do? What'd he say?"

Caper breathed deeply once again. "He got to the top step and seemed winded by the climb. Looked around the place almost as if Manfred and his pool-pal weren't there. Stretched his arms. Probably cracked his neck, left then right. Took in the interior as if he were thinking of painting it."

"No dressing-down?"

"He squinted for a long time. Gazed over at the window as if puzzled, as if"—Caper quickly consulted his own wristwatch, and appeared to be satisfied with the results—"he had somehow forgotten that it existed, but was now quite relieved to recall that it was still there. He turned to Manfred and pointed at the open window, the back of his hand poised confidentially next to his mouth. 'Just came up here'—quick toss of the head and eyes to the window— 'to take a leak.'"

Zing-a-ding-ding.

Core in an uproar.

Langwein, unrepentantly delighted that the story had taken a sharp downward turn into even ruder matters, still had the wherewithal to shout, "What's all this got to do with Van Der Meyer, Cape?"

But Caper saw it coming from a mile away. "Not much, Lang, from one point of view. Those of you trapped in the clutches of a literalist world-view might indeed see little in common between a teacher who is currently feeling a lot of heat from St. Louis homicide detectives"—he paused to take a refreshing gulp of air, as well as another bite of cake—"and an eighth-grade boy who made a most unfortunate decision from a second-story garage window on a fine summer day in Pittsburgh, back in the days when the Ford administration was discharging its abbreviated duties." His body offering foreboding hints each day that it would soon unleash some terrible ailment reserved especially for people who had dared to drift into their 50's, Caper found himself in need of another large dose of oxygen.

"Fair enough, C. How 'bout you give us the non-literalist take on this?"

"Happy to. Those of us of the non-literalist persuasion might begin by pointing out that neither Van Der Meyer nor Manfred had any sort of *intent* to harm anything or anyone. No one could possibly utter the phrase 'malice aforethought' in their direction. Not by a longshot."

"Fair enough, again. Is that all you've got?"

"No. Not at all. I've 'got' quite a bit more, Lang. For the moment, I'll limit myself to the observation that both of the accused—"

"Bell, Cape. Bell. Any second."

"—both of the accused were guilty of little more than failing to *notice*—to anticipate, this is what we're talking about, isn't it?—the absence, *or* the presence, of a particular person. One didn't see a gardener down bel—"

Bell.

"I'll finish this lesson tomorrow, lunch!"

* * *

The last day of September in 1972 was damp, gray, and cold in Pittsburgh, even by Pittsburgh standards. Young Morton Caper played a football game in the morning for the St. Bernard's junior-varsity team, and recalled being as muddy as anyone else on the field at the final whistle. Now that the football segment of the day had been concluded (Caper and his father would not, as was their custom, remain to watch the varsity game, nor even go home to shower), their focus turned towards Three Rivers Stadium. Quite aside from the fact that he bore damp, tangible evidence of the prevailing climate conditions upon his person, he would have had good reason to remember the date's clamminess, as he was keenly aware that that particular September 30th either would or would not mark the occasion of Roberto Clemente's 3,000th hit. It was the final game of the regular season.

Of all the benefits that retrospection can impart to the person who chooses to indulge in it, Caper considered the power of reappraisal to be of prime importance. Without that, why bother to remember anything? Why? Nothing but dead wood, fertilizing nothing. But getting long-dormant moments up and living again didn't come without genuine re-evaluation. As it happened, his view of Three Rivers Stadium underwent a significant transformation more or less at the moment it was demolished. It wasn't that he had developed a sudden fondness for the now-razed concrete circus. (He had not.) But anyone who lamented the fact that the slate-gray structure was just plain ugly (as Caper had done many times in his teens, nursing the hapless idea that some ideal Forbes Field would reappear Brigadoon-style, but also somehow manage to materialize for more than a single day), should well consider the possibility that it may have been the perfect stadium complement to the Pittsburgh climate, and therefore had every right to consider itself a textbook example of "organic" design, environmentalists and hippies be damned. If some armed, bearded, and completely deranged architectural terrorist had entered a well-lit design firm somewhere in southwestern Pennsylvania, loudly declared himself a member of the "Pittsbionese Liberation Army," and proceeded to demand that someone build a sports complex that strictly conformed to the local biosphere, that extremely unbalanced person would have had very little to complain about once he saw that his ransom demand had resulted in Three Rivers Stadium. Like Riverfront, Veterans, Busch (architectural *cognoscenti* may feel free to keep their mouths shut), and probably one or two other examples, it was routinely decried as an abominable "cookie-cutter" structure, on a certain par with St. Louis' Pruitt-Igoe housing projects, so predictably abhorred in so very few, so narrow, and so very convenient, ways. But now, looking back on that cold, wet September 30th, sitting and then standing and doing everything but kneeling in the damp concrete donut, he couldn't help but recognize how right it was that there were fewer than 15,000 fans in attendance, hands in pockets, shivering and staring at the occasionally glistening Tartan Turf, some of them maybe wondering if the game would be called. The gray stadium most certainly "completed" the climate. September 30th served as exhibit A.

The game wasn't called. The Mets were in town, playing their very last game of the season. Three years past the "Miracle," they still possessed the vestiges of an assassin starting rotation. Seaver and Koosman sat shivering in the dugout. The much younger Jon Matlock was on the mound, finishing out a year that would not result in a Met playoff appearance, battling cold and achy air. Whether he knew it or not, he was also dealing with the expectation that the "Great One" would hit the hit that everyone in the sparse crowd yearned for. Presiding at the mike, Bob Prince would make the call (whatever it turned out to be), but in a rare lapse in preparing for the game, none of the Capers had brought along a transistor. Everything would depend upon their own eyes and ears.

In the fourth inning, Clemente stroked a double to left-center field, as Caper's father's whirring, purring, clicking SLR captured a half-dozen or so discrete moments of the swing. Each image reveals just how many empty seats there were, how scanty were the people who showed up in the cold damp for what turned out to be the last hit.

Caper, gazing backwards, no longer thought that it was a shame that so few had gone to the trouble to witness the milestone. (Roger Maris, too, didn't fill half a Yankee Stadium on a different and earlier season's final day.) In fact, he probably thought something close to exactly the opposite. No one in the pictures was decked out in the obligatory team gear. It was not a "sea" of Pirate black and gold. Good, and good again. It wasn't a sea of anything. Evidently, not many people felt obligated to be present. Good for them. Those who wished to behold Clemente's 3000th hit went to the game and defied the very un-baseball-like weather, crossing their fingers; those who did not did other things. Nothing at all amiss there. In fact, something quite civilized, commensurate.

As far as Caper could recall, people didn't used to "bleed" team colors in zany ways, nor paint their faces and/or their bodies, nor purchase oversized, pricey jerseys with names stitched to the back. But such stirrings were undeniably to be felt *at that very second* in Steeler Country, as well as in Fields and Stadiums all over the nation, something that, in the ensuing decades, would eventually manifest itself in loud, twangy music assaulting one's peace of mind between at-bats, just as soon as the promotional announcements on the upcoming nacho giveaway had run their course. Paying customers were now dressing up as gorillas, inanimate gridiron-related objects, or just about anything, for that matter, that would signal one's comically fanatical devotion to the team. Others were motivated to tote all sorts of gear from home, like props for a play. Caper, then and now, held no strong opinion concerning this sort of behavior. It was none of his business. But he occasionally entertained the possibility that there might be a campaign afoot to exterminate the simple pleasures of watching an athletic contest, of availing yourself of the opportunity to talk in a civilized tone of voice to your son or daughter or the stranger sitting next to you, perhaps recalling (or lying about) other games you had attended, other great catches or costly errors.

Forget about it. Ruthlessly programmed noise had become the rule of the day, kudzu-style; complaining about it would only add to the volume. But was it still worth quietly remarking that the English language once made room for words like "diversion" and "amusement," and that the activities thus designated were not necessarily a tacit invitation to go shirtless in subzero weather, your index fingers and your crimson belly jiggling in unison?

Never underestimate the small, unassuming pleasures of the past, Caper thought. Always, forever, and without exception, deeply suspect claims—every last one of them—about the glory and the grandeur of the old days. Things were never, and would likely never be, sweet and fitting. But they were sometimes quieter and a little bit less orchestrated, and worth remembering for that reason.

*   *   *

"Get back to that garden caper, Cape. Scene o' the crime, my man. I can't hear *enough*," Langwein gushed, "of that…that…tell us about that scream again. The scream."

"Love to, Lang, love to. But today I've got a different crime to tell you about. It was committed about a year prior to the garden drama, but it, too, featured a memorable, shocking, and bloody scream. May even have surpassed Edvard Munch's rigorous expectations. It occurred as I was acting in my one and only theatrical production." Caper gazed at the faces gathered about the lunch tables, every one of them skeptical. "In this instance, as in so many others, I find that it's best to finish one story by telling another. *Thousand and One N—*"

"Cape was once up on the boards?"

Caper beamed. "You're looking at a one-time thesp, Lang. A killer, in fact. Cassius." He held up an invisible dagger in his right hand and bared his teeth menacingly.

"Pretend murders don't count," Schroll protested.

"Agreed," Caper responded. "But on this particular occasion, the assassination went horribly awry. The thing actually turned bloody. Not *much* blood, but still…"

"Any whizzing?"

"Can't have that in every story, Lang. But I appreciate your input. Will the blood suffice?"

"Gonna have to. You're on a Sheherzara…

"Sheherazade," Van Der Meyer assisted.

"What Van Der Meyer said. You're on a Sheherazade roll. Bring on the blood, my man."

"I'll do my best." His eyes narrowed as he attempted to transport himself back to the spring of 1974. "*Julius Caesar*. The entire year in

38

sixth-grade English was devoted to the performance scheduled for late May or early June. Every single class period. No diagramming of any sentences; no vocabulary exercises. The students who formed the Roman mob—and don't forget, this was the vast majority of the sixth grade—did nothing all year except make mob noises on cue. Miss Harrigan," he confessed with a perplexed sigh, "was more single-minded than Ahab." Caper interrupted his own train of thought. "Methuselah's long-suffering wife—if, in fact, he had one—had nothing on her. Wonder why she never became a nun?"

"We're all wondering the same thing, Cape. But we've got a staged murder to talk about, don't we? Word is, real Roman blood was shed."

"Affirmative, Lang. Yours truly was assigned the role of Cassius, second-tier assassin. Unsurprisingly, the best actor in the whole grade played the title role. But what made him truly perfect for this particular part was his body type. He was a corpulent young Roman if ever anyone was. Put a crown of anything green on his head and you're looking at *Pax romana*, Pillsbury-edition."

"So what happened?"

"Murder happened, obviously. After nine or so months, the time had come to kill brave Caesar yet again, on stage and before a public audience, for the umpteenth time. But Miss Harrigan proved to have, as do all people who devote themselves relentlessly to a single idea, an Achilles heel."

"Goodness. And exactly what was Miss Harrigan's fatal weakness?"

"Costumes, my facetious friend. Props. For whatever reason, she didn't care about the visual aspects of drama. It was all about the words."

"Fair enough. What brought on the blood?"

"A knife."

"Someone brought a knife?"

"Brutus made one. At home. And, in our opening matinee performance, he stabbed Caesar with it."

"He *made* a shi…?"

"Allow me to explain. On the day before our opening performance, someone worked up the courage to ask Miss Harrigan about costumes. She completely discounted anything having to do with all of that wardrobe foolishness, adding that each one of us could simply don a sheet or something of the sort, and don't go to too much trouble while you're at it, young man. Very, very casual. Like I said, for her it was all about the words and their proper delivery."

"So get to the knife and the blood, Cape."

"Just about there, Lang. One of us—the assassins, I mean—then took the opportunity to ask about weapons. Same thing. She waved her hand dismissively and said something like, 'Any ol' toy knife will do.'"

"Who doesn't have a rubber dagger," Van Der Meyer pointed out, "lounging somewhere about the house?"

"Exactly. So sixth-grade Cape—a.k.a., Cassius—drops by the hardware store on his walk home, where he purchases a rubber bayonet, one that looked like it would serve as a perfect complement to a rubber M1 carbine. But Miss Harrigan had already, as I've said, spurned the whole 'ought we not make at least a passing effort to look just a little bit like first-century B. C. Romans?' question."

"Okay, so your rubber bayonet didn't do the damage. But you're telling us the kid playing Brutus went home and made a knife?"

"I am."

"Out of metal?"

"No. Well, partially. But sharp things don't have to be made out of metal, do they? Jus' looka me, for instance."

"So true, sensei. So wise. It's just that I was curious about the weapon that drew blood."

"Your curiosity does you great credit, Lang. As a storyteller, I prize it above all things. It seems that Brutus," he resumed, "having foregone the rubber bayonet route, instead fashioned a dagger out of thick cardboard he'd picked up at his family's bakery, covering it in heavy duty aluminum foil." Caper winced and smiled. "The thing must've really had a point."

"And?"

"And, as events were to prove beyond any doubt, Miss Harrigan should have conducted a weapons check. But she didn't. And don't dismiss the possibility that Fate may've had a hand in this as well. The moment," Caper said with a hint of trepidation, "had arrived for the storied assassination. If I remember correctly, I was the second backstabber. I delivered my lines as instructed, then the rubber bayonet. Caesar was now down on both knees, heroically and stoically awaiting the unkindest cut. Who knows how many hundreds of Caesars have uttered those three immortal Latin words, each one fraught with disbelief, unspeakable sorrow?" Caper bit his lip. "But in the full course of the past four centuries, with a few decades to spare, there cannot be more than just a few Caesars—and quite possibly only one—who, after Brutus has swooped in and dealt the mortal wound, have stunned the audience with such a piercing, shocking howl: 'Ou-ch!'"

Caper's echoing cry was accompanied by a great burst of English department merriment. He attempted to add a crowning remark, something to the effect that, as brief as his dramatic career turned out to be, he was ever so fortunate to have taken part in one of the most amusing slaughters in the history of theatre. But his own laughter wouldn't permit language.

* * *

"Carnal abandon."

Caper had just asked a roomful of teenagers a question about a notoriously disgruntled Yonville denizen—the beautiful, bored, and tormented Emma Bovary—when a studious, slender, and bespectacled young man raised his hand and proceeded to utter a two-word phrase that the teacher had almost certainly never heard any person say aloud. Caper could further attest to the fact that seeing the phrase in print (a none too common occurrence, mind you) would be sure to bring a bemused grin to his face, even as some region of his brain would summon an image of a fat, leather-bound, and oft-handled eighteenth-century novel. But still, how was it that that particular combination of words, articulated by a committed young man given to wearing tee-shirts of an evangelical stripe ("Got Jesus?"), had triggered small-scale paroxysms that simply refused to go away? It couldn't possibly have escaped the notice of all the students gathered in his room that for the rest of the hour, Caper proved to be unusually susceptible to loud, suspiciously lengthy coughing fits, often at the most inappropriate moments. Flaubert's cold, dark masterpiece—mercilessly constructed so as to elicit muffled, sardonic laughter—had been transformed into a minefield of knee-slappers for the snorting teacher. (Student: "...which is why the botched operation on Hippolyte's club foot contributes to the motif of—" [Caper outburst #7]. Some other student: "…just after Emma swallowed the arsenic, and the black bile began to pour from her mouth, I was reminded of the burning tar of the boat ri—" [Caper outburst #9]). He had begun the class hoping to discuss some of the literary benefits of free indirect discourse; what he had to deal with now was an intractable case of the giggles.

The young man in question went by the name Hoerstler or Holzworth or something beginning with an "H." In an instant, and with no intent to disrupt the educational process, he had pretty much rendered the rest of the class period unteachable. Steadily and inexorably, the teacher succumbed to a torso-cramp. Who could talk about debauched provincial Frenchmen when earnest H had uttered words dripping with…Caper couldn't quite say what they were dripping with. Archaic kitsch?

Kid says two words, and all at once your whole being is possessed.

*　*　*

"A body," Caper was in the process of saying to Van Der Meyer and Schroll at one end of the line of tables, "definitely cannot be both present and not-present in a particular place at a particular time. I get it. Believe me, I get it. Cops don't work in a world in which quantum exceptions to this law mean anything." He carved the air crisply with his right hand. "But just the same—"

"'But' nothin'," Van Der Meyer cut him off. "No 'just the same' on this one. Not a poem they're dealing with. It's a prosecution."

"Duly noted, counselor. But they also work in a world in which people make big—but sometimes very small—mistakes. And those mistakes can be accounted for. Juries are made up of people. And every one of the people who make up the—"

"Nope. My guy's gonna walk."

Caper stirred his black plastic fork in circles, yellow crumbs forming neat spirals. *Over.*

Six months gone. *No way out*, he thought. Nothing to do. Just take it. Six months gone.

After a few moments of collective departmental quiet, Caper shook his head energetically, holding the tines of the fork between the thumb and index finger of his left hand, as if it were a baton. "Don't even think about it," he insisted, slicing the air for emphasis. "Not once more." He looked at the remainder of his lunch as if annoyed by its existence. "Not once again. Not for a second." He continued to shake his head with spirited authority. "Forget it. I probably did the same thing yesterday. No joke." He now switched to nodding his head up and down. "Not only that," he added with determination, "I've had kids in my classroom who weren't even on my class roster." He looked to the other teachers for tacit signs of empathy. "And I didn't notice."

"Happens to me all the time," Donnelly joined in.

Nodding heads around the table. "For*get* it," he repeated. He turned to the remains of the spread arranged in front of him, placed the black fork on table surface, and indiscriminately pinched a few crumbs of yellow double-layered. He washed down the meager residuum with Black Cherry pop.

"Don't go gettin' haunted by it."

* * *

Ghosts in the building. Caper supposed that he was more susceptible than most people to imagine that he detected, or perhaps even fabricated, the presences of the past. Not a whole lot different from reading a poem or a novel. A good deal of what you see you are in some ways bound to see, by training or sensibility or both. Whether trained, or predisposed, to conjure up what he imagined to be merely dormant, he was likely doomed to seek out and to discriminate layerings of the past for the rest of his life.

The sheet-metal tanker desk manufactured by the Tennsco Corp in Dickson, Tenn., at least a half-century earlier, and part of his everyday life as a teacher for the last eighteen years, was perfectly suited to his ruminative habits. It was not at all difficult for Caper to imagine bottles of Scotch tucked away in one or more of the drawers many decades ago, nor to fancy that those bottles did not lay undisturbed. Stories he had heard—some, admittedly, at second or third hand, but some not—only strengthened his suspicions that things told stories, if only you bothered to listen and to retell them. Sometimes it was nearly impossible *not* to re-imagine your surroundings almost entirely, once you had been provided with some heretofore hidden but quite straightforward fact. Example: concealed above a ceiling drop, the main teachers' lounge only a few dozen yards from Caper's classroom still housed a custom-made, heavy-duty air-ventilation system, specially designed to address the staggering volume of cigarette smoke produced on a daily basis by the LHS faculty—a system, it was averred by more than one old-timer, that was never quite up to the job. Entrance to or exit from the lounge was invariably attended by feathery clouds of second-hand Marlboro, jazzy ventilation system or no. Of course, the Lindbergh School District had withdrawn its official sponsorship of the five-minute faculty nicotine dash a quarter century earlier. Not only that, previously inconceivable organizations, operating under exotic and puzzling-sounding names like "Wellness Committee" and "Faculty Fitness Club" ("Exercise to Energize!"), were now brazenly peddling their robust services in broad daylight. Nevertheless, it meant a great deal to Caper to be able to imagine that a future archaeologist might one day stumble upon this very spot, only to congratulate herself for having uncovered such weighty and tangible evidence that some kind of arcane, collective, and smoky ritual was once enacted on these premises (no doubt religious in nature), one that must have centered upon a commodity dearly prized by scholarly initiates.

Arriving at Lindbergh in the late '90's, Caper caught a last glimpse of a breed of teacher pretty much now extinct, one who had indeed been a devoted and daily communicant in these time-honored tobacco rites. It would be tempting, but also inexcusably sloppy, to say that they were "products of the '60's," although that far too narrow way of putting it at least had the virtue of indicating a certain willingness to defend and promote the profession in ways that were probably distinctly different from the previous generation. But the "60's" tag ran the deeper danger of suggesting a *Room 222* "grooviness" that Caper never really encountered in any substantial way. In high school, his most memorable teachers seemed at least as much out of the '30's (in sensibility and temperament) as the '60's. His junior-year history course didn't settle for a token glance at either the Homestead strike or the battles that shaped the New Deal. Nor did it make room for lengthy teach-ins dedicated to raising awareness about Kent State or Woodstock. At Lindbergh, moreover, this generation was likely to be considerably less concerned with things like "self-esteem" and "differentiated instruction" and "learning styles" than more recent arrivals, even as the latter were also more likely to be, regardless of their decided advantage in the "tolerance"-related matters, politically conservative. The Old Guard wasn't weaned on sensitivity-training.

Jack Benning, next door to Room 55, was in his thirtieth and final year when Caper arrived in the late summer of 1998. He was a pain in the ass for the principals, and he cherished the role. Always happy to tell a story, he was quite eager to share with his department colleagues his opening day remarks to his students, evidently delivered with a great deal of *gravitas* each year. Having dispensed with the necessary business of handing out "Rights and Responsibilities" books, syllabi, course descriptions, and so forth, Benning would somberly intone that he wished to have the undivided attention of everyone present. He would then take advantage of a few long silent moments. "I would like all of you," he would begin, "to take notice of a very important line in this room." Uncertain, silent faces. Benning would walk over to the wall adjoining the core, point his left index finger straight to the floor tiles, and walk solemnly across the entire classroom, all the while staring down his new students. He had just invisibly divided his own desk from all of the student chairs. "This line divides me from you, and you from me. You are never—not once—to cross this line to ask me a question. Or to touch anything. Or to do anything. Have I made myself clear?" Nodding heads all round. "This is Benning territory." Pause. "Fort Benning." Only a few laughs. "My office."

It was from Benning that Caper would steal a line he would thenceforth use twice a year, whenever state-mandated tornado drills were conducted. "You heard her," Caper would say to his students after the drill-principal had announced over the loudspeaker: "Lindbergh High School students and staff: We are now experiencing a tornado."

"Ladies and gents, what's the greatest danger posed to us by a tornado?" Caper would briskly ask his charges as they grumbled their way under the desks. Once in a while, someone with a Scouting background would reply post haste: "Flying debris!" But not often. So Caper would seize the occasion to thunder, "Flying debris!" Pause. "And what do we do when we're in danger of being maimed or killed by flying debris?" Without fail, a host of incoherent answers would step on one another's toes. Pause. "No, no, no! What part of 'protective human shield' don't you understand? Caper in the middle, safeguarded by an unbroken circle of student armor. Now let's get it done!" Sometimes a modicum of laughter, sometimes not.

Benning's version was more elaborate and probably a lot funnier. Naturally, the doyen of classroom non-encroachment zones would occupy the epicenter of safety, girls forming a tight inner ring, boys a defensive periphery. "It is imperative that I be protected, because if there are casualties, I'll need to be safe so that I can take charge."

* * *

Van Der Meyer's demeanor had palpably changed for the worse. Everyone in the department knew that the half-year old drive-by was weighing on his mind. It wasn't that he had suddenly started behaving in a gruff fashion, tossing off curt replies to solicitous questions. Quite the reverse. Repeated and unmistakable signs of politeness had been noted by several of his colleagues. Cursing had become the exception. Clothes were occasionally pressed. Colleagues had every reason to worry.

Three days after Gurney's most recent visit, one that looked to be the final courtesy call from St. Louis' finest, Caper entered Van Der Meyer's room once again, toting his copy of *The Inferno*.

"Sorry to interrupt," he began. "Still like to go over the quizzes."

"Let's get it done," Van Der Meyer cheerily replied.

They spent only about five or ten minutes getting their grading plans in sync, agreeing to a schedule of one quiz for every two circles or so, capped by an in-class essay. They would pass out a couple of different visual maps of hell, one in a conical shape cutting into the bowels of the nether regions (adhering reasonably closely to Dante's vision), the other a more conventional grid, easier to read, perhaps, but losing most if not nearly all of the element of perilous descent. If the kids actually bothered to read the poem, they should have no problems.

The ensuing weeks in senior honors now settled, Caper pivoted.

"Luebbert said that the cops said," Caper paused, arching his back as he pondered exactly what he ought to say next—"that they're positive that the guy Mulnay shot—" he tapped the red paperback on the surface of Van Der Meyer's desk— "was—and this is Luebbert quoting Gurney, just a few minutes ago in his office—a 'colleague in the gang trade.'"

"'Colleague'?"

"Yep. 'Colleague.'" Caper stared at the novelty clock on Van Der Meyer's wall, the numbers arranged in reverse order on the face. *Luebbert said the cops snapped 'cooperation,' mumbled 'attrition.'* "Not very collegial on May 5ᵗʰ, was he?"

Van Der Meyer looked at the deranged clock and said nothing.

Caper continued, tentatively. "Would that little fact make you feel any..."

"Don't know."

Caper nodded slowly. "I don't, either. But you're going to have to do some honest forgetting—good, clean forgetting—on this thing. You didn't do anything. It's all pretty messy anyway." He tapped the spine of the red book on the desk once again. "Can't let the needle skip back over and over and over. It'll drive you nuts. Only one path here. Clean it out. No regrets on this one. None."

"I know."

"Forget it."

"I know."

"It's not what you did or didn't do. It's some kid who...I don't know what it is, but you've got to cut through it." Caper's voice trailed off. He looked at the clock again, half-expecting help but getting nothing of the kind. "See you at lunch."

*   *   *

When he arrived at Lindbergh High School in the autumn of 1998, Caper was approached by a kind of informal "Welcome" team eager to discover whether he would be interested in providing introductory material for a library display. Simply a help-us-get-to-know-you effort, if you don't mind too much. Caper found the 50's-era glass presentation case very congenial to his tastes, to say nothing of the circular library space. Precisely his sort of architecture. The whole idea seemed very amiable and Midwestern. He joined the cause with enthusiasm.

Provided with an introductory form, he tried to provide all the data they needed. Under the rubric "Favorite music," he answered, "Hawaiian." Just for grins. See if anyone said anything. Caper even brought in a vintage Hawaiian shirt as evidence of his musical preferences. It was duly placed in the presentation. In addition, he provided a Pittsburgh Pirate baseball cap to verify his diamond loyalties. An 8 x 12 framed photo was featured in the center of the case. Caper and James Ellroy, shaking hands in a local Barnes & Noble, with hard-bound copies of the novelist's work visible in the background. Caper attached the caption: "James Ellroy is delighted to meet me at a recent book signing." No comment from anyone.

Caper had also indicated to the "Welcome" people that he and his wife had recently been developing a modest vintage vinyl collection. True. But he had forgotten to bring in an album by way of illustrating his LP tastes. Sinatra or something. Maybe Lou Rawls. One of the library's assistants, forced to address a vacuum in the display case, took it upon herself to supply one of the records from the available collection. She (or was she merely the instrument of Providence?) selected Flip Wilson's *Cowboys and Colored People*. Arriving at the high school the following day, Caper was utterly mortified to see this album, heretofore unknown to him, curled up next to his name, his photos, youthful paraphernalia, and so forth.

His mind was a swirling torrent of…torrentially swirling stuff. In the first place, he was fond of Flip Wilson. Geraldine and all. And as both a Roy Rogers devotee and a mid-60's record collector, he knew he would have to acquire that LP eventually. (He did, some years later, when the library made its final dump of every last disk of vinyl.) But the very existence of such an artifact he did not find "offensive." Nor the fact that a public high school library would have it in its collection. He had had enough politically-correct preening to last several lifetimes, and further supposed, were he forced to take a position, that people should not forget that that phrase was once common currency. Flip Wilson, among other people, had had to deal with it. Caper's current predicament was born instead of something both simple and obvious. This particular album cover did not serve as an ideal way to be introduced to a new community of colleagues.

Cut her a break, Cape. Besides, maybe she simply grabbed any old record that was handy and didn't even bother to look at it.

He asked to see the person in charge of the display. After they had both walked over to the cabinet, Caper cupped both hands in the direction of the comedy record. "Did you put that album in there?"

She looked squarely at the cover, then back at Caper, and said, "Yes." Nothing. No indication that anything might be amiss.

"Would you like to pick out another?" she asked cheerfully.

"Yes, please."

"Would you like to pick it out?"

"No, no. Anything else you've got'll be fine. Rod McKuen. Whatever." The next day he brought in *No One Cares*.

* * *

Caper's father, like his father's mother, was given to viewing the world through a certain set of ethnic lenses, most especially when the matter of Irishness was involved. His grandmother (née Nell Duffy) probably said the phrase "nice Irish boy" at least fifty thousand times in the course of her long life. Utterly unconscious of his own habit of mind, his father would often scold himself as he paced the kitchen floor, a white telephone receiver slung over one of his shoulders like a bawling newborn, trying to retrieve a customer's last name from some shaded corner of his memory. "The hell is it, Charlie? Rimini? Rinaldi? Ruggier...? Damn." Alternate shoulder. "All kinds o' spaghetti in it." Undeterred, he would spin the receiver a complete turn, the generous cord noodling into ever more knots, a pendulous intestine occasionally kissing the kitchen's well-used linoleum. And yet the dogged incantation turned the trick more often than not. In no time, a person whose name began with an "R" and ended in a vowel would discover that his telephone was ringing.

Caper remembered in particular a dour November afternoon when the Steelers were playing the Cleveland Browns. His grandmother knew and cared very little about football, and was pleased to remark on that fact on a regular basis. Devotedly, however, she would sit at one end of the davenport and rub his father's head on Sundays, probably for the entire course of every televised game. In particular, she got a big bang out of how everyone—especially Caper's mother, who could reliably be found watching the game on the 4-inch black & white in the kitchen—would yell and scream at the television at critical moments. "Get him!" his mother would holler. "Him" would be pronounced "hiiiiiiiiiiiim." His grandmother relished every last second of it. She couldn't get over people screaming at a television.

Late that afternoon, Franco Harris took off on an improbably long touchdown run to give the Steelers a lead. As the household applause began to subside, Caper's immensely gratified grandmother, whose Irish sonar was perpetually on high alert (even if her vision had waned just a bit over the years), made certain that others, too, take note. "Listen to that, Charles," she said. "Nice Irish boy made a touchdown." Everyone laughed, but no one corrected her.

But make no mistake: this was the year when the colors of the Italian flag reigned supreme. Those three shades were to be seen on every corner of the city, on hard hats, knit hats, scarves, and flags. The "Italian Army" was really only about 1972, when even Frank Sinatra visited one of the Steeler practices in mid-December. Summarily enlisted in the Army as a field commander of some sort, Sinatra's presence had obviously not gone unnoticed by the Almighty, Who would conspicuously intervene in a playoff game only a week or two later.

Franco Harris had, as everyone knew, a black father and an Italian mother, who'd met in Italy and then returned to the US at the end of his military service in the 40's. Caper had heard from friends of his—friends of Italian extraction—that when Franco was on a tear, the house would ring with rambunctious cheers: "Run, paisono, run!" When, however, as was not infrequently the case, Franco made a particularly exasperating step out of bounds to avoid a tackle, or otherwise comported himself in ways displeasing to his "compatriots," other epithets would be heard.

He wondered if this were true, and if the practice were widespread.

If someone were to ask Caper's father what he did for a living, he would say, "I sell bulldozers." His Caterpillar customers were largely if not overwhelmingly of Italian descent, with first names like "Nino," nicknames like "Tubby," and last names like "Bozzo." Not all of them were believed to limit their business pursuits to construction and coal mining.

One time late in the 80's, long after the glory days of the construction of I-79, Caper and his parents were approaching Pittsburgh no longer as inhabitants but as visitors, and from an unfamiliar northern direction. It almost seemed a foreign approach to their former hometown. They had come across a brand new stretch of concrete highway, still bright white, and not yet on the Rand-McNally. Best guess would be that it was a new extension to one of the parkways, now serving booming suburbs up north. His mother, ever worried about the possibility of getting lost, looked anxiously at his father. "What does this mean?"

The old man didn't miss a beat. "A lotta happy Italians."

*   *   *

Intersection of Hempe and Gravois. His car stationary and trained obliquely at the city's heart, Caper briefly lost himself in a desultory hunt for the name of that nice little restaurant, the one that used to be just down there on the right. Roberto's? Rap—? In front of him, ten miles or so to the northeast, he could make out the crowning sections of the Gateway Arch, its sharp, stainless folds slinging back the low rays of the sun behind him.

Never catch this light, Caper silently griped for the umpteenth time. The northeast corner of the intersection sported a vintage Dairy Queen. Caper treasured it. Concrete block affair painted white. Blue and gold neon striping. A lot of walk-up business. And seasonal. Only open from May to September or something. Customers ate on picnic tables arranged nearby, if they even bothered to stay. Simple, small, dignified. Want to live in a world where that DQ is the norm. Functional.

Northwest corner was a Baptist church. An electronic message board had been installed about three years previously. Scriptural and/or exhortatory punning was its forte: "To Prevent Sinburn Use Sonscreen"; "God Answers Knee-Mail"; "The Wages of Sin is Death. Repent Before Payday."

Wages.

Southwest corner had a small flower shop. Southeast corner once featured a grand old dive known as "The Back Door," fondly remembered by imbibers of a certain age. It was succeeded by a bar garishly adorned by an alligator fetishist true and loyal, proudly advertising its unwavering

"T esday Kara ke Nite" for most or all of its nearly ten-year run. Van Der Meyer, long a connoisseur of such establishments, reported that longneck bottles of Natty Lite were the house specialty, conveniently submerged in an ice-water wash tub placed close to the entrance. Twin sawhorses provided e-z waist-level access to the reduced-calorie A-B beverage, coldly lolling atop the polished concrete floor. If either the front or back label still adhered to any given amber bottle, the brew would have been deemed "fresh" by veteran customers. Caper's four-year old son Paulie never tired of beholding the brightly-painted, towering 'Gators carousing luringly on the roof, their tenuous verticality sustained by strategically placed guy-wires. For a long while, every time they waited at the light he would shout with gusto: "Alligators, Daddy!" As time passed, he began to pester his old man with urgent requests: "Daddy, when can we go to that alligator house?"

Payday.

Some day, Paulie, Caper would reply. Some day.

Quite recently, however, and cruelly rendering such blithe paternal assurances into the emptiest of lies, the structure had suddenly taken some time off in order to explore what life was like as an unoccupied building. The alligators had vamoosed, whereabouts unknown. But it was the "The Back Door" incarnation that would live on in the hearts and minds of south St. Louisans, cherished in select circles as a good place to get a lip-smacking brain sandwich. Indeed, upon his arrival in the summer of 1996, Caper had discovered that the city nurtured a longstanding and proud brain-eating tradition, and could furthermore provide "head cheese" lovers with a plentiful supply of the mysterious delicacy. The joint used to have a sign painted right onto the exterior wall, or maybe hanging from an eave: "Best Brains in St. Louis!" it boasted. "Only 25 cents." How many men had caught a glimpse of the sign, he couldn't help but wonder, only to bethink themselves: "Say, that sounds like it'll hit the spot right about now. And only a quarter to boot! Why, I'll just give Dottie a call from inside and tell 'er I'll be a little late tonight."

"Best Brains." Good thing. Hate to eat run-of-the-mill brains.

* * *

A student who applies for admittance into the Program for Exceptionally Gifted Students (PEGS) in St. Louis must have achieved (among other criteria) a score of 140 or higher on the Wechsler Intelligence Scale IQ/Index. Because the Lindbergh School District served as one of two main hubs for the program, Caper had come into extended contact with a very high percentage of these brilliant young people, many of whom graduate a year or two younger than eighteen, some of whom take advanced calc classes at Washington University in the morning before being driven down to the Lindbergh campus for the afternoon, and a few of whom make the local papers for doing things like racking up a perfect ACT/SAT perfecta at the age of fourteen.

Prior to his arrival at Lindbergh, he had had little occasion to think either about the merits or the liabilities of intelligence testing. He was of course aware how certain debates might go. Cultural influences and so forth. Test biases. Certain kinds of intelligence being privileged, others ignored. He had some vague recollection of reading something which dwelt on the fact that the "original" pool of IQ test-takers consisted exclusively of British military men, and that they were tested during or after the Great War. He didn't know if that were really the case, but was absolutely positive that it would fuel the ire of the anti-IQ crowd.

One certainly didn't have to have an unusually high IQ to understand that this scale, like all systems, would break down at a certain point. How, after all, could anyone discriminate between a 180, say, and a 185? No one could design the metric to allow such fine-tuned scoring, or to interpret data retrieved from such lofty heights. All systems are leaky. Nonetheless, Caper's opinion of the IQ index improved the more he got to know the PEGS kids. No real mystery conscript in the whole bunch. That's saying something. Kind of like a quality-control system. He would grant in a millisecond that all sorts of "exceptionally gifted" young people were being unfairly screened out of giftitude simply because their minds didn't square—or square precisely enough—with a particular test. On the other hand, this intelligence machine didn't spit out clunkers at the top end.

Caper thought about the cut-off line. Were the PEGS people strict in keeping the 139-ers out of the land of Gift? Ask Roegner. -oe. Like to sit in on some of those meetings. Were there feisty arguments about

145 or 150? "Maybe you're right, Helen. We *should* kick it up to 150. Too many stragglers otherwise."

What was his own IQ? No idea. Definitely lower than theirs.

He had his own quite unscientific scale, to be sure. The *Blackadder* test. On days when big projects were due—say, the *Hamlet* essay—he'd generally reward students with some sort of video treat. Sometimes *Mystery Science Theater 3000*, sometimes a requested movie. More often than not, however, the classic Rowan Atkinson series would be on offer. Hysterical. Caper never wearied, even after years of repeats. Nevertheless, that a certain type of young person would fail to be captured by the series was a fact he simply couldn't ignore. Perhaps a few minutes' attention would be paid to the British banter before some other activity—catching up on a biology lab, or reading a vampire tale, or perhaps a novel featuring dragons and thrones—would be sought for diversion. Too much trouble to enjoy. Another stripe of student would very likely, but not always, really dig the bawdy wit-fest. Cerebral and coarse all at once. They'd *love* it. Of course, Caper was well aware of the pitfalls of extrapolating from a casual taste test. At the same time, he wasn't sure that that sort of thing was entirely avoidable.

Among his own favorite episodes were those featuring Rik Mayall, British vulgarian *par excellence*. Caper could never show these in class, given that Mayall's trademark shtick was to deliver lines like, "Am I pleased to see you, or did someone just put a canoe in my pocket?"

Can't share everything, Caper reflected.

*   *   *

"Don't truck with the Mother's Club."

Benning's gaze moved in a slow horizontal arc, left to right, and then back again. "Have no *truck*," he repeated, like a conscientious thespian still working out the kinks of a new line of dialogue, "with Lindbergh's Mothers." Each syllable had long been steeped in some unspeakably haunting experience, a trauma the tormented old teacher could never vanquish, trapped as he was in the clutch of a terrifying maternal malevolence. He had a thousand-yard stare.

Caper stood next to another newly-hired teacher early in his first year at Lindbergh High School, a young female whose name he had long since forgotten, absorbing the grave warning of the elder statesman. He took the words on faith, and always, even to this day, gave a very wide berth to that venerable and nurturing institution. "They will cut your balls off," Benning had grimly added. *Nelson.* At which point he turned to the dismayed young woman, permitting himself a lingering pause. "Even if you don't have any."

She squinted, but in exactly the sort of way that compelled one to acknowledge just how impoverished the word "squint" could be made to appear.

Nevertheless, as the years passed, Caper discovered that he never really had any reason to dread the Mother's Club. Its members faithfully provided delicious lunches once a year for the entire staff. Their baked mostaccioli knew no peer. With patience and grace, they served as caterers for those evenings when teachers were obliged to stay for parent meetings. They seemed to have a lot of scholarships to offer deserving seniors. Would even purchase stuff for your classroom, if only you asked. Not really, Caper couldn't help but conclude, a very frightening bunch. Exactly what was the source of Benning's awful proscription?

The Marching Band. The Spirit of St. Louis Marching Band. Now *that* crew strutted to its own private beat. Lookin' to replenish your club's dry coffers, are you? Widen your revenue stream? Accrue liquidity? This synchronized outfit can make it rain cats and dogs whenever and wherever it pleases, never deigning to break a sweat. Think about it. Got their very own trucks snuggled tightly inside their very own parking area (custom chain-link encasing included)—trucks driven, for all Caper knew, by their very own in-house Teamsters. Mess with them, your ass is grass. And they will definitely march on it.

*   *   *

Payday. Death.
Wages.
$9.81? Or $9.82?

Caper was genuinely disappointed with himself for not remembering to the penny how much his hourly wage was in that first summer. It was one of those two numbers. He could say for certain that he would have far preferred the lower number. Paradox.

In early June, on the morning after his high school graduation, Caper reported for work at the Dimezzo Coal Mine in southwestern Pennsylvania. Once a deep mine, its focus had turned entirely to stripping. With the rest of the summer-season workers, he toiled in the tipple, together with a supervising crew of regulars. He was the youngest worker at the mine. The tipple was universally regarded as the worst station to be assigned.

The reasons for this last assessment were not difficult to find: the tipple was the dirtiest, loudest, and most crushingly boring station in the production of coal. Now in his 50's, three decades and more removed from his very short mining days, Caper couldn't deny the fact that he bore a dim but still lingering resentment of all energy-consumers who never gave a thought to the elaborate (if also surprisingly simple and ancient) procedures that power the whole grid. That would very likely be a substantial number of people.

When the coal at Dimezzo was just about to be processed for use by Duquesne Light (or, back then, by a few of the remaining Pittsburgh blast furnaces), it went through one final stage of separation. At this culminating point, the product torn from the ground consisted exclusively of coal, slate, and dirt (or, depending on the weather, mud). The shiny black *raison d'être* for the entire operation was now destined to be dropped in one of two bituminous piles, one comprised of refined—that is to say, finely crushed—coal (the money pyramid), the other a bastard heap roughly suggestive of unevenly sized shards of hardwood charcoal carelessly mixed with bits of cinder (think "Isle of Misfit BTU's"). The latter mass, in turn, would be referred to as "slack," "slag," "culm," or "the other pile," depending on the age and disposition of the speaker. Perhaps some outfit purchased a quantum of this "other" stuff, confident that it knew how to turn a profit on lower-temp burns. Or perhaps the slack was simply waiting for a last-minute, sixth-circle reprieve. Caper never asked and didn't care. The fine stuff, by contrast, had a firm date with a power plant, or an open furnace. From this pile, and on a regular but unannounced basis, a man hired by the energy company would collect a random sample in a slender tube-shaped bag, only to drive away discreetly in his pickup. Caper's foreman was made keenly aware that this mound had to be kept quite free from taint. It should consist of coal and pretty much nothing else. More than once, gazing at this conical pile of cultivated coal, his father had remarked, "Might as well be gold." Meanwhile, a third mass, less defined than the other two and notably less shiny, slouched about the four main supporting beams of the tipple, and was comprised of jagged, heavy slabs of slate, still in the 70's and early 80's being discussed as a possible "alternative" energy resource. Shale and petroleum or something of the sort. Caper didn't know whatever became of that discussion.

Inside the tipple, his job was so simple as to be comical. He, with a half-dozen other young men and a couple of supervisors, would stand along a conveyor belt. After the coal trucks dumped the coal/slate mush into giant "pans" located above and to the side of the suspiciously flimsy-looking tipple, the dark material would be subjected to impolite treatment by thunderous "shakers," thumping iron grids whose sole purpose was to bounce, crudely sift, and otherwise brusquely shuttle the mongrel material to the enclosed and elevated ashtray where Caper and other tipple workers awaited. Their job was to separate, first visually and then manually, coal from slate. ("Slate picking," if you must know, has served for well over a century as the highly technical phrase to describe this advanced skill. Some of its earliest practitioners were once known as "breaker boys," at this distance a name as poetic as it is poetically misleading. The "boys" were actually boys, often as young as eight, their lives as expendable as the feet they flung over the picking tables, the better to conduct their bare-handed sifting of slate in Pennsylvania's anthracite fields.) This was the final step. Depending on their assessment, material would either be pulled into a vertical chute (that was the slate), or continue on into the "coal crusher," a mechanical device specifically designed to crush coal. Now and then, dear reader, stray elements of this universe make perfect sense.

It took maybe two or three days to develop the skill of discriminating which black slabs were slate, which were coal. Of course, it would be quite a big deal (really, the only big deal that could possibly happen in the tipple) if a large piece of slate were to introduce itself to the coal crusher. Coal crushers, he was reminded, were not slate crushers. And should a sufficiently large piece of rock induce the cessation of coal-crushing, the entire mine would lose its mojo more or less instantly. Some sort of coal crusher specialist might have to be brought in, and lots of unsavory talk from the bosses would ensue. Therefore, when any doubtful black cake came down the belt, six or eight or more lively hands would reach out as one, and the suspect mass would either a) be permitted to approach the crusher, because the tipple workers' experienced touch instantly recognized it as a beneficent lump of energy-producing carbon, or b) and, much more ominously, become the focus of urgent and collective physical labor. In the latter instance, the pickers would wordlessly identify the best chute for the collective heavy rock dump, and push and pull the weighty mass to its slaty grave.

You had better wear your rubber gloves. Neither slate nor coal are friendly to the palm. One co-worker, dubbed "One-Armed Bill," would routinely don only one rubber glove, each finger and probably also the thumb bedecked with ventilating "windows"—little squares that Bill had affectionately cut into each rubber digit for cooling purposes. An experienced hand in the tipple, he had concluded, presumably, that he need use only one of his two arms to remove slate from the belt. He was mistaken. One incident like the one described above left a very ugly laceration between thumb and index finger on his unprotected hand. Caper remembered that the resulting mixture of coal dust, blood, and soft tissue suggested a kind of glutinous and most unappetizing cranberry sauce, heavily seasoned with crushed black pepper. Straight to the emergency room with Bill. The bosses were pissed. After he was taken to the hospital, everyone else's hands were subjected to ungentle inspection. Keep your fucking gloves on your hands, assholes.

The cacophony produced by the coal trucks, coal pans, coal shakers, and coal crusher would be difficult to exaggerate. Black filth was ubiquitous. Eyelids, nasal crevices, lips, hair, and everything else, were subject to incessant caking. Caper's snot was black crude. Hard hats were required by law but rarely worn. The weight of the miner's helmet was palpable and unwelcome. If occasionally one of the upper foremen did attempt to enforce the wearing of some sort of substantial cranial protection (let's say by dropping a chunk of coal or slate onto one of their heads, a mode of physical persuasion hatched in the teach-by-pain school), that effort would yield predictable results.

No one in the tipple, after all, was in danger of being crushed by a tumbling ceiling of coal, shale, and/or dirt.

*   *   *

On one warm autumn day shortly after they had purchased a used 1996 Buick Roadmaster Estate Wagon, Caper and Iris decided to put the "wagon" element of the beast to some useful purpose. They drove a short distance into St. Louis Hills to investigate an estate sale recommended by one of their neighbors. Stan Musial's old neighborhood. Unfortunately, very little of the goods on offer interested Caper, with the singular exception of an agreeably patinated (the seller said "from the '30's") Immaculate Mary statue in the back garden. Caper didn't quibble and paid the full $99 on the price tag. Pleased with the acquisition, though a little disappointed that he hadn't found an opportunity to pack a large haul of dressers and ottomans in the cavern behind the front seats, Caper returned home.

He and his wife both had a taste for a certain stripe of Catholic *accoutrement*. Caper's was rooted, among other things, in being one of eight children. Iris' was developed in the southern border area of Arizona in which she had grown up, a culture steeped in Mexicana. In grade school, she and her sisters and her brother were often the only white kids in class. Their friends' houses would be tricked out in all manner of sun-baked mariolatry, mixed together with bountiful helpings of Sacred Hearts and bright plastic rosaries. As a result, the Caper dining room was adorned with a sizable number of Mexican retablos, fetched from vendors on a number of cross-border shopping raids. There was something about art painted on tin that they both liked, as well as the usually flat, "primitive" quality of the images. And the painters could and did paint anything they wished. The Caper favorite was a relatively large piece of tin—just over a square foot—featuring a levitating blue-and-white Blessed Virgin presiding over a successful and illegal river crossing into the States. Mary is floating over the Mexican side of the river; a somewhat smaller blue-and-white helicopter hovers over the other. The 'copter shines a powerfully angled floodlight down to the blue and brown Rio Bravo, but fails to detect the northbound Mexican, who is just setting foot on American ground.

His hat already on the northern shore, the immigrant is pulling himself up by a sturdy and (one could only suppose) miraculously placed tree branch. Inauspiciously, however, there's a trooper car lurking behind a small hill to the north, blue and white, too, but with a cherry daub of red on the roof. On the lower border of the retablo, in four lines of closely-packed Spanish, the scene is celebrated and dated (Mayo 1950). Evidently "Mendoza," as the man is identified, made it across for good, in spite of the best efforts of border authorities.

This newly acquired BVM would serve as a perfect capstone for a traditional "Mary Garden" Caper had been cooking up, and had the additional virtue of having an impeccable provenance: St. Louis Hills. If there were a residential ground zero for St. Louis Catholicism, this had to be it.

But this was no ordinary Immaculate Mary. Caper may have been denied a voluminous haul to satisfy his wagon-craving, but the extraordinary density of the statue largely made up for what it lacked in cubic measure. Heavy as they come. Heavier. The rear springs of the Roadmaster could, of course, easily accommodate the substantial Queen of Ivory. But pulling her out of the low rear door had gravely endangered Caper's lower back region, as well as other parts of his anatomy. Having arrived at the home garden, and just prior to planting her in the spot before which the Lilies of the Valley would be planted, Caper requested that the scale to be retrieved from the bathroom. He wished to document his pain. "One thirty-three," he announced to his wife after the weigh-in.

One hundred thirty-three pounds packed into a two-foot, nine-inch tall Lady.

Subsequent springs would prove unequivocally that the weigh-in had not been a fluke. If the earth got sufficiently wet, and then froze, and then got wet again (a not uncommon sequence in, say, March), the seasoned queen would fall backwards, her face to the heavens. Himmel. Wait. Himmelkamp. Himmelspr—? No. Himmelpflug. Fleug—? He shook his head and gave up the hunt for one of his former student's names. Just grateful no child had been caught in the squishy buckling of the concrete, celestial mother.

He had heard more recently, moreover, from a retired cop in the neighborhood, that two houses down on Eichelberger had had their garden Maries stolen. Very, very dirty pool, Caper thought. Was there some sort of underground Mary market? Chop shops where "hot" Maries were processed for illicit trade?

And yet his eyes sparkled as he considered the delectable possibility that someone would attempt to pilfer his high-density, don't-make-'em-like-that-anymore Mary. Spellbinding entertainment. He'd insist on a front row seat. Caper envisioned himself lounging in a low comfortable chair on the back porch, feet resting lazily on the squat concrete wall, breezily egging on the burglar. Ice-cold Manhattan in his right hand. Pistachios in a tastefully decorated bowl in comfortable proximity. "Go ahead," Caper would say in his best Eastwood to the hapless criminal. "She's all yours." Pause. "Free to a good home. Really."

"Oh," he would add offhandedly. "Just don't forget your one-way ticket." Puzzled thief. "Herniatown." Still mystified. "Population: *you*, 'bro."

* * *

One day in particular stood out in Caper's memory of tipple-work. Perhaps because there was for one reason or another a skeletal crew, the sharp-eyed slate pickers had been caught off guard by a very large, extremely heavy rock heading straight for the crusher, where it would undoubtedly bring the entire mining operation to a halt. There was a greasy, smeared red button on the wall by the entrance door to the tipple, designed precisely for this sort of situation. It was a kind of "emergency stop" knob, of the sort one might still see in a train or elevator or streetcar. Casual pressing of this device was very strongly discouraged by the bosses, and would be sure to trigger a genial visit from men who were otherwise tipple-averse, as well as a cordial chat with the senior tipple-supervisor. But then again, conclusive evidence of the terrible damage they had prevented would have been sitting there right on the belt. Many hundreds of pounds of proof.

Trouble was, every single hand in the tipple was desperately clinging on to the rock against the power of the conveyor belt, and not one could be spared to attend to the magical mechanical button. The crew was caught in a losing tug-of-war, and the entire scene seemed to Caper, with the luxury of reflection long after the event, like some dirty industrial update of an ancient mythological allegory. An urgent struggle was already underway, even as a solution was tantalizingly close at hand. One of the two supervising regulars was even straddling the belt with his rear end to the crusher, pushing back and yelling something no one could understand. Looked kind of heroic. Big John stuff, in a very distant sort of way.

With great exertion, they'd somehow managed to get the muddy monolith onto—but not into (the rock was stupendously large)—one of the chutes. They had then hit the "stop" button only because they were breathless, *after* the crusher-danger had passed. The rock was still perched there at the end of their shift, a weighty taunt not only to the practice but to the very idea of separating gross "impurity" from precious "product." And yet, when the workers arrived the next morning at 6:45, it had vanished.

How in the world? Couldn't have blown it up into small pieces, even with all the explosives lying around. The tipple, after all, delivered all of the combustible side benefits of a grain silo, but with a sooty carbon bonus. Zero chance of getting any heavy equipment up there, let alone to engineer any sort of removal scheme.

Gone. The thing had simply dematerialized.

How'd the night crew pull it off?

Should submit it to one of those "brain teaser" books.

* * *

$9.82 or $9.81 an hour? That little penny made all the difference. Given that coal crusher-threatening slate attacks were relatively rare, most days were spent in a kind of filthy delirious daydream. In the tipple, all talking was, perforce, shouting, and therefore tiring. Whole stretches of hours would thus be spent in an isolated noisy wordlessness. Even the regularly rotating grease breaks were mainly communicated with simple swirling hand gestures. "Your turn; see you in an hour," delivered with an index finger and a spinning hand. Caper's imagination, in a way that it has never done since, turned to math. Cold, hard math. He would silently calculate how much money he was making per minute.

Per second. (The odd wage would therefore be vastly preferable to the even-pennied one, given that it would immediately introduce fractions, which could only lead to more intricate and difficult divisions—an extremely desirable result.) He rejoiced in the fact that the UMW contract stipulated that the final 45 minutes of the 8-hour day would be paid time and a half. Mathtastic! Now he could do the same time and wage operations with *new* figures. Better. He could figure in the final 45-minute pay boost and average out his hourly pay to some new adjusted figure, and then go to town on that number.

He had any number of friends who came from far more well-to-do families. Kids who didn't really need to work, and therefore didn't. Or kids who didn't really need to work, but did so anyway. Far more commonly, kids who needed to horde a certain sum in order to make possible a specific collegiate goal. But no one—absolutely *no one*—was earning anywhere close to the money than he was pulling down at the coal mine. This was *major* dough. A month or so after he started in the tipple, his first pay came through. Fourteen hundred bucks, and change. It was a Friday, and his father for some reason or another couldn't pick him up at the end of his shift. No prah-blay-moe. He caught a lift into McDonald with other miners eager to make it a lovely end-of-the-work-week fiesta, and promptly cashed the plush promissory note. And he wasn't the only one. One thousand four hundred and who cares how many more bucks right into his unwashed mitts. A score of Grants, each one bound up in a thick white-and-red ribbon splashed with nifty markings, the whole lot capably assisted by an equally numbered pack of unshackled Jacksons. The remaining straggle of presidents were of no moment. He then proceeded to walk across the street from the bank (he'd of course never heard of the fine institution, and even more of coursely didn't have a checking account with the worthy establishment) and, at the age of 18, ordered a beer with the rest of the fellas. His proof of ID was liberally smeared all over his face. His smoky, splotchy face. It wasn't so much that the coal dust thickly overlaying pale white skin beneath "added a few years" to his appearance. Nor that bright, viscous jelly-eyes outlined in silky black paste provided extemporaneous adult-camo, bamboozling bartenders and bank tellers alike. Instead, the charcoal mask appeared to have taken the matter of age out of the question entirely, quite as if Caper hadn't been issued one—somehow hadn't been allotted, not once in all his born days, a bona fide birth. How on earth could this be so?

Only with the benefit of hindsight would he divine that wily old Kronos had been up to one of his most ancient tricks, furtively metamorphosing the minor less into a major than into a material object. Cocooned in crud, quite likely wanting even the trace of a navel anywhere on his person, Caper ran absolutely no risk of a barkeep demanding any form of official documentation of his humanity; to any inquiry regarding the length of his sojourn on this planet, he was invulnerable. A lowly coal shovel would have had more fitting cause to fret that an overzealous local magistrate, armed with a writ of summons, would presently beckon it into a court of law, bidding it tender forthwith a record of vaccination, if not a validated visa. To card the tipple-worker would be tantamount to carding a steel-toed boot, a slab of slate, or a grease gun. Time, at a single stroke, had been completely obliterated by grime. Might it even be conceivable, he pondered many years later, that a McDonald toddler—let's say, an uncommonly proactive tot who had somehow connived to buy (or, heaven forbid, to steal) an adult-size portion of tipple-face—might it just be possible that this admirably enterprising little fella could toddle into a bar and successfully order up a bracing boilermaker or two? And could we pwease hode the chit-chat just this once, Mistoow Gwown-Up?

Beyond conceivable, Caper concluded. More like borderline certain. Highly probable, at a minimum.

"Gimme a goddamn Rolling Rock!" he bellowed silently from his barstool, even if—courteous young person that he was—he didn't even dream of saying anything half so crass. "And be quick about it! I *earned* this time-unimpeded beverage! Look a' my face!"

He hitchhiked home from the ancient hotel bar late that afternoon, fourteen hundred bucks and more in his pocket. Only moments after he turned to face westbound traffic on Noblestown, the short first leg of a northeastern journey to be spent mainly on Robinson Highway, Route 22 and others, his first lift very nearly skidded over to the side of the road. As Caper took his seat, the pickup driver was already engaged in hurried private calculations. "Coal-washing plant?"

Not initially comprehending the question—not entirely sure, for that matter, whether he had in fact been asked one—Caper tried his best to offer a coherent response. "No," he responded, tentatively. "I'm up—"

"Tipple guy, heh?" The Dodge-driving samaritan's face swiveled left out the driver's side window, smiling and exhaling cigarette smoke all at once through the louvred triangular glass above his left wrist. "Shoulda known." It was then that Caper realized that his face was also a dead giveaway, at least to those who knew the local landscape.

As it turned out, the considerate driver was also employed at Dimezzo (and neither at the adjoining Kleer-Dite coal-washing plant nor, for that matter, at the closest deep mine, each one of whose three entrances almost met at a single point a short distance from Robinson Run). Far more to the point, the man was none other than the dragline operator. Himself. Just thumbed a ride with a real-life Mike Mulligan! But this time, the old steam shovel's been given a major Gulliver upgrade!

They headed north towards 22. If he had had the courage, Caper would have grilled his temporary chauffeur about every conceivable aspect of the job. Did you ever just scoop up 49+ tons of earth and move it way over there, just because? Did you ever drop a tubful in the wrong place by mistake? That would be cool. "Sorry about the 99,000 pounds of ground I should have dumped somewhere over there. I'll try to pay better attention next time." Did the bucket ever hit anything by accident? Buh-bye bulldozer! But Caper, not for the last time in his life, allowed his desire to appear calm and composed to outweigh his inquisitiveness. Big mistake.

At the 22 intersection, Caper needed to head east, and the dragline operator didn't. No matter. Once again, he hitched a boost in seconds flat. This subsequent and final ride took him all the way to his house, well out of the accommodating driver's way. While not a single molecule of gray dust could be detected inside the car, the guy rhapsodized about coal mining for the entire trip—how his grandfather had been underground for his entire life somewhere up near Scranton, how his father had managed to get out of the mines in his late 20's, and how unusual that escape was. He said he could never forget being just five or six, and how his father would come home after a shift, and walk straight up to him and give him a big bear hug, and how his mother would give his dad hell for not washing up before he touched anyone or anything. For his part, Caper remembered thinking that had the trip been twenty or thirty miles longer, the driver would have been more than happy to complete the journey, talking coal and his grubby daddy and charming domestic disputes. He also remembered feeling a bit embarrassed that he couldn't pass along at least one colorful story about some dangerous doings underground. Dude would have eaten up every single word, and asked for more. Instead, Caper had no choice but to admit to the mining devotee that his sole job was to separate chunks of slate from coal with his hands, standing next to a conveyor belt, and (apart from a one-hour tour of duty with a grease gun) nothing else. It's really fucking loud, he repeatedly emphasized, making sure his listener had a sufficient grasp of the deplorable conditions under which he labored. Fucking filthy, too, he added, squinting tautly into the sharply slanting light. (He briefly entertained the idea of sharing some of his math exploits, but refrained.)

When they arrived at Caper's suburban home, perched on a steeply descending slope, the driver's coal fixation remained undiminished. The pocket-flush 18-year old rightly felt obliged to hear out the grandson of a nameless, lifelong Scranton miner probably long dead, yet still very much alive in the recollections of his son's son. All the way to his door! That's something. Yet the fact that his own thoughts were themselves intensely focused on two delightfully overlapping circumstances (Major premise: Caper had a most unusual assembly of Grants and Jacksons on his person; Minor premise: Caper didn't have to work the next day; Ergo: Eureka! Logic can take a fucking holiday!) didn't prevent him from perceiving that the driver, completely oblivious to the hitchhiker's all too fleeting nirvana, had probably taken one look at the bituminous shade standing on the shoulder of Route 22, thumb extended, and immediately rocketed backwards in time and space. Who knows? Maybe he never found a chance to reminisce about any of this stuff with the people who knew him well.

Strange thing all the way around. Caper's charcoal face actually served to endear him to people—certain people, anyway. Dirty black mug with coal mascara must be perceived as trustworthy, or something. Guess you knew exactly what you were getting when you picked up the hitcher. Some kid who'd just finished his dirty shift. No way he's a psychopath. Wouldn't look like that.

Twenty-two years later, speaking to the gathered and quite vast Caper clan at his parents' 50-year anniversary, he had somehow managed to allude to the mining days. When it came time for the bride and groom to speak, his mother couldn't bring herself to address the throng. Probably too happy and too overcome to say anything. His father took the mic and, in the course of his remarks, said something that had never occurred to Caper. He was just a little defensive in his tone when he talked about his sons and mines. Had six, plus two girls. Had to get 'em through college. People must've said things, or maybe given him strange looks, when he mentioned the jobs he secured for his sons through his construction and mining contacts. Caper now imagined long-ago parental exchanges.

"Hey, Charlie. Long time. Great to see you! What're your boys up to?"

"Great, great. Mort's goin' back to Virginia in the fall. I got 'im working at the mine this summer."

In their minds, the conversation probably went like this:

"Hey, Charlie. Long time. Great to see you! What're your boys up to?"

"Great, great. Mort's goin' back to Virginia in the fall. Tryin' to get him cancered-up in the meantime. Take it easy, Rich!

Caper's brother Joe graduated from Yale in 1979. The largest Caper. He had, Mort recollected, a 20-inch neck during his collegiate wrestling days. People would often remark on it. Literally. Like, "You've got a really thick neck."

"Thanks."

By the middle of the wrestling season, he'd have cut weight to 190. In the meantime, he had no choice but to wrestle "Unlimited" until he got down that low. That would be about 30-40 pounds of wrestling your way down to 190.

Upon graduation, Joe had not immediately found any suitable work for his economics degree. Senior thesis was on coal, or depletable energy resources, or coal-fired energy plants. With the aid of some paternal connections, he got a job at the Morton mine, a deep operation whose main entrance was close to where his father now lived. Quite a few times, Caper would get questions about his older brother from friends and neighbors who knew that he had graduated from Yale. Hearing that he was underground, they responded—quite understandably—with extreme skepticism. There was the time, too, that the mine's fairly longstanding safety run ("No industrial accidents in 337 days," the sign outside the entrance might boast) came to an abrupt halt. Two fatal electrocutions within a short period. But the far bigger story was of a miner who, for reasons never clearly established, was being chased by his foreman. Climbing the stairs next to the elevator shaft, he had stuck his head out for a glimpse of his pursuer. Elevator car coming down the shaft at that very instant sliced the miner in two.

Had to hide one that from mom, Joe said. She'd ask, every so often.

Joe's gonna have to lie, Caper remembered thinking.

Years later, Caper envisioned an unheard-of Yale secret society: Bull Dogs who had graduated and then gone on to work in the deep mines. Not a whole lot of Elis at that gathering, brother. But who the hell wants a crowded secret society?

No need for a secret handshake. They could have their own secret cough. Lung & Bones? Coal & Wheeze?

* * *

Plum & Plummer.

Morton J. Caper, Ph. D. put on the dog the way other people put on their BVDs. That he was the most audacious and charismatic dresser in the history of the Lindbergh School District was an incontestable fact, one that might conceivably serve as the starting point for some other discussion (concerning snakeskin shoes, for instance), but not itself available for any sort of deliberation. Just as it would never occur to educated people to chat about whether a + b=b + a, or to debate whether or not history has anything to tell us concerning the wisdom of invading Russia, Caper's overwhelming dominance in sartorial matters was candidly, calmly, and universally recognized. Indeed—to Caper's mind, at any rate—his stylistic supremacy might even be said to be *a priori*-er than the vast majority of axiomatic propositions one could possibly imagine. His claim, unique in the world of axioms, had the additional and great virtue of being subject to falsifiability experiments and repeated testing, and was therefore also a prime example of natural science at its best.

One day early in the fall of 2010, and for reasons he would never completely fathom, Caper announced to a senior honors English class that he had decided to name the get-up he was wearing (an especially dangerous orange-red-maroon combo) "Autumn Apocalypse." This otherwise unremarkable event would surely have perished into oblivion that very day, were it not for a vexing young lady, who wished to know on the following day the new "name" of the eye-catching attire he featured yet once more. "Autumn Jubilee," he had managed to blurt out, after a confused pause. Straightaway, he realized that he would soon run out of autumnal phrases, and that if these christenings were to keep up, he would need to adopt a far more forward-looking stance. For the next school day, he arrived on campus armed with "Burgundy Blitzkrieg."

What happened in the ensuing weeks, months, and years was elaborately chronicled under the "Caper's Wearhouse" rubric ("You're going to love the way I look. I guarantee it.") Captions soon began to explode in a variety of directions, which, while they betrayed no clear or dominant theme, still managed to reveal a few readily recognizable patterns. Literary allusions, not surprisingly, were in plenteous supply: "All Stylish on the Midwestern Front"; "Their Eyes Were Watching Gold"; "Something Worsted This Way Comes"; "Quoth the Maven, 'Never Bore'." Cinema, too, received fashion *homages*: "Back to the Fuschia"; "Urbane Cowboy"; "Full Mental Jacket"; "Reservoir Duds." Nor did the music of Caper's own high school years ("Blue Polyoyster Cult" ["Don't Fear the Teacher"]; "Pink Flaired" ["Hey! Students! Leave those threads alone!"]; "Bachman Turner Overdressed") go wanting. Beatles fare ("Yellow Submaroon"), soul food ("[If Loving Blue is Wrong] I Don't Want to be Right"), in addition to jazzy standards ("Why Not Take Olive Me?"), were prominently featured on the menu. Additionally, theme weeks were soon in high demand, so that James Bond *aficianados*, to take one example, could bask in the pairing of "On Her Majesty's Stylish Service" with "You Only Dress Nice." Both American history ("Brown v. Bored with Education"; "Manly-Vest Destiny") and the musical genre ("Oklahomer!"; "The Look of Mormon") were respectfully saluted. Even the Old Testament left its thunderous mark in the classroom, whether Caper commanded "Let There Be Light (Blue)!," or "Let My Purple Go!" On rarer occasions, more or less ephemeral current events ("Don't paisley, 'bro") as well as seasonal tributes ("Fleece Navidad!"; "Xtreme X-Mas!"; "Peppermint Bark…With a Holiday Bite!") received the spotlight. Adages ("Those who can't blue, peach"), dicey questions ("Does this warm-up make me look fast?"), indelicate colloquialisms ("New shirt, Sherlock!"), and classical ideals of female beauty ("V-Neck de Milo") were welcomed into the diverse fold. Finally, to be sure, one had to acknowledge that the teacher occasionally slipped into unaccountably bizarre terrain: "Teal meth do us part—this one's cookin'!"

Given Missouri's reputation as one of the great cradles of methamphetamine recreation, this last label was offered with a small dose of dread: would parents respond? As it happened, the ill-conceived crank caption engendered no lasting consequences. And indeed, for the most part, his Facebook appearances were generally greeted with either indifference, silence, or minor annoyance. But when Caper donned a vintage tan sweater that looked like something John Denver would have worn in the late 70's, and matched the chunky, wooly number with the question, "Voulez-vous crochet avec moi?," history finally caught up with him.

He was called into Luebbert's office on the following day, all togged up in a blinding combination he had styled, "MADRAS: Mothers Against Dressing All Sloppy." Luebbert sardonically acknowledged Caper's high wattage by remarking, "Colorful today," to which the teacher gave his customary response. "Thanks for noticing."

He was introduced to a Mrs. Oberholtzer, who remained seated. The surname, of course, had every bit of the south St. Louis teutonic aroma anyone had a right to ask for. But even as he was noticing that the fine lady was showing unmistakable signs of distaste for his electric slacks, Caper was also making a mental note of the fact that he didn't currently teach any students named Oberholtzer.

"How can I help you?" Caper said to both Luebbert and Mrs. O.

"Mrs. Oberholtzer contacted me yesterday afternoon regarding a post put up on Facebook. It's a picture of you with the caption" (here the principal composed his face so as not to smile), "Voulez-vous crochet avec moi?"

Luebbert's French pronunciation did not leave one green with envy. But Caper had other things to think about. Who was this lady? Wait a sec. Got it. There's been a divorce somewhere in there. Son or daughter goes by some other Germanic last name. Mystery solved.

"I know it was a little cheeky," Caper began to explain. "But it's all in goo—"

"I don't want my daughter to be seeing things like that online," Mrs. O cut in. "It's just the sort of—"

"I'm sorry," Caper countercut. "Who is your daughter?"

"Katie Oberholtzer."

Caper's mind raced. Nope. No Katie Oberholtzers in any of his classes.

"I'm sorry again, Mrs. Oberholtzer," he continued. "Do I know Katie?"

"You know her friends. They're in your class. And she's been looking at the pictures that go on Facebook."

Luebbert was nodding his head unhurriedly, eyeing neither the teacher nor the parent.

"Well, I certainly didn't mean to offend anyone with the caption," Caper said by way of explanation. He drifted back to the previous autumn's "Octodressy," which appropriated what was certainly the most salacious of the Bond titles and, well, dressed it up. "I'm sorry if Katie—"

"It's not just Katie, Dr. Caper," Mrs. O. said peremptorily. "It's anyone who might come across that sort of filthy joke."

"But I took the naughty bit out," Caper attempted to explain. He turned both palms upward and then back. "And I substituted a wholeso—"

"Morton," Luebbert now interrupted. "Maybe the Facebook operation should be shut down." Caper nodded in the affirmative, looking at both Mrs. O and the principal. "Maybe this should be the end. All good things, you know."

"No problem." Caper looked directly at Mrs. O. "Mrs. Oberholtzer, no problem. I didn't mean to offend anyone. I hope that's clear to all involved. And I think Mr. Luebbert's got a point. Perhaps it's time for 'Caper's Wearhouse' to shutter its doors."

Mrs. O seemed to be satisfied by this conclusion. Caper remained in Luebbert's office for a moment or two after her departure. After Mrs. O's "Goodbye" and "Thank you for your time," he asked the principal exactly how one would go about getting offended by a slightly tweaked French question, one occasioned, moreover, by a snickering 70's sweater? Did she think he was making some sort of sublimated overture?

Anyway, didn't matter. The "Wearhouse" was over, at least in its current form. On the way out of the principal's office, he encountered Van Der Meyer, who immediately gave visual approval to Caper's madras slacks. "These the 'Pants Macabre' you were talking about?"

Caper exhaled through his nose, nodded his head, and smiled. "Afraid not. Those were to be worn on Halloween. Sweeeet black and red plaid pants."

"You're not going to wear them?"

Caper shook his head. "No, I'll still wear 'em. Jus' no more captions."

Oberholtzer. Oberdorfer. Udelhofen. Caper mused. He mused about the word "muse." Wonder what the German verb for "muse" is? Ask Conti. Funny. In this sea of South County volk, the German teachers are die Frauen Conti and Garcia.

Gundelfinger. Gottemoeller. Groeninger. Lotta G's. Vogelgesong. And Z's. And kamps. Dieselkamp. Mittelkamp. Emmelkamp. Goldkamp. Word for "field," isn't it? Campus? Or maybe "battle." No, kampf. Keller is cellar. Kaiser from Caesar.

Nearly every day Caper would scan the 'Post-Dispatch' obituary page, eager to award the DOD: Deutscher of the day. More often than not, he'd give the prize to the four-syllable dreadnoughts that sounded like some demented Bavarian Dr. Seuss (Suess?) had invented them. Beckenbauer. Baudendistel. Brandeweide. Fenstermacher. Hoernschemeyer. Dudenhoeffer. But you also had to appreciate the Muellers, the Meiers, and the Mundts; the Theisses, Weisses, and Fleisses. Schindlers, Schwindts, and Schillers. Beck. Leck. Peck. Especially when a really cool first name was attached: Elmer or August, Edna or Eunice, Eugene or Theodore. Bernice. Adolphus. It was a sea of Krauts. Krautensee. Or maybe, since this was the heartland, Krautenland? Was he teaching in the midst of a secretive bund? An enclosure? A sausage outfit? Theisser, Weisser, Fleisser. –Erer.

Klipspringer. Jay Gatsby could boast of only one piano-playing seduction aide. Caper had whole classrooms brimming o'er with Klipspringers. And Krulls and Kohls and Klugs. Lehrs and Lahrs and Mohrs and Bohrs. "I work in HR." Got a Feltz, a Beetz, a Butz, and a Bartz. Goetz. Geetz.

Gatz.

With covert and cunning design, Caper pondered the tantalizing possibility of wooing the elusive Daisy, luring her away from both Gatsby and Tom. "Come with me to St. Louis, baby," he would entreat the careless belle. "I'll cover you in Klipspringers." He imaginatively jumped to a Capered-up revival of 'Meet Me in St. Louis,' Busby Berkeley-style. Spinning whirligigs of serenading teenage Niederbergers and Freunds, Schweighoeffers, Ziegenheims, and Vollenweiders, Schodls, Vogls, and Knodls, each one earnestly striving to lend assistance to the English teacher's highly improbable romantic quest. Each singing, "♩You never loved them…" How could the rich and aloof blonde resist their enticements?

Caper descended to the far more mundane welt of spelling. He felt certain that he trafficked with the "oe" vowel combo at least as much as any other teacher in history. "Ndt," too. And "pf." Pfeiffer. Kempf. He made the "pf" sound. What would the linguists call that? Labiodental something. Fricative. Be funny as a kind of contemporary art project. Go find every red "Class Roster" book he'd ever had—eighteen years—and write down every single German surname. Who has those books? VDM. Then maybe make a kind of mini-Vietnam Wall type of thing, except for Germans. Or put it to music, like that Irish song. Bing Crosby. "Dear Old Donegal." Madigan, Cadigan, Lafferty, Rafferty…stuff like that. Could you do that with German names? "Dear Old Prussia"? Dieselkamp, Mittelkamp, Something-kamp…Doesn't trip off the tongue.

Lebensraum. There was more than enough raum around here for the most ground-greedy German. The Führer was looking in the wrong place. Lindbergh's high school campus had untold acreage. Should ask someone how many. Let's see. Two full-size baseball diamonds. Two main football and soccer fields. One, two, three, four, five practice fields—each one larger than a football field. Large wooded area. Huge tower on the northern edge of the campus. Aviation signal? Maybe television tower. That spring day so many years back when a worker climbing up had plummeted down during fifth hour. His very first day on the job, they said. Pretty much had to shut the whole campus down just to get the ambulance back there by the tree line. Way too late.

Fifth. Lunch hour.

Van Der

Dang.

Caper abruptly changed tack to the east. Make that two Dangs. Xiong as well. And then there was Zhong and Kung and Hung and Sing. Lee. Li, too. Guess it depends on who's in charge of the anglicizing. Le. Lei. Fei. No, *both* Feis. Ha. Ho. Barbeau, too. No shortage of French names around here, for that matter. Lai. Asian invasion. Tran. Nguyen. "It's a nguyen-nguyen situasian."

Toss in Amleshi and Benegal, Bala and Balaji, Srivastava and Dommaraju. Momeni. Sulaiman. Nezam. In no time you find yourself encircled by a pack of hardened creants.

Caper occasionally wondered if some sort of rebooted 21st century Axis Pact were being stealthily reassembled in his school district, in his classroom, under the radar. Masses of south St. Louis Germans + updated and different asiatisch peoples=same will to dominate the world.

Oh, East is East, and West is West, and ever the twain shall meet,

In Caper's classroom, if nowhere else—they're hoggin' all the seats!

Supreme Leader could be Schnguyendangerer, an irresistible German/Asian amalgamation, impervious to pity.

But wait. What about the troops of Il Duce? Were they being marginalized by the new Pact, treated in the same fashion as they were some seventy-five years ago? Doubt it. Plenty of surnames ending in vowels. Have to conduct a last name inventory.

Lindbergh himself not likely to earn a spot on the Reich's arch-enemies roster. Swedish.

Why do I give way to these sorts of…?

Mind's not right.

*   *   *

Two years prior to his own tenure as a tipple-worker, Caper's brother had told him a story about the blasting crew that he'd never forgotten.

One of the foremen of this outfit—a nomadic band any tipple-worker would kill to join—had suddenly and somewhat inexplicably taken vacation days in early July. A week and a half or something. (Every summer, the miner's two-week holiday shut down regular operations for the first half of August. Additional vacation time was typically taken in the autumn—deer season, whatever.)

Someone at the mine learned that the foreman had been arrested and charged with making "obscene phone calls." (Caper catapulted: completely vanished art. Like bunting in baseball. Or puddling steel. When was the last time anyone made an "obscene" phone call? Was arrested for landline lechery? Hell, aspiring heavy-breathers didn't have a prayer of honing their craft these days. Didn't seem fair, did it? Perhaps the tattered remnant should consider forming some kind of Luddite organization: start smashing up smart phones and stuff.) In any case, the foreman was convicted and sentenced in some fashion that didn't involve jail time, though he had been obliged to miss work because of the legal proceedings. Word spread at the mine. When the gentleman caller returned to work on a Monday morning, every single miner in the locker room had come equipped with a little plastic telephone, of the type that used to be given to infants, pink or blue with little curly plastic cords.

Perv enters the dressing room, and all the workers make the cute li'l phones ring right on cue. Each picks up a receiver in synchrony, thumb and index finger burlesquing a teacup posture, angled pinkies held aloft. "Hello? Oh, yeah. Just a second. He's right here. 'Hey Roger, it's for you!'" A hundred plastic phones thrust in his face. Thunderous laughter. Rehearsed laughter. Laughter that would not subside.

Insufferable, unremitting torture. Guy would've been better off in flasher-jail. Plastic phone hijinx had to go on for months. The fellas would never forget, and would never fucking shut up.

No escape.

*　*　*

Not one member of the 99.9999-whatever per cent of humanity who have never worked in a coal tipple could possibly know the glorious, delirious ecstasy of receiving the tidings that tomorrow morning, O young man, you'll be reporting not to the tipple, but to the explosives shed. Hallelujah! Hallelujah! Free at last! I'm goin' to the promised land, and I'm gonna help blow it up!

Blasting crew, baby. Had any people ever been more chosen? With this intrepid and turbulent tribe, Caper delighted in working under skies that were anything but clear blue, breathing air that could in no way have been described as either "bracing" or mote-free, but which had the immeasurable advantage of not incessantly suggesting that you had somehow been duped into toiling within the confines of a woebegone canto, whose only mark of distinction was a Roman numeral affixed to it by a power neither known to you nor available to your entreaties. Outside, for fuck's sake! This exquisite edict was delivered to Caper only two or three times, and only because the unruly outfit was for one reason or another short-handed. He fervently wished there had been some sort of blasting crew waiting list, because "Caper, M." would have staked out its territory in the very highest rank. "Preferred substitute," or something.

These beatific respites provided him his first opportunity to see the dragline in action with his own unlined eyes. Caper immediately intuited that no human being—not even the most unwavering environmental guardian of our delicate planet, a person solemnly pledged to protect its ecological integrity—could observe the insatiable coal fiend go through its paces without at least a tinge of awe. Like seeing an aircraft carrier up close. Or New York City. He remembered his father told him that, as big as it was, there were much larger draglines skulking in the hills of West Virginia and Kentucky. Although he couldn't quite bring himself to believe that his pop was intentionally lying, neither were any of the reasonable alternative possibilities terribly comforting. Was the old guy going soft in the head? Maybe, as Caper preferred to believe, his father had simply been misinformed. Badly. Then again, perhaps someone at the Caterpillar office was having a bit of fun with him, pulling his chain by fabricating looney heavy machinery tales. After all, each scoop of earth, rock, coal, and slate moved nearly fifty tons of southwestern Pennsylvania from one spot to another one pretty far away. Quietly. It spun quickly, nimbly, effortlessly. The machine had no wheels—not a chance!—but rested upon two colossal rectangular feet, themselves attached to two incomprehensible cams in one manner or another.

"Tub machine," the workers at the face called it. When the dragline had completely annihilated all of the land in its reach, it would be walked *very slowly* to a new location, whereupon it would resume its inimitable mayhem. The really big ones, according to his father (how could they manufacture a larger version?!) could move nearly four times the load with each scoop! It seemed utterly impossible. You could probably fit a sizable house in the bucket, attended by a three-car garage and an in-ground pool.

Relishing every second of these all too temporary reprieves, Caper's job was to do whatever the hell anyone else told him to do, as the dynamiters carried out a very orderly and systematic program of blowing up the more than gently-rolling hills southwest of Pittsburgh. In effect, they were rendering the landscape all the more digestible for the stupendous coal leviathan, with its 9-story boom and what looked like a quarter mile of very thick cable. The drillers would be directed to create a coal "map" of a particular chunk of land. In order to do so, a grid of the land would be diagrammed, and carefully measured drill samples would be taken and interpreted. The invisible and constantly slithering layerings of the top of the earth's crust would thus be rendered "visible"—or at any rate, profitably destroyable.

When the blasters entered the scene, the top foreman would drop a plumb line into every single hole, determining exactly where the three-tiered explosives would be placed. The main blasting truck—a squat, square rig packed with tiny white balls of fertilizer and diesel fuel in separate compartments, the one on top of the other—would pour its goodies down to the desired depth, cutting off the earthquaking flow when directed by the foreman. At this point, eight or ten feet of dirt would be shoveled on top by Caper and any other available non-skilled workers. More explosives. More dirt. More explosives—the top layer wired to go off a microsecond before the middle, the middle before the bottom. Wires were wired to colorful wires and more wires, and were spread all over the dirt or mud surface like a nest of twisted and neglected and altogether sinister Slinkies, each one ultimately reporting back to the single detonator, itself resembling nothing so much as a forlorn lunch pail. Dull, dusty metallic exterior. No Farrah or Fonzie for you, my melancholy friend. So sorry. Perhaps things that make other things go "Boom!" are destined to play the wallflower.

Doing his best to adopt the bearing of a person who was not at all fazed by proximity of tons of high explosives, Caper also endeavored to do two other things: stay the fuck out of the way of the way of the men who knew what they were doing, and pretend he knew what was going on, mainly by nodding his head whenever anyone told him to do something. Primarily owing to the fact that no workers were killed on any of his two or three blasting shifts, he judged himself to be a seasoned and highly valued veteran of dynamite work. None of the explosives, to his surprise, looked like those he had so often seen in the movies or on tv. Like really big firecrackers, in other words, perhaps bundled into a tightly knit TNT gift package, ready to be heaved by John Wayne at the last instant over the barricaded wall of the bad guys. Some of the stuff, indeed, bore a strong resemblance to one-pound packages of Jimmy Dean sausage, the kind you slice up into little disks. Each fat little sausage-digit had a light but visible powder-layer on the outside. Caper didn't know what this was and never would, but was cautioned never to pick up any of the stuff with his bare hands. Yes, sir. It would burn your skin immediately, and would not wash off easily.

After a full day of explosives rehearsal, everyone would retreat from the piece of land that was about to change forever. Sirens would warn any stragglers, though there never were any. The upper blasts would loosen up the surface for the lower blasts, make it "lighter." Everything would go ka-boom! Caper learned then that when you blow up the earth you also blow it up a couple of sizes. It "lifts." Bloats. At least 15 feet. The crew, at the end of its shift, would return to the lockers.

Behind the retreating workers, the landscape, now doing a pretty respectable impression of Passchendaele, awaited the beast. The tub machine would be served.

The greatest irony of these days of escape was abundantly evident to Caper only an hour into the new job. How much quieter and cleaner it was to work on the blasting crew than in the tipple! Yippie-ki-yay!

*   *   *

That Caper had a propensity for loud clothing no one could doubt. His favorite color was orange. Each September or October he would wear all three of his pairs of orange pants on consecutive days, patiently responding to anyone who inquired that no, these weren't the same pair that he'd worn yesterday.

He was on the second pair of corduroys when he spotted a slick, powder blue sports car pull into one of the visitor parking spaces in the lot just outside his classroom. On the move with several errands to accomplish during his conference hour, Caper took no further notice of either the car or its driver, walking briskly toward the guidance office to meet with Dr. Riethmeier. Just as he was entering the office, a voice resounded from the parking lot entrance.

"Dr. C!"

Caper smiled and waved and began to walk very slowly back toward his classroom. Guy was huge. 6' 4" or 6' 5", and wide-bodied. Looked like he played tight end for Ohio State. Caper didn't yet recognize the boomer. Halfway there, he began to distinguish a familiar face.

"Peter?"

"Yes, yes, it's Peter!"

Peter Kempf. All-round sterling student. Marching band phenom. Now up in Minnesota, junior-maybe-senior year.

Caper repeated, "Peter?"

"Yes! How are things!"

"You look like two Peters," Caper marveled. "One and a half, anyway."

The two shook hands in the middle of the hallway. Kempf's casual grip raised the real possibility that the University of Minnesota now offered a blacksmith major.

"What'd you quit school an—"

"What's the name?" Kempf interrupted.

"What?" Caper's unwary right hand was now paying the price for his never having taken a proper CPR course. The strangled flipper thrashed about, desperate to coax a fix of blood and oxygen back into one or two of its throttled joints.

"What's the caption? The pants. Still lookin' sweeeetly orange." Kempf swept his arm toward the fluorescent cords.

"Oh." Caper nodded appreciatively. "Can't do that anymore. But if I could, I'd—"

"Can't what?"

"Do the captions. Long story." Caper shook his head uncertainly. "Short story, actually. Kinda boring anyway." He paused, then added, "I'd been saving 'Agent Orange' for a while." He gazed meditatively down the hallway. "Maybe add something about a 'license to enthrall.'" Then, as if suddenly recollecting something he knew his former student would appreciate, he tapped one of Peter's newly reupholstered shoulders. "Hey, I brought back the Western Wednesday tradition." Kempf eagerly nodded his approval of the midweek cowboy salute, temporarily revived after a year or two hiatus. "What d'you think of 'Butch Cassidy and the Sunkist™ Kid'?"

"Golden. Do it."

"Can't," Caper quickly replied. "The 'Wearhouse' is no longer in business. Don't worry, I'll—"

"What happened?"

Caper shook his head. "Don't worry. Like I said, boring story." Caper now waved his hand inquisitively across the new and improved and altogether family-sized Peter Kempf. "So what's the tale here? What's your jacket si—"

"Remember *Mein Kempf*?" Once again, Peter nodded his head up and down and smiled broadly.

Caper did. On certain days, when papers were due, he would offer his students the opportunity to play "Literary Hangman" instead of *Blackadder* reruns. Boys v. girls, usually. One student would perform as a kind of Vanna White gallows-keeper at the board. The answers would riff off authors' names or novel titles or literary devices. Clue might be: Smelly *bildungsroman*? Answer on the board would eventually be revealed: *A Portrait of the Artist as a Dung Man*. Two-for-one dungs. Pretty snazzy. You had to get the answer exactly right, or the other team would get all the points. And if Caper could work in a student's name, all the better. "Peter's teutonic struggle?" had yielded *Mein Kempf*.

"I do. I do," Caper responded. "Not the most baroque combo I've ever done, but punchy. No one says," he added, "that 'Hangman' has to stop. So I'll keep the tradition alive."

Kempf nodded his head appreciatively.

"Gopher Band, right? Golden Gophers?" Caper returned the conversation to the present.

"I'm impressed, Dr. C. 'Pride of Minnesota.' You've got a good memory. Yes, having the time of my life."

"Good crew up there?" Caper asked.

"Oh yes, most definitely. In the clear. The practices eat up every hour I've got."

"Not at all surprised. Marching bands probably practice more than football teams. And," Caper added, "*you* look like you play football for the Minnesotans. Strongside linebacker or something?"

Peter laughed. "One or two people have remarked that I've put on some pounds."

"Some pounds? You look like Schwarzenegger." Caper stepped back a foot or two. "*Young* Schwarzenegger. 'Course you're much taller, so that's even better," he added reassuringly. His face now took on a pensive cast. "You're not thinking of going into politics, are you?"

Kempf laughed again. "I've been working out a lot, I guess." He didn't appear eager to pursue this line of conversation any further.

"If you've got a minute, follow me into the guidance office," Caper offered. "I've got many a form to drop off."

"I'm heading there myself. Transcripts."

"Oh, yeah? Who needs to see 'em?"

"I'm thinking law school. One of the coasts. Not sure where yet. Not even sure I'll go that route."

"Lemme know if I can help out, when the time comes."

Caper had umpteen pieces of paper for the guidance staff. These days, applying for college was more than a full-time job. At least for some of his students. To those who bothered to ask for advice, he routinely recommended that they apply to three or four colleges, tops. With rare exceptions, these same students paid him no heed whatsoever.

Guidance work finished, he met up with Kempf on the way out of the office. They walked back towards Caper's room. At the eastern entrance to the school, Caper stared out at the parking lot.

"Your convertible?" He looked at the expensive-looking blue ride. He made out "Lexus" on the front lip of the hood.

"Yeah," Kempf acknowledged.

Fairly long pause.

"My parents gave it to me," Kempf said by way of explanation.

"Pretty cool. Looks fast."

"It is."

Caper eyed the license plate. Personalized Show-Me. MOPEDS.

"Take it easy, Peter. Hope to see you soon."

"Take it easy, Dr. C."

Caper watched Kempf trundle back to the blue coupe. He waved through the too-bright windows.

* * *

"Ready, harch!"

Marching band command. The traditional "h" substitution probably goes back a long way, Caper figured. How far certain sounds "carry" had to make a big difference in that line of business, more than enough to trump standard pronunciation.

Peter Kempf was, by his own humble admission, as well as the testimonies of his peers and bandleaders, as devoted to marching band excellence as anyone Lindbergh had ever had in the ranks. In stark contrast to his classroom demeanor, which was unfailingly generous and considerate and accommodating, Caper had heard, as early as the first month of the student's junior year, that there was a second, and quite different, Peter. "Band Peter," they said. The Enforcer. The beloved Mr. Spiegelman was in charge, to be sure, and the drum majors were the leader's lieutenants. But the tall and lanky drummer made sure that commands were carried out.

How'd he get so thick? Caper flashed.

"Reset!"

Caper would have liked to poach some of the tactics of his colleagues in band, theatre, and coaching. A "long ranger" megaphone would certainly come in handy now and again. You could wake up the echoes, and perhaps a drooping student or two, with one of those volume virtuosos. Nor should the pleasure of barking out some universally understood command be ignored. Two syllables and everyone's back to the beginning of a new literary drill. Cool. Nothing like that in a discussion of George Eliot. "Reset!" would be met with puzzled and perturbed gazes.

"Let's do it from the top!"

Exactly how might that work in an English seminar? Caper didn't know, but he'd like to be the first to try. Say Canto XVII, Circle Seven (Round Three) is up for discussion. "Okay, okay. Let's go back to those wicked usurers. People, listen please! Usurers! Why are they *down* this far? Usurers, people! We're in some seriously deep hell here! Money parasites! And a-one, and a-two..."

And then, a bouncy performance of the latest literary routine, Florentine style.

But classrooms were neither playing fields nor music rooms nor theaters. For better and for worse.

*   *   *

Standing outside a classroom in the bottom floor of Sperring Middle School at the close of a "team meeting" with all of the district's "Communication Arts" teachers—K through 12—Caper was talking about the upcoming high school drama schedule with Jessica Laney, Lindbergh's theater maestro. One of the middle school instructors enthusiastically approached the drama teacher, introduced herself, and said with a beaming smile, "I'm so sorry, but I've *got* to ask you a question. Have you ever heard of the actress Jennifer Beals?"

Laney nodded her head politely. "Yes. Yes I have. I know." Her facial expression clearly indicated that she was in on the secret. "I look just like her, right?"

"You really do! I mean it!" The middle school teacher couldn't get over the resemblance.

"Yes." Laney hadn't ceased nodding her head. As the astonished instructor was walking away, Beals added, "Except she's a lot older than I am."

Caper, who knew enough about women to know that he knew very little, and who would freely acknowledge the fact to anyone who cared to inquire, sensed possible gold in this little exchange. Pittsburgh. 80's. Oversized "shirts." Legendary leg-warmers. Have to pass this tidbit around to the fellas in the department. Could be some serious needling.

Plus, women never bring up age unless something's in the breeze. Wait a minute. Maybe I *do* know something about women. *Cherchez la femme* and stuff like that.

Probably not. But how to exploit?

Patience, Cape.

A few days later, he shot Laney an email ostensibly discussing the staging of the ghost scene in *Hamlet*. "How would you position the prince vis-à-vis...yakka yakka yakka." Deftly, cleverly, he closed the missive with an oh-by-the-way inquiry. "Hey, how often do you get that 'you-look-like-Jennifer-Beals' kind of remark? Interesting."

Laney replied on cue. "I get that 'you look like that girl from Flashdance' at least twice a week. It is incredibly annoying. Über annoying. Woody Allen-at-a-blockbuster-movie annoying (: '"

How to increase her annoyance? Gold. Surprise department birthday party, with a blaring rendition of "What a Feeling"? Too ham-handed.

Caper had always regarded *Flashdance* as a ludicrous piece of 80's schlock. But who hadn't? Movies are "pitched," aren't they? Can you imagine? "Okay, okay, okay. I got a great one. Main character's a broad. Lives in Cleveland, Pittsburgh, Buffalo. Whatever. Wants to dance in the ballet. Workin' in one o' them steel mills, if you can believe it, so this whole ballet thing is a real long shot. Now here's where it gets real innaresting. Moonlights as a pole-dancer. It's dance, yeah, but not like the classy kind she wants. *She's* classy, but she's not doin' classy dancin'. Follow me so far? Then...no, then, *owner* of the steel mill falls for her. Not sure how yet, but still he falls for her. Bing, boom, bam. They fall in love, gonna get married, happy music over the credits. Whaddya think?"

Pittsburgh's imploding, but the movie uses the steel working jobs as "gritty" backdrop for *Pretty Woman*-style romance. Pretty sure JB had some sort of "industrial" loft apartment. Former air brake plant? Didn't matter. Just make sure the place produces lots of clanking, loads of clunking. Metallic authenticity, don't you know. Freight elevator doors thwapping shut like they were doing auditions for San Quentin.

Everyone wears leg warmers on Laney's birthday? Impractical. Weird. What about the exotic dancing angle? Make a wisecrack about goin' east of the river to the gentlemen's establishments? Nah. Bad taste.

"Laniac"? Everyone sings and dances at a department meeting? Probably more than we could pull off.

Got it. Get one of our tech-savvy kids to photoshop Van Der Meyer into that leggy Beals pose with the huge shirt and the hands between the legs and the head-tilt and everything. For the ages.

Better leave it alone, he finally concluded. Not everything pans out.

*   *   *

When the time came for the miner's vacation—a two-week stretch at the beginning of August—Caper's job shifted to a task he had been gravely cautioned about by his older brothers. With coal production at a standstill, the summer crew was targeted for the only job worse than working in the tipple: cleaning the massive grease pan of the dragline. On a daily basis, and round the clock, the tub machine's 66 billion ball bearings required slavish human attention, else the lilliputian drones who crawled about on their teensy, tracked "heavy equipment" playthings flirt with the terrifying possibility that its dirty carbon deeds go unconsummated. Fifty weeks of grease, spread out over an acre-sized pan, awaited the tipplers, each one of whom was armed with nothing more than a heavy steel spatula and a single five-gallon bucket. Their task was to remove the previous year's ointment, one bucket at a time, in order to ensure that the following year's gloop would find a spacious new home in the belly, as the saying goes, of the beast. One final insult increased their torment exponentially: the overhead metal covering of the pan was just low enough to prevent anyone from moving about on hands and knees. Even Gary Coleman's gonna get his tummy sticky.

Unlike the tipple, protective headwear was absolutely essential in the grease pan. Unless you were willing to flirt with a severe military cut, some sort of improvised, multi-layered babushka would need to be employed each day, simply to keep the slime at bay. As a result, all five or six of the grease-collecting slitherers practically oozed a most disquieting aura (déclassé sheikhs? mentally disturbed serfs?) wriggling about on their elbows and stomachs in a couple of inches of gray-yellow goo. For that matter, total body coverage in clothing that you would most certainly dispose of at the end of the two-week lubricant hiatus was the only way to go. The oversized overalls that Caper had purchased for this filthy fortnight could capably stand, after the first day's work, all by themselves, in the basement of his house, which they proceeded to do each night until he lifted the stiff, cold, greasy garment—to all appearances, a looted, oily mummy—back into the trunk of the family car at 5:30 each morning. He wouldn't climb back into these work clothes until he and his father had arrived at the face, dead in the heart of an almost completely abandoned mine. Even his old man, whose Ford LTD coupe always betrayed copious evidence of driving expeditions through strip mines and construction sites, insisted at the end of each shift that Caper strip off not only his outer clothing, but replace his undergarments as well, just in case they, too, had sopped up some of the grease. He then put on a third set of clothes and sat on a canvas cover acquired just for this occasion. That canvas, too, would be tossed when regular mining resumed.

On the last day of grease detail, his father snapped a photo of Caper and his 89-year old grandmother standing inside the bucket of what was reputed to be the world's largest high-loader—an experimental International Harvester mammoth of which only a handful had ever been manufactured. Even the equipment operators in that section of the mine remarked with awe on the unrivaled capacity of the machine, though seldom without the softly disdainful addition that it mainly remained comfortably idle, for the simple reason that it was too massive to be genuinely useful. So quickly could it load a coal truck that it was actually detrimental to the efficiency of the whole operation. The rhythm of blasting, dragging, loading, and sifting the coal could not be violated without consequence any more than a musical composition could be trifled with without notice. Caper regretted that he never got to see a loaded bucket lifted on high, brimming with tons of shale and coal, one moment prior to dumping its rude contents into the coal truck's bed, whose every spring and axle would instantly feel the pain. How it came about that he and his grandmother had been positioned inside the bucket on a hot August afternoon in order to be photographed no one would ever to able to say with any certainty. Probably the sheer freakishness of the image had been more than his father could resist. Caper remembered that the blade had been stripped, the machine's imposing steel teeth scattered about in the gray dirt. He would pay a lot of money to see the lost snapshot once again. That surreal image, as well as the fact that at the end of the second week's grease days, he and another worker had climbed to the top of the dragline's boom to eat lunch (nine stories, plus the drop of the face, beyond doubt the most heart-pounding mid-day repast he would ever experience), marked the only two moments of redemption in ten workdays otherwise devoted to unbroken drudgery.

*　*　*

"Like a ship at sea, Ophelia ran from the castle."

Paradoxically, slogging prose such as this made an English teacher's life worth living. If all of Caper's students produced sentences of this stamp, he could teach forever. But they didn't, and he wouldn't. Pure poetry. Sailing and walking. Same thing, when you think about it. A ship is a vessel that moves on a body of water, and usually contains a crew of some sort, as well as cargo and perhaps passengers. And so is Ophel—

Well, okay. But still. It might all work out in the end. Journeys and destinations. That was just the point. There's something to work with here. There's a viable suggestion being made, a connection between two moving entities. Moreover, the "ship at sea" business, for all its silly lyricism, also manages to convey Ophelia's isolation with respect to her father, her brother, her lover. Good chance to talk about metaphors. In short, there's something to *revise* when you compare fair Ophelia to a ship.

In the fall of 1986, grading his first set of essays at the University of Pittsburgh (of the "what-did-you-do-during-the-summer?" variety), he had been ambushed by an alarming sentence: "Last summer, my mother had four disks removed from her back." Except that the word "disks" was the victim of a typo, and would be readily recognizable to all English speakers as a vulgar way of referring to an aspect of the male anatomy. Or, by a smaller number of English speakers, as a now archaic term for "detective." Typo-a-go-go. Gold. He shared this sentence with all of the other teaching assistants who were, like him, beginning their first year of teaching, and who were also being paid a princely stipend of $7000. They had to take their pleasures when and where they could.

But typos are typos. They happen. Indeed, Caper fervently hoped that they would happen far more frequently, that he would always have a fresh stream of unintended error, continually delivering defibrillating jolts to his soul. Mistakes can make sentences really last. Art by error. No doubt he'd made some professors drop an essay or two to the ground in shocked and guffawing disbelief. Where's the harm? Far more troublingly, however, lurking patiently in that same batch of freshman essays, an insurgent sentence or two launched itself with the word "granite." "Granite," one of his students may have reflected, "I've had more than my share of…" Or perhaps: "Granite, the Pirate bullpen has not been up to the task recently…" Such statements begat a mystical state of mind in the neophyte teacher, enkindling in the process an abiding agony, one that he was now sure he would never satisfactorily assuage. What universe were these writers living in? What did they think they were saying? In their daily experience, did words bear any relation whatsoever to thought or reality? Or were "words" merely clusters of colliding sounds, random sequences of phonemes to be processed in ways human beings had more or less memorized? Giving the slip to such gnawing questions was far easier said than done. And yet at precisely this juncture, Caper seized the opportunity to consent, with all due humility, to the overwhelming wisdom of these granite peoples: You magnificent bastards! Bestow upon me, if you please, even more of your timeless insights! Ain't no schoolmarm. Teach this humble servant!

But the gods of language, reigning in splendour from celestial thrones marked "Written Word" and "Speech," had only begun to toy with the anguished teaching assistant. In no time, the "grant it" faction made its appearance on the field, and Caper would find himself sucked back into the verbal vortex yet again. "Grant it," one of them might command, "a Pirate playoff appearance is long overdue." Caper obediently granted it. One also had to grant that the "grant it" adherents were playing ball here. The verb "grant" was present and accounted for. But now a different question reared its confounding head: Did these people ever read anything? If they did, did they pay absolutely no attention to writing conventions? But yet once more, with equal force and with right modesty, he retreated from easy derision, and vowed never to indulge in this lowest and laziest form of smug gratification.

Truth be told, unintended turns of phrase would take their permanent and quite welcome place in his memory. Sometime in the late '90's, a student had written the following sentence on an Act V *Hamlet* quiz: "The Danish prince emerged from the shadows, and exposed himself." Caper, who now had in his possession sound reason to suspect that the fair Ophelia had taken the right way out after all, also knew, instantaneously and unshakably, that lewd and lascivious conduct would never have a more appreciative audience. And even if it were the case that every time he revisited the hotly contested gravesite of the young maiden (always in the escort of a couple dozen trusting teenagers, each one of them new to the hallowed tragedy), who could possibly blame him for the unbecoming grin that habitually visited his face, at a moment fraught with so much death, so much sorrow? More recently, he had the startling privilege of reading a final exam addressing Lermontov's *A Hero of Our Time* and some other novel he couldn't remember, which managed, against all odds, to begin with the word "estrogen," only to proceed to be a pretty damn good essay. Most people, Caper reflected, couldn't do that if they were commanded to. Certainly some people, meanwhile, hearing about these entertaining nuggets of unbridled literary analysis, might find themselves tempted to think, "Say, maybe teaching English ain't such a bad job after all."

There's the, Caper would silently soliloquize, rub. Aye. Civilians, in fact, would never be able to appreciate the life of an English teacher. This was an immutable truth. Nor would instructors in other departments ever be capable of understanding how qualitatively different their day-to-day lives were. Caper didn't blame them; it wasn't their fault. Hemingway's most disillusioned and alienated Great War veteran stood a much better chance of developing a simpatico relationship with a cheery, anodyne, small-town Minnesotan, than the most eloquent English teacher would ever be able to adequately convey the lived experience of grading innumerable essays to anyone else back in the world.

For every Danish prince committing an unspeakable act at his erstwhile lover's grave, for every anatomically impossible surgery, for every misspelling that left the reader in awe for its inventiveness, there were thousands and thousands and thousands of sentences and paragraphs that cut the soul with more thousands of cuts. One must always remember that reading a moribund essay is not at all like watching a delightfully awful movie. There's very little Ed Wood or Roger Corman or *Point Break* in the life. No Utah; no Bodi. What small doses of charming schlock one might be fortunate enough to encounter in no way made up for the eternal task of reading, grading, marking essays that seemed to breed of their own accord as they snuggled inside one's briefcase. One is, no matter one's station in an English department, ever in danger of being assaulted by paragraphs that burp themselves onto the page, without ever bothering to say, "Excuse me." Paragraphs authentically deathless precisely because they had never been alive. Sentences that appeared to have been sentenced to begin, "This just goes to show that," and to end, "helps to make it interesting." "Camus uses diction," any number of writers might "explain," "in order to make it flow." Or, in response to some other diction-user, one much less adept in making it flow: "It seems to not flow." Indeed, "it," "this," "use," and "show" served as the coal, slate, mud, and dirt of the essay tipple, but when they trundled slowly by on the essay belt in sufficient quantity—as so often they did—they had little hope of creating any measurable BTU's.

Never, Caper wistfully observed, had the equivalent of a blasting-crew respite entered the classroom workspace, some tempting opportunity to assist a gang of destructive brigands who happened to be short a hand. (Administrators? Nah.) No pedagogic foreman had ever burst into the core whilst Caper was marking essays, only to bawl the mellifluous command: "Caper! Tomorrow morning get your ass straight down to the essay demolition!" No engraved RSVP had ever arrived in the teacher's mailbox, an enticing invitation to join an ace troop of boomers as they expertly wired up mountains of barren examinations, readying the material for consumption by a prodigious paper shredder.

He had chosen the life, and he liked it, but it was no gravy train.

* * *

City of Engels
Caper dropped by the high school's main office for a quick check of his June mail. Best-case scenario? Nothing whatsoever in the "Caper,

90

Morton" slot, a receptacle more depressing than ever now that a brassy magnetic name-tag had usurped the rightful place of its embossed vinyl Dymo-Label predecessor. But Caper had long since given over any full-hearted lamentations for the steady disappearance of poetry in everyday life. In this particular instance, the best thing for it was to hope that his mailbox contained no urgent requests for his presence in a momentous "Individualized Education Program" meeting. No peppermint mints enticingly scotch-taped to a fundraising postcard for a StuCo-sanctioned "Christmas in Cancun!" No "We Appreciate All the Work Teachers Do!" 10% discount voucher from McDonald's.

Not so fortunate this time, Cape. A teeming mass of lit-infested pamphlets, just waitin' for your timely professional response. Needing both hands, he removed the ungainly heap. Hang on! Tucked in amongst the glossy and unsurprising array of literary conference invitations and district flyers was a piece of yellow legal pad paper, carefully folded into a four-square. Note from a student, probably. Cautiously opening it, Caper was puzzled—very pleasantly puzzled—to discover that the text had been typed. Typed-on-a-typewriter typed. On yellow legal paper. Apples and oranges. And thin green lines on a lemon backdrop.

"Herr Doktor," the note commenced. *Former student*, Caper vaulted. Used to mess around with different types of address. "Cäper," for instance, or "Cåper," if he were in a Scandolicious state of mind. "Herr Doktor," if his temperament happened to lean toward the Germanic hordes. A few grins never hurt anyone, did it? Besides, any language teacher who failed to underscore the fact that more than five vowels puttered about the planet was derelict in duty, no?

"Greetings from the not-so-distant past. I write to you in order to correct some deliberate misinformation you may have been the victim of in the past few years. I think you will remember Max Fei, a Lindbergh student who graduated in 2009. He went on to Wash U, and has been informing anyone who asks that he graduated last spring." Caper, of course, *did* remember Max very well, and taught his younger sister Francesca more recently. And unless his memory served him poorly, the teacher received a visit from the fine young man early in the latter's undergraduate career, during which Max had firmly declared that upon his graduation from Washington University, he would be applying to

91

one and only one law school: Stanford. Very big ambitions to go along with a very big talent. "This is a lie. He did no such thing. In fact, he stopped attending any classes at Wash U early in his sophomore year. I'm talking about Absent Without Leave, Doktor C. By the end of that semester—his third—he was dismissed from the university. He has never attended any college or university ever since." Not blinking, Caper lifted his numbed gaze back up to the dark, empty rectangular slot that had, until just a few moments before, lodged this neatly folded scrap of lunacy. "In addition," he discovered himself reading once more, after an unknown lapse of time, "Max is telling some people that he wants to attend or is going to attend Stanford Law. Another lie. But he does have a lot of money, and he likes to spend it. He is a criminal."

Evidently, the typist felt the need to give the carriage return lever a bit of a workout. About two inches below the "criminal" allegation, Caper read the solitary sentence that brought the madness to a close: "I thought you should know this."

The letter simply ceased. No signature; no closing. No "Insanely yours." No "As ever, with affliction." Caper glanced at the back of the paper to ensure that he wasn't missing something, reread the bizarre missive, and stood motionless as he gazed once again into his empty mail slot. Nor an "I remain most methamphetaminely in your debt."

What the hell was going on? Le Max was an all-time great student. A proud drum major in Spiegelman's marching band. He'd be the very last person in the universe to drop out of school. Wonder, Caper wondered, did he jilt some little Miss Maxine, and now she's gettin' some payback? Couldn't be. She'd win first prize in the "World's Most Pathetic Vengeance Seeker" competition. What would *I* do with this information? Besides, the typist didn't even bother to indicate what *anyone* could or should do with this faux Fei-dirt. Far better to boil a rabbit on the Max's stovetop and really flip his lid. Direct action trumps written retaliation, or something like that.

"I thought you should know this"? What the hell?

* * *

Late in his first semester in Göteborg, Sweden, during a time when the sun would cast its feeble light for only about six and a half hours per day, Caper began teaching a large gathering of undergraduates in the 20th Century American Lit course. The focus of the second class meeting was William Faulkner, and the novel on offer was *As I Lay Dying*.

Because the enrollment was large enough to make anything like a genuine seminar set-up pretty impractical, Caper had been more or less obliged to conduct lecture sessions. At the very beginning of the second half of this two-hour class (just after the 15-minute hiatus that the Swedish university referred to as the "academic break"), Caper discovered that a new student had arrived, one who had either enrolled at the very last minute, or (the far more likely possibility) the lady in question was a member in good standing of a quite sizable tribal diaspora of students, one insufficiently studied by anthropologists or sociologists. Spread all over the globe, these scholars adhere to the credo that a given academic course's first couple of meetings are, for reasons presumably sanctioned by both tradition and repeated practice, completely optional. In this particular instance, he was made aware of this new, belated arrival primarily because the young woman began (and here our language possesses no other verb that will serve quite so well) to cackle. She cackled enthusiastically and at great length, all the while rocking back and forth in her chair. It was likely the only Swedish cackling he would ever hear. At one point, she lay on her side length-wise and propped her head up with one hand, like a maniacal model striking a Garbo pose. Not surprisingly, all present appeared to be visibly disturbed by the newcomer, none more than the instructor. Lending an extra layer of eeriness to the entirely batty gestalt was the cackler's uncanny resemblance to Glenn Close.

At the end of the meeting, Glenn—whose actual name turned out to be the beautiful Swedish "Ingela"—approached Caper and proceeded to batter the poor teacher with a series of incoherent questions, all the while grinning insanely. She was mad and Caper was a timid foreigner, making the encounter all the more unfair. No other Swedes came to their lektor's aid; they simply departed when time was up. How the rest of the one-on-one "conversation" went the American couldn't remember.

What happened at 8am on the next morning, however, was forever cauterized into his memory. Still pitch black out of doors, and with daylight not due until about 10am, Caper arrived at his spacious department office for one of the relatively rare early morning seminars he would have to teach in Göteborg. Because of the "break," class wouldn't actually begin until 8:15. Having just placed his winter coat on the standing rack, he turned to the spacious window that opened onto a garden area separating the offices of the U-shaped English department. Drawing the curtain, he was in every sense of the word shocked to be looking once again into the grinning visage of Glenn Close, only inches from the window. Even as she was enjoying a cigarette on this fine black cold Swedish morn, Caper's nervous system was reeling from a near-fatal dose of adrenaline.

The first phone call came, he thinks he remembered, that evening. The cackling was back in spades, and Ingela spent most of the mad chat explaining how it was that she was able to get his home number. (Not a small feat, since the telephone would not have been registered in Caper's name.) Near the end of the call, she volunteered the information that she was phoning from a bathtub. (This would appear to be true, as Caper did think he'd detected splashing noises in the background. Moreover, once the police became involved, they confirmed that she had been repeatedly admonished by the staff working in the institution in which she didn't sufficiently reside to refrain from making bathtub calls to outsiders.) In later telephone banter, Ingela made no secret of her admiration for Caper's hair, specifying that she'd like to replace her own blonde with his brown, adding that she possessed the very shears to make that desire a reality. Utterly confounded by this turn of events, Caper approached the irreproachable Harriet Sjöblom, head secretary for the English department. Harriet had already taught Caper that you could say the Swedish word "skit" (shit) in relatively polite conversation, an invaluable lesson all on its own, but also one that Caper often repeated to his American high school students, by way of exploring cultural differences in cursing. Now he needed her for very basic counsel. A flurry of maternal phone calls ensued, to the police and a local mental hospital, among other places.

For the first and only time, he went to a Swedish police station. The officers he met were well aware, thanks to Harriet, of Caper's situation. If only he could have managed to say in Swedish something along the following lines—"So happy to be in close proximity to all of you valiant policing humans! Could you please assist in the disappearance of a most singular girl on my phone and against window where I have job space? She maltreats her bathtub to make ring my telephone. Even she breaks up my language attempts in the teaching with witch-laughter, and I crave for a stoppage in her chortles. She envies my scalp. *Please sustain me*"—he would have. That he could do nothing of the sort made absolutely no difference. In very clear, ABBA-inflected English, they explained that laws recently passed by the Riksdag, and advanced largely for reasons having to do with cost-savings, had opened the doors of some mental institutions more widely than in previous years. Patients such as Ingela had a great deal more freedom in coming and going, despite the advice and desires of their supervising physicians. Swedish polis could do very little about it.

They did, however, advise Caper that they'd done their best to warn her to stop the stalking. Apparently it worked. Her intrusions came to a swift end.

* * *

How Green Was My V- Neck

For four years, from 1959 to 1962, a quarter century and more before Caper himself would teach on the very same campus, his father taught a course at the University of Pittsburgh titled "Open Pit Mining." The number of full-time professors who offered classes in mining engineering was exactly one, his father remembered, and that lonely member of the faculty devoted nearly all of his efforts to the intricacies of surveying technique. Pitt's mining engineering majors thus required, in addition to the usual array of calculus and trig courses taken by all engineering students, at least a few more classes specific to their chosen major's needs, taught, it would appear, by part-timers. In such circumstances, Caper's father's field experience was precisely what made him an appealing addition to the classroom. As the July 1959 issue of *The Dealer* (a trade journal catering to the needs of heavy equipment operators, although the fact that the magazine's cover featured not only a CAT D8 in all of its earth-moving glory, but also a bevy of attractive young women draped over most of the machine's surfaces, seemed to provide a telltale indication that its editors were taking measures to appeal to a wider general audience) boasted, Chuck Caper taught "the country's only college course in open pit mining." Surely, it was no small thing to conduct the nation's (the world's?) only course in a particular field, especially when casual, masculine reference to "D8's," "D9's," and "DW21's" would have been one's classroom stock-in-trade, and at a time, moreover, when so many young women had begun to succumb to strip mining's powerful allure.

Looking back, his father admitted that a more apt title for his course might have been: "How and Why You Should Purchase Caterpillar Bulldozers For Use in Your Strip Mining Operation, Particularly If You've Set Up Business in Southwestern Pennsylvania and/or Northern West Virginia." The general emphasis of his teaching was on things like how the cost of moving a cubic yard of dirt would affect your desire to get down to and remove large quantities of the Pittsburgh coal seam in a profitable fashion. As it happened, his father inherited the notes of a fellow who had taught a similar class at Pitt decades before, but these were predictably and sometimes comically outdated, occasionally featuring intricate problems which assumed that you could get a railway built right out to your mining operation.

Fact was, an innocent, dewy-eyed observer visiting a strip mine for the very first time, an open pit situated in an otherwise isolated area (as the vast majority of them tend to be), might well be puzzled by quite a few things. Perhaps if he cast his eyes at the dragline, this naïve newcomer would tilt his head quizzically and calmly bethink himself: "How the fuck did they get that battleship with the bucket secured to it all the way out here?" The answer, once he received it, would likely embarrass him, since it would instantly appear to be glaringly obvious. The machine was not, of course, shipped "out here"; it was assembled on site. But even born as he was into a populous family, a sizable brood largely dependent in turn upon a significant number of people purchasing open pit mining equipment, and with three brothers, moreover, who had worked above and below ground before him, Caper had a great deal of difficulty comprehending how, broken down into "smaller" components, some collection of coal-craving humans conspired to get the mammoth contraption up and walking. No "Wide Load" big rig he had ever seen in the intervening years trucking down this or that interstate could begin to approach the proportions of most of this machine's constituent parts.

The fleet of bulldozers constantly buzzing about might also attract our novice visitor's uncertain attention, as their actions might not initially appear to be altogether consistent with the mine's overall objective. Curiously, not all of them would seem to be relentlessly bent upon the task of extracting coal from the earth. But the bulldozers, he would quickly discover, in spite of whatever side jobs that might be thrown their way, really had only one major task: Protect the Coal Star. Clear all decks, now and forever. The tub machine had, one could not help but notice, an epic posterior, a galactic derrière. Tuchus? Tremendous. Gluteus supermaximus. The plain fact was, it had no choice in the matter. Countering the weight of the boom, the line, the bucket, and all ninety-nine thousand pounds of material tossed about with each shovelful, meant that the behemoth was perpetually crouched like a gravely insulted sumo. That, in turn, meant making utterly certain that its revolving backside had beaucoup room to spin about. Should any entity ever be so unfortunate as to make contact with the wheeling caboose of the dragline, it would instantly and irrevocably be dispatched into the next dimension, leaving behind no trace of its ever having existed in this. And let there be no mistake: the tub machine's feet had to be absolutely flat on the ground. As far as Caper knew, no dragline had ever gone off-kilter. But if ever one did, you had better run for the hills, if any were left.

This is where Caper's father came in. It is not necessarily a simple thing, once you know that a particular bit of land contains coal in sufficient quantities for you to unburden it of its energy-producing matter, to decide how to sequence your actions, particularly when you've got an extraordinarily large and extremely heavy queen bee on the premises, and—no small matter—the dirt you want to move around is not good ol' flat Midwestern loam, but instead, pesky, rocky, hilly southwestern Pennsylvania earth. The conventional windrow practices of your experienced and capable Illinois bulldozer-operator are not always going to get you where you need to be.

Caper's mine was in many respects quite typical of Pennsylvanian coal extraction. Flexible. If one way of getting the stuff out of the ground no longer made economic sense, mining operations were either completely discontinued in favor of some other chunk of ground, or traded in for another method of removal. His father was intimately aware of, and emphasized in his teaching, those moments when stripping (or deep mining) delivered diminishing returns. What to do? You know the desired commodity is there. In some cases, you can literally *see* it, from the top to the bottom of the seam. It's visible from your current cut, and you might even be able to touch it. Lovingly caress the buried commodity. But because of a steep incline, let's say, you can't entice the coal out in a way that satisfies you. Too many bulldozers pushing too many cubic tons of dirt, in order that the colossus might drag it out. Precisely at this point, you may well decide to send down an elevator shaft. Happened all the time. Go back to the old ways, the Welsh ways. But you'd better know the lay of the land. Literally—and in explicit detail. Go for the Compton augur? Take your chances, pal. That's sloppy mining in any case, even by mining standards. You're leaving a whole lot of product in the ground, and you're rendering the seam unmineable forever after. Waaay too dangerous to go back in there afterwards, with man or machine. Absolutely no prospect of providing any kind of overhead cover.

Strippers referred to the material lying above the coy carbon seam as "spoil." "Overburden." What one did with spoil and overburden, if one were an open pit operator, was assay to get rid of it as efficiently as possible. Move it the fuck out of the way. But move it where? And when? Indisputably, a dragline could move heaping masses of material out of the way, and do so with a great deal of panache. But it also weighed a hundred million tons. Remember: it had to move somewhere else after it had had its fun. You've got to think a few moves ahead, minimum.

Coal votaries, indeed, had even more to think about. Dirt doesn't behave the way you might wish it would. It swells when you dislodge it from its native habitat. It swells a lot. The "freshman 15" may or may not be a myth, but the "overburden 25" is cold fact. You're disturbing millions of years of dirt nap, and the spoil tends to wake up a little bit grumpy. It's going to grow by a quarter. This fact may in part have justified the strip miner's view that everything over his product is a "burden." You're going to deal with dirt bloat, and you're going deal with it right now. Your machine is squatting in the middle of it. Worse news. Really desirable coal very rarely presents itself in the form of a convenient outcropping. When it does, the BTU's are quite unlikely to knock anyone's socks off. Seems your authentically covetable coal likes to have a whole lot of spoil on top of it. Something to do with all the pressure changing the chemistry of the stuff.

It is, in short, hard to get. The open pit operator *wants* sufficient spoil, but he is surely neither happy with all the expensive fuss involved in pushing and hoisting it, nor in the way it behaves afterwards.

*　*　*

Yellow strikes again.

Walking past the glass block wall of the main office, Caper could see from a distance that a sharply folded yellow corner was sticking out of a small pile of mail waiting for him. He quickly determined that the other stuff could either wait or be discarded, and began a brisk walk back to his classroom, where he anticipated another dose of yellow legal pad dementia. Not even halfway to his destination, Caper suddenly pivoted and quickly returned to the main office.

"Kathy," he asked the secretary, "didn't happen to notice any of our students—or any other young person—drop off a letter for me, did you?" He held up the unopened yellow square.

"No. Students aren't allowed to—"

Caper nodded vigorously. "I know. I know. But I've received a couple letters." He looked at the paper. Then at his mail box. "Strange stuff. Keep an eye out, will you please?"

Kathy assured him she'd do just that, and Caper retraced his tracks. Even he was a bit surprised at how eager he was to discover the contents of Yellow Legal Paper Rant: The Sequel.

Reflecting back, Caper could hardly believe how late in his life it was that he got wind of the landmark Swedish "erotic" film, *I Am Curious (Yellow)*. Only days into his first year in Göteborg, he had been invited to join a department sailing expedition one sunny afternoon along one of the stunning southern waterways. Somehow, the English department chair and others got into a discussion of a film Caper would later learn was a notoriously campy dirty movie. From all accounts, it wore its jazz-flute existentialist sensuality on its sleeve (or on some other metaphor truer to the condition of sleevelessness). Several of his colleagues observed how relatively tame the whole affair was, especially a quarter of a century on. Much more recently, *I Am Fabulous (Yellow)* was the only tag that he had surrendered, entirely of his own volition. The outcome of not doing so was simply too predictable to ignore. Virtually no one would know what the four strangely sequenced words referred to, ensuring a couple of things: a number of people would look it up online, and someone in authority in the district would eventually want to know exactly why Caper felt that it was school appropriate to make a goofy allusion to a slice of vintage Scandinavian smut. But now, Caper reflected, he could honestly say that he was curious (yellow), whatever it was that those two words were striving to signify. Who's in the typist's sights this time?

In his room, he unfolded the four-square and immediately glommed that it was going to be "Max, Part II: The Son of Fei."

"HD," Yellow now typed, addressing Caper in what could either be a more intimate or more abstract fashion. "Max Fei is a fraud. I have already told you that. But I can tell you a great deal more. And I will."

Caper now wondered if he were dealing with the next iteration of Deep Throat. If so, what -gate scandal would unfold in the press? What the hell was Yellow playing at?

"Fei's a gangster. Eventually, I'll take it from the top. For now, all you need to know is that he's spreading lies in every direction, and the result is a brand new Mercedes-Benz convertible. Fei's a money pimp. Check out his car. Baby blue beaut. While you're at it, have a look at his license plate. RINSO. Very funny. He's a funny man. And his clothes won't disappoint you. Who knows? Maybe he wants to be the next HD Caper."

Yellow cut off the Fei narrative right there. But more was coming. This one *was* "signed." Never assume, Cape. The typist pecked out a cliff-hanger *au revoir*: "Until I write again, he that thou knowest thine, Horatio."

The *Hamlet* handle was, for the moment, simply annoying. Ham-handed. Caper would stick with "Yellow" for the time being. Other things to think about. Take "money pimp." Was Yellow just a sloppy writer? Can money be "pimped"? And what was the origin of that word?

Check it out later.

Typewriters had unexpectedly become interesting machines, hadn't they? Caper recalled all those Ellery Queen-type stories. Bad guy's betrayed by some anomaly in his typewriter. Like the detective happens to notice that the capital "R" is slightly out of line in the ransom notes, and the kidnapper is eventually snared by his own quirky Underwood. Caper scanned the new note for some sign of a typewritten "fingerprint." Nothing out of line. Look again at the previous letter.

Nowadays it'd be your go-to method of remaining anonymous. No cyber trail. Pretty much no trail at all, or as close as you can get.

What'd he have on Yellow so far? Access to a typewriter? Check. Unorthodox command of typing-paper etiquette? Check. Knows *Hamlet*? At least in a SparkNotes sort of way. Former student? Good chance, but not a cert. Aware of my stylish rep? Obviously. Fei fan?

Sorry, Max. These ain't no mash notes. Yellow's yearning for your skin, all right. But kind of like Elliot Ness pined for Al Capone's hide.

Why?

Caper was curiouser (yellow).

*   *   *

Jessica Laney exited the main theater room and walked in as straight a path as possible over to Caper's building to deliver a peculiar letter. She found Caper's room empty, dark, and locked. Turning, she walked less certainly across the hall to the high school Writing Center, hoping someone would know his whereabouts. As it happened, Caper and Van Der Meyer were there, chatting with a couple of seniors who also served as writing tutors.

"Cape, could I talk with you for a few minutes?"

"Absolutely. Come on in."

Laney looked uncertainly at the others present, not quite sure whether they ought to hear what she was going to say.

"Nice pants," she remarked in a desultory fashion. Caper immediately apprehended the fact that, in her agitated state, Laney hadn't given the wine-dark, plaid bell-bottoms the attention they deserved. "New acquisition?"

"Thanks for noticing." Caper looked down at the slacks. He searched his memory. *Don Burgundy*, wasn't it? Something like, *If you do, you'll always stay classy!* "No. I've had these for quite a few years. How can I help you?"

Laney remained a bit tentative. "I had a really weird letter delivered to my mailbox sometime yesterday." She held out the now-familiar yellow square, folded. "I think it was meant for you." She shook her head. "I mean, I'm sure it was."

Yellow strikes again! he thought. Then, "Yellow strikes again," he said coolly.

"What?" Both Laney and Van Der Meyer asked the dapper one for clarification.

"Yellow. I know this guy. We're pen pals," Caper explained. "'Cept I don't know his name, his address, or even if he's a he. But we're bff. Trust me."

Caper held out his hand to accept the latest installment of Yellow fever. Fei-ver? *Do me a Fei-ver, pal.* Yes! He'd use a line just like that should he ever get a chance to write back to Yellow. And he would be sure to type it on oddball paper. Goldenrod, let's say. With vertical lines. "This is my third post. It would appear that Yellow's not happy with his previous delivery service, and that Mrs. Laney's been tapped for postal duties."

Laney handed Caper the folded yellow square, whose lax crease suggested that it had in fact already been opened and read. Meanwhile, it was Van Der Meyer's turn to be visibly perplexed. "I didn't think you'd ever do that."

"Do what?" Caper replied.

"Talk like that."

"Talk like what?"

"Like someone who says 'bff'."

"You're right. I don't talk like that." Caper stared at the corkboard on the Writing Center's wall, searching for an answer sidling somewhere in the deeply mottled nooks and crannies of the board's surface. "What's wrong with me?"

"I don't know. But get it fixed."

Caper nodded solemnly. He would get it fixed.

Still ruffled by some aspect of this recent turn of events, Laney's attention continued to focus on the yellow paper. "Cape," she asked with evident concern, "are you okay?"

"Mrs. Laney," Caper responded, "I enjoy the best of health. Best of health." He rotated the yellow square with both thumbs, compressed index fingers forming an impromptu axle fitted to an imaginary hub. "Neither severe chills nor dangerous draughts of air pose any real threat to me, as far as I know. Why do you ask?"

Laney stared down at the seated teacher. "Can we talk alone?"

"I trust Van Der Meyer with my life, Jessica. If I were to ask him to leave, it would—"

"Cape."

"Okay, okay. Sorry." The rotating came to an abrupt stop. Slowly, Caper stood up. "Sometimes it's difficult for me to resist taking a trip down *Godfather* Lane."

*   *   *

Only occasional remnants of the legendary highway remained, and they weren't in good shape. About two miles west of Caper's house, the Midway, the Prince, and the Lennox motels could still summon, fleetingly, the look and feel of a 40's or 50's motorway, abandoned ghosts awaiting shadowy cars no longer looking for a night's respite, not in that part of St. Louie. Still keeping guard over low-slung single-story rooms spread out over extensive lots, a few signs spoke of earlier eras: "Color TV"; "Air Conditioned Rooms." The kicks these motels once promised, if the grand old song were to be believed, had long since been sought elsewhere. He had heard or read that one of the local ministries had purchased the properties for its homeless clientele. Unusually heavy pedestrian traffic in that area of the road suggested that this was true. The "mother road" was still serving those who had been displaced, at least in some spots, but the itinerant were now back on foot.

In the mid-90's, just prior to the arrival of the Capers in St. Louis, the last truly great reminder of 66's glory years was demolished only a quarter mile east of the Midway. The Coral Court Motel, known to one and all in St. Louis as *the* no-tell motel. Eight point five acres of "*sssshhhhh.*" Caper had seen pictures and posters and even a documentary on local cable. It really did look like a James M. Cain locale. Deco style to spare. Each room came with both a garage and—this is the important part—a garage door. An unknown percentage of the guests were reputed to stay for less than 24 hours. Untold infidelities. Somehow, too, it had been mixed up with the Greenlease kidnapping. Lindbergh. The drunken perpetrators of the Kansas City abduction staggered to the gas chamber, holding hands, in record time. Bruno-something, wasn't it? Steeply slanted ladder leading to a second-floor window. Kaufmann? Somewhere in Jersey. Another notch on the belt for Old Sparky.

Caper had heard that the last owner of the Court was widely regarded as an extreme eccentric, who for one reason or another was hell-bent having it demolished. Who knows? It was said that wealthy Japanese and German businessmen had attempted to intervene, keen to preserve this irreplaceable piece of Americana. Business Axis.

No soap. Its once sweeping grounds were now as nondescript a piece of suburbia as one could find. Voodoo of place such a fragile thing.

But whatever his myriad failings, Caper was an adept when it came to salvaging small consolations. Responsibly reporting for one of his biannual dental check-ups, he could reassure himself that he did so in an office located on a road that people from Japan and Germany (well, certain types of Germans and Japanese) would affectionately regard as the central auto pipeline of a treasured mythic America. Dr. Mraz. No glockenspiel in *that* name. Not a bit. In fact, had Caper's dentist grown up in another time and place, he may well have been coarsely subjected to a term of verbal abuse that seems to have faded from the scene: "hunky." This noun was quite often but not always accompanied by the modifier "mill." First cousin to this abusive epithet was the disparaging "bohunk." By the 70's, both labels had the air of the relic about them, a faint whiff of a smoky past. Yet they soldiered on. In earlier decades, of course, they would have been readily recognized as having every bit of the sting as "polack," "dago," "guinea," or "greaseball." To the best of Caper's knowledge, however, people did not avail themselves of the "hunk"-rooted insults any longer, with the possible exception of a few sentimental folk who might embrace them as quaint artifacts from a sepia-tinged past. Surely they had lost the old venom, or most of it. Nor would he be surprised if "bohunk" were to be found on some sort of "Endangered Slurs" list. These days, people would very likely have to ask you what you meant by that cute little "bohunk" word, and in an instant all of the derogatory intent would simply melt away. Two-to-tango, baby, whether you're partaking in scorn, dance, or romance. Offense must be taken for you to give it.

Pittsburgh once had names like Mraz like Doan's had pills. Hriszt. Sopchak. Snatchko. St. Louis had more than its share Central and Eastern European immigrants, but the western Pennsylvania landscape was awash in consonants that could barely make room now and again for a vowel or two. The "ch" sound was ever in the air. In addition, appearances suggested that a bare minimum of at least one "z" or "k" in one's last name was a non-negotiable prerequisite for membership into this stalwart group, although one could not doubt that intensely condensed packs of these letters, combined together with a liberal sprinkling of "c"'s, were held in the highest regard. Meanwhile, prohibitions against possession of the letter "v"—if, indeed, any ever existed—or the syllables –ic, –ak, –ich, and –sky, appear not to have been strictly enforced. Perhaps because he was a person unusually susceptible to contemplating letters and sounds and syllables and words, Caper couldn't help but speculate, when he was introduced to a person with a clipped name composed almost entirely of consonants—Glab, say, or Drovl—that two or three or more syllables had been amputated by an exasperated official back on Ellis Island, and that as a consequence, an unknown quantity of z's and k's had disappeared forever from the face of the earth.

In the late '70's, one of Caper's older brothers received a lot of needling from fellow air-tool salesmen solely because a worker at the Wheeling Pittsburgh Steel Mill in Mingo Junction (guy was known to everyone on the floor as the "gay hunky"!) regularly complimented his "rugged good looks." Seems that this memorable steelworker, who was known to favor purple work clothes, didn't take exception to the epithet; he even took some pride in it. Beyond any question, he was (quite bravely, one should not need to add) "out," and would also answer to the name "Munzie." Short for Munszcak or something. Not only did they film a great deal of *The Deer Hunter* in and around Mingo

Junction, but Munzie liked to tell anyone who would listen that he was a regular drinker at the very bar where quite a few of the drinking scenes were shot. He would eagerly inform you which scenes required fifty-two takes, which ones featured lots of improvisation, and which were sealed at the first go. Said he drank with De Niro and Walken.

Unequivocally, Caper reflected, the demise of ethnic slurs whose existence he had once taken for granted was a good thing. How often does one get a genuine opportunity to bid permanent adieu to a thing you wish would go away? Inveterate word mutationist that he was, he would occasionally find himself hunkying-up his last name, chiselling it into a more sinewy, flinty format. He would gladly sacrifice at least one vowel, or warmly embrace an orphan "z." Cpka might do the job. Capzic. That ought to answer. Right? But would these consonantal alterations be enough? Enough to make his Bohemian bones?

He conjured up brusque confrontations with would-be purveyors of ethnic invective, dust-ups intended precisely to display to his central and eastern European cohorts his own loyalty to the cause. "Name's Cpka," he'd phlegm with consonantal swagger. "Got a problem wi' that?" Or maybe he'd just channel the master himself. Travis Bickle. "You callin' me a bohunk? Huh? A bohunk?" Swivels around. "Well, then who the hell else are you slurrin'? I don't see anyone else." Swivels again. "I'm the only one here. 'Kay?"

And when the pitiful fool failed to volunteer an explicit and spirited denunciation of even a hint of anti-hunky bigotry, Cpka would make the vowel-dependent softy wish he'd never been born outside the Ottoman Empire. He would have demonstrated his fidelity, and he'd be on the inside.

Then again, Caper reflected in moods marginally less touched by delirium, maybe words have a life in them that he was underestimating. In the early '90's, at one of the Three Rivers Arts Festivals, a large statue of a broad-shouldered puddler, equipped with the title "Hunky Steelworker," was unveiled. You might have thought that since the southwestern Pennsylvania steelworker was at that very moment a critically endangered breed, and that the statue was a fawning (and mawkish) tribute to the mill workers of yore, not a lot of uproar would attend the unveiling. You'd have been, as the saying goes, wrong. Caper didn't know the exact details of the outcome of that artistic/ethnic spat, but seemed to recall that the offending adjective had been blow-torched into oblivion.

* * *

Laney and Caper looped to the right and back across the hall into Jovanovich's classroom, turned left when they reached the rear core entrance, and then took another quick left into Caper's room 55. The new mandatory-lock system had introduced a hint of the labyrinth into previously straightforward tasks.

"What's up?" Caper asked once both teachers were inside the classroom.

"Who's this 'Yellow' dude you're talking about?"

"That's my own private moniker. He's written me twice. Now thrice. Real strange-o."

"What's he writing about?" Laney now looked more disturbed than she had across the hall.

"Well, in the first place, as I believe you know"—Caper paused as he pondered how to begin, wondering what this most recent letter would provide in the way of dire accusations—"he's not writing so much as typing. Typing. Typing on a typewriter. And the cat types on yellow legal." Caper held up the third missive as exhibit A, fully aware that he had B and C in his briefcase.

"So what's he been typing about? Before this one, I mean."

"A whole lotta crazy. Definitely has it in for a kid I had a couple years ago. Several years ago. Max Fei." Caper paused, looking up at the white and blue cinder blocks that formed his classroom walls. Down through the years, graduates had hand-painted their names along the upper ribbon. "I'm getting old." He visually located the name he had just uttered, one that had been sounding inside his head ever since the first letter arrived from Planet Dizzo.

"Twice now," Caper began again, after another pause, "Yellow's somehow managed to drop off some zany messages focusing on Max. Put 'em in my mailbox without anyone in the main office noticing. They read sorta like ransom notes, except no one's been kidnapped, as far as

I know, and no one's asking for money." Caper looked at Yellow #3. "I suppose that could change."

Laney digested the new information, her face the picture of strained serenity. "Zany how?"

"Like, he's a liar, a criminal, a gangster, a dropout—"Caper ticked off the Fei accusations briskly, each calumny accompanied by a new finger on his left hand—"and get this, a 'money pimp.'" Yellow's financial slur earned Caper's thumb. He shook his head and smiled to indicate his bemusement. "Meanwhile, Mr. Max Fei is Boy Scout material. *Very* smart Boy Scout." Caper paused. "Oh, and Yellow signed the last one 'Horatio.'"

"Does it again on this one, too." Laney leaned back, screwed up her eyes deliberately. "That would be *Hamlet*-Horatio?"

Caper smiled again. "Yes," he confirmed. "*Hamlet*-Horatio." He stared at the notes he had written earlier that morning on the whiteboard, words and phrases and clauses that would only get in the way of his next lesson. "Wait a minute. You might be on to something. Could be Horatio Alger, couldn't it? Guy owned the patent on Gilded Age rags-to-riches tales." Caper interrupted himself a second time. "No. Couldn't be. Definitely *Hamlet*. Yellow signed off the second letter with a memorable line from the play. 'He that thou thinkest…kinder…kin… so," he changed the subject, "what's it say?"

"What?"

With his right hand, Caper tapped one of the corners of the latest letter steadily into the center of his left palm.

"It's not real clear to me what it's all about. Most of the stuff is pretty aggressive and creepy. All of this 'Herr Doktor' business and PEGS and—"

"PEGS?" Caper interjected. "Yellow's typing about *PEGS*?" He began to unfold the paper. "This secretive snitch just keeps on giving, doesn't he? Maybe kidnapping *is* just around the bend. But what I don't get is why the talented and treasured Mrs. Laney found herself the lucky recipient of this most recent exposé. Has the squealer typed up malicious accusations against our beloved theater program as well? Bemoaned its malignant, anti-family influence? Laid bare its morally corrosive agenda?" Warming up to the idea, Caper stepped on the gas, beseeching the young theater teacher to confirm his newfound suspicions. "Please tell me that insinuations have begun to spread, and that I hold here in my hand a litany of grievances pertaining to the depravity of Lindbergh High School's dramas and musicals." He looked at the yellow paper and then quickly back at the theater teacher. "Laney," he paused dramatically, "have you been shaking down our wee, vulnerable teenage actors?"

"No, Cape, I'm sorry to disappoint you." Laney smiled, but more weakly than Caper would have liked. She stared absently at the yellow paper, the letter still not completely opened in Caper's left hand. "And I'm afraid that my receiving it was simply the result of the deliverer's being in a rush. My mailbox's right beneath yours. I checked. Who knows what happened? A little bit of panic on Horatio's"—Laney politely corrected herself—"on *Yellow's* part."

"Seems likely enough. But don't be too quick to rule out mild dyslexia." No laughter or smiles from Laney. "Caper and Laney and all. Who can say for sure? Easy to mix up." Still not amused. "But I won't deny being a bit disappointed. Having another teacher subjected to the shady yellow typing treatment would have been a hoot." Laney either didn't share Caper's enthusiasm for the new pen-pal possibilities or wasn't listening to him at all.

Nothing to get sore about, Cape. Happened all the time. He waited patiently. "It's too much like the last time," she finally whispered. "Before I came here. It was my last year at La Brenton. Just like last time. Shades of…"

Laney mumbled something, but Caper couldn't make out exactly what it was that it was shades of.

* * *

"Aeneas undertook a similar journey, my chilluns. Penned a couple thousand years ago, and then some. And don't forget, Odysseus sailed on a memorable excursion to Hades long before that. Encountered his poor mother there. Very sad. Heartbreaking, in point of fact. And then there's the underworld in *Gilgamesh*, scratched on tablets thousands of years earlier still." All across the horizon of his sunless classroom, smooth, placid faces contracted; mouths pinched; arrow slits usurped serene, egg-shaped eyes. Each student a strict sentinel, each also appeared to register the fear that unforeseen reading and writing assignments would soon be wheeling into view. "We're gonna read just a little bit of that old stuff. Just to get a taste of what Dante was working with." Caper grinned reassuringly. "And against."

"Which little bit?" One or another version of this question was moaned from several sectors of the classroom.

"*Aeneid.*"

"Whole thing?"

"Nope," Caper responded soothingly. "Just Book VI." This calm assurance wasn't enough to quell the steady grousing of overtaxed teen scholars.

"Isn't one journey through hell enough?"

"Enough for wha—?" The teacher began to return fire, but abruptly ceased. "It's enough to discover," he Caped, "that you probably need more than just one. In fact" (why not lay it on thick?), "it's enough to realize that you can't profitably travel through hell until you've already accomplished the task at least once." Instantly aware that he would be hard put to explain the significance of what he had just said, Caper took comfort in the fact that the whole thing sounded pretty damn profound. What more could you ask? He allowed himself a shrewd grin. "And the others aren't even hells, in any ca—"

"Your face," a disruptive young voice interjected.

"Yes, Flo, what about my face?"

"It's strutting."

"Strutting?"

"Yes. It's like it's this incredible...this boastful.... swaggering... mixed metaphor."

"Did I have any role in teaching you any of this irreverent nonsense, young lady?"

"I don't know. Maybe."

"Okay. I'll accept the uncertainty. *Only,*" he added pointedly, "if you continue to mix things up inventively. Artistically and ambiguously. Keep it within the penumbra."

*   *   *

110

I'll be damned, Caper thought. Wiki comes through again. "Pimper." French verb, infinitive tense. Presumed to be the source of the modern English noun. Who knew? Says here that the word goes back to the 17th century: "to dress up elegantly." Hell, been a prize-winning pimp for a long time now and didn't even know it. Procured me some *fine* clothes. Le docteur is *in style!*

Caper squinted his eyes advisedly, tilting his head to the right as he did so, as would an accused racketeer listening to his attorney's private counsel. That must be Dame Prudence whispering in my ear right now, he surmised. The wise lady's cautioning me to withhold that interesting little etymological factoid from my impressionable young wards.

"Money pimp." This new French angle made Yellow's phrasing all the more troublesome. Gonna have to deduct some points from the youth's next gonzo letter. Maybe jot down a note in the margins: "Awkward phrasing, Yellow." No, better than that. "Rephrase, young typist: money can't be dressed up elegantly, now can it? Prime example of a mixed metaphor, my friend. And," he would add indignantly, "I'm not 'bout to 'llow that, am I?"

Words beget words, including the no-nos. Wherever there's the one, there's the other. No exceptions. Propriety forever handcuffed to profanity.

*　　*　　*

"Veiled, at first. Barely. But still veiled." Laney looked at the legal paper. "And then not veiled at all."

Caper nodded empathetically. "What was he after? What did he want?"

"Turned out that he was a 'she.' And she wanted her son to be cast as Romeo. Or else."

"Else *what*?"

"Else she'd make me wish I'd never..." Laney shook her head, unwilling or incapable of completing the thought. "I'd 'never direct another fucking play in the district.'" These latter words were uttered rapidly and as if scorched in her memory.

"So," Caper continued gingerly. "You began to receive drama threats? *Typed* drama threats?"

"Yes."

"Yellow legal pad paper?"

"No. White paper. But it was some sort of fancy linen stuff. It looked and felt expensive. Every letter I received had the texture of a formal invitation. With the bile of a death threat."

"Worthy of La Brenton, isn't it? Comfortable citizens are the rule, I'm told. I'll bet she typed on a stylish Hermes. Or maybe a rare vintage Smith-Corona."

At a glance, Caper had no difficulty comprehending that Laney ignored his speculations completely. "Insane," she continued. "Certifiable. I almost went to the cops. My job was on the line. But then it occurred to me that I might deal with it on my own terms, so I held off."

Caper allowed some time to pass. "So what'd you do?"

"Made the young man my Mercutio. As you're well aware, Cape, Romeo's hotheaded friend is killed at the beginning of act 3." Caper jerked his head back and to the left, his face the very map of impatience. *I know all about act 3, Laney. Stop wasting my time.* "Stabbed on four separate occasions from Thursday to Saturday, in a public place, and believe me, it couldn't come soon enough. Each time he slumped down to the Verona *terra firma* I thought of Mommy dearest." Caper, even while displaying telltale signs of endorsing this vindictive turn of events, still seemed puzzled. He was working uncertainly with each one of the digits of his left hand. Laney recognized his difficulty. "You're forgetting the Saturday matinee, Cape." *Yes*, he acknowledged wordlessly. *I was forgetting that.*

"Revenge," Caper said aloud, and approvingly. "Being a director must be pretty cool. You get to call all the shots." His vision temporarily took flight to some distant region located outside the windowless walls of his classroom bunker. *Somewhere, some place out there*, his eyes almost audibly implored, *there's a domain where others are obliged to say what you tell them to say, to sing to your tune, to march to your beat. To provide a snappy answer to your question, "Just what is your objective, you actor-in-name-only?"* "But how," he continued, catapulting back to this planet's inexorable dictates of time and space and tangled actualities, "did you identify the mother as the culprit?"

"Not really very difficult, Cape."

"You're right," he hastily agreed. "Cherchez la Texas cheerleading murderer... Texas chain-murder moth... cheerleader murderer... The mother's," he regrouped, "got to be pretty easy to spot when these sorts of things occur. Who *else*," he wondered aloud confidently, "would it be?"

"Exactly."

Benning. "The only odd thing to me is that the whole vindictive mess took place in posh little La Brenton. You'd've thought that such refined folk would recoil from that sort of uncouth behavior. Flagrant demands for attention? Pah! Unseemly threats betraying nakedly ambitious plans for their pampered offspring? Pah, again! It just doesn't seem part of a winning strate—"

"Cape, you've got absolutely no idea about the ambitious and the well-to-do. How far some people are willing to go in order to guarantee the fortunes of their—"

"I'm sure you're right," Caper interposed. "I really am. I've got absolutely no idea. One must walk in their shoes—or drive in their Bavarian cars—before one casts any judgment upon their actio—"

"Or teach in their school districts."

"Bingo, my young Laney." Caper sat up straight in his chair to indicate that he was about to put on his own one-man show. "The gripping dialogue always unfolds something like this:

Wounded mother and/or father: 'However did it come about that our dear, brilliant li'l Leo wasn't accepted to Princeton?'

Laney (*face racked with shame and sorrow*): 'Because I failed to exert my considerable influence at that unparalleled New Jersey university. I'll never forgive myself for neglecting to alert my well-positioned contacts in the admissions office to pay special attention to young Leo's application. How shall I ever live this down?'

Moderately accommodated parental unit(s): 'Well, at least you acknowledge your complicity in this horrible trauma. Perhaps next time you'll be more attentive to our needs, and better organized.'"

*   *   *

Alone with the stealthy Yellow for the third time, it occurred to Caper that he had better start keeping some sort of cataloguing system for the steadily amassing incoming missives. No margin holes had been punched in the legal pad paper, so a folder would be more practical than a binder. Should start dating the arrival time, too, since Yellow wasn't observing most of the time-honored letter-writing conventions. If this anonymous typing keeps up long enough, Caper calculated, he might eventually have the material for an epistolary novel. An updated *Dracula*, as it were. Let's see what Bram Stoner—Bram Toker?—'s been smokin' lately.

"Herr Doktor," chapter III began. Back to the goofy formalities, Caper noted. Not a consistent Yellow, are we? "Long time, still no see. I'm going to guess that you are a bit skeptical about some of the things I've said about Max Fei. If so, I'm not insulted. The Max you knew in high school exists no more. The Fei I've described is nothing like the PEGS-prodigy you knew." Caper paused and grinned. Check out the vocab on Yellow! Let's hope he *is* an ex-Cape. Maybe he's retained a thing or two. Calls himself "Horatio," too. Okay. A little bit irritating. But still. "He has been replaced by an entirely different Max."

Wrong again, Capester. Not talkin' 'bout the legendary Transylvanian bloodsucker, but an updated version of Jekyll & Hyde. Yellow's soundin' better all the time. Bring it on, Robert Looney Stevenson! "I'm going to ask a favor," Yellow continued. "It's as much for me as it is for you. I need you to be certain about the truth of what I'm saying. Why not take a trip up to Wash U? Ask for Max's records. Snoop around a little bit; see what you uncover. I'll give you a few days. Then we can begin to talk about XXL PK."

Holy pumped-up Kempf! Yellow's hep to Peter's surging pec portfolio! But exactly who's "talking," Yellow? I'm just reading the diary of a madman, my young friend. You've turned me into a legal pad voyeur, with no opportunity to reply. Thanks for sharing. Shows you care.

PK. MF. Now why did the teacher suddenly feel that Yellow wanted him to serve as MC?

Caper now knew a couple of things. He had to find a way to type back to Yellow. Rattle his cage with a little C-sage, tippy-tapped away on his own vintage Royal Companion. Made in Holland, baby. Yes, indeed. The typewriter dance would soon commence, one way or another. Knew that little steel beauty would come in handy one day. What to type on? Yellow's got the copyright on the legal approach, so forget that. Why not treat him to a dose of orderly graph paper? He could use a little bit o' grid. Good for his unhinged mind. Might even give him a little balance. And let's make it green, Cape. Oh, yeah. School colors, Yellow. You and I are goin' to dance a little typewritten Lindy Hop. Might even make it one of those marathons.

But how to get the tightly-squared paper *to* him?

In the meantime, Caper also knew that he would take up Yellow's Wash U invite. Could it be that Max really was a dropout? Impossible. But have to verify. Besides, logging some time on the Metrolink should soothe his agonized soul.

Yellow signed off: "Just trying to report the cause aright. Horatio."

Fair enough, Yellow. You've read your Shakespeare. But I remain unsatisfied.

*   *   *

Secretive and sinister typing, folded neatly and hand-delivered for quick readerly consumption, sent Caper's mind soaring back to his very first job. In fact, he was once quite the capable paper folder himself, adept at both the conventional tri-fold (wherein the newspaper would be contracted into more or less equal rectangles, the frayed side slipped into the smooth-sided fold), or the more flashy and advanced "tomahawk" iteration, whose end product was an obtuse triangular frisbee—in experienced hands, capable of being tossed a great deal further. (Given the right conditions, in fact, the tomahawked newspaper could also probably break an otherwise sturdy window, although happily such an event did not take its place among Caper's many delivery *faux pas*.) That typewriters and paperboys made their exit from the stage more or less at the same time was surely no accident. From the mid-60's to the early 80's, the six Caper lads delivered the now-extinct *Pittsburgh Press* seven days a week. Each of the boys had taken his turn, Caper's tenure extending from sometime in 1971 to August 1977. One of the last papers he delivered—and quite possibly *the* last—brought tragic news from Memphis. The King was dead.

When, many years later, he came into contact with Pittsburgh-native Andy Warhol (née Warhola)'s "Death and Disaster" series, he immediately sensed an uncanny echo of his own paperboy past. Warhol's grainy and extremely grim images trained one's attention on an often violent underbelly of American culture—electric chairs, spectacular car crashes, race riots, assassinations. Caper's newspaper route memories centered precisely on just these sorts of sudden, unpredictable turn of events. Clemente's plane crash was, of course, paradigmatic. The Patty Hearst "kidnapping" spree received particularly intense attention from the Scripps-Howard *Press*. J. Edgar Hoover's death, while not perhaps terribly surprising to grown-ups, somehow earned an unusually chubby headline, one that bewildered Caper. Exactly what had this old bald guy done to deserve such fat letters? Wasn't this the sort of treatment you reserved for a victory over the Orioles in the seventh game? And just who makes these alphabet decisions? Had the printers downtown no sense of priority? Headline perplexities aside, Caper could say with utter certainty that the Director's death took place on a breezy spring afternoon, in sharp contrast to Clemente's cold, icy plunge. At any rate, that was how he experienced them as he delivered the sobering news door to door. Freddie Prinze's suicide was dead freezing. Nixon's resignation was sweltering. Caper couldn't remember what the weather was like when Jimmy Hoffa went missing.

But above and beyond all other news stories from his childhood, the single most dominant event centered on one Joseph "Jock" Yablonski, the assassinated UMW president. While most of the history textbooks still appeared to teach the long-accepted claim that the Vietnam War differed from all previous American wars because "it was watched on television while families were eating dinner" (or some such formula), Caper would have sworn that they were all missing the far more pertinent mass media development—viz., that everyone in the universe had absorbed every single detail about the triple homicide in southwestern Pennsylvania, its tragicomic aftermath, as well as the hubris of the guilty contract killer, William A. "Tony" Boyle. It was simply impossible not to know this tale of a hit gone crazy, as both the wife and daughter of the union boss were shot and killed together with the intended target. The slaughter had taken place on December 31, 1969, precisely three New Year's Eves prior to Clemente's ocean crash. From the police point of view, the triggermen couldn't have been more considerate, as fingerprints were reputed to have been conveniently placed on every available surface of the home, as well as on beer cans breezily tossed out of the getaway car. Caper was too young to deliver the murder itself. But the Yablonski family homicide story had legs—Joey Heatherton legs—and it seemed as if all Pittsburgh news outlets were legally bound for four or five years to report the latest on this particular case before any other stories could so much as be mentioned. Pentagon Papers? Sure, right after the latest Boyle-buzz. Christmas bombings? Good stuff. Let's see how it fits with coal-mining murder trial. Hotel break-in near Washington, DC? Fascinating. Think it might be related to the hired killers?

Yablonski was Pittsburgh's gruesome answer to Tate/LaBianca. It had no Charles Manson and no "Helter Skelter." But Caper expertly folded and delivered the murder's aftermath for a solid three years. His 70's were unimaginable without it.

* * *

How to get word to Yellow that he wanted to get words to Yellow? This asymmetrical correspondence was very difficult to abide, but also very difficult to alter in any way. Yellow was holding all the cards. If only he could type back to the Fei-foe, Caper felt, he could begin to get on top of some of the rumor-mongering.

Before he could make headway on any sort of workable reply scheme, Caper received entry #4 of the Yellow pages. Curiously, the latest installment came the old-fashioned way. USPS. Neither snow nor rain nor heat. . . nor random and callous defamation. It looked like postman Bill would be taking over delivery duties from Laney, though he couldn't possibly be aware of his service as an emissary of venom.

As it happened, Caper had for a long time quietly nursed a desire to employ the phrase "drop a dime" in casual conversation. Surely, the very act of uttering those three words would serve as an ironclad guarantee that a really cool verbal exchange was in progress. Couldn't really be exceeded on any hard-boiled language (HBL) metric. "Hey

Cape," Van Der Meyer might one day find himself saying. "Heard about Roegner's run-in with that nasty PEGS-parent? Takin' some heat from administration 'cause one of her pint-size geniuses has his knickers in a bunch."

At which point Caper would nod with impassive ease, shifting the toothpick that just happened to be loafing in his dental region. "Kid drop a dime on 'er?"

Alas, each new dawn brought with it dramatically diminishing chances of ever fulfilling this dream. When you reflect on the fact that the best any surviving payphone could hope for was a stint in the Smithsonian, doin' easy time, you also have to concede that very few of the extant metaphorical "dimes" we're lucky enough to possess might ever again be "dropped." But hey, new vernacular windows open when other slang doors close. Thus reassured, Caper resolved to deliver the news, should the opportunity ever present itself, that "Yellow licked a stamp on Fe—" Nah. Loses the alliterative pep. And that's just for starters. "Stuck a stamp"?

Work on it, Cape.

Opening the white business envelope (Was Yellow losing a step? No "Special Delivery" trappings available? "Luftpost"?), Caper saw the 90-degree fold. Wasting no time, he flipped the envelope back again. Return address was stamped in large print: LHSSoSLMB on the top line, over the high school's address on South Lindbergh Boulevard. Spirit of St. Louis Marching Band. Didn't know they had their own special address. Then again, why not? On most days, one of the band's spiffy big-rig trailers was conspicuously parked right outside the Music Building. Why not a PO box to go with it?

Back to the letter. "Herr Doktor," Yellow resumed. His manner of address was beginning to stabilize. "Please forgive my intruding upon your home address. But I feel the need to remain mobile in my communications." Fair enough. If Caper were in Yellow's position, and for whatever reason wished to besmirch Max Fei's reputation via a series of inflammatory messages, he, too, would shift his artillery position so as to avoid detection. Caper was nothing if not an empathetic soul. "I've got much to say about another former student of yours, Mr. Peter Kempf. I think you'd be surprised if you bumped into him."

Oh, but I have, Yellow. I have. "You'd bounce off." Touché, mon jaune ami! You're beginning to have a way with words.

"But let's dwell on Max just a little bit more. I used to respect him. I really did. He was a leader, and a worthy one. I'd have marched through a wall for him. I thought we'd be friends for a lifetime. But the PEGS phenom has betrayed our calling, and made a mockery of his musical leadership." Suddenly, Caper felt compelled to pause. This one's getting tough to assess. Second PEGS allusion. In normal circumstances, he'd have spotted Yellow's particular brand of resentment a mile off: PEGS-envy, pure and simple. Not all that uncommon, as a matter of fact. Would-be exceptionally gifted youth takes out his frustration on one of the Wechsler *wunderkinder.* IQ cravings beget catty accusations. But Yellow's Max-mania seemed of an entirely different stamp. Clearly he wasn't interested in disparaging Max's intellect. Instead, moral despondency was the overwhelming theme. "When you confirm what I've said about Max at Wash U, and when you begin to develop a trust in all that I've got to say about both Max <u>and</u> Peter, I'll allow you to play a more active role in our little investigation. Who knows? Soon you may know more about the musical cesspool than I do."

"Our calling"? Yellow's marching band feathers were ruffled in a very big way. Why's he want me to be involved? He'll "allow" me to play a role? I'm no made member of the band, Yellow. Wouldn't know a reed if it slobbered all over me. And I ain't no detective. So you can keep on workin' the angles all on your own.

Today's sign-off? "Alas, I thought I knew him well,
Horatio."

Shakespeare allusions continue unabated. Would love to parry on that turf. But how to reach out and touch Yellow?

*　*　*

Max.

A worthy name; a commendable syllable.

"Wardrobe Maxfunction." Not the only Timberlake-infused ensemble Caper had ever sported. "Justin Timberlook" would also pay homage to the "Suit and Tie" crooner. Then Reinhardt and the "Mirrors" video. What're the odds?

Now, once again, he was homing in on the "max" syllable, but with an entirely new aim. How to run those three letters up some useful flagpole to see if Yellow, and only Yellow, would salute?

Where, Caper wondered, were the snows of yesteryear? Could personal ad space in the *Post-Dispatch*, or the *Riverfront Times*, have the remotest hope of delivering any sort of signal to Yellow? *Horatio: I'm just your* type. *But if you insist on remaining a one-man* band, *how can we take our relationship to the* max? Just try to imagine the replies that would arrive in the P. O. Box. "I'll be your Horatio, honey. Will you be my prince? Felicity is my middle name. Upon what ground shall we meet?" Did a world once really exist in which the newspaper personal ad was a viable communication option? Authentic correspondence delivered with reasonable precision, reliable anonymity, and occasionally something like intimacy? It wasn't an easy thing to conjure up such olden ways, nor to fully appreciate the behaviors of people who inhabited that universe.

Gone, Caper reflected. Couldn't dream of any secure secret diplomatic communication anymore. "The most appalling spying machine that has ever been invented." Say Assange's right. Still, could Cape somehow turn Facebook to his own purposes? Fair chance that Yellow had access to his posts. If so, even better chance that he or she might now be monitoring Caper's activity with greater attention than usual. Checking to see how C might respond to the secretive and aggressive Max-attacks. Could Caper turn this to his advantage? Maybe float an otherwise indecipherable syllable, word, or phrase?

"What's on your mind?" the spy machine perpetually asked. Can't simply type "Max" or "Fei." At best, a few "likes" and Fei-friendly remarks would ensue, with nothing to show for it. Plus Max might respond with a chipper "What's up, Dr. C? What can I do for you?" Caper didn't want to communicate with his former student just yet. *"Horatio"*? Needs to be more specific. *"I must reply to your accusations. Let's set up a P. O. address. Your choice. Maximum discretion."*

Caper laughed even as he typed out the words of the enigmatic offer. If Yellow reads that, he'll most definitely get the message. Equally certain to cause puzzlement in quite a few quarters. Especially the finale. Sounds hinky.

With an audible exhale, Caper posted the curt invitation. He waited for another covert surface mail response.

Communication was rarely—perhaps almost never—an easy game.

* * *

Perhaps three weeks into his tenure at Göteborgs Universitet, Caper embarked on a carefully designed campaign to improve his rudimentary grasp of the Scandinavian language. He had, of course, learned from his Berlitz Swedish language kit how to ask very practical questions: *Does this hotel room come with a bath? Is this the train to Stockholm? How much does this _____cost? Is this _____ (the final tram this evening/skim milk/herring/a Cuban cigar)?* But even here, he discovered, "practical" was a very relative term. He wasn't initially in any position to take any trains to Stockholm or Oslo or Helsinki, and by the time he was, he quickly observed that only an imbecile would have occasion to ask if this train or that were the Stockholm train, since the word "Stockholm" would be plastered on the front, back, and both sides of the engine and cars. Nor, as it happens, did he have any cause (or any money) to stay in a hotel. The "how much does _____ cost?" formula, by stark contrast, was worth its weight in gold. It should be the very first utterance all people learn when studying a foreign tongue.

From new colleagues in the English department he learned to make very handy inquiries, such as, "Excuse me. Where is the bathroom?" (The Swedish people are an extraordinarily kind folk. Indeed, one of their faults is that they *underestimate* their kindness. For some people, this is a very refreshing break from the norm.) Another national characteristic staining the Swedish reputation is that its citizens like to practice their English too assiduously. Caper would often make his Swedish inquiry concerning the location of "toaletten," and almost invariably be answered in perfect, and frequently British-flavoured, English. That's right. A suspiciously large contingent of Swedes spoke like Julie Andrews or Christopher Plummer. And forget about getting a quick, streamlined response. Something along the lines of, "Down that hallway and to the left." Oh, nej. You're going listen as Miss Andrews works on her periodic sentences. Tjej would say, "Right, brilliant. If only you'd walk past that oak-topped counter paralleling the mirrored side panel, turn *slightly* left when you see the brass umbrella stand (and do be careful to avoid the swinging doors—they move very rapidly from the kitchen and back!), and continue just beyond the foyer outside the elevator entrance, you'll find the door to the gentleman's WC on the left." Andrews would grant herself a satisfied smile after this Ciceronian excursion. Caper would simmer.

His new and more formalized strategy was to encounter the Swede in a series of increasingly lengthy and sophisticated "conversations," each one building on the last, and each designed to bolster his confidence. It seemed to be a sound plan of action. Baby steps. Order a certain pizza, for example, with a few mundane toppings. Don't get greedy, baby. Take the easy wins; bask in each small triumph. Next time, add a new wrinkle: at the last moment, as an afterthought, ask for anchovies. Better: *half* anchovies. Mutter something—something *very simple*—about your wife not liking them. Then shake your head and offer a second mutter: "Kvinnor." ("Women.")

Caper mentally scripted these encounters down to the last detail, even choosing his locales with great care. His first maneuver was set for a Friday afternoon in early September, after he had taught his last class of the week. It would take place on Avenyn (Göteborg's central and justly celebrated shopping boulevard). Department store. Conversation had to be airtight. He designed it so that it made absolutely no difference whatsoever what the Swede said in response to his question. This was vital because Caper had no hope of understanding anything in any case. Simply nodding his head would be his way of "responding" to his interlocutor.

It would go down like this: Caper would enter KappAhl from the street, locate where the men's sweaters were displayed, show signs of interest in one of them, and then approach the salesman. (For some reason, he assumed that some middle-aged man named Lars would be working the floor.) He would then roll out "Operation: Successful Swedish Chat."

Caper: Hur mycket kostar denna tröja? (How much does this sweater cost?)

Swede: Boinga boinga kronor.

Caper: *(Nods head. Pretends to absorb price information while visually inspecting sweater. Then, while considerately placing the sweater back on the rack)* Tack så mycket! Hej då! *(Exits store. Congratulates self. Plots next department store incursion.)*

Reflecting on the language crime that came to pass, Caper humbly acknowledged that he didn't really deserve to make any sort of allusion to the "best laid plans." This was a crap plan, on several levels. It was like taking an X's and O's diagram of a football play way too literally, as if your opponent is actually a square or a circle, and therefore won't move at all until you run over there to block him, right on time for the running back to exploit your perfectly executed interference. It was perhaps the single clearest instance in his experience illustrating life's most profound lesson: plan stuff, but be flexible. If you fall for too much planning, you'll never be in a position to exploit any good luck that might come your way.

As it happened, not one element of the orchestrated language event he concocted bore any relation to reality. Entering the store, he immediately deduced that he was in the women's department. Intimates and so forth. Life was definitely not imitating—not even politely cooperating with—his finely wrought art. *How much does this sweater cost? Thanks so much. Goodbye!* He was repeating these sentences in his head so urgently that he was probably saying them aloud. As he turned to the right in order to seek out and price a men's sweater—*any* men's sweater—he heard a woman calling out some sort of warm and chipper greeting. Even though he could have safely presumed that she probably only said something in the neighborhood of "How are you this afternoon?" and even though he knew that "Bra, tack," would pretty much cover all bases, Caper began to panic. *How much does this sweater cost? Thanks so much. Goodbye!* He was now in danger of shouting his question to the poor sales clerk, should he ever find a goddamned sweater. *Hur mycket, hur mycket!*

Caper came to the end of the aisle, and had no choice but to turn left, deeper into the heart of Swedish garments. Someone was now following him, maybe the friendly female voice working lingerie, maybe a store detective. He tried to check his stride. Don't want to look like I'm running. Ahead, he saw what had to be men's coats. Looked like something your everyday Gunnar would wear in the woods. Yes!

Definitely. Big Swedish plaid *jackor*! And pants! And *tröjar*! He had arrived in the blessed land of Swedish sweaters!

Slightly light-headed now, his breathing probably showing signs of strain, and his pulse most definitely on the uptick, Caper walked straight to a circular display of Scando-themed sweaters. He picked up a gray-and-brown number, with metal snap buttons along the shoulders. The thing positively reeked of pickled herring, akvavit, dill sauce, lingonberries, and sauna interiors. Caper immediately proceeded to feign some interest in it. As he turned around, he was just a little bit startled to discover that the sales person—a woman, but perhaps not the one who had chirped "Good afternoon" in Swedish a few moments earlier—was standing close by, waiting to aid him in his sweater quest.

She said something very quickly, smiled, and nodded. All of Caper's short script vanished into thin air, more completely than if someone had written it down, torn it up into little pieces, and tossed it out of a moving carriage. He nodded and opened his mouth. Nothing. He stared at the sweater he was now holding high into the air with his left arm, as would an insane and woefully incompetent Scandinavian bullfighter. He nodded his head for what had to be a very long time.

Finally, "Är detta en tröja?" escaped his mouth. ("Is this a sweater?") The panicked foreign syllables had not even cleared Caper's lips before he knew that the chances for anything like a graceful exit from this conversational wreck were zero. Lacking anything else to do or say, he continued to stare at the sweater while he moved his lower jaw into different configurations, as if he suddenly needed to stretch his mandible muscles. The clerk, meanwhile, was in the periphery of his vision, a bit blurry, and he wished to keep it that way. The word "Ja" loitered somewhere in the department store air, an affirmative response to Caper's question that still managed to sound more like a question than Caper's question. While he couldn't say exactly when it had been uttered, he did think it likely that she had taken a tiny step backwards. After an indefinite period of time had lapsed, Caper replaced the woolen mass on the circular display, turned, and marched out the nearest exit.

Over the course of the next 33 months, he never once returned.

* * *

Only the inexcusably obtuse, the willfully naïve, or the disgracefully unobservant, Caper well knew, could ever be duped into believing that the highest ranking officials of Washington University in St. Louis—Chancellor, Provosts, Deans, and so forth—had anything to do with the actual management of the place. It would be far closer to the truth to regard these men and women (and the academic titles attached to them, purely for appearance's sake) as little more than pawns or puppets, ever at the beck and call of the all-powerful Gothic Revival mafia that ruled the institution with a masonic fist. Like many other such cabals, this sect needed to present to the public a few unobjectionable faces, in order that it might be about its real business of blanketing every square inch of the Gateway City with ceiling bosses, pointed arches, tracery windows, and ribbed vaults, unmolested by inquisitive outsiders. That very few of even the made members of the architectural family had access to the complete and exact composition of the Revival register was a probability; that this crew could be prevented from fully implementing its ambitious architectural scheme was a matter open to debate; that it existed was an absolute certainty. Thus it was that one could assume with unshakable confidence that every single Wash U string worth pulling dangled from a decorative finial, to be handled only by lawfully consecrated hands, each one of them a link in a continuous succession traceable back to John Ruskin.

As he walked the familiar path from the Skinker Metrolink station onto the large rectangular campus, Caper noted once again that, like certain hospital sites, Washington University appeared to be functioning on a mandatory and permanent construction schedule. Cranes everywhere. Orange "Detour" signs prominently gracing well-nicked scaffolding at every turn. Not one of the new and/or refurbished structures was permitted so much as to whisper any element of style that didn't begin with the prefix "neo-" and end with the syllables "goth" and "-ic." Not one. How the Olin Library's modernist heresy managed to erupt (undoubtedly back in the '60s, when an unhinged, barbaric, and hygiene-challenged group of radicals had somehow conspired to hijack campus design decisions, if only temporarily) would be an interesting tale to investigate, probably involving murderous vendettas and architectural firm explosions.

As thin slabs of neo-stone facing were being hoisted to the third floor of what he took to be a new dormitory, Caper wondered if a few of these smart young kids would take it upon themselves to hang up a Farrah Fawcett poster in the new digs. Seems like something a certain type of hipster might do, no? You could signal your sly historical awareness, for one thing. Your ironic sensibility. Who knows how many conversations of 70's cultural flotsam would be triggered by those teeth, that hair, and other things? Then again, he'd bet a very large amount of money that, whether or not Farrah made her feathered presence felt in any of those rooms, the mind-bending works of M. C. Escher were certain to be found on every floor. In the first place, it had to be an incontrovertible truth that of all the Escher-print posters ever printed, well over 90% were to be found in dorm rooms. But now we're talking about Wash U dorm rooms. Gothically delicious! On the inside, the maestro of geometric distortion would effortlessly provide all the angels and demons and twisted staircases and towers anyone could possibly need. All the while, those ever-whirring construction cranes would take care of the exteriors. Heaven and hell! Somebody put a Dio LP on the stereo, and be quick about it! I'm going to descend those staircases one more time, and I need some proper serenading!

If only one could monitor conversations from all over the world between college students contemplating the Dutch master's manipulation of space and perception. "Oh, maan! Dude, how'd he *do* that?" Those very words, in dozens of languages. Better, narrow the scope just a bit by cross-referencing "April 20" and "Escher-print conversations." It'd be dorm-tastic. In any event, if one day someone managed to invent an Escherometer, a device designed precisely to gauge the Escherdensity of any given geographic area, Caper felt certain that Wash U would acquit itself quite well. Perhaps even intercollegiate competitions were not out of the question. ("Best Tessellation" category; "Best Overall Paradox"; and so forth).

The Bears of Wash U would have the eyes of the world upon them. And they would make St. Louis proud.

* * *

"Let's talk about PK, shall we?"

No greeting at all this time. Not a problem. Formalities are made to be set aside, aren't they, Yellow? Far more to the point for the teacher: would the second letter to his home, and the fifth overall, acknowledge Caper's outreach effort? Or was he still trapped in a one-way pen-pal relationship?

"I'd like you to understand one thing. It's not me doing the typing." Whoa, Yellow! You're not goin' all Milli Vanilli on me, are you? Type-syncing? That's just not right. Might have to burn your letters in protest. Besides, I was hoping to take a break from Germans. "It's never been about me. It's always been what Spiegelman taught every one of us. Once in band, always in band." Caper reflected on the enduring influence of the beloved band leader. "I'm typing for the cause."

At least Caper could put the typing-integrity anxieties to rest. Nonetheless, in a far more troubled fashion, he wondered how on earth had Max, and apparently Peter as well, violated the "cause," at least in Yellow's eyes? What had they said or done? Clearly, Yellow's mission was to set things right. And Caper had definitely been right about another thing. This was no by-the-book PEGS takedown.

"Herr Doktor," he delay-greeted Caper. "Have you bothered to check the Minnesota Golden Gopher record in band competitions lately?" Sorry, Yellow. Been remiss, I admit. No excuses for not keeping abreast of the latest marching band news from the land 'o lakes. Please, tell me what I've missed. "Their percussion section has racked up win after win over the past two years. The year prior to that, they came out of nowhere to consistently grab second and third place honors." That's terrific news, Yellow. The Golden Gopher percussion section has certainly done the North Star State proud. Exactly where are we heading with this riveting reportage? "This miraculous"—easy there—"performance coincides, I am certain you haven't failed to note, with the arrival of Peter Kempf."

PK's band credentials were known far and wide. "Band Peter." Oughtn't we to be proud of our former colleague, now doing such first-rate work up north?

"PK, as I've already mentioned, now comes in a plus-size." Yellow continued to wax witty. "But don't go blaming Moon Pies, Ding Dongs, and Sno Balls. All the extra Kempf comes in the form of <u>lean</u> muscle mass." I'm aware of that, too, my colorful friend. If only you'd bother to listen. But you don't bother, do you? Still, I'll rise above the fray and say, Thank you, thank you. In spite of your callousness, you have repeatedly reminded me of what an underlined word looks like hot off the presses of a gen-u-ine hunt-and-peck machine. Takes me back. "The truth is, the entire Gopher drumline is equally large and very much in charge. Think about it, Dr. C." What happened to my German credentials? "Peter arrives, and soon all the Gopher drummers are doing a very capable Steeler O-Line impersonation." Nice touch, Yellow. Pittsburgh allusion and football coach lingo all in the same sentence. You're hitting all my buttons. "I mean, they're collecting awards like Lance Armstrong used to collect yellow jerseys." If only you knew, oh jaundiced one.

"They're the loudest drumline in the nation, bar none."

Then, an abrupt postscript. "I accept your offer. You will receive notice from me of our shared P. O. Box as soon as I am able to complete the necessary paperwork."

Yeller! Old boy! You had me at Yellow! Never thought for an instant that you'd disappoint the old man. Can read you like an open book, my friend. And soon you will make the acquaintance of *my* deathless prose!

Gentlemen, start your typewriter ribbons! Stool pigeon just got himself a new correspondent.

*　*　*

The land upon which the Dimezzo Coal Mine stripped its coal had once been a deep mine, ceasing operation, Caper's father told him, in 1910. Of course, that earlier mining effort had been carried out under vastly different circumstances for the workers. One—but only one—indication of the historical chasm that separated him from the miners of seventy to one-hundred years previously, was the fact that the underground workers had been obliged to leave about 50% of the coveted carbon product in place, so as to minimize tunnel collapses. Because the Pittsburgh seam was 5-6 feet, enough coal remained to be profitably removed, by other means, in the 60's, 70's, and early 80's.

At the face, one would more than occasionally be reminded of the long-dormant precursor. A fat stick of dynamite, a heavy equipment blade, or (rudest intruder of them all) a heedless, rasping steel tub, would suddenly expose stunted passageways that had never before been visible from the earth's surface. Fresh dirty air would be introduced into the cramped old warren, not bringing anything back to life, except perhaps an odd reverie or two. Caper's musings were always of the most pedestrian variety. Wonder who worked those tunnels? Wonder when? Wonder what was their equipment? Where'd they live?

Had to be sleeping right over the seam, available for the next shift.

Mandrels? The British had cool words for everything. Modified picks, made for use in close quarters. Add or subtract two or three inches, depending on ceiling height. A pool shark's private cue, except this one was fashioned to slam the seam, and the most experienced eyes would know just where to strike it, or so the stories went. He'd once read that a transcontinental "Great Seam," or some such mass, shot up from deep southern Europe, made its way to Wales, turned left under the Atlantic, only to "resurface" (close enough to mine the stuff, anyway) in Pennsylvania. Dirty black shadow companion, carbon doppelgänger, to the Gulf Stream. Warmers both. Was the Pittsburgh seam *that* seam? Pretty damn cosmopolitan coal if so. On easy terms with a quite a few languages. It'd have its own special passport and maybe a Baedeker. The old man frequently remarked (no matter its geological pedigree, about which he wouldn't have given a shit) that the stuff burned very hot, that it couldn't be beat for coking. That's why they still mined it; that's why you have a job in the tipple.

Wonder did many of those guys live past 60? Lungs took a terrible beating. Something -osis. One of the few places where being short paid off. Built like bulls. According to the old legends, the really skilled ones, the virtuosos, would confidently eyeball the face, take the measure of the dark horizontal ribbon—nemesis and beloved all at once—before cracking it dead-on on some invisible sweet spot with their customized underground picks. Calmly, of course, utterly certain of the consequences of their perfectly executed stroke, they would watch the stuff fall by the ton. Take that, shiny black bituminous son of a bitch! Romance of the underground. Lawrence always banging on about their bowed legs.

Was all that canary business true?

*   *   *

To the novice, a quick study of a map of St. Louis would probably produce one of a handful of visual comparisons. Some might describe the city as being football-shaped, set on a tee and waiting to be kicked. More fastidious map-readers might politely remark that footballs are nearly always quite smooth, and suggest instead a lemon analogy, bumpy rind and all. No doubt certain botanically-minded observers could name some appropriately shaped leaf, pointed at the ends, bulging a bit in the middle, and scruffy about the edges.

All along the eastern border of the city, stretching north to south for many softly curving miles, the Mississippi River "keeps rollin' along." While it is undoubtedly true that one of Twain's great themes underscores the mighty river's ever-shifting course (and furthermore, that his bottomless affection for the unflappable river pilots grows precisely out of their ability to master the always-changing channel), it is also true that from the point of view of the cartographer, the river has served as an admirably stable element of the city's "picture." For the most part.

In an 1867 map of the city framed and hanging in Caper's dining room, the lemon is, not at all surprisingly, a decidedly skimpier one than that which awaited the family upon their arrival in the mid-1990s. Judging from this post-Civil War rendering, St. Louis' western edge was marked by Grand Avenue, more or less thirty-six meandering blocks to the left of the rather more hippy river. It depicts a city largely designed upon what were to Caper's mind sensible grid patterns, a feature especially prized by people who are not St. Louis natives, and who therefore rely upon an abstract "idea" of the landscape far more than locals. He took pleasure in locating both his Eleventh Street apartment and his Pestalozzi Street house, though the latter would not be built for another quarter century, ten blocks due west of the Anheuser-Busch brewery. He took further pleasure in gazing at two spindly islands depicted in the middle of the Mississippi River. *Huck Finn*sville, baby, but each arguably better than anything Hannibal had to offer. The more northerly land mass is marked "Bloody Island," a name which of course could not be improved upon in any way whatsoever, while the southern isle—only partially rendered—is simply marked "Arsenal Id." These now expunged habitats simply had to be investigated, a task that Caper took up the minute he purchased the map.

"Bloody Island" did not disappoint. Turns out the place was a favorite haunt of duelists, who presumably prized the fact that neither Missouri nor Illinois claimed the sandy, woody river mass as part of its territory. Ergo, resolute and vindictive honor-preservationists could ply their trade with impunity. All sorts of prominent affronts were settled here, including one duo that perished simultaneously after their weapons discharged from the target-rich distance of five feet (Wonder what their seconds said to one another in the aftermath of this impressive display of marksmanship?). In one of the endless attempts by the Army Corps of Engineers (Mississippi Valley Division) to render the Mississippi ever more navigable, Bloody Island disappeared sometime later in the century, but poetic justice received her tribute: some of the island is now part of Illinois, while a bit of the southern end became a small chunk of Missouri.

Less colorfully, but no less interestingly to Caper's mind, Arsenal Island had a sometimes conflicting set of stories attached to it. Once a military cemetery, it had also apparently served as a quarantine space when cholera epidemics hit St. Louis. The "Arsenal" name seems to have been owing to the simple fact that the island was situated directly east of the St. Louis Arsenal. This latter institution, meanwhile, played a very important role in the Mexican-American War, a less important role in the Utah War, and a complicated role in the Civil War, one reflecting Missouri's own fiercely torn positions. Its military service continues to this very day.

As the lemon has grown more plump over the many decades, and as the major north/south axes have been carved into the cityscape every twelve blocks, from Grand to Kingshighway and Hampton and beyond, St. Louis has enacted on the micro-level the great refrain the nation has always been repeating: western expansion. But that expansion has never been free of sometimes strong counter-expansive forces. Perhaps an archer pulling back on the bow would serve as the best, but still quite proximate, visual analogy. If so, that bending and increasingly tightening western string has its own extremely complicated tale to tell, one that would require not only a thorough account of St. Louis' tangled role in the Civil War (as well as the years immediately following), on the one hand, but also of far more mundane—or perhaps only seemingly mundane—matters, on the other: tax policy, municipal service, and—not least of all—who gets to be in charge of the city's police department.

Caper and his family now lived about half a football field to the south and west of that bow string, a distance that can make all the difference. The city line cuts sharply back to the Mississippi on a diagonal, slicing through dozens of houses in his neighborhood. One's place of residence, for not a few of the neighbors whose abodes sit quite precisely on the city/county divide, depends entirely upon the location of one's bedroom. If the master is to the east of the line, you're a city slicker. You get city garbage pick-up, city taxes, city schools, city landscaping services. If to the west, you're a staid suburbanite. Your bills and services will be coming from and going to other locations. This geographical and architectural quirk, in turn, occasionally leads to some visually counterintuitive residencies. One home sitting on a lot unmistakably further to the east than another across the street might nonetheless out-master bedroom its neighbor and thereby earn "county" status, while a more westerly structure might surreptitiously boudoir its way inside the city limits.

Interesting locale, Caper thought, for local government to make the final "cut." Not that he had any objections. It's just that the kitchen might have certain claims in this matter. Even the biggest bathroom.

*   *   *

Yellow's next contact was easily his most abbreviated thus far. No greeting, narrative, or sign-off. Nothing on Max or Peter or fidelity to the marching cause. Pure information exchange, neatly typed in three single-spaced lines. But the paper remained the same. Old Faithful had nothing on the band loyalist.

"Horatio," the first line read. Some things never change.

"P. O. Box 034100." Got it. Now to the heart of the matter.

"Vineland," line three announced. Oh, the poetry! But which are we...

"NJ." Are you kiddin' me, Yellow? Jersey? So you *like* summer weekend traffic jams? *New Jersey* is going to be the lucky recipient of my first typed pages since...I don' know. The *Challenger* exploded?"

"08362."

Beautiful. But it didn't really mean anything, did it? P. O. Box addresses about as reliable as ninth-graders who've gone full non-compliance on the ritalin. Yellow's actual location remained as undetermined as ever. Might be living down the street, opening my "New Jersey" letters just as soon as they ricocheted back across the Mississippi. Not likely, of course. If anything, Yellow was probably still in district, holed up in the parental basement. Whatever his locale, the cat was getting more interesting all the time, wasn't he?

All indications, in any event, pointed toward a new communication era. Caper thought it wise to seize the lead, aiming to keep Yellow moving backwards...and in high heels.

"Dear Horatio:

I don't know where to begin. Perhaps I should take a moment to explain my choice of paper. To say the least, I cannot hope to match, let alone exceed, your own exquisite stationery. In fact, I am willing to go on record right now by declaring my own steadfast belief that you've touched off, intentionally or not, a new writing craze. Once I reveal to the world your incomparable epistolary habits, hipsters near and yonder are sure to seize the yellow baton with zest, soon inundating one another's mailboxes with mysterious four-squares, each one containing malicious and unsubstantiated allegations against third and fourth parties. Each one, indeed, composed on a typewriter. So, congratulations! You are a true trendsetter!

My own choice of little green checked paper is in part a belated offering to my father, who avidly wished that I would become an engineer. Alas, I failed to deliver on that paternal desire. But the least I can do is to employ one or two tools of the trade. Perhaps I'll also purchase a calculator and pretend to apply an equation now and again—or, far more to the point, a slide rule. That's just the way we play! (NB: expertly executed underlining job.)

I would be remiss, however, if I kept secret my other motivation. A great Canadian once said that "the medium is the message." I do hope he won't mind if I attempt to apply this dictum in a quite pragmatic manner. Even if he would not approve, I can still comfort myself by noting that, like all would-be reformers, I am attempting to alter your course of behavior with the very best intentions. Put bluntly, you have drifted far off the rails, Horatio. Very far, indeed. When I reflect on the fact that you are the one responsible for introducing a Shakespearean note into our written communications, I also feel compelled to observe that your letters only serve to make your dear, melancholy Danish friend look like a paragon of even-tempered rationality by contrast. Therefore, it is my own dearly held wish that your own poisonous and erratic conduct be influenced, even if only subliminally, by the orderly, squared sheet of paper you are currently holding in your vindictive hands.

I have long been aware, for example, that Mr. Peter Kempf is held in the very highest esteem by both his band colleagues and his band leaders. 'Band Peter,' I learned in his junior year of high school, was an epithet born out of respect for his discipline, skill, and leadership. I have no reason to doubt that his Minnesota colleagues feel the same way, and for the same reasons. That he has unflaggingly applied himself in the weight room during the past few years cannot be doubted. Indeed, quite recently I had the pleasure of "bumping into" Peter (as you so delicately put it), and genuinely appreciate your sly observation that I would be obliged to "bounce off." Ol' Man Caper, rest assured, has no desire to collide with the freshly hewn Herr Kempf. Neither, however, is he at all pleased to be subjected to unsubstantiated suggestions about the imposing drummer. Please do me the favor of either supporting your wily (and quite woolly) intimations in your next letter, or terminating them altogether.

But my desire to write to you about your former drum major has been set to the side for far too long. Whence the malice towards Sir Max? A dropout, you say? A liar? A dandy driving an expensive ride? You will doubtless be gratified to learn that, even though I anticipate bureaucratic and legal roadblocks, and in spite of my certainty that everything you say is baseless slander (what your motive is I cannot begin to guess), I am going to attempt to avail myself of Washington University's student records, in order to catch the alleged truant—no, I know, that's not it. That's not quite the "dropout" word you have used. But I don't know where any white-out might be sleeping its long coagulated sleep, and I don't think I could be bothered if I did. At any rate, you know what I am driving at, since you are the prime cause of all this nonsense. Allow me to try again: I will attempt to obtain evidence of his having been drummed out of the university for chronic truancy in his second year, an occurrence that will explain, in turn, how and why Brilliant-and-Ambitious Max more or less instantly metamorphosed (according to you) into Gangster Max. Caper is on the case, in other words, so at least one of your stated desires has already been fulfilled.

Can't wait to hear the latest from the Garden State!

Yours,
The Doktor

P. S. Please take note of the color scheme we've set up—we're Lindberghians through and through!

PSS. Careful proofreader that I am, I have not neglected to spin my typewriter's cylinder back and forth to identify any stray errors. The word 'favor' caught my eye. But I will leave it alone."

* * *

"Godless. Totally."

Such was the unflinching verdict volunteered by a parent of one Caper's students upon the otherwise illustrious and expensive institution known as Washington University in St. Louis. It had been uttered at the beginning of one of those semi-formal parent-teacher conferences one routinely has in the autumn (if one happens to be a teacher), in response to Caper's perfunctory inquiry as to whether or not the young person in question would be attending that prestigious university in the subsequent school year. After all these years, Caper couldn't remember what he might have said in response to this grave accusation, if indeed he were motivated to say anything at all. But it certainly seemed reasonable to conclude that the youth, whose tee-shirts made no bones about his own fervid devotion to wolves, stock cars, and birds of prey, found himself matriculating at a more openly devout university the following fall term.

At the moment, on the trail of Fei, Caper thought it prudent to proceed under the assumption that the Wash U grounds might very well be totally mapless. Tentatively heading west, keenly aware that a teeming variety of architectural styles would not provide a visual boon in distinguishing one building from another, Caper expected he'd have to rely on a friendly undergraduate to help him locate the Ann W. Olin Women's Building, on the bottom floor of which, he had been informed by a clear and knowledgeable voice working the Registrar's phone lines, the indispensable keeper of student records had been ensconced for sixteen years and counting. Once you toss in all the construction projects underway in every single art and science, in law and in medicine, in education and engineering, it was little wonder that Caper surmised he would have to depend upon the traveller's most ancient crutch: "Pardon me, but could you please point to...?" Making matters worse, a soft autumn rain falling in the sinking dusk appeared to have thinned out the number of helpful pedestrians one might otherwise have expected to encounter for directional aid. It looked like it would be Caper, his own waning vision, and dumb luck.

Arriving at what he took to be the halfway point in the quad, he was pleased to discover that he had had little reason to worry after all. The groundskeepers of the fine university had anticipated ignorant visitors like Caper, and provided a sturdy "You Are Here" map of the area, complete with backlighting. The raindrops on the less-than-pellucid plastic surface may not have been particularly welcome, but the teacher did eventually manage to locate building #128.

As he approached the main entrance to the structure's southern face, Caper made out large capital letters carved into the lintel: WOMEN'S BUILDING. Closer to the ground, the cornerstone sedately informed all who entered: 1927. At eye level, twin acrylic modifications, limpid and bright, had been affixed to each side of the main door, bearing witness to a much more recent (and privatized) rechristening: "Ann W. Olin Women's Building." Once and still the only housing for sororities on the St. Louis campus, the structure also served as a reminder, to those who bothered to notice, of those distant days when the university grounds were more or less divided into discrete men's and women's "sides."

The building directory near the elevator indicated that the Registrar could be found on something called the "Garden Level." Walking down a curving flight of capacious marble stairs, chaperoned by an intricate cast-iron railing redolent of Henry Clay Frick, Caper intuited that "Garden Level" was the phrase Washington University residents employed when they meant to say "basement."

Garden. Steep slant.

He had, make no mistake, quite low expectations with respect to uncovering Fei's undergraduate student record. At the moment, however, he had no other choice than to try to corroborate Yellow's accusations, in any manner available. Furthermore, and never to be underestimated, he had at his disposal the formidable Caper charm.

Below.

"Sorry to bother you, Renate," he said to a woman who had the name tag "Renate" attached to her brown blouse, and who was sitting behind the front desk. "I was hoping to get just a little bit of information about a former student of mine at Lindbergh High School." Thumb raised, he casually lifted his left hand up to and over his shoulder, as if the Lindbergh High School campus could readily be glimpsed just behind him.

Renate nodded her head ever so slightly two or three times, absorbing the rhythm of the slick performance. "Max Fei," Caper continued. "One of the best I've ever taught." Suddenly, even the mini-nods ceased. Caper entertained the possibility that Renate was incapable of speech.

The Scream.

"I'm sorry," she replied after an unnervingly wordless interlude, thus bringing to an unceremonious end yet another one of Caper's suspicions. "May I help you with something?"

"I'm sorry," Caper repeated, clumsily, officially making this an inordinately sorry start to the conversation. "I should have been clearer. Should have gotten straight to the point." Mini-nod. "Is there any chance—I mean I know I can't see any transcripts or anything, nor do I want to—" Caper uttered the latter five words with a noticeable uptick in emphasis. "I just wonder if I could find out when Max graduated. Word from some of my current students is that he finished early," he added unnecessarily and unhelpfully. He smiled.

Gently but quite firmly, the woman shook her head. "I'm afraid that that sort of information is private," she said, an assertion, Caper immediately realized, whose exact formulation she kept very close at hand at all times. "With a very few exceptions, the student himself or herself must initiate all record requests. We're bound by law to keep all records confidential."

He wished to indicate that he was quite aware of what he had no right to ask about, but was distracted by Renate's appearing to take sudden notice of his attire for the very first time. White cardigan, green polo underneath, chocolate corduroy pants. Green shoes. Something very close to this get-up had once done duty as "The Full Minty." Caper speculated that Renate would not find this information amusing.

"Isn't there a way I could find out the year of his graduation? Some sort of list? Old graduation program or something?"

Renate had already begun to speak assuredly into a sleek wrap-around microphone gizmo, attached, it would appear, to an invisible node on the back of her head. So thin and form-fitting was the device that Caper didn't spot it until she fixed her eyes on the neatly arranged items on her desk, all the while addressing something or someone (Major Tom?) in a manner that exuded perfect reassurance.

Before she had ceased speaking, or seemingly so, Caper was approached by a man exiting the office immediately behind Renate's desk. He introduced himself as Albert Frederick, Assistant Registrar. Renate, who had stopped talking to the device, looked at neither of the two men.

"I'm sorry," Frederick said while shaking his head in a welcoming manner. "May I help you with something?" A woman opened another office door, stepped halfway into the main compartment of the Registrar, and made it plain that she would be listening to and observing the unfolding conversation.

Caper nodded in a similarly warm fashion. "Yes. Please." He continued to nod. "I'm trying to find out about—" here he reconsidered his phrasing. "I'm trying to get in touch with a former student of mine." He grinned a wide teacherly grin. "Great kid. I think he's at Stanford now. Stanford Law. But he graduated from here probably in twenty-thirteen." Caper paused, before beaming, "I'm sure with 'honors.' Magna cum this or summa cum that." Frederick's smiling visage managed to conceal its granite composition not a jot. The woman monitoring the encounter did not even share Frederick's smile. "I'd like to ask how things are going. See if he looks back on his Lindbergh years with warmth." He grinned again.

The simmering Fei scandal would not be settled with any help from this basement crowd, Caper privately confessed. Still, he would attempt to extricate himself from this Yellow-induced discomfort with at least a scrap of dignity intact, even as an angry new letter was already being typed in his fevered imagination. *You'll pay for this, my vindictive friend. I'm-a be the guy standing with his hand out in all your Garden State Parkway nightmares. Tollbooth revenge! You gonna think twice before you type out any more accus—"*

"Yes," the woman standing in the doorway said clearly and confidently. She was holding her eyeglasses in her left hand, poised horizontally against her left hip, and staring directly at Caper.

Attempting to ascertain whether in fact he had recently posed a question, the teacher nonetheless wished to convey his gratitude for the concise positive response, whatever it was she'd just agreed to.

"Great. Thanks," he managed. Not certain who should say something next, he slogged on. "So, is there a piece of paper I should fill out? Some sort of formality?"

"No," the doorway answered. Nothing else.

Inexplicably, Caper nodded his head as if he understood.

"I believe that Olin Library maintains a file of all of our graduation programs. Mr. Fei's name will be in the 2013 program," the woman explained. "*If* he graduated."

Silently, Caper continued to try to locate the interrogative daddy of the orphan "yes" she had uttered only a few seconds previously, and was coming to the tentative conclusion that it must have been a belated response to his wondering aloud (for the benefit of how many listeners?) whether there were public records available concerning Washington University graduates.

"Where do they keep graduation programs?" Caper ventured.

"I wouldn't know," the pit boss answered. "Perhaps you could find out for yourself."

"Yes," Caper responded. "I'll make a point of doing just that."

"Good."

"Yes, good." Caper cast about the office. Renate's lips were moving again. "So how are things down here at the 'Garden Level'?"

"*Take a lea—*"

"Fine, thank you," someone said.

"Nice to hear." Caper continued to gaze through the windows of the two visible exits for evidence of plants, flowers, herbs—vegetation of any kind. "Where's the garden? I'd like to see the grounds."

Pause. Possibly pregnant, but far more likely barren. And certainly provoked.

"Years ago, there used to be a…"

"I'm sure there was."

"Now, you can't discern the…"

"Interesting. What're you growing just now?"

Doorway wasn't in a serene state of mind.

"Is there a problem, Mr…?"

"Not at all." Caper fleetingly inspected the Registrar's Office for the last time. "Just thought you might've gone to the trouble of plonking a bag of mulch on the floor, just to make it look like a garden is actually down h—"

The man from campus security had entered basement airspace without Caper taking any notice of the fact. He announced his presence by thrusting his thumb at the teacher, looking at Renate, and asking wearily, "This the guy?"

The secretary, working the microphone once more with some unknown, invisible party, put on full display her unsurpassed multi-tasking skills, neither pausing in her current conversation nor even bothering to glance at Caper or, for that matter, at the recently arrived agent of the teacher's removal from the premises.

Effortlessly, she executed a crisp affirmative nod of the head.

*   *   *

Five days after having had the pleasure of dispatching his inaugural letter to Yellow, one that at least nominally went "back east," Caper received the first post-P. O. Box response. Wonder if the messages crossed in the mail? Or, as was the teacher's strong preference, did Yellow have the opportunity to read Caper's gridded greeting? Would the unopened envelope he was presently clutching prove to be an angry riposte?

Please say yes.

He stepped with purpose into his living room, wisely reckoning that it just might be a good time to take a safe, comfortable seat.

"Herr Doktor," Yellow resumed. So far, so neutral. "How are things back in St. Louis?" Very clever, my insidious friend. But until I see a few grains of certified New Jersey sand in this envelope, or at the very least a notarized boardwalk splinter tucked in among these yellow pages, I'll continue to assume that you're typing away right here on the western side of the Mississippi.

"'Band Peter'?" Yellow jumped right into the fray. "I know all about 'Band Peter.' I knew him well. That's past tense." I can read, Yellow. And you might think about giving the underlining just a bit of a rest. "Very well did I know 'Band Peter.'" Right, then. The jury had now decisively returned a verdict on the question, "Did you know 'Band Peter'?"

"But as much as it pains me to say it," Yellow continued, "you're missing the point, Herr Doktor. We're no longer talking about 'Band Peter.'" *You* are. "All along I have been writing about a very different person." Max? Me? Van Der Meyer? About whom have you been writing, O flaxen one? "'Bad Peter.'"

141

Ahhh, "Bad Peter." Well done, Yellow. One simple subtraction, and you've turned the tables completely. Let's see now: any chance that a host of sinister insinuations are mustering on the field right about now, soon to enter battle against this yellow backdrop?

As it turned out, no. Nothing remotely insinuating about this particular installment. Perhaps the wounded one had opted for a more aggressive prose style, hoping to sway Caper under a barrage of direct recriminations, each one launched straight from the shoulder. "PK," Yellow j'accused, "is a juicer. He juice, they juice, everybody juice-juice." "Old MacDonald" had very likely never been subjected to this sort of insouciant treatment before. From the aging Caper, however, such a perverse hijacking of the ancient children's song could not be granted any immediate attention. Acutely aware of his own severely limited grasp of contemporary "street" lingo, he could still apprehend the general thrust of Yellow's taunting allegation. Young Peter, Yellow was making it abundantly clear, ingested the naughty stuff, the pills or liquids or powders, or maybe shot something through a needle, or rubbed in some sort of ointment, anything to make the muscles dance a happy dance. Human growth something. Doping. All kinds of steroids and who knows what else. Lance. Named after Rentzel, wasn't he? Just what were Mama and Papa Armstrong thinking? Surname's just a bonus irony.

"You asked for a more direct approach, and now you're going to get it. PK headed north after high school, hooked up pretty quickly with a juice supplier (who the connection is and what exactly the substance is, I admit I cannot say), and soon started to pack on lean layers—many lean layers—of muscle mass." For the first time, Caper found it difficult to deflect this allegation as a possible explanation for what his own eyes had witnessed. Suddenly, and for reasons he couldn't pinpoint, it simply felt like Yellow was landing a pretty solid punch. Had Caper himself been diverting his own attention away from the obvious, afraid to gaze at the awful pumped-up truth? How else could one account for the dumbfounding expansion of his former student, a one-man Louisiana Purchase in the flesh? But if the puffed percussionist had in fact scored a similar physique acquisition, who had served as the stand-in for the famed Corsican general who gave up the land to the founder of the University of Virginia, and who would crown himself Emperor of France shortly after closing the bad bargain? Whatever the answer to that question, there remained the matter of motive. Would Peter—or anyone else, so far as that is concerned—really take the stuff to enhance drum performance? Was nothing in this world sacred? What all-American pursuit would be the next to sell its soul to Dr. J? Cheerleading? Baton twirling? Curling? Cradling his chin between index finger and thumb, Caper slowly rocked his head in disbelief. Could steroids really be corroding the outwardly wholesome world of collegiate marching bands, soon and forever to befoul an unsuspecting public's appreciation of half-time excellence?

The Spirit of St. Louis Mar...

Yellow stayed on the attack. "It's a whole lot worse than you could possibly imagine. Not only has Peter 'made some bad choices' (as we used to say back in primary school), but he's managed to get the rest of the drum section to go along with him. If this keeps up, Minnesota's running backs might soon be the first in the country to have their linemen drumming interference." You just keep on giving, don't you, Yellow? The marching band might actually refuse to yield at the end of the half, huh? "But here's the kicker. He's a major dealer. He's pushing some sort of drummer-juice for a huge chunk of the Midwest." That's a spacious patch o' dirt, my dear Yellow. Just ask Boney. "And he's pulling down some serious—I mean, major—scratch."

Mr. Dime, meet Mr. Payphone. Not failing to appreciate Yellow's sharp turn towards hip vernacular diction, Caper also decided that it was finally time to deliberate calmly over some of the evidence that would surely be brought to bear in the landmark legal case of "Yellow v. Peter." Exhibit A? May it please the court, we would like to submit into evidence the fact that the accused hastily and with anabolic forethought engineered a gargantuan new Kempf, an intimidating percussionist compelling nearly all of those in his vicinity to feel miniscule. In addition, he has been observed tooling around in a flashy Lex, teasingly garnished with a "MOPEDS" vanity. Nonetheless, Your Honor, we remain well aware that in this instance, as indeed in all prosecutions, we are duty-bound to exclude all reasonable doubt. Should we not therefore carefully weigh the possibility that with respect to the license plate, young Mr. Kempf has simply seized an opportunity to advocate for environmentally sensitive two-wheelers, motorized cycles embraced by low-emission transportation proponents all over the globe? That he is guilty, in other words, of nothing more than proudly displaying his concern about the many harmful effects caused by atmospheric pollutants?

Given Peter's current inclinations, counselor, this possibility seems extremely unlikely, would the levelheaded judge say. A Lex devotee is ill-suited to serve as a booster of super-economy transportation.

Well and timely observed, Your Honor. But perhaps we should take into account the (admittedly remote) possibility that the plate merely celebrates the verb "to mope"? In this particular instance, dressed up (once again, improbably and incomprehensibly) not in its infinitive but in its past tense, and what's more, in a plural format? If this unusual combination of circumstances should prove to be the case, a person who found his attention captured by the tag might well be put in mind of multiple sulking life forms, all of them doing said sulking in some unspecified bygone time?

World's most surreal vanity plate, counselor. Magritte himself couldn't possibly dream up such an irrational combination of semantic elements.

Once again, an astute observation, Your Honor. But should the court take up the matter of a possible pediatrics angle? Perhaps the defendant is merely offering a friendly DMV "shout out" to the well-trained and capable "Show-Me" medical professionals who tend to our precious childr—

I've had enough of your silly speculations, counselor! Clearly, you're grasping for meanings that simply aren't—

Suddenly, Caper's eyes seemed to recede into a dazed stillness, gazing into a space they hadn't ever been in a position to see before. He rotated his head slowly upward, sitting on the yellow davenport in his living room, not blinking but also not seeing anything in the room. The ceiling, illuminated by a single shining lamp, seemed unusually bright.

Guidance.

"Clearly…"

"In the clear," Caper repeated, for the first time. Then again: "In the Clear."

Peter's in the Clear. In the Clear in Minnesota. Now is it just me, Caper silently but decisively queried, or does the big dude seem an unlikely spokesman for the Church of Scientology?

The Clear. MOPEDS. Mo' PEDs. More performance-enhancing drugs.

The cheeky juicer!

*   *   *

Escorted outside the Women's Building, Caper took note of six or eight or perhaps even more lawn installations of some sort, spread out over more than an acre of quad turf. They didn't appear to be part of any of the myriad construction projects underway in every direction. But increasing darkness might be playing with his eyes more than he knew. He felt, at any rate, that the temporary structures, in the dim light resembling oversized painting easels, would make a good point of conversation with the campus security officer, who, as it happened, hadn't yet said a word to the expelled Registrar visitor, not even to indicate where they might be heading.

As Caper reached the bottom stair of the main entrance, he turned to ask about the wooden frames. Security appeared to be moving on to other more important business, as he was presently heading back into the Women's Building, evidently leaving Caper to his own devices.

"Aren't we going anywhere?" he asked the campus officer, who had one foot already in the building.

"Excuse me?" The man leaned back so as to make himself heard.

"No holding cell?"

He grunted a laugh. "What for?"

Caper paused to consider. "I don't know." He cast about for some sort of serviceable violation. "'Registrar loitering'?" He raised his right hand suddenly. "No. Got it. 'Vagrancy.' Campus Vagrancy. I believe the Inclosure Acts came down very hard on that sort of thing." The very idea of being charged with such a Dickensian crime provided immediate satisfaction to the ejected teacher.

"What?"

Caper shook his head. "Nothing." He then held up his right index finger in an inquisitive manner. "May I ask you a question?"

"Yeah." Signs of impatience from the campus officer.

"Is there a drunk tank around here?" Only Caper could possibly know that his motivation for asking this question rested entirely on two things. One the one hand, the pleasure of saying the phrase "drunk tank" to a man who was almost a cop should not be too quickly dismissed. Indeed, he had no reason to presume that such an opportunity would ever present itself again. On the other, he had been increasingly cognizant of a rapidly developing need to endure some sort of traditional 'Dark Night of the Soul,' one that would require a suitably forlorn setting. In one way or another, he had to hash out the existential implications of Steroids, Inc ("The quicker jacker-upper"©). But one can't simply have one's Edward Hopper moment in any old place. Caper would readily concede that a drunk tank might not score high in the originality column, but he also took some solace in the fact that, quite apart from originality being an overrated commodity, such rough confinement would certainly stand a good chance of getting the job done.

"No." The security officer's face now bore an expression which suggested that he might be toying with the idea of escorting Caper to a special cell after all. He stood, as he had been, halfway in the Ann W. Olin Women's Building, watching the teacher walk uncertainly towards the suite of outdoor easels.

In the rapidly diminishing light, Caper walked slowly from one display to the next, gazing at the jumbled images, painted headlines, small bits of text arranged on wooden surfaces. Some of the stuff appeared to have been silk-screened with early Warhol echoes in mind. Each seemed in any case to be devoted to energy production around the globe, working conditions in coal and oil, the effects of global warming in specific and different parts of the planet, and so forth. Coal mining in India was the subject of the first display he glimpsed. Some text he couldn't quite make out focused on child labor conditions. Others focused on South and Central America. Some took up Asian regions; others Central Europe. More than a few featured startling imagery and tables of data to reveal the processes by which the global air conditioner was kept humming along. Ameren Missouri, Bank of America, Chevron, and Herculaneum—names and phrases to be found in large block letters on nearly every work—provided something like a unifying theme.

Turning back east toward the Metrolink station, Caper determined to check on this area once again when he returned to the main Olin Library in the coming days. Max Fei's name would be found on one of those graduation programs, or would be found to be an absentee. Caper would then bring to an end at least part of this noisome business.

*   *   *

"Gum disease may be linked to heart disease."

Caper had had a student years ago who had written a 4000-word essay on precisely this topic. *Wesselschm—?*

An admirable little sentence, when you think about it. It suggests a connection between two distinctly undesirable conditions that one wouldn't, in the regular course of things, necessarily connect. It also suggests that if you take the trouble to look after the smaller and quite treatable thing (gum disease), you might be able to affect the bigger and more dangerous and more ominous thing (heart disease). Finally, it retains the inestimable virtue of not being an entirely settled matter ("may be linked"). In other words, many of the properties you look for in good writing are captured by a single straightforward declarative sentence.

At present, however, sitting alone in Dr. Mraz's waiting room, with little else to do but scrutinize every photo, notice, and university degree scattered about the office's coffee paneled walls, Caper found himself dwelling upon a distinctly different pleasure. Wasn't it just a little remarkable that such a dire health warning, writ large on a faded poster, and accompanied by an outsize photo of some poor creature's retreating, swollen gums (the stranded ivories, most discourteously, abandoned to their own devices), could catapult him back ten or more years, summoning him to recall a student he would otherwise not have occasion to remember. *Weitz—?*

The other signs and pictures scattered about the walls were cheerier and cleaner in every way imaginable. Highly effective teeth straighteners made out of invisible cutting-edge plastic alloys, probably first developed by NASA for the space shuttle. Brighteners and whiteners of every description, each offered in an array of shiny options.

Caper's eyes drifted back to the older, worn, and far more sinister image. "May be linked." Yikes. The vintage poster relied unapologetically on the tried-and-true "scared straight" technique put to such effective use back in the day, whether the problem at hand were imprisonment, drinking-and-driving, or VD. Floss and brush and rinse, my pretty, or the gum succubus just might get you. And your little heart, too!

Caper smiled mischievously. Why not let's try one of these public service announcements on for ourselves? Sure we could come up with something. Let's see. How 'bout, "Max Fei may be linked to Peter Kempf"?

Oh yes, he thought. Yes, indeed. Gots me a prize-winning poster right there. Maybe attach side-by-side shots of a snazzy Benz and a silky Lex. Would make a top-tier wall-hanging in the workhouse downtown, don't you think? Or maybe in one of our fine juvenile detention centers would appreciate the cautionary message. Why not my own classroom?

I'm really quite gifted, Caper congratulated himself, after an appreciable pause. I am. Really. Not PEGS-gifted, mind you.

But that poster's gonna fly.

*　*　*

"Dear Horatio," Caper began his second "New Jersey" letter. "I type to you with mixed emotions. On the one hand," he pecked, "I am obliged to confess that your most recent post struck a deep chord in the Doktor's soul. My ongoing doubts as to your motives cannot be allowed to overshadow entirely the substance of your accusations." Caper recalled once more Yellow's badly bruised band ethos. "Something there is about PK's physique that doesn't add up."

"On the other hand," Caper's fingers now worked with a more fevered intensity, "I must inform you that I was a recent visitor to the enchanting grounds of Washington University's Danforth Campus, where I discovered a) nothing whatsoever about Mr. Max Fei's undergraduate years, and b) that not being detained by local campus security officers might have, contrary to one's expectations, the effect of damaging one's self-esteem."

Caper now did his utmost to adopt the tone of the sage. "I wish you to know that I no longer doubt the veracity of what you've written about PK. What remains unclear, however, is what you would have me to do with this newfound knowledge concerning a few of my former students. They are not, after all, my current students. I find myself no longer able to issue three-hour detentions to either of the young men, as much as it would delight me to write the word 'Juicing' under the 'Reason for Referral' column. What, in short, do you imagine I should do with respect to Peter and Max?" Caper's typing came to an abrupt halt. Then rapidly recommenced. "In fact, if I may be permitted to paraphrase the words of one of the characters from a play I have too often taught: 'I hate to seem inquisitive, but could you kindly inform me what Max has got to do with all of this?'

'Gangster'? 'Money pimp'? Kindly inform me what these accusations are meant to indicate."

Twice he shifted the carriage return lever to the right, making room for the sign-off.

"Do tell.

Yours,

HDC"

*   *   *

Back to the scene of the non-crime and the non-arrest. The clear, cold November air would provide a much better atmosphere for Caper to view the energy displays just west of the squat geometric profile of Olin Library, and just to the south of the Women's Building. Wearing a period curling sweater that, even by his own spirited standards, he judged to be uncommonly dangerous, Caper paused with his right foot on the low granite step outside the library's main entrance. On the back of the blistering torso-toaster, each thread seeming to vouch for a foregone and long-forgotten sweater heraldry, a robust stag had been stitched by an ingenious needlesmith, whose natural gifts were only accented by the fact that they would forever remain unalloyed by any earthly name. The stately beast reared on its powerful haunches, presenting a stirring *buck rampant* attitude to anyone fortunate enough to be walking behind the stylish teacher. On the front, a large woolly

149

bust of the same eight-pointed forest-roamer had been knitted to the left of the sturdy zipper, a visage whose features were unquestionably noble in proportion. On the right side, woven into the top edge of a commodious pocket, the name STAN—each letter about an inch in height—informed all who dared to look of the identity of the winter masterpiece's original owner. Garbed in the majestic *tour de force* for the first time only a few years earlier, Caper had christened it "Stanley Kowoolski." Not even Brando himself, he felt sure, had ever bedecked himself in anything half so damaging.

From the shaded terrace of the library, Caper could now see that each of the easels had been arranged at a certain purposeful distance from one another, and that a neatly serpentine sawdust path had been provided to connect each separate station in a certain sequence, something over a dozen in view. The idea, it would appear, was to enact (or better, to re-enact) a well-trod journey. Particularly with the weather so grand, he resolved to take the edifying stroll after he had settled the Fei matter, one way or another.

As it happened, the Olin Library had always held for Caper a wonderful mixture of attractions. He had been visiting each summer for years now, in order to meet with a small number of his International Baccalaureate students. They, for their part, would be doing research for an essay of between 3000 and 4000 words, due on the ensuing ides of March. Obviously, the resources offered by the university's library made it a very useful place for young researchers to get a jump on the monster essay, almost certainly the longest they would have written in their young lives. Caper, all the while, welcomed the chance to mess about with any informal academic project he had cooking. Olin had everything he could possibly desire—not least its effortless ability to offer a refreshing, dark respite from the relentlessly oppressive St. Louis summer climate—as well as the further charm of projecting just a little bit of Bauhaus self-restraint into the midst of a Gothic orgy.

Entering the dark and invitingly cool space of the library, Caper reflected on the global supremacy of the American bar—at any rate, the bar of the old school. Dimness was to be unceasingly maintained at all costs. Darkness, and cool temperatures. Low ceilings. Quiet. The only sounds to be heard would be those of the necessary preparations for the cocktail hour. Clinking teaspoons, thin and long, suggesting ice cubes in transit from one container to another. Lightly frosted, wispy glasses carefully shuffled inside an icebox. Ever a hint of Marc Chagall in the air.

STAN's sweater was in its element.

Approaching the main desk, Caper forthrightly identified himself as neither a student nor a member of the faculty of the splendid institution. Just a teaching stiff from a local public high school looking for some information on a former student, one who had graduated from Washington University quite recently. He would be indebted, Caper said by way of clarification, to any obliging and knowledgeable librarian who might help him locate graduation programs from previous years. Indeed, he had been informed by the caring and attentive staff of the Registrar over yonder that he would be able to peruse said programs somewhere in the Olin archive.

The young woman to whom he spoke appeared never to have been apprised of these graduation booklets; she seemed to be endowed even less practical awareness of the existence or purpose of curling sweaters. Her eyes skirted from the tan STAN lettering to the buck's stern, woolly face, and thence to Caper's. In one of those millisecond flashes one occasionally has, he wondered if there might not be a secret push-button behind the library checkout counter (of the sort that one has been told that bank tellers have ready access to), and whether she might not be pushing it with uncommon vigor just at the moment. If so, she was masking her alarm admirably, turning her back to Caper in order to gesture to one of her superiors that she would like some assistance—right away, if it wouldn't be too much trouble. An older gentleman answered apace the wordless plea from one of the offices glassed off some distance from the desk.

When, however, Caper repeated his request concerning old graduation programs, the man tilted his chin in a deliberative fashion as he pondered the location of the desired documents. "I know what you mean," he said tentatively, stretching the last word into two syllables. Then, with sudden certainty: "Not any more." Noting Caper's puzzled expression, he kindly repeated, "Not any more. They've got those over at the Archives Building." The librarian pointed his finger due west. "West Campus. Across Big Bend. Sorry," he added. Before Caper could ask for any more specific directions, he continued, "They switched those to Archives about three or four years ago. I don't know why. Sorry."

"No, not at all," he replied. "It's certainly not your fault."

Caper looked uneasily in the direction the librarian had pointed. "May I ask why," the librarian continued, "you're interested in them?"

"Oh, I'm trying to find out if a former student of mine graduated from here in '13. Great kid." After a pause. "I'm sure he did. But maybe he transferred."

The librarian nodded his head. "Have you looked at any of the *Hatchets*?"

"Excuse me?"

"Our yearbook. *The Hatchet*. We've got a full collection in 'Oversize'."

Hope springs… "Are all graduates listed or pictured or . . . accounted for?" Caper's question may have been uttered with a barely detectable trace of urgency. "What's 'Oversize'?" he added with a jerk of the head.

"Books or documents that require a roomier shelving. Irregular or extra-large codices. I guess you could say that it's storage space for special-needs texts." Uttering this last phrase, the librarian worked his index fingers in a lively quotation mark dance, shook his head, and smiled in recognition of his own droll description. Caper grinned archly. The bibliophile, however, soon showed signs of being much less certain about the contents of the yearbook. "I'd have to look into the matter. I can't say for sure that all graduates are pictured in any given *Hatchet*. As such. Probably most of them, anyway," he added after a brief pause.

"Where might I find 'Oversize'?"

"Level B."

"Level B?"

"Yes. Bottom floor." The librarian turned to the desk computer and very efficiently entered some data. "LD 5798." The librarian pointed to the staircase. "Down those stairs. Oversize. Bottom floor."

Caper, writing down the call number, thanked him for his troubles. Garden Level Redux. "You've been a lot of help. I appreciate your concern. Thank you," he said, turning toward doors that led to another staircase, another tight descent.

* * *

In the spring of his sophomore year of high school, Caper arrived early one afternoon in Mr. Franco's classroom, vaguely aware that the *Death of a Salesman* segment of the "Great American Writers" course would soon be coming to a close, and that the ensuing text on the reading list would be Tennessee Williams' *A Streetcar Named Desire*. He knew next to nothing about the new play, apart from the few remarks his instructor had made at the end of the previous day's class meeting, remarks emphasizing, as Caper recalled, the fact that both of the landmark dramas had emerged in the same tumultuous theatrical period following the Second World War.

The new play, it turned out, was indeed brand-spanking new, as evidenced by the fact that one of the custodians wheeled in several large, unopened boxes of books just as Caper was taking his seat. Franco deftly produced a handy box-cutter from his desk, and immediately proceeded to slice at the taped midsections of several of the boxes, seeking out shiny copies of the dark New Orleans melodrama amidst other neatly bound collections of *Catch 22*'s, *Catchers in the Rye*, and a pack of groovy-looking books whose cover featured gnarled hands partaking of an advanced game of cat's cradle. (Caper would not learn until much later that Tennessee had in fact spent a large chunk of his formative years in a river town in Missouri, a thousand miles and more up the Mississippi from the Crescent City, and that he was known to indulge in frequent expressions of unvarnished contempt for the city situated only a dozen river miles below the Missouri's westward drift, a city as well known, in Tennessee's youth, for its shoe manufacturing as for its beer brewing).

Having located the laminated cache of tawdry southern tragedy, Franco (whose build might well have been described as "portly" by those of a diplomatic bent, though it would more likely have been granted a less oblique description from coarser natures), straightaway exhibited unmistakable signs that something had gone horribly wrong with this most recent parcel delivery. Somehow managing, in spite of his evident dismay, to distribute a copy of the play to each of his students, the teacher appeared to be utterly incapable of making heads or tails of the book's cover. He repeatedly examined it front and back, hoping, it would appear, to discover some clue that might put to rest his state of consternation.

For their part, the students couldn't help but cut silent, quizzical glances at one another, perhaps in the expectation that someone else in the room had detected the same problem—whatever the hell it was—and would be considerate enough to share the information. No dice. They, too, gazed at the book's cover, probably with greater intensity than was their wont. *Is this the wrong play?* some of them must have wondered. *Is there some other book called 'Streetcar Named Desire,' and in a moment of mental distraction, Franco had somehow managed to botch the order? What gives?* Meantime, Marlon Brando, freshly laminated and shirtless (or was he adorned with an improbably torn tee-shirt?), couldn't possibly have been less intrigued by all of this speculative hooey. He glared back at each one of them with peerless smolderingness, eyes cloaked in the smoky darkness of a fiercely tilted neanderthal brow. Indeed, had the inanimate text in question, itself only a few moments removed from the sealed and sheltering gloom of a UPS box, been capable of speech, it would doubtless have been bawling, "STELL-LAHHHH!" But none of the juvenile and benighted students could possibly have suspected any of this as yet, and therefore could do little more than tacitly offer their best wishes in this mysterious search for the text's flaw, so disruptive to Franco's peace of mind. Seething, motionless, and relentless, Brando kept the needle on maximum-Kowalski.

At long last, the teacher appeared to be ready to share with his students exactly what it was that so nettled him about the recently delivered texts. With his countenance continuing to serve as a guarantee (or so it seemed) that some unfortunate individual would soon be the recipient of, at the very least, a strongly worded letter, Franco brusquely cleared his throat. "Ladies and gentlemen," he announced to his baffled audience. "May I ask you to examine—to examine *warily*—the front cover of our new book?" Even though they had all been doing exactly that for the past several who-knows-how-many minutes, the students renewed their hunt for the publishing blemish that so irked their corpulent instructor. Franco then directed them to refine their search. "Please look with extra care at the neck area of the actor portraying one of the protagonists of our next play." All of the students did so, to no avail. "Deceitfully," he launched into the inspired conclusion to his masterful performance, "the publisher of this edition of *Streetcar* has decided to allow the profit-motive to override all other considerations." He paused; the neck mystery would have to wait just a little bit longer. "You will notice," he resumed, "that the designer of this book's cover has shamelessly superimposed an image of Marlon Brando's head"— holding the book aloft for all to inspect, he sternly placed an accusing index finger next to the actor's neck—"on *my* body."

Unfazed by the uproarious laughter triggered by this earth-shaking allegation, the victim of the photographic crime calmly assured his audience that the offence would not go unpunished.

*   *   *

In the first years of the 1990's, at or around the same time that a cultural tempest was triggered by the unveiling of a certain statue depicting a hefty and chiseled mill worker, the Pittsburgh Pirates earned a spot in the National League playoffs, bringing to an end a long dry period of postseason blues. Not since the illustrious days of Willie Stargell, Kent Tekulve, and "We Are Family" had the Pittsburgh nine been in such an enviable spot. The Pirates were hosting the Cincinnati Reds, and scheduled to sing the "Star Spangled Banner" was none other than the "Polish Prince," Mr. Bobby Vinton. The Prince stepped to the mic at the designated time, but not before a Pittsburgh mensch known to the world as "Mister Rogers" threw out the ceremonial first pitch. Attending the game, Caper remembered thinking that no baseball city on the globe could ever dream of matching such an intoxicating duo. The Reds, it was clear to anyone who was paying any attention, were doomed.

Very early in his rendition of the anthem, however, Vinton betrayed unmistakable signs of lyric panic. He was belting out one or two too many "o'er the lands," the "twilight" wasn't quite aligned with the heavens, and the "banner" was probably waving a couple of lines too early. Disconcerting stuff for the Pirate faithful. In Caper's outfield section, an already well-lubricated cluster of Buc boosters responded to the discord by singing the line "Home of the brave" o'er and o'er again, beginning at just about the moment when they ought to have been corroborating how the red glare gave proof. In solidarity with the struggling crooner, the entire section joined in enthusiastically, home-of-the-braving it all the way to the stirring conclusion. When the final and actual "Home of the brave" had been croonily delivered, the crowd went berserk.

The Reds, it was plainer than ever, did not have a prayer.

Jack Buck, who was announcing the game on one of the national networks, and who would become a great deal more familiar to the Capers upon their arrival in St. Louis, killed it. Something like, "Well, I guess if you're Polish and you're in Pittsburgh, you can sing it any way you please!"

That's what words are for, Caper thought when he learned of the "controversy" the next morning. Crisply delivered entertainment. But organizations had gotten involved, statements had been issued, the Falcons were outraged. Apologies were offered.

The Pirates did not make the World Series that autumn, and would soon return to the league's basement, where they would remain for an even more protracted period.

* * *

Bowels of Olin. Cool and dark. Cold, to be honest. STAN's BTU output would not go unappreciated.

The "Oversize" section positioned to the left of the entrance from the Level B stairway. Heading west? LD 5798. Cooler treatment. Isolation. Be funny if it were Oversize PK 5798.

Caper silently reprimanded himself. No, it wouldn't.

He quickly found the LD aisle, tightly squeezed between mobile shelves on either side. Texts arranged in this fashion have got to learn to get cozy with one another. It was difficult, he privately conceded, to withhold one's admiration for this kind of book storage, taking as it does maximal advantage of limited, low-ceilinged space, and offering the additional boyish pleasure of effecting very substantial shifts of bound paper merely by pushing a button with an arrow on it. The whole room's contents performed like a nimbly ponderous accordion, stacks of books contracting and expanding with each studious visitor, submitting to every research whim without hesitation or complaint.

Should Caper take it upon himself to slide thousands of pounds of Heraclitus, Herodotus, innumerable Hedonists, or some other aspect of Hellenistic culture with his little right pinky, he would encounter no obstacle to hinder this commendable desire, one that seamlessly mixed equal portions of the erudite and the Herculean. Should he decide instead to give way to whimsical philosophical contests, he could direct Nietzsche's entire Germanic œuvre to reverse course in the open field, suddenly and shamelessly outflanking Kierkegaard's unsuspecting Scandinavian meditations and dialogues just across the aisle. *Take that, you intellectually enslaved Dane!* the German would no doubt mock the stunned theologian. *Now where's your 'God'?* Or Caper himself could enter into an updated jousting contest with some other hapless Garden Level visitant, Dewey's decimals taking the place of honor and crest on research's battleground. Rightleftright. *Prepare to die, Poindexter! How do you like the tang of these steel shelves?*

Caper's fanciful, if also disturbingly vicious, meditations underwent their own sudden swerve toward more familiar and decidedly more cinematic combative clashes. He conducted a hurried private inventory of the action-thriller genre, a form which so often favors "highly unlikely" backdrops for intense deadly action. The abandoned amusement park, to be sure, whose long-idled rides might unexpectedly come to life, catching one or both of the do-or-diers off-guard. Or perhaps a limestone quarry, whose conveyor belts would somehow be running full-tilt in spite of the complete absence of any workers, thus conveniently lending a hauntingly depopulated industrial texture to the Magnum-fueled mayhem. Large-scale dams had proven themselves quite serviceable, providing thunderous symphonic accompaniment to unpredictable derring-do. Elevator shafts could never be dismissed, descending into impossibly murky vanishing points. Harry Callahan or Harrison Ford or Bruce Willis pursuing or evading the bad guys, and the decisive weapon turns out to be—who knew?!—a rusty old crane hook (once used to unload railroad freight), or the final pursuit a gun battle taking place—can you believe it?!—on rival tugboats!

Why not, Caper meditated with deepening absorption, a university library stacks area?

Hell, Caper silently effused, I gotta start writing this stuff down. Moderately intelligent people with expendable incomes might dally with the idea of forking it over to me. *Publish & Perish*? Not bad. Perhaps a bit too adapted to the academic crowd. Need to appeal to a broader base. In any case, need have a snazzy catch-line to put butts on seats. *Check Out with Extreme Prejudice!* Better: *Research and Destroy*. Subtitle? *Study Hard*? *Live Free or...*

LD. K to M aisle. Right. Somewhere in the middle. Walking north, probably, two stories beneath the quad surface.

Just about halfway between the K and M offerings, right where he would have expected to find it, Caper came to *Hatchet*-ville. One, two, three, four, five shelves of yearbooks, from 1903 to the present da... Check that. An unnerving number of *Hatchets* appeared to be playing hooky. Or—the far more disquieting possibility could no longer be kept at bay—had they been abducted? Wash U undergraduates purloining irreplaceable *Hatchets*? Caper shuddered to contemplate such base behavior from comfortable young Bears.

The books were stacked from eye-level to ankle. Curiously, the top shelf supported the concluding volumes of the "British Parliamentary Papers: 1816-1896." Each volume embossed with thick gold letters: "EDUCATION: POORER CLASSES." Looking left over his shoulder and down, Caper saw another four shelves of jumbo codices devoted to the British lower orders. Early post-Napoleon to late-Victorian. Eagerly, Caper cast his eyes about the quiet book vault, stem to stern. Who, in these circumstances, could say for certain? Perhaps the spectre of Disraeli himself might be haunting these cool, dark depths, wearing a perfectly tailored burgundy velvet jacket, longing to engage someone in snappy political repartee. Killer cravat. Dressed to the nines, crackin' wise about the Corn Laws, or Gladstone's mistresses, or the Suez Canal.

Alas, the dazzling Prime Minister, his coat cut to just where it ought to be, was nowhere to be seen.

Sitting down at the nearest cubicle, Caper inspected the most recent addition to the *Hatchet* shelves. 2013. The first flip of his left thumb took him to a couple of pages devoted to an event called *WUStock*. Outdoor concert. Get it. Clever, I guess. Student musical group called the "Noam Chomskys." Why, that's a good name for a band, you madcap young…Flip #2 brought him to something called *Spring WILD*. Big party. Outdoors again. Most of the students muddy and, one might prudently suppose, not entirely free from other liquid influences. *Sports.* Washington Bears. *Clubs & Organizations. Greeks.* "Alpha Omericron Pi." Sorority. Women's Building. No soap. *Seniors!* Yes! Grids of faces. 7 x 9. Head shots aren't the same as in high school. Turn. Turn. Still B's. Turn. Turn again. Finally the E and F graduates have the decency to show their faces. Edelmann. Down. Esselman. Down. Fang. Down. Fehr.

Down. Caper's shoulders briefly rose and just as quickly sank, the unbroken movement accompanying a deep inhale and release. No need to descend any further.

Fein.

No doubt about it. A piece of Max was visibly present, in a manner of speaking. But it was a piece that did anything but argue for his presence in May 2013.

For reasons that he would have been unable to justify, Caper retraced his descent down the same column of names, fully aware that the repeat journey would once again fail to yield the only one he was seeking. Still no Max. Grids of faces, every last one of them still strange.

Seated at the underground cubicle, he looked back over his right shoulder, back to the Oversize shelves, as if they might yet offer some last-minute explanation.

He stood up slowly, revolving gently to and fro, the library chair still beneath him. Still no hint of Disraeli; not yet. Perhaps, Caper thought, he had always had it all wrong. Perhaps books, even extra-large volumes printed and bound in Victoria's very own century, and arranged on custom-built shelves stories below the earth's surface, could no more summon the past than any other fabricated objects. The great prime minister, hall-of-fame dandy, time-tested wit, remained—no matter his inseparable bond to the weighty parliamentary papers—a no-show revenant.

Caper brought his slow hip rotations to a stop. Circular ceiling lights receded and narrowed in front of him. They went all the way to a wall he couldn't see.

No Fei. Without leave.

* * *

Leaving campus during fifth hour owing to an afternoon conference he'd been invited to in a neighboring district, Caper approached the lone security gate that admitted visitors to the LHS campus. He lowered his window and prepared to slow to a very deliberate speed in order to be identified by Herb, the security guard, his departure requiring only a visual recognition and a wave of the hand. As he got closer to the gate, Caper could see that Herb was leaning outside the booth's incoming window, handing a yellow-and-green visitor's badge to the driver of a vintage European sports car. Old school charm. It had the air of something Jean-Claude Killy would have driven to the Alpine ski lodge, way back. Or Richard Burton tooling around Puerto Vallarta, Liz, Shakespeare's sonnets, and Scotch whiskey competing for his attention. The driver of the shiny yellow coupé was wearing sunglasses and brandished a large, fulsome black beard. The plates, alas, were neither French, Swiss, nor Mexican, but Show-Me state: T-BONE.

For the record, Caper was a Porterhouse man. Saratoga Rib-Eye a distant second. The remaining cuts distributed themselves evenly along his own private steak metric. But then he never really understood why anyone ever took the trouble to go the vanity-plate route—for any reason at all—let alone to proclaim to the rest of the motoring world one's beef preference.

Wait a sec. Could be his nickname. "Hey, T-Bone, what's in the breeze?" Plays the blues or something.

Still.

Caper scanned the chic Euro-sled for make and model markings. Nothing presented itself on the hood. Lower, just above and a bit behind the front wheel well, something in metallic cursive writing underneath what appeared to be an air vent. Oh, my my. Fix It Again, Tony. Yes, indeed. Italian blast from the past. You couldn't possibly argue with it. Behind the wheel of *that* auto, Caper thought, you'd know what it felt like to be Joe Willie White Shoes, wearing a fur coat on the Jet sideline. You'd be your own private Broadway Joe. Seraph of style.

Motoring slowly off the campus in his '99 Crown Vic, Caper wondered would he ever get the Riviera of his dreams? Mid-60's number. Two-tone. George Shearing and Nancy Wilson on the radio.

The world would be verdant and bright. He'd be driving on 66, east or west or just idling at a stoplight, with no particular destination.

He would be at the wheel.

* * *

"Herr Doktor," a greeting now familiar to Caper, commenced what he hoped would be the letter that would clarify Max's role in all of this PED-pandemonium. "When it comes time for you to meet Max Fei once again, you will not discover, as you did with Peter, that the former drum major has ballooned into a drum double-major." Oh Yellow, did I have any hand in your verbal dexterity? You're blossoming. I see great things. "You will find, however, as I have already indicated, a radically new Max. A Max who knows how to make money do funny things. Funny money. Very funny." Got it, Yellow. We're in Jerry Lewis' neighborhood. Any chance you gonna get to the next block? "He makes dirty cash all bright and fluffy." Where's he going with this? Tide-town? Proctor & Gamble? & Fei?

"Peter's got the juice job running on all cylinders. He's using the stuff, as you can well attest. And he's got the rest of the battery bursting at the seams as well, pounding the drums like nobody's business. But he can't handle all the business coming down the PED Turnpike from outside sources. And as you know, Herr Doktor, Max has always had a good head for figures." Good head for pretty much everything, Yellow. So's Peter. "Therefore, Peter hires Max and makes him his own personal cash-cleaning service." So Max *is* stronger than dirt. Ajax, wasn't it? Muscleman for the Greek mob. "When you add his scrubbing powers to Peter's juicing venture, you've got yourself a strapping little syndicate. And that's exactly what Max is doing, and has been doing, with all of Peter's muscle money. Both are getting very, very rich."

Yellow kept this one brief. No sign-off, but one final sentence set apart from the rest. "To think that they were both band leaders."

Fei and Kempf. Marching band apostates.

Yellow. Keeper of the flame.

Who would be standing at the end?

* * *

If, in 1962, one had a subscription to *Inside Story* ("The Magazine That Takes You Behind-the-Scenes"), one would have had the pleasure of reading dauntless and probing investigative reports casting light on **The Strange Life Rock Hudson Is Hiding!** as well as **Sex in Russia: How K Made It Kooky (An Eye-Witness Account of Love Among the Reds)**. One would have learned that while "poor Rock has a phobia for the fair sex," he hadn't allowed this fear to sidetrack his movie career. Not at all. Because "if there's anything that paves Rock's rocky road to stardom, it's dames. Oodles and oodles of them." As for Kruschev's Russia, "If it's a bed-and-broad deal you want, stay away from the Soviets—they sneak their fun on the run." But lest one be tempted to conclude that this upstanding magazine peddled a single line of goods and services, keep in mind that it was *IS*—and **NOT** one of its wincing competitors—that first broke the story that shook America to its core: **CASTRO ARMING SOUTHERN NEGROES!** Humdrum scandal rag, you say? It was oh so much more.

And yet, notwithstanding its manifest record of delivering wide-ranging and trustworthy investigative reports, *Inside Story* might have fallen achingly short of your exacting cultural standards. Perhaps one should weigh the possibility that (for reasons you were under no obligation to explain), your tastes leaned toward *Top Secret*. You'd have been clued in to the **New DRUG Sensation! ORAL CONTRACEPTIVES FOR MEN!** You'd have been one of the fortunate few to discover some of the startling answers to the question, **WHAT MAKES SHIRLEY MacLAINE RUN WILD?** You would have carefully pondered matters many of your fellow Americans had never thought to think: **ARE "THE UNTOUCHABLES" REALLY UNTOUCHABLE?** You would've been grateful that someone had at long last paid heed to **THE BLACK KU KLUX KLAN**—had, indeed, exposed just how passionately this secretive organization **HATES WHITES!** Unlike your ignorant compatriots, you would unflinchingly confront the awful possibility: **Did U-2 Gary Crash the Red Party—Only to Become a Soviet VIP?**

In the autumn of this Red-hot year, a certain Caribbean island was observed to be playing host to a flock of missiles, an event that would itself spark one or two other headlines, their urgency to be gauged less by the conspicuous use of exclamation points and underlined capital letters than by the possible imminent delivery of oodles and oodles of megtonnage. Plump, squalling Morton Caper, nowhere close to occupying a position from which to appreciate the impressive array of mad poetry found in the day's gossip sheets, was also decades away from learning to fathom just how target-rich the time must have appeared to headline-hewers. A passing glimpse over at Hooverville would have instantly provided a sufficient indication of the possibilities. (**J. Edgar's Bonnie's a Clyde! Sub: Tolson's in Charge of <u>Personnel</u> & <u>Discipline</u> [& Who Knows What Else?]**) But Caper was not so foolish as to wish to meddle in any way with the time and place accorded him, to look back and yearn for maturity when he had none, or for knowledge and perspicacity when his lot was comfortable, diapered ignorance. He would have to settle for the brinksmanship, loopy paranoia, and suicidal glamour of Camelot from a crib's-eye point of view.

It was perhaps not so foolish, however, to wish to tinker with bygone days and ways, so long as one had distinct present-tense aims in mind. Accordingly, he found himself tempted to compose a few headlines for his own sizzling (albeit completely imaginary) rag, one which would do full justice to the sordid marching band vortex he had been sucked into. He needed, in the first place, a catchy name. *Caper Confidential*? Why not? Not terribly original, but it gets straight to the point. Besides, the real meat and potatoes of the operation would lie in the juicy stories no one else dared to print, not in the name on the masthead. He went to work on a few of the upcoming headlines. **KING KONG KEMPF'S PHYSIQUE PACKS A NEW <u>OOMPH</u>! (Klue: His Secret Ingredient's <u>Not</u> Vitamin K!)** Or perhaps, **GOLDEN GOPHERS GO <u>APE</u> ON THE BONGOS! Drummers Beat the Skins Louder than "Bonzo" Bonham!** Keep stringing the story along, each successive issue featuring teasing but also legally elusive suggestions. Never print anything substantial enough to hang a defamation suit on. That Rock Hudson two-step really couldn't be beat, when you think about it. Could do service as the very first lesson in "Tabloid 101." First you traffic in already swirling rumors, adding some new wrinkle along the way. Then you pen a story that cuts *against* the grain of both the rumors and your winking and screaming **HEADLINE!** Beautiful. Not only would the Rock be very hesitant to raise a ruckus about his romantic life, but you could even claim that,

163

unlike other rumor-peddling magazines, you actually went to the trouble of promoting the star's prowess with the "dames." Caper now worked on his third Kempf entry, for the March issue of *CC*. **GOLDEN GOPHERS' PAUL BUNYANS BANG THE DRUMS <u>SAVAGELY</u>! North Star Percussers Lay a Concussion on Competition!**

Max, all the while, would garner a lot of ink for his cash-cleaning services. **FEI'S THE FOCUS FOR FED PROBE: Does <u>He</u> Have Any Dirty Laundry?** Swiftly followed by, **PEGS PRODIGY PLAYS WITH FUNNY MONEY! DA Denounces Dirty Dough**. With readership skyrocketing, *CC* would gin up the pressure on the sawbuck scrubber: **FEI'S FEELIN' LUCKY (LUCIANO, THAT IS): Soiled Lucre Gets the Lux Job in Speedy Laundromax!**

The righteous tabloid punishment Caper now allowed himself to ponder was tempered by a sobering strain of thought. Had Peter and Max absorbed absolutely nothing in his classroom? Not just a wee something about pride? About how it precedeth a...Hubris? Hubris, anyone? Just one residual fiber from the *Poetics*?

One thing was certain. The juicer and the cleaner were about to experience a sharp and tragic turn of fortune, courtesy of Caper's fateful Royal Companion. Definitely in Dutch with your former teacher, my young hooligans! That's right. 'Bout to learn how one resolute old man, sitting before the keyboard of his old clicking machine, is going to wake the old phrase "Chicago typewriter" out of its long winter's hibernation. Guess you didn't figure on the C-Man takin' both o' you for a ride, did you?

Or did the teacher have it all wrong? Could it be that the delinquent duo was lurking somewhere out there, idly paring their nails (or paying others to do the paring for them)—just waiting for Caper to make a move?

*   *   *

Having climbed the stairs back up to the ground floor, Caper turned toward the southern exit for what he hoped would be the final leg of this day's journey. Only steps from the library's security gate, he was politely hailed by the same helpful librarian who had alerted him to the *Hatchet* archive.

"Excuse me!"

Caper walked back toward the main desk signalling that, yes, he'd found the yearbook cache, and, yes, he'd managed to retrieve some useful information. He nodded a thank-you. Thinking the thumbs-up was all the librarian needed, Caper pivoted again to head back out the bank of doors.

"Excuse me!" the librarian repeated, with just a bit more volume.

Caper spun about once more. He returned to the desk with a somewhat puzzled expression.

"Found 'em," he said in gratitude for the yearbook tip. "*Hatchets.*"

"Wonderful," the librarian replied. "May I ask what your name is?

"Sure." He'd been caught just a bit off-guard. "Caper. Mort Caper."

"Great. Do you plan to head over to Archives?"

"Yes," Caper replied. "Have to. I'd like to confirm his…" He looked at the librarian. "If I can."

The librarian nodded. "Your student wasn't in the Senior section of the yearbook?"

"No," Caper said with a clipped head-shake.

The librarian nodded again. "While you were downstairs, I called over to West Campus. They're open now, but not for long. Close at noon on Saturdays. And they don't have any other weekend hours. Your access is limited."

Caper indicated that he understood that the West Campus hours were tightly restricted, and that he had better make his way over there presently.

"I'll call back to Archives right now. Are you walking or driving?"

"Walking."

"Great. I'll call Dan. He's the curator. I'll tell him to keep a lookout for you."

"Thank you. That's very considerate." Caper shook his hand. "Thanks for all of your help." He then approached the exit for the final time.

Outside the library, splashy autumn colors and crystal sky and chill temperatures imparted to the Washington University grounds a quality well-nigh otherworldly, almost as if, Caper thought, he were standing inside a numinous three-dimensional model labelled "College Campus:

American Incarnation," built for the benefit of gods who wished to consult a platonic ideal of the thing before constructing their own. Disappointed that the case against Fei had not been firmly settled one way or another, but increasingly resigned to the high probability that the brilliant honors student had ditched the crenellated campus walls long before he should have walked across any graduation stage, Caper could also find simple consolation in the fine, bracing air, as well as the consideration that his next two destinations more or less lined up. He could walk through the outdoor exhibits, and then continue west to the Archives building. Once there, he hoped to confirm or to rebut Yellow's accusations. He would be satisfied, he had to admit, that Yellow had been typing the truth, so long as all ambiguity were removed.

"Indian Black Gold," the first wooden display announced in large black letters. Painting, or a print? Ask Iris. Can artists print on plywood? Some sort of stencil? In much smaller white circles, presumably representing coins (Caper supposed they were meant to indicate rupees) the phrase "Money for School" was written in a jumbled heap. In the lower right of the artwork, a diminutive Indian coal miner was pictured balancing an overflowing basket, or maybe a bucket, on his head. The text printed on the backside of the freestanding installation outlined the practice of "rat hole" mining in India, an activity in which tens of thousands of workers under 16 were contracted. Many, indeed, were likely quite a few years younger than that, given that being about four and a half feet tall qualified one as an ideal fit for the job.

The dangers and horrors of the lives of these young workers were outlined in incisive detail. A typical wage of 200 rupees a day (about 4 bucks) for a 12-hour shift. A figure almost certainly more, the text emphasized, than the combined wages of any family members the petite miner might have. Caper momentarily allowed himself to indulge in his old carbon ciphering routine. That'd be about 16 rupees an hour. About a quarter of a rupee per minute. He halted. He'd leave the seconds all to themselves for the time being. Not one of those small boys, of course, would have anything remotely like the luxury of his own stultifying tipple-boredom to carry out such fastidious calculations. Kid would want every single rupee he could lay his hands on. Fuck the fractions.

Short- and long-term ailments galore, all of them acquired in the almost inconceivably dangerous conditions in which they toiled: utter darkness below, dimly pierced only by the lights loosely fashioned to their heads. Caper drifted. Buddy system? Butty system?

Turning to face the next display, he saw the words MISSOURI and AMEREN and LABADIE COAL PLANT in large lettering. Abruptly, he decided he would move on to the Archives. Walking purposefully in as straight a line as he could manage, towards where he thought the Archives Building would be located on the West Campus, Caper occasionally peeped at the passing displays now receding behind him. Equador and Chevron. Tar sands and Alberta, Canada. Scandinavian Sami Culture. Swedish reindeer herders no longer able to herd. Wash U undergrads urging divestment.

Going west, west, past large dwellings now serving as university centers for counseling and housing and a host of religious organizations, west through blocks occupied by large dwellings that held steady as large dwellings, west to the old Famous Barr department store building in Clayton, a curvy deco extravaganza, currently housing posh estate auctions in the upper regions, a well-stocked wine, cheese, and liquor store on the ground floor, and, on the Garden Level, the Washington University Archives.

Descending via the lobby's lone elevator, Caper walked along well-lit and well-marked underground hallways, wide and tall at every turn. It was an easy thing to imagine bustling department store workers wheeling unwieldy open carts laden with blazers or sweaters, maneuvering their wares towards the upper floors. He opened the steel-and-polished-glass entrance to the main Archive office, most of whose catalogs and records were housed in wooden file drawers aligned in precisely spaced semi-circular patterns, each arc becoming slightly smaller as he walked closer to the main desk. The entire arrangement appeared to have been dictated by the curving outside wall of the spacious room, something on the order of a shrunken and bisected British Museum Reading Room. He continued to advance towards the center of the straight wall. Above the main desk, separated by a sizable gap, the words DESK and GUIDE, fastened to the wall in brass capital letters, seemed to indicate two separate workspaces. At the moment, however, only one man was behind the long, flat wooden counter, watching Caper approach as if he were anticipating his arrival.

"Been expecting you. Beutrich called me from Olin. Danny Voergel." Caper shook the hand held steady over the counter. "He said you're hoping to locate a former student?"

Caper smiled. "Yeah. I've been told that you've got a file of old graduation programs. Any chance I could have a look? I'm really only interested in one year. 2013."

"Not a problem." Voergel leading, both men walked back toward the outer wall entrance, located in the middle of the arc. His lively pace spoke of an eagerness to help. Evidently, one of two cabinets arranged on the furthest and thus the largest of the arcs at the rear of the room held the documents Caper was seeking. "Mr. Caper, is it?" Voergel didn't turn around; his gait remained sprightly.

"Yes," Caper said to the other man's back.

Voergel may have nodded. He then slowed noticeably and pivoted back to the right to peek at the visitor. "Milton?" he asked, in a tone of voice suggesting that he liked the name. At the same instant, the guide appeared to absorb for the first time the splendid buck's bust woven into the left side of Caper's sweater. His eyes quickly dropped down to the STAN-lipped pocket.

Caper shook his head, sorry to disappoint the man who would soon provide him with the incontrovertible evidence he sought. "Morton."

Voergel turned back to face the rear wall they had nearly reached, eyes skeptically tapering. "Oh." And then, "I'm sorry." He had arrived at the cabinet he sought. "Morton. Right back here."

Once opened, the tall oak doors revealed an array of shiny gray shelves. All sorts of pamphlets and programs, brochures and handbills and announcements, were standing at attention. Stiff cardboard organizers were well represented. Voergel's probing finger ranged with unmistakable purpose to a spot that held Washington University graduation programs.

"Here we go."

He grabbed bundles of manila folders labeled "Commencement Publications," and announced with confidence: "2013 should be in here."

Voergel fanned out the graduation programs as if they were a poker hand he was proud to display. "Here it is."

Just as Caper reached for the desired year, Voergel snapped up the proffered program. "You're gonna have to fill out a 'Patron Use Form.'"

The teacher nodded. "Okay," he agreed. "Where do I do that?"

"Here," Voergel explained.

"Okay," the teacher repeated. He looked around the basement space. "Where?"

"In the Reading Room."

"Great. Lead the way."

The two men now headed to a very brightly lit square space set to the side of the curvy archive room. Neither slowing down nor turning his head back toward the trailing Caper, Voergel said something that the teacher couldn't quite make out. In response to the latter's "Pardon me?" the archive guide barked in a loud voice: "No pens."

"Got it."

On the first of about nine or so regularly spaced plain tables, Voergel had already placed an official-looking form clearly marked "Patron Use: Dept. of Special Collections." He had, in addition, even begun to fill out the formal request, placing check marks in boxes labeled "Non-W.U. affiliated" and "Purpose: Public Domain." Caper was given a pen and promptly signed and dated where he was instructed to sign and date. The pen was repossessed. There was no one else in the room.

He was now granted permission to peruse the graduation program. The first thing he observed was that the discriminating people at Washington University most certainly did not scrimp when it came to graduation programs. The 2013 edition appeared to have been handcrafted on high-end vellum. "One Hundred Fifty-Second Commencement," the front cover commenced. "Friday May Seventeenth: Eight-Thirty Friday Morning," it redundantly Fridayed.

"Per Veritatem Vis," in a circle. Truth and Strength.

Virtue. Man. Virile.

Would Max finally be absolved? Found virtuous? Man-up?

Turn. "1963." Columns and columns of names. Why? "Fiftieth Reunion." Makes sense. How many of those names even thought about the anniversary? Were still alive?

Columns of names now arranged by major and degree. Bachelors. Masters. Doctors of Philosophy. Summa Cum Laude. Magna. Everyone else.

BA. BS. Subcategories. Honors degrees. Engineering. Max-ville! Bio-Medical. Chemical. Mechanical. He had to be somewhere on the rolls.

Caper checked every line. Every way. Left to right. Bottom to top. Fiala to Ernst. Fang to Freund. Not accounted for. Fei-less. Max-Free.

He put down the pencil he didn't even realize he was holding. He left the program on the bare table, open to the page where Max Fei's name should have been, confidently reposing just beneath some impressive Latin phrase. He walked past the main desk in the larger room, nodded his thanks to Voergel, and made for the elevator.

Back up on the street level, Caper's spirits were buoyed just a bit when he observed that he had walked so far west of the Wash U main campus that he could reconnect with the next homebound tram at a station only a hundred yards or so from the Archive Building. His well-exercised legs and feet would welcome this unintended convenience. Not having to make up lost ground, he reflected with a smile. Not exactly the gaudiest of gratifications to be had in this world. But pleasures could also come in far lower calibers.

About ten feet from street entrance was another door leading to an enticing collection of cheese, wine, bread, coffee and brandy. Earthly delights. Garden. Why not?

*   *   *

Full circle, Caper shrewdly observed as he approached his faculty mailbox. Looks like Yellow didn't repeat his earlier error, giving Laney another unintended jolt of typewritten terror. And with stamps being so expensive and all, he didn't blame the aggrieved marching band whistle-blower for returning to discreet, hand-delivered drop-offs. Yellow paper folded sharply once again, cantilevered just a bit, jutting out the way certain modernist architects might have designed it. Wonder if he'll indicate why he's decided to switch back to his original courier plan?

"Dr. Caper," Kathy said from the interior meeting room next to the large bank of faculty mail slots.

"Yeah?" Caper responded to empty office air.

"Dr. Caper," Kathy repeated, "I think I saw who might have left a letter for you yesterday afternoon."

"Yeah?"

"Yeah."

"Who?"

"Bearded guy. Big bearded guy. Came through here pretty quick. Left by the Athletic Room door."

"Big bearded guy?"

"Yeah, bearded." Kathy stuck her head out from the meeting room. "He was wearing sunglasses."

Tony. T-BONE. Big Tony T-Bone.

"What'd he—" Caper stammered.

"I just saw this guy walking through. Pretty fast. I began to ask for his n—"

"Get his name?" Caper interrupted.

"I began to ask for h—"

"Get his name?"

Kathy shook her head in a slow and admonishing manner. "No," she said. "I didn't get his name."

Thus chastised, Caper nodded in a self-deprecating way meant to convey that, yes, he understood perfectly well why it may have been difficult to discover the big bearded guy's name.

"Anything else?" the teacher asked, tapping the edge of the yellow square against the thumb and index finger of his left hand.

"No, sorry," Kathy answered. "He left quickly." After a brief interlude, she added, "He seemed to know his way around. Entered through the main door and left by the athletic office. Didn't really come to a stop."

"Thanks. I really appreciate your paying attention. And thank you for telling me."

Caper descended the double staircase down to his classroom, ready to tackle the latest episode in Yellow's exposé of degenerate band behavior. Especially because he and the secretive one had very nearly crossed paths, the teacher was all the more keen to read and to respond to the most recent delivery. Tony T-BONE! Vintage yellow Fiat! It was simply too good to be true. How should Caper play this one? Offer no clue that he knew anything whatsoever about the dashing Italian wheels? Put forward teasing hints? Make casual mention of the beard? (Please tell me it's a fake, T-BONE!) The simple act of pondering the various new Yellow angles provided a refreshing breather from the juice-and-launder morass.

In his classroom, he prepared to absorb the latest dispatch. "Dear Doktor," Yellow began. "Because it is always a pleasure to revisit my alma mater, I felt it would be appropriate to hand-deliver my latest letter while taking care of other business. Two birds, as they say." Caper's mind whooshed to a brand new opportunity, one made possible by the single advantage he held over the canary: he could easily recognize the splashy car the ardent carnivore was driving, and might well be able to discover the lad's identity, if only he could spot the head-turning Italian ride in the parking lot one fine day. For that matter, if he were merely lucky enough to see it cruising about some south St. Louis street. More whooshing: could a body find out the name of a fellow motorist by getting access to some sort of reverse license-plate directory? Not a chance, C. Not without cop help. And even that's got to be illegal. Final whoosh: do an online search of the history of Fiat makes and models. Could he put a year and maybe a model name to Yellow's stunner?

"I may be talking out of turn" (typing, Yellow, not quite talking just yet), "but I feel that the best thing to do now would be to confront Max and Peter, probably in that order." Who's going to do the confronting, T-BONE? Where will these confrontations take place? To what end? And why the Fei first, Kempf second sequence? "You may be the only one who can bring them back from the brink." Check. "Maybe you could invite Max to meet you at a local drinking establishment. I hear he's developed some quite sophisticated tastes." Sure, why not? I'll order a Sidecar. Max'll sip on a frosty Gimlet. We'll get along famously. "You could break the ice, chat about the PEGS program" (PEGS again) "and eventually—wham!— let him know that you know exactly what he's up to." But I *don't* know exactly what he's up to. But why should we allow that to ruin a perfect plan? Then what's gonna happen, T? "It may be a long shot, but I'm hoping that the shock of a Herr Doktor intervention will break the crime spell, and restore Max to his senses. He might still turn out to be the leader I once knew." The letter was coming to a close.

Why Max should be approached first was a matter that would have to wait for the next delivery.

"I think you're the only one who has a chance of finding out the very cause of Max's defection." Cause and effect, Yellow. My specialty. I'll be sure to apply my finely tuned analytical skills.

* * *

In the summer of 1979, Caper and three of his friends took a trip to the New Jersey shore. Comfortably ensconced in a shiny new red and white Buick Electra 225 (graciously provided by a colorful business associate of one of the teen's fathers), they drove east along the Pennsylvania Turnpike for several hundred miles, whereupon the Garden State obligingly assumed tollbooth duties. They reached the Ivory Motel Inn in Wildwood just as the sun was setting. Exactly why any of their parents agreed to this scheme was a question that would forever go without an adequate explanation.

Most likely owing to the fact that the drinking age in New Jersey was 18 at the time, the four green Quaker Staters must have looked to be easy prey for the unscrupulous boardwalk barkers who manned nearly every darkened doorway along the shore. Yelling, gesturing, pointing, and wheedling, the shore shills appeared to be of the uniform opinion that the single year's difference between 17 and 18 was the very essence of the word "negligible," an insignificant accident of the calendar that should in no way be permitted to interfere with anyone's enjoyment of shoreline festivities, let alone four first-time visitors from another state. In any case, when in Jersey...Several of the more aggressive procurers went so far as to attempt to engage in out-and-out hoodwinkery, literally steering the lads towards the doorway of this or that bar. But the young vacationers, as they would all dutifully confide to their parents, would have none of it. They were perfectly content to sit at the outside tables provided by many of the establishments, drinking pop or lemonade and enjoying the musical acts, some of which had indeed set up their stages for *en plein air* relaxation.

Not surprisingly, many of these beach cafes featured Bruce Springsteen cover bands, a fact that gratified Caper immensely, at the same time that it confirmed in the most tangible way that he and his companions had actually arrived in south Jersey. But several drinking and dining venues also promoted groups that specialized in covering the music of The Babys. Caper did not know why this was the case, since he was completely unaware of any sort of Jersey connection. Even so, he was pleased to hear several of the band's catchy tunes while enjoying his holiday. Just outside one of these Babys establishments, as they were listening to the throbbing beat of "Isn't It Time?", all of the Pennsylvania youngsters were made aware, albeit in a very indirect fashion, of some terrible news.

Half a dozen or so young men from New York City entered the premises, accompanied by a great deal of hubbub. The caps they wore made it quite clear that, one and all, they were proud partisans of the Bronx Zoo team that made 'The House That Ruth Built' its home. With thick, perspiring accents, these gentlemen commanded the attention of everyone—even the band stopped playing. They raised shot glasses snatched—or so it would appear—from the mystical New Jersey air, chanting in unison, "To Thurman Munson!" Everyone in the outdoor bar followed protocol and loudly repeated, "To Thurman Munson!" Not a Yankee fan among them, the four Pittsburgh boys were nonetheless willing to play along with this *ad hoc* tribute to the all-star American League catcher, and held aloft their soft drinks. It was not until the following morning that they would discover why Munson commanded this noisy and unanticipated salute: a deadly plane crash in Ohio. Roberto.

Caper was spooked. Only a year before, on the first family vacation that the Capers had ever taken, a trip that also provided his 50-year old Iowa-raised mother her first glimpse of an ocean—*any* ocean—he had received similarly jolting news from the West Coast: Bob Crane had been bludgeoned to death. Klemperer. The Jersey shore giveth, but she also taketh away.

Although not by design, Caper had no occasion to return to that haunted region of the East Coast for another three decades and more. Who knows how many celebrity lives had been spared by his absence from the sacred shore of Skee-ball? Dozens and dozens, he conjectured. Then, in 2011, he returned as a responsible parent and family man, renting a house this time, rather than a vintage-if-also-more-than-a-tad-ropey deco motel room. He said nothing to his wife about the previous baleful shore visits; he braced for the worst.

On the third day of their Stone Harbor sojourn, word came from overseas of Amy Winehouse's alcohol poisoning.

Crane-Munson-Winehouse. Caper's Jersey shore trinity.

Fei-Kempf-T-Bone. Caper's Axis trinity.

Benz-Lex-Fiat. Asian kid's carryin' a torch for an expensive Bahneville racer, if Yellow could be believed. RINSO tags. Old-time kitchen product? German's got a Japanese jones, Missouri MOPEDS front and rear. Advertising his goods and services right out in the open, courtesy of the DMV. Yellow's rolling in the world's toniest meat wagon.

Whoever the steak-lover turned out to be, he would definitely feel right at home on the race track with the marching band recreants. Caper even began to suspect that a fourth former student would soon re-enter his life, scooting around town in an eye-popping Volvo, if such a thing existed.

What about Yellow's suggestion? Why not catch up with Max, offer to meet him at a place in the city? Couldn't be easier. Facebook. Message. "Hi, Max! What are you up to? I'd love to hear about the law career. How 'bout we meet at…?"

No harm, after all. It wasn't as if he would be entering some underworld scene. Just a chat.

* * *

The Notorious E.G.G.

Caper wondered whatever had become of the bright yellow cardigan that had served, together with his mustard snakeskin shoes, as the yolk element of the alarming ensemble. He felt fairly certain that the suave white pants were somewhere down in the basement in one of the heaps of clothes that clogged the house's lower landscape. But the sweater was nowhere to be seen. Had it gone AWOL?

The teacher had arranged to meet Max Fei, after a quick one-two online exchange, at 11:30 am at the Royal Flush on Kingshighway. He arrived 15 minutes early, precisely in order to watch Fei arrive. Maybe there was something screwy, something that had eluded all of his snooping around, something not accounted for by Yellow's accusations, something that explained Peter's new...Maybe, somehow, Fei *had* graduated from Wash U and *was* en route to Stanford Law. Just maybe.

On a quintessentially sweltering St. Louis July day, the cool, dark bar was an especially welcome antidote. The staff was in the middle of preparations for the lunch onslaught. A few drinkers, sitting on tall stools along the main bar, were already at it pretty hard. No bad whiskey. Quiet drinks in quiet joints. Tinkling glassware and flatware noises were accompanied by buoyant, sibilant lyrics:

Money, money, money
Must be funny
In the rich man's world...

The Maxster arrived, as Yellow would have sworn he would, in a shiny blue Benz two-seater. And he parked, as chance would have it, right next to Caper's white Crown Vic, which had been protecting and serving the Caper clan for 16 years. Illinois tags on the blue speedster. RINSO. Bingo. Lid was down on the coupé. Really wouldn't want a convertible in this city, Caper reflected. Wind blowing through your hair nearly always laden with oak pollen and heavy steam. Where's the payoff?

He watched as Fei casually stepped out of the sleek bahn-burner, the restaurant's sound system persisting in its claim that for some lucky people, money must be funny. Max was definitely dressed to the max. Everything about him—posture, clothes, demeanor—seemed streeted-up. To his knowledge, Caper had never had a student go from merit scholar to presumptive gangster, and so quickly. Sunglasses looked like something Keith Richards would wear.

Money, money, money
Always sunny
In the rich man's world...

"What'll you have, Max? It's on me."

Moments after the young man entered the bar, still blinking his eyes into focus, Donnie Iris took over Royal Flush vocal duties.

Do I have to say it?
Don't you already know it?
Do I have to spell it out?
Don't you think I show it?

"What'll you have? It's on me," Caper repeated, as Fei took a seat at their window booth. Max made no effort to conceal the fact that his attention was devoted to the layout of the joint, one he had clearly never before seen, rather than to the existence of his former teacher. He appeared to be a person sensitive to ears and eyes that might be in the vicinity, serving the needs of people who were not his friends. He was behaving like a nervous undercover cop.

"Bloody Mary," Max answered, his chin swivelling calmly from right to left and back, absorbing the sights and sounds of a room that would soon get a whole lot busier. He sternly eyed the rapidly approaching waitress, who had heard the two words he had softly uttered to Caper. "Grey Goose," he specified.

Caper discreetly requested a second Arnold Palmer.

He wasn't sure how to approach his former student, now dressed very closely to how Caper might imagine an Asian pimp would dress, if in fact he were ever asked to imagine such a personage.

"I'd heard things were looking unusually spruce in the land of Fei," Caper offered. "And now I see they're not lying. You're looking snappy."

"Thanks," Fei responded. "For the 'snappy.'"

"My pleasure. Sir Max-a-Lot definitely knows how to dress."

Max nodded his head slowly. "That means a lot. From you."

It was Caper's turn to nod. Then he tipped his head towards the convertible parked in full view of their window. "Stolen?" He smiled.

Fei didn't. Nor did he bother to look at the blue Benz. "I bought it from a friend."

"Live across the river?"

"Nope."

"Do you?"

"Nope."

Caper nodded again. "I was just curious about the pl—"

"It's kind of a long story. Saved a friend a little money by keeping it an Illinois transaction." He stared at Caper through his sepia lenses to signal that the license plate powwow had been brought to a close. The absorbing tale of RINSO's derivation would have to settle for a rain check.

The waitress brought the drinks. Somehow, Max had a weighty green roll in his hand, produced out of thin, if also impressively flush, air. "Max, no way. I've got—"

Too late. She had the cash in her hand. "Keep the change," Fei added. The waitress nodded appreciatively.

"Max, this just isn't right. *I'm* the teacher. People making big dough are supposed to pick up the tab. *Noblesse oblige.* Didn't I teach you anything? It's the way of the world."

Fei finally allowed himself to smile.

Still, seemed on edge.

*   *   *

"Dear Horatio," Caper saluted the bearded one. "So pleased to rediscover that you continue to visit your old high school haunts. I do hope," he continued, as one concerned about the well-being of his typing companion, "that you are taking extra precautions not to be recognized by any of the faculty and staff of your alma mater when you deliver the latest devastating news from Bandland." The beard, Yellow, the beard! You're outdoing yourself. Will I never learn?

Caper's fingertips then came to an abrupt standstill on the steeply angled, softly rounded keys of the vintage typewriter, his countenance consistent with that of a person who has suddenly been made aware of an embarrassing truth. "But just listen to me, Horatio! Me! How impertinent! To presume to counsel Horatio himself—a young person of utmost discretion, whose very name is a byword for caution—to 'take precautions.' Can you ever forgive me?"

To the present task, Cape. "I'm beginning to worry," he added provocatively, "based upon your repeated campus visits, that you just might be the type of person who actually knows some of the lyrics to the Lindbergh fight song. If so, you are more or less in a class of your own." Take the direct tack, C. "But shouldn't we hash out this sort of business in person? Isn't it time," he repeated, "that we met for a chat? It seems to me you could convey in much more vivid detail <u>all</u> of the machinations of the Kempf/Fei tag team, if only we discuss them over a good meal. With a deeper knowledge of their <u>modus operandi</u>," he suggested, "I just may be able to figure out the best course of action, whatever it is you wish me to do about the recently renovated Charles Atlas (never again, to be sure, will this drummer be mistaken for an outmanned member of the 97-pound weakling club), as well as his custodial associate, the Scrubber." Where to meet, Cape? The Fiat fiend is definitely not a vegetarian. License plate practically screams "Carnivore on Board." "Why not allow me to treat you to a nice meal—a steak down near the Landing? Ever been to Alberi's?" Last of a breed, Caper reflected. Tuxedoed waiter wheels in a square-meter tray richly laden with different cuts of animal. You recline in a booth gazing at a cornucopia of mammal flesh, a butcher's bonanza, a bill of fare capable of satisfying the needs of both the most discriminating meat sophisticates as well as the illiterate and/or the speechless. You point; they char.

"What do you say?

Yours,

HDC"

*   *   *

"I'll pay for the lunch, Houdini. You can put that green steamroller back in its magic container."

The dark Flush interior provided an increasingly sharp contrast to the glaring parking lot. Fei deftly pulled out another bit o' green from some other pocket, and, with a wordless flourish, extended his left hand towards the teacher. Leaning forward to gain better focus, Caper beheld a neatly presented chunk of mentholated Marlboro country. The cigarettes were poised in various degrees of extension out of one of the top squares of the green-and-white soft pack.

"No, thanks," he calmly declined, belying the fact that he was stunned by Fei's new hobby.

Caper observed a few moments of respectful silence as the Max-man got the aromatic stick up and glowing. "Times sure have changed," he remarked as the inaugural fluorescent orange ember began to wane.

"What do you mean?" the exhaling Fei asked.

"Menthols. Used to be strictly an Eastern seaboard affair, at least in the advertisements. Newport and Salem. Always featured fit and frolicking young people in sun-splashed ocean tableaux. Made it seem as if menthol smokes would turn you into a young Kennedy. Now," he said, pointing at Max's new hand-ornament, "it looks like even Montana's gone all minty."

Caper suddenly swept his gaze back in the direction of the Benz. For some reason, he wanted to see whether Fei had affixed a pair of Mudflap Girl silhouettes behind the rear wheels of the auto.

No. Silhouette-free zone.

"Times always change." Fei's pearl of wisdom was accompanied by another cloud of larynx-soothing Marlboro.

Caper nodded in sage agreement. "So do people."

Fei's attention appeared to be wholly consumed by the cool, refreshing tobacco flavor, courtesy of Philip Morris.

In the interim, Caper caught the waitress' gaze and motioned that he and Max would like to order. "Please don't accept any more of this young man's legal tender this afternoon," he requested. "This booth will pay for food and drink with my late middle-aged plastic from here on out, if you please."

Caper wasted no time in ordering a Reuben, together with a Palmer refill. Fei followed suit on the sandwich, but feinted to the left with a vodka Collins highball to help wash down the corned beef. Not everyone, Caper reflected, had enlisted as a gung-ho member of Arnie's Army. Nor did the house's Grey Goose bottle have any cause to feel underappreciated.

"Max."

The Benzer appeared to be preoccupied by the intricacies of the booth's ashtray, a red-and-white-and-gold-leaf number that was either a vintage TWA smoker's aid or (far more likely) a reproduction.

"*Max*," Caper repeated.

Fei acknowledged the teacher's requests for attention by staring over the top gold rim of his sunglasses.

"What happened?"

Fei's stare shifted to some unidentifiable point above and behind Caper's head. His right hand approached Caper's side of the booth, only to drop down mechanically in a steady series of tamping gestures, each one further extinguishing the mentholated flame.

"What do you mean?" Max's right hand absently reached for, but quickly retreated from, the inside breast pocket of his blue sharkskin jacket. He then clasped both hands in front of the ashtray placed between them, his extended index fingers pointing at his former teacher. The tips of the fingers were moving in a steady circuit.

"You know what I mean."

Fei's fingers slowed to a halt.

"What happened?" Caper repeated.

"I don't know." Fei sat completely motionless, his eyes gazing, perhaps, at some long-lost Max, a young scholar receding ever more rapidly into an impenetrable past. Both the Palmer and the Collins had arrived and were standing by in cold expectancy, though neither the teacher nor his former student showed any sign of acknowledging their presence. "Reset," Fei finally said, his voice barely above a whisper. His eyes remained fixed on something or someone only he could possibly know.

"Reset," Caper echoed, his own voice more of a sigh than a statement or a question.

Twin Reubens now arrived, but seemed as unlikely as the tall glistening glasses to see any action in the foreseeable future.

For the first time, Fei looked at his former teacher in a manner that suggested that he would like to engage in a conversation.

"No drink? I thought maybe we were going to share a drink."

Caper gazed at the Palmer. "I stopped ordering drinks at bars years ago." Fei, for some reason, nodded empathetically. "Not to be trusted," Caper added by way of clarification. "And since we happen to find ourselves discussing this particular topic, I'll be happy to recite the rest of the Caper cocktail credo, if you decide you wish to be subjected to it."

Fei gestured with both hands to indicate that he was all ears.

"Vodka," he said disapprovingly. "Don't get it, Max. Sorry. And I really don't get it when people appear to need to talk about it in loving detail—quadruple distilled and all that stuff." Once more, Fei seemed, contrary to his own evident liquor leanings, to share Caper's skepticism. The latter squinted back out at the parking lot. "I don't trust people who hold the margarita in high regard." He assumed the demeanor, if such a thing exists, of a man absorbed in contemplating cocktail demographics. "They're all over the place, by the way," he reflected philosophically. "You'll hear them praise this or that Mexican restaurant. 'They've got the *best* margaritas!' Translation: Sweetened lime slushies with a little something added to them." Caper's expression now took on the signs of a man reflecting on otherworldly days. "When you come right down to it, there really aren't more than about a dozen or so legitimate achievements in this area of human endeavor."

Caper changed his sitting position in the spacious booth, his face now directed toward the establishment's interior, with its softly curving horse-shoe bar and steadily increasing hum of activity. "The main thing is, Max," he presently said with a markedly new urgency, "all of this is pure nonsense. I mean having credos. Of any sort." He paused and reconsidered. "No. Not just having them. But sharing them without permission. I think that's about the most solid nugget of wisdom I've managed to acquire." He finally took the generously proportioned sandwich in both hands, held it in suspension several inches above his plate, almost as a kind of conversation prop. "It's the only civilized thing to do." He examined the Reuben, from the top to the bottom slice of rye. "Keep all that stuff to yourself. Unless someone asks."

Caper permitted himself a hearty bite of the sandwich, which necessitated in turn a protracted stretch of time to process. Sensing that his moment had arrived, he seized the opportunity as soon as his chewing would allow. "So anyway, Max," he said casually, eyes squinting against the window's midday glare. He worked his napkin in nonchalant swipes. "Have you become a gangster?"

"That's a nice GPA you got there. Be a shame if somethin' happened to it."

Grade-point shakedown operation. Yes, indeed. That's a racket with a future, Cape.

"Wanna wave buh-bye to your 'reach' school? Or maybe you'd rather play Moneyball with Dr. C instead? Some people seem to think that a big, fat C- next to the words 'Honors English' may not be the best way to cozy up to Northwestern.

"See, it just might to occur to an ambitious young scholar to bake his English teacher a cake now and again, mightn't it? From scratch, natch. And just to make sure that the gesture receives due reward (quid pro & all that), might be wise to see that the frosted delicacy gets delivered every Monday morning. On the teacher's desk. Punctually. Anonymously.

"Oh, and if one could be permitted to trespass upon the eager learner's valuable time for just a few more moments…No one need bother about any of those heartfelt (and unfailingly moving) greeting cards. 'Thank you for being the most inspirational…Never forget your fifth hour…I'll always remember how we…' Welcome relief, no? Besides, just think about all of those other teachers, the ones who care about feelings. Won't they benefit from all the surplus gratitude poured into your sincerely composed tributes?

"But those little plastic gift cards are an altogether different matter. Who's to say? Somehow they just might pay courtship visits to an unspecified teacher's mailbox, even though it ain't even Valentine season. And, you know, the funny thing is, one or two of the little court-and-sparkers has got an extra zero at the end, jus' by mistake. A teacher works up an appetite, don't you know."

Nickname? "Ace-Man"? Morton "Ace-Man" Caper. Pretty good rhythm to it.

"PEGS," Fei finally managed to say in response to the teacher's query, his voice still in the neighborhood of a whisper.

"PEGS?" The gossamer webs of Caper's day-tripping had not wholly dispersed. "Not exactly the 'yes' or 'no' I was looking for." The patient teacher observed a discreet lull, hoping that a penny might take the opportunity to drop. Unfortunately, no clinking sound was forthcoming. "PEGS," he said once more, in the absence of anything else to say.

"PEGS," Max repeated with greater volume and clarity. He looked up from his still undisturbed sandwich. "You have no idea about the expectations."

Caper nodded in acknowledgement. He was pretty sure he had no idea.

"Harvard and Stanford and Yale, oh my." Fei tilted his head back so as to ease the passage of the ice-cold Collins. The Reuben remained steadfastly on call, even as the high ball lost significant volume. "Always the same schools being mentioned in your vicinity, the same meaningful nods of the head." He took another strong tug on the Collins. "Same high expectations. Always the same chant." Fei mechanically chomped on a few stray ice cubes. "Smiles and expectations." He shook his head wearily. "The assumption that you'll do everyone—family, school, program—proud."

"You *have* done them proud, Max."

Fei showed no sign of having heard Caper's remark. "Always the burden of being 'exceptional,' of putting your 'gifts' on display. Always 'on.'"

Caper remained silent for a few moments. Then he tossed his head towards an artfully-constructed neon-script, the bar's name illuminated above the top-shelf spirits. "Poker. My son called me a 'four-flusher' the other day at breakfast. Loved it." He smiled. "Loved it."

Fei's attention had definitely been caught. "What's that?"

"Old expression. It's an insult. Describes a person who pretends to be in possession of better cards—and by extension, more gifts—than he actually—"

"How'd your son learn that one?"

"*Looney Tunes.* Probably Bugs, but I can't say for sure. Mother lode of idioms that've nearly evaporated."

"You don't mind being insulted? By your own son?"

"Kiddin' me? Not in the least. As long as it's done with style." Caper won a brief grin from Max. "For the record" (he sensed that he might be on a roll), "it was also Bugs who taught me years ago that members of marching bands were once affectionately known"—he paused, ever the dramatist—"as 'street monkeys.'" Then, seizing the opportunity to veer back to the matter of Max's burdens, he decided to take some risks. "Exactly why," he volunteered, "should anyone decide to exercise his 'gifts'—onerous or not—in the service of felony? I just don't get it."

"Cash," Fei answered impassively. "Cash and cars."

Caper glanced out at the glimmering Benz, and recalled the plus-size green cylinder tucked away somewhere handy on Max's well-clad person. "Old story," he remarked, trying to sound composed.

"Cash and cars and," Fei now corrected himself, "Cessna Citation II's."

Caper blanched. "Don't forget the cigs," he said, hoping to cover up any signs of uneasiness. "Chicks, too." Then, "Am I to understand"—he downed a slug of Palmer—"that you've taken up an interest in aviation?"

"That's a safe assumption," Max confirmed, as Marlboro Green #2 commenced its short one-way journey to the ash heap. "It's not the flashiest plane on the block," he added by way of clarification. "Not by a longshot. And it's used. We—I—bought it 'pre-owned.'"

Caper nodded knowingly, as if he were well acquainted with the fine points of aircraft makes and models. "Well, we're jus' talkin' about starter jets here, Max," he pooh-poohed. "Nothing to be embarrassed about. There's plenty o' time to get acquainted with the G550." He stalled for effect. "You're young, after all."

Fei nodded appreciatively. "So you know your aircraft."

'Caper immediately disabused him of this erroneous supposition. "Nope. Not one bit. But my little brother's a pilot. When the time seems right, I just repeat stuff he's said in my presence. Pretty good system."

"Sounds like it," Max admitted, all three syllables escorted by cool, minty, diaphanous flavor. "I'll have to give it a try."

"By all means," Caper advised. "Probably one of life's more useful tricks. But," he felt compelled to add, "like all tricks, it isn't free of danger."

"Like?"

"Like you might err in your repeating. Happens all the time. I call it 'misrepeating.'"

Fei's small burst of appreciation betrayed untapped traces of verdant tobacco smoke.

"And more often than not," Caper continued, "on those occasions when you misrepeat, you don't even *know* that you've misrepeated. So you're in a world of trouble when some attentive and knowledgeable jerk asks some sort of cogent follow-up question. You've gotta have your very best bs-boots strapped on tight just to make your way out of your own misrepetition. And even then, there's no guarantee. Don't forget," he added obligingly, "there's a very real possibility that you're misrepeating someone else's misrepetition." Caper feigned a shudder, at the same time releasing his own deep breath, bereft as it was of any smoldering mentholated tang.

Outwardly, if nothing else, Fei remained attuned to his former teacher's wisdom, born of decades of bullshitting. The latter seemed determined to take advantage of his heedful audience, by making one final pitch to his former student-*cum*-desperado. "Max," he said, gazing once more at the blue RINSO-ride. "Stay away from those flying machines. Just stay away." To Fei's puzzled countenance, he delivered the warning as straight as he could. "They're dangerous, Max. Turn water," he paused dramatically, "into concrete."

"What?"

"Nothing." Caper was forced to acknowledge that his deft turn of phrase had failed to deliver the desired punch. "It's just that they crash. Do me a favor. Stay away."

* * *

The machines dated all the way back to 1899. Pretty impressive, you had to admit. Predate Orville and Wilbur. Fiat 3.5 CV.

4.2 horsepower. No reverse gear. Assembled in Turin. Must've seemed like miracles. Irish twin to the Shroud.

What Wikipedia was good at it was great at, Caper conceded for the umpteenth time. Yellow's coupé had to be from the mid- to late-60's. Looked a little bit like a 240Z. Maybe even a lot.

Wiki organized Fiat makes and models into discrete chunks of production. Caper's survey of the 1948-1965 packet featured quite a few stylish autos, but nothing on the order of T-Bone's yellow head-turner. In fact, most of the pictured models would probably be described as "cute" or "amusing" rather than "cool." They looked to be the sort of Euro-wheels Audrey Hepburn might have found captivating, if for no other reason than that little car over there would make the perfect complement to her favorite blue purse. Or why not Inspector Clouseau, whose trench coat had every right to command some sort of amusing continental escort?

On to 1966-1979. The designers appeared to have gotten the "make it sleeker" memo. Would Yellow's ride rear its head in these tumultuous years? '66? Nothing. '67-'68? Hallo! There it is! Same color! Hello Yellow! T-Bone's driving around in a Fiat…"Dino" Coupé 2.0 or 2.4! Don't know what to call this cat anymore. Yellow? Horatio? Tony T-Bone? And now "Dino" enters the picture?

When would the epithets stop proliferating? This latest tag gave a whole new meaning to the phrase "Rat Pack." Dino was rattin' out Fei and Kempf, to be sure. But would the allegations stick?

Updated trinity: Benz-Lex-Dino. And the Italian's taken the lead.

*   *   *

In the autumn of 1969, Jack Benning had been quietly approached by a 10th-grade student named Guy, who discreetly invited the novice teacher to a tête-à-tête in one of the rear corners of Benning's classroom. As it turned out, this same student would forever etch himself in Benning's memory when, a year or two later, he was obliged to miss school because he had wounded himself whilst hunting deer. What made this painful and ignominious episode particularly indelible was the fact that Guy had managed to suffer the self-inflicted wound during bow season. Evidently, he had fallen out of a tree and landed on one of his own arrows.

At the moment, however, Guy had urgent and confidential news to deliver to Benning, all of it centering upon a family project that would require him to miss the next three days of class. In response to Benning's inquiry regarding the reason for the upcoming absences, Guy quietly explained that in this particular instance, he didn't feel he could avail himself of the normal procedural channels—guidance office forms, teacher signatures, and so forth—that usually accompany a "Planned Absence."

Why not? Benning wished to know.

Well, Guy explained, neither he nor his family thought the district would be likely to look favorably on hog-butchering as a legitimate excuse for missing school, and in any case, they were all of them already a bit fretful about any nosy neighbors who might take it upon themselves to discover exactly what it was the family was doing down in the first-floor bathroom—more to the point, nosy neighbors who might also be inclined to report their bloody porcine deeds to the police. Making this year's slaughter all the more difficult, the young man anxiously explained, was the fact that the family would be butchering Guy's little sister's pet hog, so emotions were naturally running unusually high. Benning, for his part, did his best to appear to absorb this discomfiting information in a sedate manner. Had any other student made such a request, he recalled much later, he most certainly would have responded with a battery of incredulous questions. As it was, he warmly commended Guy for the heads-up, and bestowed his blessings upon the family for good measure.

The fact of the matter was that the Lindbergh School District had, until quite recently, the designation "R-VIII" attached to all of its official documents. On what turned out to be the very first snow day of the 1998-1999 school year, Caper had been scanning local news outlets for weather updates when he saw that classes had been cancelled for something called "Lindbergh R-VIII." Puzzled by this heretofore unknown appellation (was that "R" a typo? had K through 8 been cancelled?), he felt he had no option but to place a number of phone calls to confirm that school had indeed been closed for the day, or at least to discover what this esoteric and slightly sinister bit of Roman code was all about.

Turned out that the "R" indicated that Lindbergh had for a fairly lengthy period of time designated itself as a "Reorganized" entity, and that the "VIII" further signified that there were at least seven other local school districts which had also somehow or other undergone similar "upgrades." Additionally, Caper discovered that this "R" could generally—if also quite unofficially—be understood to be a relic of those days when smaller, more or less rural areas had banded together into a single larger, and distinctly suburban, district (a process apparently not uncommon in the '50's, '60's, and 70's), and that the motivations for these sorts of organizational changes may not have been entirely unrelated to patterns of racial migration going on apace in St. Louis, at least as briskly as in any other American city at the time. Caper, who had made a two-hour lecture he had titled "The Suburbanization of the American Landscape" the centerpiece of a twelve-hour "20th-Century American Studies" course he was obliged to teach as the American Lektor in Göteborg, was now delighted to consider this compelling topic from an angle he hadn't previously considered—or at least considered adequately. Amidst all of the talk of "white flight" and "northern migration" and so forth, upon which so many sociologists and urban historians had lavished their geographic attention, perhaps good old-fashioned "non-flight" ("geosedentarianism"?) hadn't received its due. (Caper briefly entertained the prospect of staking a claim for this new and seductively useless bit of academic coinage, but quickly dropped the matter.) Perhaps, it occurred to him, it was too easy to ignore the fact that some people may have simply stayed put while nearly everyone else around them were fleeing from this and/or migrating up to that.

Surely, no suburban nuclear unit would suddenly and without provocation take up pig-slaughtering as a seasonal pastime. No one, after all, could possibly confuse this daunting enterprise with any number of current retro-trends—raising backyard chickens, for example, or some other such "slow food"-motivated domestic activity. That Guy & Kin were acutely aware that they were doing something that would be perceived to be patently scandalous by everyone else in their newly rearranged neighborhood could not be doubted for a moment, even as that awareness gave sufficient testimony to the "authenticity," as it were, of the whole butchering exercise. Doing it in the first-floor bathtub was of course the *pièce de résistance*, ironclad proof that this particular pig-killing was not in any sense an acquired taste nor a groovy nod towards locally-sourced food production. Instead, as Caper preferred to surmise, Guy & family had managed to pull off a feat that should be given due deference, if for no other reason than that it had to be a comparatively rare achievement. Whether by design or not, they had succeeded in keeping alive, however briefly and tenuously, exactly the sort of farm practice that "reorganization" should have eliminated as effectively as the most ruthless pesticide.

More than occasionally, as Caper was well aware, long-islanded patches of land tilled for agricultural purposes—stout, vegetative holdouts surrounded by "Drives" and "Lanes" and "Courts"—would finally give up the ghost, their acres fated to be graced by bird or tree or blandly aristocratic place names. Such hoary, grizzled patches would be brought to market one last time, under the species of late-blooming subdivisions. An onion field or potato patch or truck farm would metamorphose, compliantly or not, into the next Chukkar Court or Aspen Brook Lane or Windsor Estates Way. To remind oneself of these delayed terrestrial transformations was to underscore just how qualitatively different a phenomenon was Guy's family's bathtub pig-offing, which could hardly hope to occasion anyone's wistful longings for a rapidly receding bucolic past. No. It was a serio-comic eruption of a bloody present-past, ghastly in its sly insistence that it would accept no moratorium on its enactment—not even in a neighborhood bestrewn with such newly imported words such as "Manor," "Trail," and "Pointe"—all the while fully conscious of the fact that *it* was now the unwelcome trespasser, a gruesome violator of the new dispensation. It had better hide itself while it could.

One could probably safely assume that Jack Benning had been the very last recipient of the very last inside tip on the very last pig-butchering ever to take place in the Lindbergh School District. Dead certain was the fact that had the police become involved, local news stations would have gone bonkers. "Pig-Slaughter in Ranch House Bathtub! Story at 10!" Irresistible. Perhaps Guy's family would have been captured by television cameras as they were being escorted out the front door, their Miranda warnings still garden-fresh, their clothes anything but.

Yet once more, Caper gave free rein to his macabre imagination. The notorious 1970 MacDonald family slayings featured, among other things, the word "PIG" scrawled in blood on one of the headboards of one of the murder-beds; a female hippie with a floppy hat; additional hippies; the haunting hippie chant: "Acid is groovy; kill the pigs!" Every last bit of it staged (according to the prosecution), a copycat killing invoking Tate and Polanski, the La Blancas and Manson.

PIGS.

PEGS.

PEDS.

The slightest amendments could effect the most unpredictable leaps.

MO.

No mas, Caper wished he could say, bidding the Fei/Kempf mess a swift adieu. *No mas*. No mo' PED-muck.

But his own unwished-for Helter Skelter wouldn't simply dissolve of its own accord. He knew that it would require a long, hot rinse in a swine-free tub to wash away the stains and stench of the marching band miasma.

Lindbergh R-VIII, by contrast, could and did officially rechristen itself as the "Lindbergh School District." Rural roots, such as they were, were swiftly and legally expunged from all official documents.

* * *

The first thunderbolt struck Caper early on a bright December afternoon. One winter's nap terminated, he awoke to a universe forever alien, forever prone to sheets of flashing agony. His posture utterly frozen, he would later wonder why, given the otherworldly source of his instantaneous physical mutation, he hadn't simply been stricken blind. Wasn't that the more conventional method of whipcrack conversion for pigheaded souls? Clenched as he was in an unnatural squatting position on his bedroom floor, right knee, left foot, and all ten strained fingertips serving as the sole points of contact with the smooth, chilled pine surface, an intrigued observer might have been forgiven for wondering whether Caper were attempting to mimic a lost, misshapen Giacometti bronze, or whether instead he were working on a new and exotic wrestling move from the "down" position—a slick escape, say, that he had recently seen put to admirable effect by a stylish Olympic grappler—were it not for the disquieting fact that no other wrestler was present in the room to assist him in this laudable endeavor; that he was 53-years old; and that, inexplicably, he was wildly keening all manner of demonic gibberish, none of it connected in any discernible way with that august Greek sport. Groveling, prostrate, and absolutely astounded, powerless to descend one millimeter further, he was also rendered almost entirely incapable of anything that could be described as "cognition," except to recognize that only two questions could possibly hope to lend meaning to what little remained of his existence: What magical and pernicious force had knocked him into this hopeless abyss? Would the terrible punishment ever cease?

Tortures of the hip and knee he could never have imagined, even in the midst of his most petrifying nightmare, had trapped him within the confines of an invulnerable chamber of affliction. Kempf, Yellow, Fei, and all the rest of it, he may well have "thought" in some distant region of the brain not yet charted by neuroscientists (the Sado-Sensory Cortex?) would definitely have to wait. At a single stroke, this supremely potent "Herniated Disc" entity (as he would later learn to address the prime cause of all this pitiless torment) brought into being a complex and variegated cosmos. "Let there be Pain," the rogue L3/L4 area calmly yet sternly commanded. "Physicians, percocet, and prednisone. Magnetic Resonance Images, spine specialists, epidural shots, and cortisone. And," in a voice Caper was certain he heard hovering menacingly over the dark waters of his crooked future, "it was done."

Steroids. Did irony get ever get more ironic than this? At long last, the incapacitated teacher would be granted the opportunity to become intimately acquainted with the very substance at the heart of Yellow's obsession, of Peter's disconcerting body refurb, not to mention Max's newfound creativity on the accounting front. O Peter von Kempf—'Roid Baron in the flesh!—who would have guessed that we would one day have so much in common, my sometime student? So many bio-chem notes to share and cherish? Just think. Our banter will be chockablock with carefree discussions of all matters anabolic and catabolic, while phrases such as "chemical sequences" will be accompanied by knowing smiles on our highly experienced mugs. But alas (Caper now felt obliged to censure his still merely imagined interlocutor, with whom a second meeting, one doubtless far more confrontational than the last, was already being arranged), at some point we've got to be just a little bit honest with one another, don't we? Your 'roids turned Kempf into **KEMPF!** "Minnesota Muscles," pal, pullin' down more money than fleshy Fats, laboriously bent over billiard tables for decades, could ever have dreamt of. My juice, by contrast, is delivered by great big scary needles worming their way into very close proximity to imperfectly arranged vertebrae, and transform Caper into Cap...one more time, if you please, Dr. Feelgood: what are the chances that that sparkling harpoon cradled in your hands is going to help me *not* have back surgery?

As a matter of cold fact, the teacher's immediate and long-term and most pronounced physical response to the winter afternoon's back attack was to drop gobs of weight, seemingly without let-up, down and down and down, until he threatened to reacquaint himself with the beanpole figure he cut in high school. It may as well have been designated in the medical textbooks as the "Anti-Kempf Curve," a perverse deflationary process whose athletic, let alone marching, advantages would most certainly be difficult to identify. For his part, the teacher knew, from the very first instant of this novel epoch of unrelenting pain, that his bathroom scale would soon be perplexed by the suspiciously dainty feet stepping ever more delicately upon its surface, but he consoled himself with the thought that there was nothing he could do to alleviate the instrument's anxiety, and that in any case it would simply have to get used to the new math. Nor would food intake play any role whatsoever in the ineluctable plummet. He would eat whatever he wished in whatever quantities he favored. None of it made any difference. The pounds would simply melt of their own accord, from the moment he ceased lifting weights, from the instant he banished running from his weekly routine. If others might find might find cause to complain of some gross injustice in this unlikely phenomenon, that was their problem. For if staying out of the gym and off the track had always proven to be a reliable slimming exercise, far more effective than any diet he had ever been made aware of, it was neither a virtue to be admired nor a character flaw to be criticized or resented.

"It's weird," Caper said to Kempf as the latter took a seat in the warm interior of Myno's Bar & Grill. "Things don't always turn out the way you might have expected, or work the way they're supposed to work." Peter responded to his former teacher's blandly unobjectionable observation by purposely casting his eyes around the pine-paneled restaurant, with the air of a person aggressively seeking something or someone rather than agreeably taking in the convivial atmosphere.

Ooh baby, Belinda Carlisle blissfully cooed from the bar's jukebox. *Do you know what that's worth?*

Caper countenanced the possibility that the jumbo drummer might just have been casing the joint, surveying the premises for an adventitious patch of sand to kick in a skinny drinker's face, or, failing that, seeking a likely target for one of his most trusted and reliable jests: "Yer ribs are showin'!" The fact that it was a cold February afternoon, and that layered clothing was the rule, not the exception, for all paying customers, would likely serve to intensify the jollity occasioned by this caustic observation. And given that scrawny, highly experienced imbibers were likely to be in ready supply within the confines of the toasty establishment, the muscleman had every reason to feel confident that he would soon deliver himself of the beloved barb that would set the bar aroar. For the moment, however, Kempf held fire.

Noting the ongoing conversation lull, Caper, so much the elder of the two, launched forth once more into the breach. "'Dynamic Tension,' I think it was," he said, his eyes resting with only intermittent interest on a bright retro wall clock celebrating the supreme flavor of Griesedieck Beer, these days a boutique brand "crafted" in a region hundreds of miles to the north of St. Louis. Kempf finally appeared to take an interest in Caper's presence, and stared at the latter's musing face.

"What's that?"

"That's the name," Caper responded, still tentatively, "of Atlas' system. At least I think that was it." He returned Kempf's stare in a direct manner, nodding his head as if he were becoming increasingly certain of the accuracy of the phrase. "The idea was that you resisted your own strength. Pressed your palms flatly together, counted to ten, and then took a breather. Rinse and repeat. That sort of thing. Strongman system." Caper flashed back to the "Hero of the Beach" cartoon panels crammed onto the back pages of comic books. "All sorts of he-men attested to its dependably virile results."

"Atlas? You mean like the…"

"Yeah," the teacher responded. "Except this was *Charles* Atlas. Get it?" His reminiscing smile indicated that he warmly endorsed the vintage advertising recipe. Myth and marketing. "Peter, it's just as if you were to promote your own muscle-building services—with scientifically proven results, mind you," (he gently elbowed the burly younger man, in his best you-me-and-the-lamppost rendition)—under the name of…"

"Peter the Great."

Faintly caught off guard by the calm dispatch of Kempf's verbal assistance, Caper was equally quick to express his appreciation. "Well done, O mammoth one." He reinforced his approval by slowly repeating the three-word denomination, attempting, as he did so, to recall the snazzy Greek term for that particular sort of wordplay. You take the well-known epithet celebrating unsurpassed Tsarist luster ('Great' Russian reformer and empire-builder), all the while seamlessly morphing it into an unorthodox ode to Kempfean muscle mass ('Great' physique enhancer and drum-line enforcer). Impressive rhetorical turn, Peter.

Makes me feel as if a little bit of classroom instruction just might have gained a tenuous purchase somewhere in that enlarged skull of yours.

Synth-something? Syllo—?

Unceremoniously, Caper abandoned his listless search for the fancy ancient Mediterranean word for this sort of linguistic torque. Providentially, perhaps, the old motel mantra tolled with tranquil and welcome regularity in his head. *Spend a night,* it rang out. *Not a fortune.* Top-notch advertising work, Mr. and Mrs. Econo-Lodge. One feisty little "spend" conscripted into double-duty. Living proof that at least a share of those old ads packed a little poetic zing.

"I was going to suggest some sort of 'Ajax' angle. But 'the Great' is much better." The teacher also managed to repress a sudden urge to blend an acronym regularly to be found in the sports pages these days together with a certain someone's first name. *Better to squirrel away 'PEDer,'* he silently counseled himself, *for some future occasion.*

And the world's alive...

Out the window, across the street, the city's Old St. Marcus Cemetery was doubly bleached by a thin powdering of snow and a radiant, early afternoon sun. Perhaps the oppressive brevity of the day, Caper opined, was occasionally redeemed by the intensity of the noon luminosity. Just about half a block to the east, close to the road and resting atop and behind a concrete wall that was itself in need of repair, a rusted, sunken section of old Cyclone fencing stood scarcely intact, a neglected relic of an otherwise dissolved barrier. Someone, Caper thought, must have bothered to tear the rest of the thing down one fine day, and then forgot to finish the job, leaving behind a lonely remnant of diamond mesh standing in place for someone or something else to expunge. At either end, rusted tendrils of chain link fell off to the graveyard ground, joining together the earth and the fence, as climbing plants more often do. Far more effectually than a larger section of fencing could possibly have done, the corroded brown and orange stump was able—without any visible effort, Caper felt like adding—to evoke the totality of the long vanished thing, a galvanized steel enclosure that once confidently marked the graveyard's circumference.

Inside the bar, Caper contracted his eyelids and exhaled warily, not failing to take note of an entirely different aura surrounding Peter.

No longer did the Lindbergh grad exude the garrulous and infectious demeanor of a collegiate marching band devotee. Instead, an aggressive hulking sullenness provided the dominant note for the drum-line drill instructor, whose vaguely hostile posture conveyed the idea that he would rather be someplace else—perhaps in a room replete with heavy iron plates, circular and smooth, each one anxious to take its place in the beefy drummer's latest "personal record" bench press. Or, should a weight room be unavailable, a handy "rejuvenation clinic," wherein discreetly acquired vials of colorless ointments provided the primary attraction.

"You haven't said anything about my cane," Caper gently admonished the aspiring beach bully. "I'm a little put out, I've got to tell you." The teacher made no attempt to veil his hurt feelings. "Most people seem to feel that it's quite the tony accessory." He reached to the side of his bar stool and deftly brandished a maroon and gold walking implement, with matching gold rubber tip. He proceeded to hold aloft the polished walking aid, twisting and thrusting it about as if he were engaged in a heated bout with an accomplished and invisible cane-fencer. "I'm really quite put out," he corrected himself. "It's the least a young person might do as a way of commiserating with a badly wounded old man."

Peter, for all his newly acquired surliness, was now visibly stumped, either by Caper's worrying parrying antics, or by the unexpected news that his former teacher was in one way or another "wounded," or both.

"What's wrong? What happened?"

"You took the words…" Caper abruptly halted; he looped back to respond afresh. "Too much for me to say, Peter. Too many things. But," he added by way of narrowing their conversation, "I can say, and with unrestrained displeasure, that my fickle spine has betrayed me." Softly tossing his chin over his left shoulder and casting his eyes downward, just in case Kempf needed a visual reminder as to where spines were located, Caper's facial expression was at the same time unforgiving in its admonishment of the mutinous backbone. "L3/L4 herniation." Caper uttered the syllables with liturgical gravity, as if all who heard them would immediately grasp their significance, and perhaps even observe a deferential pause in their daily routine, purely as a mark of respect.

Kempf was, to all appearances, not yet fully grasping their significance.

"Surgery's likely. 85%. Meantime," Caper held back for maximum effect, "steroids"—he halted consequentially— "might be my only hope."

Kempf's face remained a blank slate.

Caper looked out the window once again and blinked. Directly across the street, only three or four headstone rows to the south of where the old fence must once have stood, a mustard-colored backhoe stood tenantless next to a stubby, frozen heap of dirt. The hard brown cone, seasoned with dry white powder, had the air of something that had been undisturbed for a long while.

"I definitely approve of the colors," Peter remarked.

Caper eyes wheeled from backhoe and frosted mound back to Kempf, with puzzled expression.

"Minnesota colors," he continued, now smiling. "Maroon and gold. If ever I need a cane, I'll be sure to get one just like that."

"Then I believe this is an instance of what they call 'serendipity.'" Both teacher and former student nodded their approval. "And a stylish instance at that." Caper then appeared eager to address some new consideration. "Peter," he added with wrinkled brow, "I do want you to know that I earnestly hope you never have occasion to fulfill that wish." After a brief pause, the teacher again held on high the thin stick that made possible his limited daily strolls, on the off chance that someone else in the bar would require visual confirmation of his reliance on a crutch.

"Golden Gophers," Kempf said in a trailing, distant voice, his eyes not following Caper's maroon and gold baton-work, but seeming to seek some faraway place, one that had been rendered cruelly inaccessible to his view.

In this world we're just beginning...

"I never felt so much like a Kennedy," Caper mused aloud—too loudly—overcompensating for both Peter's wistfulness as well as the ever-escalating bar din. Several patrons in their vicinity, proficient drinkers who had not been entirely oblivious to Caper's cane antics, turned their heads one more time, puzzled by the conversation between the hobbled older man and the brawny kid. "It's not the cane, of course," he explained in a decidedly more confidential tone to the still withdrawn Kempf. "Not at all. How could a skinny, crooked little walking aid possibly help to bolster the 'could we all please agree to drop the terrifying Cold War business we're currently managing with such stylish aplomb, and go play a raucous game of touch-football out on the lawn, and by the way, watch out especially for Bobby, 'cause he just might clothesline you if you cut across the middle' family reputation?" Though not quite wheezing, the maturing teacher did appear compelled to take a deep, rejuvenating breath. "It's the back problem. Jack had a doozy. I've even taken to referring to my needleman, the spine injector," Caper paused and monitored Peter's reaction, "as 'Dr. Feelgood'." He smiled as if soundly pleased with the sobriquet, and then opened his eyes widely in recognition of a newly arisen idea. "Unless I'm quite mistaken," he informed Kempf with evident satisfaction, "I'll soon be in the market for a rocking chair purchase as well." The teacher swayed back and forth very gingerly on his stool, as if to demonstrate for the younger man how it is that one conducts oneself while sitting in a rocking chair, how, indeed, he would be delighted to oscillate in the newly acquired furniture. "No need for any Oval Office or Secret Service as long as you've got yourself a first-rate rocker." Lost in a glamorous reverie of spine-soothing to and fro, Caper very nearly forgot that he had serious business to conduct with the Enhancer.

Kempf, impassive as before, easily managed to mask any signs of curiosity about Camelot, let alone any of its celebrated accessories.

Caper abruptly cocked his head to the side as if trying to determine what it was that he was intermittently hearing in the noisy bar. Yes, he nodded to himself in confirmation of his suspicions. Yes. No mistake. A new band had taken over jukebox duties.

And it's a hard winter's day, I dream away...

"I wouldn't care to repeat the ending, of course," the teacher picked up where he had left off.

"Excuse me?" Kempf responded. "What ending are y—"

"*The* ending. An early afternoon assassination on a fine clear day is not the way I prefer to exit the stage, should I be so lucky as to have any say in the matter."

Peter spread wide the thumbs and index fingers of both hands, gunslinger-style, to indicate that he now understood, and fully concurred with the sentiment.

Caper glanced back at the wall-mounted neon beer clock, searching for the dimly colored hands behind the thick and brightly illuminated glass.

...where the water flows...

He returned his gaze to Kempf with a mischievous smirk. "I just thought of something."

"What?"

"An all-time shocking typo. One for the ages." His elbows planted on the table, Caper held the Gopher-tinged implement in a horizontal position, spinning it between his thumbs and the first two fingers of both hands. He brought the gyrations to a sudden halt and leaned the cane against the side of his barstool once again. "Typo di tutti typi."

Kempf appeared interested. "What was it? I hope I wasn't the guilty party."

"Oh, no. Don't be silly. In fact, the offence in question was typed and submitted for a Caper critique quite a few years before wee little 'Band Petey' was born." No reaction from Kempf. "It was a trespass," Caper continued, "I encountered in my very first collection of student essays back in the '80's. The 'proto-pile,' I suppose I should consider it. Or should I say the 'ur-essays'?" He paused, but appeared to be genuinely incapable of choosing between the two. "In any case, there can be no doubt that the typing blunder I refer to very much deserves to be deemed"—Caper, softly rubbing the fingers of his left hand against his thumb, a pretense meant to indicate that he was searching for an elusive phrase, one that he would be fortunate to retrieve (*got it!*)—"the Original Typo."

Kempf appeared to be even more intrigued, his overall disposition nearly returning to his affable high school years. Caper continued to dwell on the matter, uncertain of all of the details. "I'm not sure if disobedience entered into the equation, of course. Maybe it was a simple case of a disobedient typewriter. But it certainly gave me a great deal of pleasure. And it probably makes for a good story to think that at the very beginning, ten-and-twenty years before my very own back double-crossed me, one college student committed the typing act that left the stain," he paused purposively, "for which all writers pay, quite aside from their own personal culpability." Caper appeared to be satisfied with this entire line of speculation. His spinal agony might have a sterling lineage, after all.

Kempf, listening intently, was eager to discover the rebellious act that did the whole writing race in.

"It, too, had to do with the back, Peter. Or rather its component parts. D-i-s-c-s. Or substitute a k. Take your pick." Peter silently sorted out the c's and the k's. "Spell it any way you wish. The result of this student's *mis*spelling remains the same. A most shocking surgery. One too grisly even for the tabloids." Caper picked up the walking stick, spun it.

Kempf, understandably, hadn't yet grasped the nature of the medical procedure that so haunted—or in any event appeared to haunt—his former teacher.

"What was it?"

"You're a grown man now, Peter." Caper, perhaps rashly, permitted himself to elaborate on that theme. "You are, in fact, much bigger than I am. Vast. Immense." Kempf appeared to be unfazed by these assessments. "So I think you can handle what I'm about to tell you."

One of the Myno's waitresses approached them, one hand gently tapping against the round wooden bar table. "Fellas. 'Ratskeller special' starts in five minutes. Intristed?"

"We were about to order food," Caper responded. "What's a 'ratskeller special'?"

"Perfect timing, then," the waitress answered. "Any food and beer ordered *and* eaten in the basement room is half-price. But only for an hour. Over at two."

"We want the 'ratskeller special,'" Caper answered for both. "Where are the stairs?"

The waitress gestured toward the rear wall, an area of the bar dominated by a broad patch of exposed brick, leavened by a blend of burnt wood carvings, distressed street signs, nautical paraphernalia, and rust-tinged photographs of San Fermin fests of old. Without further ado, they headed for the basement specials.

... it's over now...

The plaintive lyrics of the well-wrought pop elegy, ebbing in any case, were further subjected to insult by the descending ka-thumps of Kempf's thick-soled maroon Doc Martens. Caper and Peter would hold underground counsel with one another all right, but the spine saga, whose punchline was the Boss of all Typos, would have to wait until suitable helpings of half-price food, half-price beer, had been duly ordered, consumed.

*   *   *

In what was and would remain his most blunt communiqué, T-Bone responded affirmatively to Caper's sit-down invite ("Alberi's it is"), and even provided reservation details ("Saturday the 15th. 8 p.m."). Very thoughtful of you, Dino. Taking it upon yourself to make dining arrangements for the hobbled old man. How accommodating. I just might have to break with tradition and order us both a round of Sidecars, Hal-style. We'll raise thin, frosted tonic glasses in a warm toast to drug-free marching.

Yet again, and for the final time, the name attached to the legal-pad letter was that of Hamlet's loyal comrade. The clipped message was indeed the very last typed note he would ever receive from the steadfast marching band steward (a matter that would occasion, for years to come, a soft despondency on Caper's part), but he could still take some comfort in the fact that Yellow's actual identity was certain to be revealed very soon. Old enough to comprehend that clarification rarely, if ever, compensates for the continuation of a richly sustaining mystery, Caper well understood why it was not with unqualified glee that he contemplated the inevitable dissolution of Yellow and Horatio and Dino and T-Bone, together with their profuse associations. That warm cluster of names would soon be exchanged for exactly one actual face, whether or not it were still embellished by an lavish beard. And at that very instant, Yellow's Shakespearean persona would go the way of all flesh.

Alberi's Steakhouse, an eating establishment poised thirty to forty meters directly above the world's fourth longest river (only narrowly edged by the Amazon and the Yangtze for the silver medal), might very well be deemed to be a defensive pillbox position by future visitors to this planet, presumably built to defend the western bank of the Mississippi from expanding eastern marauders. Gazing at its exterior, many an earthling of the present day might rather be tempted to remark that the eatery appeared to be, if not a defensive fortification *per se*, at any event "connected." A concrete bunker, brutal, smooth, and squat, its few windows were deep-set in the thick exterior walls, some of which were adorned by discreet smatterings of orange and yellow neon script, not one daub of which would appear to signify anything of any importance whatsoever. A single valet stood at ease on the southern side of the building at all hours of the early evening and late night, waiting to service the parking needs of well-heeled meat-eaters. For Caper, no restaurant on this earth could ever hope to exceed its charm.

He wheeled up in his white Crown Vic, his mind divided between two equally diverting considerations. On the one hand, he was eager to enter the dark, fortified cave resplendent with truffled satisfactions; to nod his head appreciatively as the waiter, accompanied by a solemn busboy a step or two behind, and moving at a slow, dignified pace, escorted the impressively arrayed provender to his table, its very existence a triumphant mockery of the printed word in all its forms; to point his index finger, after due deliberation, at a substantial cut of animal flesh; and finally, to lean back into the softly polished maroon curvature, awaiting the moment when he would give the highly-experienced bartender's best Sidecar effort its rightful scrutiny. On the other, he wondered exactly what the valet would think and do when T-Bone pulled up in the smart yellow Fiat, emerged from the coupé in bearded glory, and handed over the boot-shaped keys. Driving that car with *that* license plate to Alberi's Steakhouse might yet provide a welcome opportunity to revisit the origin as well as the meaning of one of this globe's most timely adages: "like carrying coal," the old saying had it, "to Newcastle." But even in this instance (and isn't this always the case?), any well-intentioned attempt to impart an appreciation for historical substance (the bygone industrial might of northern England, for example) would surely be overwhelmed by the breathtaking vintage *macchina*, bustin' an eye-poppin' U-ey out on the cobblestones. Surface upstages depth almost every time.

Bad thing?

Caper entered the welcoming darkness of the riverboat restaurant of his dreams. All of Alberi's arriving customers, he was delighted to recall, were routed over a mock-up of Ol' Man River, the short bridge offering stout ropes for customers (some of whom, heading in the opposite direction, doubtless grateful for the aid) as they headed to the bar. In addition, interior wall surfaces offered a host of sentimental river tableaux, in lieu of the actual thing rolling by outside and below the thick, velvet-gray exterior walls. In this, as in so many other instances, Caper preferred the merely mock rendition to the real McCoy.

Having just crossed the bridge, he was jolted by the certainty that down at the end of the bar, sitting beneath oversized piles of fur pelts arranged on a gangplank, the beard had already arrived. He was sipping on a milky beverage...Hold the phone! Was Dino drinking milk in a bar? *Love* this guy! You wholesome, earnest, bearded Italian tattle-tale! Just think of all the Dean Martin gags just waiting to be whipped up! Delighted by these considerations, Caper also recognized that he, too, had been spotted him from across the bar, further down the air-conditioned Mississippi.

The teacher walked slowly and steadily across the bar's floor, caneless, not yet trying to put a name to a face for the simple reason that he didn't yet recognize the face. He continued to approach Yellow, even as the latter made a quarter turn on his barstool, preparing, it would seem, to greet the recent arrival.

Yellow slid easily off the seat, standing up to shake Caper's hand. Big, but no Kempf.

"Dr. Caper," he said firmly. "It's been a pretty long time."

Caper took the offered hand, squinting slightly, still put off-balance by the beard. "Nice to see you," he replied. They were still shaking hands. "Is that *you*, Ricky?"

* * *

"From her back?" Kempf asked, awestruck.

"'Fraid so," Caper confirmed the awful truth. "And there I was, a green teacher—probably wielding a green marker, now that I think about it (red markers were highly discouraged, for entirely unsubstantiated psychological reasons)—at a loss as to what to write in response to such an unprecedented medical procedure."

"So what *did* you write?"

"I can't remember, Peter. I wish I could say that I managed to dash off something witty. I don't even think I could manage that today, not even after so many thousands of pages of student writing have passed over my desk." Pausing, he appeared to be trying to cobble together some sort of clever, albeit respectful, teacherly retort to that now unknown student who so many years before had quite innocently attested to a surgery that most certainly would have been, had it actually happened, one for the medical books. All of them.

With sudden determination, Caper spun about completely and steadily on his round red barstool, a one-man rotating radar disk, recently placed on high alert for suspicious flying objects. Evidently something had just entered ratskeller air space, something that he recognized but that eluded him. "Where are they piping that in?" he asked Kempf.

"What?"

"That movie song. The Michael Jackson song." He spun around once more, a full circle, still not locating any jukebox. "*Ben.*"

We both found, young Michael was singing, *what we were looking for...*

"They've got to be piping that in from someplace," Caper resumed, apparently resigned to not finding out how or where. "That's from '72. Fifth grade, baby. Big hit with the ten- to twelve-year old set, I'm here to tell you."

Kempf kept his head tilted to the side, the better to take in the lyrics. "What was the movie about?"

"Standard boy-meets-rat picture. You've seen it a million times."

Kempf smiled in appreciation, and seemed to want to hear more. "Does he get her back in the end?"

"Can't remember, to tell you the truth. But the rat's a 'him,' in any case. And the important thing is"— Caper paused to scratch his clean-shaven right cheek— "it's never a good idea to team up with a rat, Peter. Trust me." Stoical Kempf silently digested the latest nugget from his former teacher. "I do have a vague recollection of a very fiery ending. A million rats getting torched by the cops. Very apocalyptic stuff."

Kempf's smile returned, more guarded and, Caper thought, mildly unsettled.

There's something you should know
You've got a place to go...

"It was also," Caper resumed confidentially, "many years before the King of Pop started doing some very strange things to" (again with the right cheek) "fabricate a new Michael."

Kempf maintained the smile, but now it seemed to require maintenance.

"In any case, that was a big year for me. Heavenly receptions. Fatal sea collisions. Concrete."

I used to say 'I' and 'me'
Now it's 'us,' now it's 'we'...

Kempf, puzzled by his former teacher's musings, was also exhibiting clear signs of impatience with these obscure recollections. "I'm not usually about going into the past. I'd rather be positive about the future."

Caper nodded. "Makes sense to me. You're young. Why go back to the beginnings of things? Waste of time."

Kempf nodded vigorously, signalling his strong agreement with the sentiment. In addition, he appeared to be warming up to the song.

"Genesis," Caper uttered flatly.

"What? I thought it was Michael Jackson."

"Genesis," Caper repeated, ignoring Kempf's consternation. "No. No. Sorry. That's not it." The teacher gazed at the ceiling of the underground room. Molded tin painted white. "*Bio*genesis," he said in a manner fraught, as the saying goes, with meaning.

Kempf nodded, uncertain.

* * *

"Ricky?" Caper repeated.

"Yeah," Yellow answered, in a tone of voice that may or may not have borne a sheepish note. "It's Ricky."

Eric "Ricky" Pacchia. Class of 20-Caper-couldn't-say-for-certain-which-year. Affable. Always sat in the back. Picture not likely to be found in the dictionary, especially if "industrious" found itself in need of helpful visual backing. Same goes for "studious."

Axis.

Gazing up at the painted piles of beaver pelts crowding a St. Louis wharf of yore, at quaintly chugging riverboats heading upstream, their straining engines emitting gently snaking black trails—up to the river's origin, it might be, *way* up in Minnesota—Caper was attempting to process this utterly unpredictable turn of events. So Yellow/Horatio/Dino/T-Bone turned to be…Ricky? Pacchia was the beard? *Pacchia* was Ness, taking down "Laundromax" Fei, Peter "Upon-this-juice-I-will-build-my-pecs" Kempf? Temporarily at a loss for any banter, Caper nonetheless managed to mumble, the fingers of his left hand moving up and down next to his own clean-shaven cheek, a single word: "Beard."

The hirsute one appeared to catch the teacher's meaning instinctively. "I know, I know. No one can recognize me behind this thing." Pacchia moved his hand freely over his impressively bewhiskered chin, cheeks, and neck.

Caper appreciated the conversational assist. "No way," he said, happy to confirm the truth of Ricky's newly acquired anonymity, "would I ever be able to pick you out as"—here he paused, searching for a way to end his sentence with a flourish—"the dedicated and enthusiastic student of literature I taught just a few years ago."

Pacchia smiled.

"But I *would*," Caper continued, "know you in your car. In a fashion, that is." As Pacchia cocked his head quizzically, the teacher went in for the kill. "Signor T-Bone," he said with the trace of a grin. "Don't think for a minute that that yellow set of Italian wheels cuts a homely fig—"

"How did you know—?"

"Absolutely stunning, my hairy friend. Stunning. I wanna *wear* that car, and you know how much—"

Ricky tried again. "How did you know—?"

But Caper was on a roll. "You know what that means to me, is all I'm saying." He cast his eyes back on the wall, high up, but he was not taking in any of the saccharine, Twain-tinged river scenarios. Bustling wharves of nineteenth-century Missouri were no match for the scenes unfolding in his imagination. There he was, on the open road, guiding the raffish Dino over rolling desert roads in Nevada. Or hurtling down the California coast, the Pacific on his right hand, a Gauloise in his left. "Ricky, if *I* could drive around town in that yellow meat wagon, I'd consider myself the luckiest man ali—"

"Meat wagon? What meat wagon? *Whose* meat wagon?" Pacchia's bearded countenance bore all the signs of authentic confusion.

Caper's eyes glinted; an arch smile took up residence beneath them. "Don't be coy with me, you unconscionable carnivore. Don't even try to deny it. I know your car. I know your license plate. And," he added, turning his head back over his shoulder, in the general direction of the dining area, "I've got a sneaking suspicion that I know exactly which cut of bone-in meat you'll be pointing to when our waiter escorts the inviting tray to our table."

"What tray?" Ricky wished to know. "What wagon? What are you talking about?"

Caper's eyes widened with equal measures of surprise and glee. "You mean you've never *been* here before?"

"No. Why?"

"Oh, Ricky." Caper couldn't believe his luck. "Ricky Ricky Ricky. You do realize that you've stepped inside St. Louis' most primordial meat-cavern, don't you? By all rights, there should be ochre drawings of buffalo and antelope on the walls, red and yellow and snorting savagely at the modern-day Paleos tromping through the door. Not this 'Meet Me in St. Louis' hoo-ha hovering over us, diverting our attention away from the barbarous business we've come here to transact." Caper now paused to sweep his hand over the serenely glowing river scenes, apparently reconsidering the tenor of his artistic assessments. "Don't get me wrong," he said in a conciliatory tone of voice. "I've always been a champion of mural paintings. I really have. Thomas Hart Benton's got no more enthusiastic fan. Diego Rivera. It's just that those Stone Age French caves they can't seem to stop discovering got nothin' on Alberi's, lemme tell you." His eyes panning across the bounteously be-showboated Mississippi, Caper decided that he should probably give the topic of wall-painting a rest for the time being.

Pacchia appeared to be still in the midst of digesting this heady mixture of meat and art appreciation, delivered so enthusiastically by his former teacher. Signs of confusion were legible on his brow. "But what's this wagon, the tray? What's that?"

"Two different things, you mad typist." Happy to leave visual art alone for a while, Caper believed that he divined the origins of Ricky's uncertainty. "You will soon make the acquaintance of the meat tray, my young informer, and you will thank me for introducing you to it." Pacchia was transparently befuddled, but Caper paid absolutely no heed to the youth's confusion. "Here at Alberi's, the waiting staff is not at all squeamish about making manifest exactly what animal flesh they have back in the kitchen—in any case, not so squeamish as they appear to be elsewhere." He paused momentarily. "I can't be sure," he said in a much lower tone of voice, "but I think chop houses used to be run in just this fashion, and that people like William Howard Taft were strong advocates of the system." He spun in a very measured rotation, backbone stiff, to see if one of the impressive presentations might be underway at that very moment, in order that Ricky might peruse from a distance an enticing tableside entrée presentation. Unfortunately, no diner appeared to be engaged in the act of selecting a room-temperature steak from the fulsome meat palette, nor requesting a perfectly matched accompanying sauce. "Main courses here," Caper said simply and directly and even more sotto voce, "are carted to your table, à la raw. It's what you get when you combine Neanderthal etiquette with the Montessori Method. Ingenious. Puts the 'men' back in menu."

After a few brief moments, it became plain to Caper that Pacchia had finally assimilated the fact that he needn't have brought his reading glasses. Dinner would be served even so—opportunely, deliciously, and bloodily—without the aid of script or print. But Ricky continued to show distinct signs of confusion. "What's the other 'thing'?"

"What other thing?"

"The second thing. The second 'different' thing."

"Oh." Caper now understood. "Your car thing. The Dino." He nodded up and down in an exaggerated, and very approving, fashion. "No cooler car was ever manufactured, Sir Rico of Turin. Or should I say once again…Signor T-Bone?" He blinked slowly, knowingly. "You've got to tell me that whole story, among many others. Let's start with the year. '67? '68? And exactly when did you decide to proclaim to the world that the T-bone was your cut of choice, Ricky's own distinctive grill preference, so dear to you that you would allow it to grace both the front and the rear bumpers of that magnificent Fiat?"

Pacchia emitted a bemused sigh. Somewhere a coin had dropped. "'67. And Dr. Caper, I don't really have any grill preferences. None at all, as a matter of fact. That's not my—"

"Ricky," Caper admonished. "It's no sin to be in…"

"Dr. Caper," Pacchia said firmly, interrupting. He stared directly into the spinally-compromised teacher's eyes. "I'm a vegan."

Back held erect under orders from his surgeon, the teacher had nonetheless been tossed into an abysmal tailspin by three simple words. It was as if someone had force-fed him a full tin of Skoal Extra Long Cut, only to insist that he chase the moist, flavorful smokeless dip with a generous snort of Mickey's Wide-Mouth, the better to wash it down. Reeling, he yet possessed enough of his faculties to glance over to the restaurant's entrance, in order to behold whether SEAL Team Tenderloin had yet penetrated the establishment's perimeter, eager to locate and liquidate the bearded turncoat.

"What…? Did somethi…? T-B …? Ve…?"

"It's not what you think," Ricky calmly continued. "It doesn't stand for steak or meat or anything of that sort. It's short for 'trombone'." Pacchia smiled the smile of a proud and experienced wind-brass adept. "My instrument. Always has been."

"Trombo—," was all Caper could manage.

"Yeah." Ricky held up both hands to illustrate how one properly played a trombone, his right hand moving forward and back on the invisible slide. Caper nodded gratefully for the impromptu pantomime.

Still reeling, and with Pacchia absorbed in a spirited, silent 'bone solo, the teacher struggled to identify the familiar pop strains infusing the chop house interior.

Göteborg. Ace something. "Wheel of—"?

*   *   *

"What about it? That's the name of that baseball clinic in Florida, isn't it? A-Rod and his crew?"

"Just so. But I believe" (recklessly, Caper assumed the attitude of a person forced by circumstances to explain a fine point of illicit muscle enhancement to a naïf, somehow unmindful of the fact that he was speaking to a large young man *au courant* with all of the most effective techniques conducive to rapid human growth) "that they called it a 'rejuvenation' clinic." Even as he spoke, Phil Collins' wounded voice, oblivious to the gripping PED heart-to-heart, persevered in its unquenchable despondency, three and a half decades after it had first raised its plaintive cry.

There must be some misunderstanding, he mournfully insisted, imbuing the underground cave with disbelieving grief. *There must be some kind of mistake.*

"You've got to admire that. Plucky."

"Genesis? Guess so. I never really paid much attention to their music." Then something appeared to have occurred to Kempf quite suddenly. "He was a drummer, too. Wasn't he?"

"I believe you're right. A member of the brotherhood, I suppose." Caper lifted a glass in silent tribute to Phil and Peter, Ringo and Keith, Karen and Sheila, as well to those untold multitudes of inglorious percussionists who had also valiantly wielded a drumstick. "But I wasn't referring to Phil Collins' pluckiness, commendable as it may have been." Caper banged mutely on an invisible drum.

Peter's muscular squint bespoke genuine confusion.

"I merely meant," he attempted to provide some clarification, "to call attention to Biogenesis' refreshing gall."

Caper paused to give the youth-restoring wordsmiths their due respect. "Place is closed now, one would have to assume. FBI, ATF, TSA—what federal agency *hasn't* had a look at those Miami digs?" Peter remained noticeably perturbed. "If so," he continued, confident that he would soon alleviate the young man's confusion, "those very same medical entrepreneurs should strongly entertain the idea of opening up a 'euphemism clinic,' don't you think? Could call it something like 'ProVarication™.' Or 'FalCityCorp™.'" He paused. "Better. 'MendaCitiCo—'"

"What about it?" Caper's desultory corporate musings were brought to a bouncing halt with Peter's brusque (and, the older man immediately suspected, PED-fueled) interjection.

"Easy there, chiseled drummer boy. I was just sharing my admiration for the linguistic talents of a few of our Sunshine State-based

PED-pushing brethren. Anyone who dresses up HGH as a 'rejuvenation' product gets *my* vo—"

"What's that supposed to mean?"

"It's just a metaphor, Peter," Caper patiently explained. "'Dress up' means to alter something for the better. It doesn't necessarily imply that actual clothing is invol—"

"No," Kempf interjected. "No. The 'brethren' thing. 'S that supposed to mean?"

Caper knew the moment had finally come. "Peter." He braced himself for the confrontation. "You've developed into a very *large* drummer. You're authentically Ruthian. You are. Don't try to deny it." The teacher appeared to have suddenly stumbled upon a memory he had forgotten that he'd stored away. "Last home run was launched in Pittsburgh. Did you know that?" Kempf betrayed no signs of being interested in the locale of the Bambino's final tater. "Forbes Field. Over the right field roof. He was the very first hitter to do that. And it was his final homer, mind you." The teacher stared at the bar-cellar's ceiling, as if he were watching the slow, high arc of number 714, disappearing behind the sharply angled stands. "That's poetry, my buff young friend." If Kempf were moved by the lyricism of it all, it didn't show. "But the Babe, while he most certainly ingested more than his share of—" Caper paused, searching for some sort of *bon mot*— "substances"—(whiffed on the *bon mot*)— "was not known to pad his home-run résumé with PEDs."

Kempf was granite, in more than one way.

"If anything," the teacher continued, "he most certainly hangovered himself out of more than a few four-baggers. Had to. That's what happens when you cozy up to a different sort of juice."

Kempf continued to resist any temptation he may have felt to shut down the discussion of performance supplements. Caper did what he usually did in such circumstances. He kept the topic alive by swerving about in a series of more or less contingent associations.

"Clemente played right field, as you may or may not know. Decades later, of course."

"Who?"

Kempf didn't know. "Don't worry about it. But one of the cool things was, Forbes Field was right on the Pitt campus. On the university's grounds. As it happens, I attended the very last game there. Sunday afternoon doubleheader, baby. Cubs. I still have the program."

"So?"

"So nothing. Exactly. But I still have the program. And one of the box seats."

"You stole a seat?"

"No, you droll drumsmith. But since you mention it, it would appear that *you* might be well-equipped to help yourself to heavy outdoor furniture anchored in concrete."

Still no return serve from Kempf.

"Anyway, the seat is one of ten that my father purchased when they tore down the grand old park. Two rows of five, everything painted blue. Someone in the family decided to break the rows down to—"

"So you think," Peter abruptly intervened, "that I should aspire to be like Babe Ruth." His tone was equal parts accusation and question.

Caper took his time responding. "Not exactly, no. I don't think so. In fact, Herr Doktor C would rather suggest Hank Aaron as a role model." He took a few more moments to dwell on the matter. "Yes, that's right. 'Hammerin' Hank.' You should drum like Hammerin' Hank. That's just about right." The teacher appeared to be increasingly convinced that he had provided an impeccable figure to emulate. "Could be 'Pummelin' Pete.' Something like that. What d'ya think?"

Kempf's facial expression remained the very picture of impassivity. The two stared at one another, home-run hitters' names hanging in the air, mixing uneasily with a new and yet, to Caper at least, familiar lyric, one that had snuck up on them unawares.

What's the name of the game?

Does it mean anything to you?

Kempf's cellular telephone chirped. He reached into one of the pockets of what appeared to Caper to be a tailored kevlar vest.

Peter pressed and slid an index finger on the sleek gizmo. "This is Peter," he answered. He listened to a voice Caper couldn't hear, and nodded, eyes on the basement carpet.

*   *   *

"Bill this call to four-one-two, three-two-seven, one-three-hundred."

Over the course of three decades and more, this laconic verbal command, delivered in an unvarying monotonous tempo, had been uttered somewhere between two to three million times by Caper's father into the receiver of a wall-mounted kitchen telephone, one that he would have happily deployed to reach out and touch strip-mining Turks, or Autobahn-clearing Austrians, if only the fine *beyler* or *Herren* would consent to move dirt in southwestern Pennsylvania or northern West Virginia. The sole technological alteration worth noting in this otherwise timeless delivery—namely, that at some point in the late 60's or early 70's, a square button grid had callously replaced the slow, mechanically whirring pirouette of the telephone dial of yesteryear— brought with it absolutely no alteration in the billing recitation. But those very words needed to be spoken, in that exact order, else the earth itself would find itself adrift of its orbit. It was abundantly clear to young Caper that ancient and divinely inspired scriptures were far more susceptible to capricious meddling than were those ten numbers, spoken to an invisible and yet altogether trustworthy entity somewhere else in the universe. How many thousands of telephone operators had obediently charged the home office in Murrysville for the ensuing call? How many more thousands of times had Caper himself overheard this pre-call billing procedure, the eternally abiding prelude to bulldozer seduction?

Only three more words remained to be spoken to the unseen Ma Bell worker, enunciated in a staccato fashion that would likely have thrilled—but also perhaps unsettled—Jack Webb: "My name's Caper."

As a youth, had Caper himself been asked what it was that a salesman did in order to make a living, he would have said—with the absolute certainty of someone whose knowledge had been acquired and reinforced each and every day of his existence—that such a person drove a car for well over a hundred miles each day, talked into a telephone whenever not driving, and beyond those two things, had no other job responsibilities whatsoever. Could we *please*, he would have implored this imaginary interviewer, move on to truths not self-evident to the non-dim-witted?

His father, assuming he was not behind the wheel of a mud-caked station wagon—or, somewhat later, a roomy, late model, mud-caked

Buick sedan—concentrated his sales efforts on only one other activity: bullshitting with customers. He was on the phone bullshitting very often before daybreak, perhaps as a winter-dark rerun of *Sea Hunt* hummed in the background, a welcome maritime counterpoint to the clatter produced by his landlocked progeny, and he could be trusted to be steadfastly bullshitting well into Carson's monologue each weekday night, with bonus bullshit on Saturday and Sunday, pre-dawn to post-sunset. It was a bottomless cup of bullshit, a Wurlitzer juke fed by the invisible and infinite quarters and dimes of four-one-two, three-two-seven, one-three-hundred.

If only Caper had been a writer, it would have been an easy and diverting thing to capture the atmosphere of the family kitchen on, say, a December morn in 1972. Absent the eldest two boys away at college, six children, ranging from 17 to 5, would have been crammed into the eating area. The breakfast din would have been a thing to behold, pinging spoons accompanying the consumption of vast quantities of milk-drenched O's. Indeed, a whole box of cereal may well have been depleted on the very morn it had been opened, although this outcome would largely depend, as would so many other food-related matters, upon the unpredictable inclinations of an already thick-necked and large-headed 15-year old. Next to the kitchen telephone, a plump index finger would doubtless have been approaching the well-used "0" button, that peculiar bottom-dwelling square so inconsiderately denied the fellowship of a trio of alphabet companions, and yet stoically bearing the burden of the top three numeralled layers nonetheless, with only the scant solace of the rarely employed pound and star keys. It was not too much to say that the stomachs of all ten Capers depended on the recurrent pressing of the sole button that could summon a friendly and capable telephone utility employee, who would have been expeditiously provided with the ten-number formula that would enable, in turn, ten thousand thousand long distance and long-lasting CAT confabs to occur. In a more just world, that exceptional button would have richly deserved its own siren-red—No! CAT-yellow!—coloring, the better to distinguish it from the squalid, slate-gray three-by-three grid above it. It was the one and only hotline to the commish. It was the key that greased the bulldozer tracks. It, and neither the 2 nor the 7 above it, *owned* the B, *invented* the S.

"Angelo, my man, how are you?" Thus would the bulldozer courtship be reignited.

As the half-dozen offspring were processed through the morning kitchen regimen, they could not help but overhear as Angelo, or Gino, or Nino, or any number of dirt-manipulators with special needs, received what would likely have been their first phone call of the day. The conversations could of course be about anything or nothing, and could (and most often did) run to a slow conclusion without either party so much as mentioning the fact that somebody somewhere was building something, or destroying something, or destroying and building something, or that any person in his right mind might be in any way concerned about that nettlesome overburden. Coal, you say? That black stuff laying down there just a few layers below the earth's surface—just *laying* there, waiting for the right outfit to purchase the right Caterpillar bulldozers to push all of that damnable spoil out of the way, in order that the fossilized carbon, otherwise so completely pointless, could work its profitable magic?

Who could be bothered?

"…every single person sitting in the Forbes Field bleachers knew damn well that Bobby Lane had been out all night drinking with Staut…"

The very idea that a certain brand of expensive machines were in existence specially designed to consummate the unseemly desires of ardent earth-pushers may have preoccupied other, less cultivated, minds, but needn't trouble their own more refined sensibilities. Caper's father and Angelo had far more ethereal matters to contemplate. They would tire the moon with discussions of Rocky Bleier, Billy Conn, and *Deliverance*. Or perhaps Frenchy Fuqua, Fritzie Zivic, and *The Godfather*. Eugene "Big Daddy" Lipscomb. Beyond any question, he was the largest man who had ever lived, or who would ever live. That Baltimore overdose had shocked everyone, hadn't it? But just why in the hell had the coroner down there found no needle marks? And will someone tell me how any of this makes any sense when the Rooneys said the only thing in this world Big Daddy feared was the needle? Ten-year old Morton readily understood that these questions would never be satisfactorily answered. But he knew with even greater certainty that they would continue to be spoken into the white kitchen receiver, assuming their hallowed place in the long chain of mysteries and uncertainties and sweet nothings that imbued heavy-machinery courtship with sparkle and longing.

Caper got the feeling, even so young, that if the question that dare not speak its name ("Are you going to buy a fucking bulldozer?") were ever to escape his father's lips, the heavens themselves would open, the largest high-lift in the cosmos would lift its burden on high, and an unfathomable load of unsorted coal and unpicked slate would rain down upon the Caper home, never to be seen again, not even with the aid of a fleet of D-9's. And yet that ineffable question was no less present for never having been uttered, as available to the senses as the eight-to-ten lamb patties sizzling on the stovetop grill, the three and a half gallons of milk in the icebox, or the makeshift pyramid of bread loaves on the counter. It may as well have been engraved upon the house's lintel.

The old man, one had to concede, would permit himself a certain latitude in cursing on the phone in the kitchen—he would "son-of-a-bitch" it with impunity, "goddamn" it without a second thought, "hell" it any way you please—but he would never, ever cross over to the far-flung, smoking bank of the River Eff's farther shore. Not in the kitchen! The fuck are you? An animal? That's for bars! His mother, meanwhile, ubiquitous in this domestic region and therefore, and for that very reason, invisible in the way that only the genuinely omnipresent can be, would have been recovering (in a fashion Caper couldn't even remember) from the greatest trauma both she and the Caper family had ever experienced. Only five months earlier, just after lunch on a spring afternoon, she had fallen backwards on the staircase leading from the basement to the kitchen, clasping in her arms a basket of laundry. The impact broke her back. When people heard of this horrible accident, they would very often emit an audible gasp (as perhaps some others would, too, should they have learned of this calamity by other means). Young Morton occasionally felt that he detected in that breath something extra, something more than the natural empathy due to any person who had suffered such a painful and unfortunate fate. Something in the vented air—he couldn't say exactly what—communicated to him the sense that they may have been thinking about the number eight, perhaps also about human procreation, and about labor. Had some sort of foreboding fable played itself out in the family basement? Given to wondering what other people were wondering, Caper wondered if the story struck certain sensibilities as an updated and forbidding parable, or if it simply seemed too much like a *story*. But the tale was no less true for that.

"...course, if it ever came to an actual fight, Stautner'd come to the rescue of Lay..."

Bulldozer romance, it should be emphasized, was not for the weak of heart. The men who purchased D-9's were not to be confused with prospective stereo owners, asking smug questions about woofers and tweeters. Few people would have been tempted to describe them as an especially genteel folk. When, for example, his parents were invited to put on some fancy clothes and spend an evening out with the quality, it might be to attend the annual Sewer Diggers Ball, one of whose galas was deeply etched in the minds of all the Caper children. The old man had decked himself out in a standard black-and-white tux beneath his standard-issue flat-top; his mother had on a Jackie-influenced number, long, thin, shiny gloves climbing past her elbows. The whole thing was captured in living color on the home movies, two snappy partygoers waving goodbye (no doubt with emotions not completely purged of relief) to a gaggle numbering from between six to eight, depending on the year. Their glittering departure to the event celebrating high-quality drainage in southwestern Pennsylvania was illuminated by a lamp that could have been seen from one of the moons of Jupiter, unaided by telescope.

"...how the hell am I supposed to know he wanted to trade in a D-8 for a..."

Of course, at certain points in time, some portion of the calls made on the perpetual telephone tilt-a-whirl must needs culminate in a tangible transaction, one made visible to the human eye, as well as to the manager in charge of sales commissions. The realities of this world—a realm that would not forever permit landline flirtation *sans* actual bulldozer dealings—would always have for Caper a corresponding alphabetic dictum: an expansive, mellifluous aural domain richly supplied with proper nouns ending in vowels would eventually have to yield to an army of clipped, hard consonants, these latter invariably welded to rugged integers, whether fore or aft. No one needed to tell him that Caterpillar, for pragmatic reasons, could readily be turtled back into CAT. So, too, would the D-8 have its day. Angelo, Gino, and Nino must ultimately give way to 993K, 963D, D-10.

When these latter negotiations had begun in earnest, an eavesdropper might have been excused for wondering why the people on the telephone had suddenly chucked their meandering recollections of Bob Prince and Maz, boxing and drinking and the city cops clobbering that Raider tight end (offering, in compensation, a handsome white turban, *gratis*). The pillow-talkers had suddenly taken up an entirely new line of negotiation, one that would appear to involve fighter planes, or heavy bombers, or were Soviet tanks being delivered to satellite states? Had the lines been crossed? Had the von Schlieffen Plan, against all odds, been resurrected? What the hell had happened to the merry bullshitters, happily recollecting forgotten moments from the past, sporting splendors available only to the initiated?

The end of that month would see a careening football almost hit the ground; a descendant of French counts, the flashiest dresser in the history of the NFL, refuse to divulge whether or not the ball had come into contact with his refined hands; unusually large headlines in the *Pittsburgh Press*, reporting on bombing operations not seen since the Second World War; and an overburdened plane fall to the sea, off the shore of Puerto Rico.

Very sudden shifts were the rule, not the exception. Caper would only begin to understand this truth early in his life, but would have to relearn it, repeatedly.

* * *

One early evening in 1962, in the midst of those halcyon days when he was regarded in the highest reaches of the strip-mining world as the most distinguished living professor of the open pit, Caper's father gave the telephone, the steering wheel, and the classroom chalk a brief reprieve, in order to indulge in an unhurried perusal of the pages of the *Pittsburgh Press*. Unfortunately, however, a story on page 2 sharply truncated this rare moment of repose. Pictured was a well-dressed man who made his living in the construction business, a person with whom Caper's father was at that time only casually acquainted. Directly beneath the winsomely smiling equipment purchaser, one could read an account of a murder trial that had come to a conclusion only the day before.

The newspaper article laid out the facts of the case, just as they had been presented in a court of law. It seemed that another man (neither pictured nor, alas, presumed to be sentient) had gone missing about a year earlier. This allegedly deceased individual, too, had been a dedicated professional in the field of construction, but was entirely unknown to Caper's father, as he had been conducting his pre-disappearance business primarily in the state of Maryland, an admirable chunk of dirt that could certainly stand to be improved upon by the properly acquired Caterpillar heavy equipment, but unfortunately not situated within the confines of either southwestern Pennsylvania or northern West Virginia, and for this very reason completely outside the scope of the old man's 'Dozer Radar. In any event, the *Press* story reported that federal authorities, likely spurred by the high-profile crusade against organized crime led by the nation's dashing young Attorney General, had somehow gotten it into their heads that the well-dressed man pictured in the newspaper had had a hand in making the disappearance of the Maryland businessman happen. Indeed, the trial that had just concluded was itself an extension of those misguided beliefs.

The verdict had been "not guilty."

His father sat up stiffly in his chair, and believes to this day that he may have audibly uttered the word "backhoe."

For reasons that should be obvious even to people who have absolutely no interest in or connection to the construction business, the purchase of a bulldozer is a considerably more fetching proposition (to the person selling that costly piece of earth-moving equipment) than is the purchase of a backhoe. All else being equal, a backhoe inquiry would be relegated to "back burner" status, a potential sale to be attended to in those moments when bigger game appeared to be temporarily unavailable. But then page 2 had just exploded all of this "all else being equal" nonsense, hadn't it? Caper's father, who had very likely never in his life uttered the word "alacrity," acted with it. The wrongly accused man whose flattering photograph was so prominently featured in the newspaper would have his backahoe toot sweet, and for a very fair sum.

Some ten or eleven months earlier, a very polite person with a charming accent had contacted the salesman, desiring to purchase a relatively modest piece of equipment, to be used (this bit of information would have certainly attracted the interest of those same federal authorities, no matter how mistaken they may have been in their assessment of the circumstances surrounding the disappearance of the Maryland businessman) on a modest farm he had recently purchased south of Pittsburgh. Caper's father had equally politely responded to the inquiry, going so far as to meet the caller on his newly acquired property, in order to discuss the usual matters of price, capacity, function, and so forth.

But bulldozers happen, if you're lucky, though rarely without logging some serious telephone time. Clemente and Maz, Groat and Hoak, Stautner and Lipscomb—the entire venerable Pittsburgh sporting scene, for that matter (occasionally stretching as far back as Harry Greb, the "Pittsburgh Windmill")—each must receive his tribute. It's easy to lose track of a backhoe lead when a couple of D-9's might be revving their engines, just itching to treat some overburden in the only manner it deserved to be treated. Thus had many months gone by, even as the well-mannered person, unbeknownst to his father, had had some bothersome legal business of his own to attend to. But now the jury had come back, and bulldozers, in an unprecedented turn of events, suddenly found themselves temporarily demoted (though surely not entirely neglected), while Caper's father launched a flurry of bullshitless phone calls, every last one of them centering on the expeditious delivery of backhoes.

The story ended very happily. The falsely accused construction businessman *cum* gentleman farmer was very shortly after the trial the proud owner of a spanking new Caterpillar backhoe, acquired at a most enviable price. In the ensuing years, many larger machines were purchased by the unconvicted man, and their delivery, too, was prompt.

* * *

What you gonna tell your dad
It's like a wheel of fortune

"Ricky, I'm not even going to try to remain composed, okay? You drive to Alberi's Steakhouse in *that* car, a yellow Italian streak sporting *that* license plate, and then blithely come out as a veg…I mean, I don't even know where to begin, d'you understand? Things are definitely not what they seem." Caper lurched forward as a bright flash—some luminous apparition, perhaps—appeared to have crossed the horizon of his dazed consciousness. Still leaning forward, spine held in strict military formation, he gave in to pent-up premonitions. "Uh-oh."

"What?"

"Uh-oh," the teacher repeated. "I think I'm about to make a literary allusion, one that you, my secretive 'Horatio,' will recognize immediately and appreciate with special delight." He paused again very briefly, silently mouthing the words he was on the cusp of uttering. "There are more things in—"

"—in heaven and earth, Horatio," Ricky elbowed his way into the quotation, astounding his former teacher. "Than are dreamt of in your philosophy."

"Ricky," was all that Caper managed to say, tasered by his former student's ready ease with the play that, righteously pecking away at his typewriter, Pacchia had unofficially embraced.

"Dr. C, the thing is, it's not even my fav—"

"Stop right there, Ricky." Pacchia stopped. "Stop, I say. Exactly what are you drinking? Is that *milk*? 'Cause I just might have to report you to the Vegan *polizia*."

"White Russian."

"Whi—" Caper's eyelids contracted. "I guess the rules are pretty relaxed in Veganville these days, aren't they? When vodka's involved, nobody's lactose intolerant."

"It's a White Russian made with almond milk, Dr. C. Not milk or cream. *Almond* milk. It has more calcium. And fewer calories." Pacchia smiled the smile of a man who had just won a debate.

Caper looked about the interior of the Steakhouse of Forgotten Dreams and realized that he lived and breathed in a world he no longer comprehended, not even in its most basic functions. But there was nothing he could do about it. The only thing for it was to try to stay inside the canoe, hoping that the frothing rapids of change didn't cause his vertebrae to kick out even more cripplingly than they already had.

Whatever his cocktail preferences, Ricky would have to answer some questions, directly.

"Why 'Horatio,' Ricky? And why take down Max and Peter? Why," he asked, staring at the cold, pearly rocks glass Pacchia, a swizzle-stick adept, wielded with confident aplomb, "me?"

* * *

Kempf thumbed his rectangular device, abruptly ending a phone call Caper could only occasionally understand. He slapped it on the counter's surface, gazing distractedly at the ratskeller's ceiling. The camo Otterbox was earning its keep.

"Dr. Caper, I'm going to have to go. I'm sorry. It's pretty urgent." Kempf stood up and put another bone-crusher on the ailing teacher's right hand. With his left, Peter began to work the latches of the briefcase he kept close by him at all times in the bar. Caper flashed back to Fei's pumped-up green roll, wondering if Kempf were making a bid to out-cash the cleaner. Was he toting a stylish valise crammed with carefully arranged green bricks, a gangster accessory of the first order?

"Stop right there, Peter. Your greenbacks ain't no good down in this cellar. Let Ol' Man Caper settle the tab. Besides, there's that 'ratskeller special' mixed into the equation, so they'll go easy on me."

Kempf responded by smacking a stout, sealed amber jar down on the table's hardwood surface, his facial expression a gloating testament to his conviction that he had just won something important. But what, exactly, was the prize?

Caper remained seated and silent, an expectant pause padding leisurely between the two soon-to-be parting diners. He stared at the bottle, whose contents may well have been vitamin E, or cod liver oil, or cough syrup, or snake oil, or perhaps some fifth thing he hadn't yet contemplated. He waited patiently for the clarification that was sure to come.

Kempf, if anything, gloated more triumphantly. He appeared to be determined to withhold any explanatory remark, confident that his former teacher was in the weaker position. Bending slightly at the waist, he spun the bottle a quarter turn so that Caper could better read the label. He then resumed his satisfied stance, ample forearms crossed in front of his chest, rocking ever so slightly from the heels to the balls of both feet, and then back. He beamed.

Caper took a moment to put on his reading glasses. "Testost-o-Maxx"?

"Best stuff there is." Kempf's swaying motion was now a swagger. "*Best.*"

"Not gonna argue that point, my muscly young friend." Caper leaned in to inspect at closer range the bottle's label. The lettering was done up in a kind of mock-vintage military stenciling, of the sort you might expect to see on a sturdy box of hand grenades, circa the Chosin Reservoir. "Best," he asked uncertainly, "for what?"

"Building muscle mass."

"Muscle mass," Caper repeated, picking up the weighty jar filled to the brim with glistening golden pills, though the dark glass may well have been playing color tricks. He nodded his approval, not taking his eyes off the label. Who could possibly take issue with the highly commendable goal of building greater muscle mass? And if Testost-o-Maxx could produce more than satisfactory muscle-mass results in an astonishingly short period of time (the bottle's label left absolutely no doubt on this point), only a squishy longhair would bother to kick up a fuss. "It's testost-o-legal, of course?"

"Of course. Completely above board." Kempf picked up the bottle and held it against the ratskeller ceiling light, admiring the beauty of the angled rays slicing through both the bottle's exterior glass as well as the translucent pills themselves, whatever their unvarnished daylight color might be. It was clear to Caper that this was not the first time that Kempf had gloried in the intoxicating appearance of the..."the prohormone supplements"... is that what the label said? ...the "steroid alternative."

"Legal steroids."

"Why are you showi—"

"I'm not a juicer, Dr. Caper. I'm—"

"Are there really legal steroids?"

"Definitely. Absolutely. That's what they inject into—"

"My back, of course. My spine." Caper nodded his agreement. "True. Shrinks inflammation, if you're lucky. And I have been, so far. But believe me," he suddenly felt the need to assure Peter, "the needle's no shrinking violet." His two hands speedily assumed a standard "almost-caught-a-fish-this-big" formation. "Could bring a dinosaur to his—"

"Steroids can do *all* sorts of things, Dr. Caper."

The teacher nodded unhurriedly once again, paying due tribute to the multitudinous capabilities of the anabolic family.

"No doubt about that. All sorts. Home-run production," he held a single pinkie aloft, "might well see a notable increase. I believe that a few people have noted an interesting correlation." A second finger joined the first. "Lithe cornerbacks might develop crackerjack Hulk impressions." Third. "Even drumlines might show signs of—"

"I got big legally," Kempf asserted flatly. "Nothing to apologize for."

"Not lookin' for any apologies, Peter." Caper spun his chin in a slow, measured denial. "Don't want one."

"Good."

The waitress returned with the rat-bill. She handed it off to Caper.

"*An den See,*" the teacher said absently, his eyes casting about for something residing just past the edge of his vision.

"What? Something wrong with the bill?"

"No," Caper laughed. "Not that I—no. I'm sure it's fine." He gave the bill a cursory inspection. "Looks like they weren't lying about cellar deal." As he pulled out his wallet, he picked up the other line of discussion. "'An den See.' That was it, I think. 'To the sea.' Maybe 'on the sea.' That was Peter's answer."

"To what?"

"To the question."

Kempf squinted impatiently. "To *what* question?"

Caper's gaze resumed long-range mode. "Wohin geht Peter?"

Kempf now indicated that he understood the question, and with it the answer. "When did you learn German?"

"I wouldn't say that I 'learned German.' Not very much, anyway. But I had a few years of it in high school. Almost forty years ago now." He waved the bill and a plastic card in the general direction of the waitress, who was doubling up as a tender behind the ratskeller's own satellite bar. "I remember several of the conversations we were forced to memorize. 'Where is Peter going?' 'To the sea.' 'Wo ist Monika?' 'Im boot.' Pretty engrossing stuff. I guess they were working on a sort of catechism model."

"Did it ever get more complicated than that?"

"Oh, yes. Immeasurably so. I'm quite fluent, as a matter of fact. So long as you play by my rules."

"Such as?"

"Go ahead. Ask me if the post office is open. In German."

Kempf composed himself, slowly choosing his words. "Ist die Post offen?"

Caper suddenly realized that something was amiss. "Sorry, Peter. I forgot. You're supposed to address me as 'Otto.'"

"Otto. Got it." Peter cleared his throat. "Ist die Post offen, Otto?"

"Nein," Caper aggressively führered. "Sie ist am Sonntag geschlossen."

Kempf laughed appreciatively. "But it's not Sunday, Dr. C."

Caper was undeterred. "Peter, it's *always* Sunday when anyone asks Otto that question. Next question."

Nonplussed, Kempf still managed to ask the next question. "What's the next question?"

"Sorry. Should've thought of that." He collected himself. "Lemonade," he softly mouthed. "Okay," he announced confidently. "*I'll* ask the next question. Ready?"

"Ready."

"Trinkst du eine Limo mit mir?" He smiled triumphantly.

Kempf laughed again. "Glad to, except we just had a couple beers. Make that *Biere*. So I'm feeling a little bit bloated." He turned toward the staircase leading up to the main floor of the bar. "Gotta go. Sorry."

"No need to apologize." Caper drained what remained in his tall glass. "Bloated," he casually repeated. "Not juiced."

Kempf stopped in his tracks, his back to the teacher, facing the staircase. He didn't turn around. "That's right."

Caper took in the shoulder-to-shoulder span. Had to special-order his shirts and jackets, that's for sure. Maybe there was a clothing line specializing in linebacker. "Wohin," he said in a modulated tone of voice, "Peter?"

"Not going to the sea, Dr. C."

"Fair enough," the teacher responded. "But are you heading north, back up to the land of 10,000 lakes?"

Kempf restarted his trek to the staircase, still not glancing back. "Yes," he said in a tone just a bit too loud. "Back up."

"Max," Caper said firmly to the retreating drummer.

"I know," Kempf answered. "I know." He stopped and turned around. "The stuff's the very best. Just do what the label—"

"No," the teacher corrected. "I'm not talking about your 'Testo-stereo,' or your 'Testox-o'—" He took in a deep breath. "I'm not talking about your pills. Or powder. Or whatever it is that delivers the testostero. I'm talking about Max. Not M-A-X-X. Max Fei."

Peter turned very slowly, then continued his steady climb back up to the first floor.

*　　*　　*

The northernmost Romans (as Caper and his wife knew from having walked the entire length of Hadrian's Wall from east to west, from Newcastle to Plymouth—the same direction which the legions themselves followed when they built the coast-to-coast marvel, a thousand years and more before anything like those two proper nouns came into existence) had never made it, as far as anyone could tell, anywhere close to the southern coast of Sweden. It should in no way detract from the illustrious reputation of those indefatigable wall-builders and road-pavers to make note of this fact. But it should also provide people given to pondering such things fresh reason to wonder why the second-century emperor chose to mark the northernmost border of the western empire where he did. Hadrian's decision, after all, was an imperial act subject to a variety of interpretations, from anything between "*That* ought to keep those pesky barbaric Caledonians up where they belong (and by the way, please don't fail to recognize our unsurpassed engineering skills yet again)," to the tonally more modest, "This is about as far as we need to go in any case—let the northern hordes have the remnant." The wall and its attendant vallum were undoubtedly protective, and therefore couldn't help but suggest at least some element of vulnerability, no matter how you chose to take the measure of the igneous rock structure. But it was hardly impossible to ignore the soft sniff of the boast, the unspoken (because it didn't need speaking) assertion that victors leave the last mark, and do so according to their own temperaments and wills. Caper was especially taken by the incontrovertible evidence that the wall-builders had—about halfway through their task—had the confidence to change their minds, to pare down the proportion of the wall itself both in height and width. Suddenly and without any warning, the barrier assumed a substantially smaller profile, though it remained unbroken. He construed this reduction as a sign of sanguine composure, not a blushing concession, or some sort of diffident downsizing. The Romans went on to finish the wall at the newer, less robust scale. Not finishing would have been entirely different. But completing the task accorded a dignity to the calculated decision, a quiet grandeur that may have cut against one's learned expectations with respect to the Roman temperament, but which nonetheless reflected well upon the wall-makers. Somewhere in that on-the-go adjustment one had to appreciate the dexterity of people who knew what they were about.

But as his copiously mapped dining room could attest, some Germans most certainly did make it further north, made it up all the way to southern Sweden, and then some. Nestled between a vintage print of postbellum 19th-century St. Louis and a tin-painted depiction of a successful mid-20th century Rio Grande crossing (the latter carried out beneath the aegis of a levitating blue-and-white Virgin), a finely wrought replica of an 18th-century map of Göteborg, created by proud and unashamedly imaginative German cartographers, held sway. "Anno 1744," the map announced. At the top, etched in large, inky gothic lettering, the dedication was hard to miss: *"Dem Königl. Friedrich."* "The Great" may have been in the early days of his reign, but already he would have had a dandy map of the barbarian northern lands to hang up in his Prussian dining room, or wherever else he ordered the thing to be nailed to the wall. The mapmakers themselves (brothers?) were commemorated in not-so-great print: *Max. & Pet. Efken Kartogr.* Together they had produced a picture of the southern tip of Viking World that most certainly would have rattled the ribs and shivered the oars of any trireme unlucky enough to pull itself up that far. That the illustration of the ancient fortified town was laced with Latin place names, Latinized German proper nouns, and both Latinized and unretouched Swedish regional names, made it an appetizing linguistic goulash to Caper's palate, even as it confirmed that here, as elsewhere, the Romans made it a lot further north than they may have supposed. The German map-makers made certain that the ancients' language gave its stamp to regions far borealerer than their most remote stone wall. *SEPTENTRIONALIS OCEANUS,* the sea off the west coast was imposingly labelled. And lest one were under the false impression that these northern waters were uneventful (a not unlikely possibility, if one knew that both the Celts and even some Germans had also referred to this ocean as the "dead sea" [*Morimarusa*]), a cluster of Loch Ness-style marauders were plying their destructive craft just off the coast. These Deutsch-imagined leviathans were multi-humped and, based on the evidence of their very sizable canines, not to be trifled with. A scary See, indeed.

Dangerous place to sail your ship, southwest Sweden must have been. But why didn't the map warn of Vikings? In the perfervid imagination of the Brothers Efken, weren't those dragon-faced longships still marauding the northern seas? Heathern prows still molesting wayward searfarers, just as they had been doing in the deeper past?

Oh well. Whoever said that picturing forth perilous threats would yield consistent results?

Quick dispatch to unwanted depths, to undesired territory, seemed—and seems—to be the rule of the day. But as to the means of getting there? It was likely never the same for any two travelers.

*   *   *

One student in particular stood out in Caper's father's mining engineering course. Burmese and brand new to the States, the young man repeatedly made it clear to the Past Master of the Pit that, per his student visa, he needed an A or a B in the class, else be sent back to Burma, which was not at the time enjoying a period of peace and prosperity. Lots of loud talk of communists, fascists, crypto-communists, coup d'états, and all-round political instability. Caper's old man listened carefully to his new student, and warmly assured the visiting undergraduate that he would do everything in his power to aid him in his mission to remain in North America.

Problem was, he also soon proved to be the worst student Caper's father had ever encountered. "Open Pit Mining," by the instructor's own admission, could not possibly have been the most demanding course on any engineering student's schedule. He handed out A's and B's like they were CAT hats. A little bit of algebra; a willingness to raise your hand now and again in the lecture hall; scoring reasonably well on the midterm and final; and handing in one or two short writing assignments: Presto! GPA-booster.

Above and beyond reminding his instructor that he "needed" that A or that B but definitely not any C or worse, the anxious young man did very little else. (Teachers the world over are, of course, well acquainted with this person, be he Burmese, Myanmarian, Missourian, or Moscovian. Even Mormon. Your job, you are made repeatedly aware, is to satisfy that "need," quite aside from any efforts that may or— far more likely—may not be put forth to secure this student's grade fix.) His algebra capabilities remained largely unknown, given that he was completely silent, often absent, and prone to skipping writing assignments and tests. It was now Caper's father's turn to deal with increasing anxiety. The kid was putting him in the uncomfortable position of being a *de facto* deportation official.

In a last-ditch effort to find some sort of excuse to give the student a hold-your-nose B-, Caper's father concocted a "field study" assignment, one offered solely to the young man from Burma. For the first and only time, the open-pit *auteur* took one of his students out to an actual job site—as it happened, to the very same mine the Caper boys would come to know well years later. Although he couldn't remember the nature of this assignment, Caper's father did recall that the work was not completed. Furthermore, the student was openly appalled by the conditions prevailing at the strip mine. It seems that it was a loud and dirty place, crawling with loud and dirty equipment. A sizable percentage of the workers were loud and dirty.

Most unbelievable to his father was the fact that this first-time strip mine visitor appeared to be completely oblivious to the existence of the dragline. He didn't even watch as it conducted its ruinous business. This would be akin to submitting oneself to all of the time-consuming steps required to see *Jaws* in July of 1975 (patiently waiting in a very long line outside the lone downtown theater showing the blockbuster, in order to purchase tickets for the 3:45 p.m. screening; killing the three or four hours until then by looking at albums in the National Record Mart and/or eating cake and ice cream at several local establishments; finally seeing the shoreline sizzler from the very top row of a completely packed house), only to fail to observe that the movie was about a ravenous shark. Keep in mind: the young man had enrolled in a course called "Open Pit Mining."

The semester came to an end. The moment of truth had arrived. The old man, who had never dipped down into the C bucket, let alone D or F, had every cause to deliver the worst. But he couldn't quite bring himself to do that.

Could he give a B- for no-Burma?

No. He recorded his first and last C-. Never again did he see the young man.

His son Morton, who was first told this story on a silver summer morning, riding shotgun in a dirty white LTD Coupe, heard it with the ears of a person condemned to the tipple. You mean some prick was driven to the mine, taken all the way out to the face, and didn't cherish every single instant? The ungrateful bastard! Caper would instantly have seized every opportunity to grab a shovel, ostentatiously move some dirt from one spot to another, pretend to be useful to the b-crew. Anyone need me to schlep some wire? Stand guard near the drill-holes? Anyone? Anyone? Pretend to be useful? Anyone?

It took a long time for Morton to realize that everything is relative. Everything. The young Burmese student would have had had his own very different story to tell. Probably, in the course of things, he would have several stories, and maybe not all of them would strike everyone as terribly convincing. But then all the choices you may have assumed that he made may not have been choices. Who knows?

In any case, Caper did come to know that C- choice pretty well. It could mean a whole lot of things, the majority of them impolite. And just how many teachers wish they could have that Burma card, or something very like it, in their back pocket, every single semester, and with every single student? Grades that determined where students lived after the semester was over? Kidding me? "Got a 79% right now, Billy. Dangerous territory, my man. Gotta pull that number up on the final or it's Borneo, baby. Get to work."

Caper's father hung up the chalk that spring, never to return to the classroom again.

*　　*　　*

And what you gonna tell your dad
If this wheel lets you down?

Gloriously emboothed in a maroon-leather horseshoe, one arranged not for the preservation of good luck but for maximal Porterhouse presentation, Caper had no choice but to quietly agonize over the very real possibility that Eric "Ricky Trombones" Pacchia—aka, the "Brass Vegan"—would find it impossible to order an edible meal here in the bowels of the Mississippi meat bunker.

Stop acting cool
Just bet you might win
I'm not too cool

"Ricky, why me?"

It's like a wheel of...

Caper remained privately and primarily engrossed in frenzied calculations as to whether Alberi's could possibly provide Ricky with at least a couple hundred non-animal calories, enough to get him back into the Dino, and thence back into whatever 'bone-haven Yellow was residing in in the Greater St. Louis metropolitan area, that one consecrated space wherein he could exorcise the demons that had overcome the better angels of Max Fei's and Peter Kempf's souls. No question, Caper was gratified to reflect, they've got mushrooms on the premises. After all, Mala's strips and chops and filets couldn't very well be burnt to order unaccompanied by lesser offerings. Truffles, too, would be readily... Stop right there, Cape. Hadn't some sort of underground fungi shortage hit southern Europe? Evidently not even food nobility with a pedigree as exalted as truffles was exempt from the blighting effects of dramatic climate shifts. Just imagine. All of those highly trained Gallic pigs, illustrious stewards of centuries of arcane fungus knowledge, now cold-bloodedly thrown out of work by unrestrained greenhouse gas emissions. Where was this planet heading? If ever there were justifiable cause to call for a good old-fashioned French general strike, this was it. To the barricades, my porcine amis!

And don't count your chicks
Before they're hatched baby...

Caper managed to grab the reins of his galloping imagination just as Pacchia was in the act of ordering his third White Russian, hold the moo juice once again, if you please. Gotta do something, Cape! Can't let the kid get back in that gorgeous Italian ride all bent out o' shape, nothing in his belly except malice for Max, rancor for the drummer, and three vodka almondines. Urgently, he turned his thoughts back toward very pressing food matters. How about 'Alberi's Vegan Surprise, à la Caper'? Potatoes: check. Truffle sauce: if we're *really* lucky. Served on a bed of mushrooms? Shouldn't be a problem. Backup vegetables, just in case? Surely asparagus and/or eggplant had been permitted to proceed, with due suspicion and pique, through meat-security, and would now be available for duty, if specifically requested. Ricky, he decided, as Ace of Base's throbbing anthem approached its conclusion, would simply have to make do.

It tastes like steel
Like a stab from a knife...

Meanwhile, even in the midst of these silent frenetic menu adaptations, Caper could not help but anticipate that his own dinner order, whatever it turned out to be, would display a total disregard for every single one of the most deeply-held dietary tenets of the youthful trombonist. Veal chops, veal dumplings, veal sauce—all of these and more were still in play. One couldn't simply disregard the fact that one was seated in a leather horseshoe in *Alberi's*; abstract ethical speculations on humane nourishment could hope for very little purchase in such conditions.

Yet the recipient of Yellow's painstakingly typed marching angst desired above all else that their upcoming conversation focus not a bit on meat matters, even as he leaned ever more confidently in the direction of the veal chop, served with—Yes!—truffle sauce. Things might turn out okay after all.

"Why," he asked Pacchia once more, "bring Herr Doktor C into it?"

Ricky responded by taking a long, slow draft on the cruelty-free cocktail. Caper's equally wordless reaction: taxicab.

"Lost purpose," Ricky mumbled.

Caper nodded. "I see." He had absolutely no idea what Pacchia was talking about. "I know, I know. I've probably lost sight of some of the most important things about teaching, but I—"

"No," Ricky interrupted, White Russian #3 now safely stowed in the dustbin of history. "I'm talking about band. Marching band. Marching isn't—or *shouldn't* be—jazz exploration. It isn't the place for Bird Parker or Miles Davis." Pacchia jerked his head sharply back, small, clear, wet ice cubes clicking and sliding down along the sides of the etched rocks glass. He leaned back forward, chewing.

Caper shook his head, puzzled. "I don't see why—maybe it's just that I'm misunderstanding your meaning—but I don't see why you're suggesting that Peter has taken drumming in a 'jazz' direction." He peered quickly up the frescoed river. "Jazz? You're the one who's been insisting all along that it's nothing more than a hostile juice takeover."

"Same thing, sort of."

"Don't follow, Ricky. Don't follow at all. Besides"—Caper reached inside his blazer, fumbling for a piece of paper—"he says it's all on the up-and-up." The teacher put on his glasses to read his own hastily scratched notation. "Something called 'Testost-O-Maxx,' Peter says," (Caper paused to allow Ricky sufficient time to absorb the most recent performance-enhancement rationale), "is the one and only active ingredient in his hasty transformation." Caper handed over the crumpled paper, just in case Ricky wanted to check the spelling. "It's the best."

Pacchia snorted. "Believe that?"

"No." Caper arched his spine, pulled back his shoulders, and appeared to have reconsidered. "That is, I don't believe he ballooned in a legal fashion. As to how well Testost-O-Maxx stands up against the Testost-O-competition, I claim no expertise. Peter himself—make no mistake about this—swears by it. The Maxx," Caper paused dramatically, "is 'the best.'"

"Believe me, you go up to Minnesota, you'll learn the truth about the Golden Gophers drumline. I did. They'll turn doubters into believers. But quick. They're *huge*, Dr. C. And they've done a lot of damage." He took another snort of melted-ice water, laced with traces of almond milk and even fainter traces of vodka, never taking his eyes off Caper. "Not in spite of, but *because of*, their denials." Every fiber of Pacchia's being bore the stamp of someone who had done his homework.

Motionless, Caper took in the young man's confident testimony. "Ricky?"

"Yes."

"Were you actually paying attention in English class?"

Pacchia smiled, then tossed back what remained of the shiny cubes once again. "It's a great road trip, Dr. C. You know you're gonna take it. You've got to see for yourself. Scene of the crime and all. And there's a bonus, maybe two."

"What's the bonus, Ricky?"

"I've already done the trip myself, so I guess I've paved the way for you a little bit. Guess how many miles it is up to the Minnesota campus?"

"I don't know, Ricky." Caper gazed again at the upper regions of the painted Mississippi hovering above them. "The river's all over the place in this place. It's rollin' outside the restaurant; it's on the floor of the bar. And someone painted it on the wall in here. Feel like I'm being surveilled by a mole code-named 'O. M. River.'"

"Five fifty-five," Ricky half-*non sequitured*. "At least that's what it is from my house."

"That the bonus?"

"No. But it like sounds like it ought to be some of kind of omen, doesn't it?"

"Guess so. Three sixes, of course, would have been far preferable, at least from one point of view."

"I know. I know. It really would have made Peter's arrogance all the more—"

"No," Caper interrupted. "Not just his arrogance." His elbows rested on the booth table's surface, index fingers and thumbs forming directive

O's, like a conductor's. "His refusal to serve." Hands and forearms moved in a steady rhythm.

"Okay," Ricky answered. "His refusal. But refusal to serve what?"

"Ricky, that's what I've been wondering all along. I still don't understand. I don't quite get why or how this has gotten under your skin so...so..."

"You wouldn't. And you can't. You've never been in band. Peter's broken ranks. He's no longer interested in...in...dressing a line properly." A waiter passing in the vicinity of the horseshoe caught Ricky's eye, which caught, in turn, Caper's. "For Peter, it's all just about the noise, the volume." Pacchia's gaze remained fixed on the waiter. "He didn't used to be that way."

"Give the White Russians a rest," the teacher sternly advised. "Go for splash of almond milk on the rocks instead," he suggested. "New cocktail I just invented. 'Virgin Vegan Russkie'." He quickly reconsidered. "I'll work on that name. Maybe splice the adjectives into 'Virgan'." He gave himself a few moments to drive the name around the block. "Virgan White Russian," he announced confidently. 'Great for calcium. Low on calories.™' I definitely think you should order one."

"Will do," Ricky responded, raising a hand to order his fourth beverage. The waiter was advised to hold the moo one more time, but this time keep the Russians out of the mix as well. Very likely the first time he had ever received that particular beverage request, Caper guessed.

The two diners stared at the breadbasket in tandem, neither bothering to lift up one of the corners of the bread napkin. "Bonus?"

"What? Oh, yeah." Ricky flipped one of the napkin corners to the side of the basket. "I really think you're gonna like this." He picked up one of the bread slices and began to chew, butter not an issue. "Already paid for the Fitzgerald tickets for you. You're gonna love it." He reached into the inside pocket of his jacket.

"Love what?"

"The walking tour. Birthplace home, too. Plus the museum. It's all in St. Paul." Ricky spread a number of pamphlets, tickets, and maps in front of the teacher. "So when you drive up there to verify—"

"To what?"

"To verify Peter's dropout status, you'll also be able to take advantage of the literary pilgrimage that all of the tourists—"

"*Peter's* dropped out, too? What about all of the percussion awards? The loudest and—"

"Dropped out. *Dropped out.* He's now in full-time juice-mode. Spreading the word all over the Midwest about how to increase percussion volume."

Caper, blankly staring at the vertically rendered Mississippi, registered not a single one of the painted details. "He never said anything. We talked for a long time and he never said anything. Said he was heading back up north."

"He wouldn't. Probably couldn't if he wanted to."

Eyes still fixed high up the painted map, up close to the ceiling, Caper remarked in a distant and lower tone of voice, "And Max is learning to fly planes."

"What?"

"He's becoming a pilot." Caper dropped his eyes suddenly and stared at Ricky's blazer, then the suit as a whole. "Very nice," he remarked. "Seersucker. Never saw one that color before." He took in the lightweight suit, appreciating the overall effect. "Yellow?"

"Goldenrod." Ricky placed a thumb behind each lapel, pulling the front of the jacket forward a couple inches. He seemed to think that this would give the teacher a better view of its virtues. "Gold and white stripes."

"Very nice," Caper repeated. "There's an old gag about that stuff, you know. 'Sears put it on the rack and some—'"

"Some sucka bought it," Ricky finished energetically.

"You've heard that one somewhere, have you?"

"Yeah," he smiled. "Somewhere."

"My memory's not what it once was." Caper's nodded his approval once again. "Where'd you get it?"

"Dr. Caper, I thought you above all would never stoop to—"

"Got it, Ricky. Exactly. Touché. None of my business."

Caper watched as the polished stainless meatwagon approached the crescent booth. "Here comes the murder-cart, my animal-product abstaining friend. I'm afraid I'm going to be participating in the bloody festivities. But we'll see what we can do to accommodate trespassers like yourself."

Ricky nodded patiently. His expression made it clear that he had been the odd vegan out on many a previous dining occasion.

"And Ricky," Caper asked for the third time, but still almost as an afterthought. "Why me?"

*   *   *

Things accumulated for everyone, Caper reflected.

He sat in the core, stiffly, on a swivel-chair whose age rendered it quite proficient in generating a wide array of noises, depending on which way you spun the seat and whether you sat up or leaned back. He was staring at two tall bookshelves, most of the texts his own, books that had massed and piled and staked a claim to their own small piece of territory over the past eighteen years. One pile of paperbacks, spines crinkled pale, stood with doubtful stability where it always did, at desktop-level and to his left. Somewhere in it, nearly every one of John D. MacDonald's twenty-one Travis McGee adventures (the rainbow's never complete, is it?) stoically awaited one more fledgling reader, a young person not yet properly schooled in boating, poker, Florida, swindlers, gin, knight errancy, and economics. It was a lending library of the most primitive sort. Take one of the titles if you like (*Green Ripper* grab ya'?); try not to lose any additional pages; bring the thing back when you're finished. But a different slovenly stack crowning one of the shelves, so high as almost to touch the ceiling, now held his undivided attention. It had assumed a more or less pyramidical structure, the same way, probably, old clothing found itself crudely arranged in long-inhabited houses, or pots and pans piled upon one another in some kitchens, seemingly of their own accord.

It was a study in shabby horizontality. Thin and thick rectangles pressed downwards, some having to bear an unfair burden, especially considering their relative wispiness. It would be one thing, after all, if all six volumes of Gibbon's massive *Decline and Fall* supported a mantle and crust of slim and slimmer volumes of wan poetry. It was quite another if Algernon Swinburne were made to bear, Atlas-style, thick blocks of the *Encyclopaedia Britannica*.

In the middle of the conical stack was an admirably annotated copy of *Gilgamesh*, a volume Caper prized. It was the oldest thing going, a document in foregone adventure. Somehow, it had managed to pull off the extremely improbable feat of bringing a vanished universe back into a form that suggested you were getting at least a glimpse of a world unseeable, at the same time that it relentlessly hammered home the point that it was all a hoax. Not even a millisecond's flash could ever be granted to any of us literate folk. Irretrievable ancient dreams, forever so, but also and teasingly familiar. Flood tale and underworld journey and legendary rivers take their stations alongside other commonly encountered elements of epic poetry, all of it scratched into stone tablets long before anything like an alphabet came into being anywhere on the planet, and long after oral versions of the tale had been passed around Mesopotamia for times unknown. Homeric and Mosaic texts were centuries and centuries away. Sadly, the chief function of this redoubtable saga was at present a mundane architectural one—to support the mostly thinner, shorter texts above it, and to be supported by the mostly stouter, taller books below.

But a different and also quite singular book at the very bottom of this irregular structure, tightly nestled inside a stiff, black protective portfolio, attracted his specific notice, and would soon be freed from the weight of all the other layers above it, with due consideration given to the elevated height of the pile, as well as to the special solicitudes due to his own disorderly spine. F. Scott Fitzgerald's *Ledger* was unlike any other text he had ever come across, and at 15 by 10 inches, would be a prime candidate for the Olin Library's Oversize shelves. Caper's facsimile copy was "No. 61," bound by "Brown, Blodgett & Sperry Co.: Manufacturing Stationers." It was printed in St. Paul, Minnesota. Caper knew that he would be bringing the *Ledger* with him on the northern pilgrimage, hugging the Upper Mississippi, his 555 highway miles (or some total very close to that provocative three-of-a-kind) shadowed by the immeasurably more ancient and far more serpentine 664 river miles (or some trey temptingly close to that). His motive was vague and untenable but still commendably straightforward: Why not bring along a talisman if one were handy?

Had any other writer of Fitzgerald's stature ever left behind such a document? Caper couldn't say for certain, but he doubted it. If asked to consider Fitzgerald's relationship to the characters he created for *Gatsby*, most readers would rightly pay careful attention (if they happen to be careful readers) to the intricate bond between Nick Carraway and the author himself. A perusal of the *Ledger* would be sure to complicate that task, but in all the best ways. One would find oneself in the (for Caper) unusual position of dwelling upon Scott's eerie aping of some of aspects of Jay's—or, far more to the point, young James Gatz'—daily habits. The oversized text is a record (incomplete and puzzling, but that is a redundant observation) of the Minnesotan's life from about 1920 to "Dec. 1936." (Some few stray figures dating from 1937 make their way into the handwritten record, but appear to be haphazard data, added as an afterthought.) The entries contained between those dates are various, but heavily dominated by revenue matters. Fitzgerald nowhere dwells upon dumbbell routines or elocution improvement or studying electricity. Nor does he resolve to rid himself of any vices. Money, however, is a different matter. It's all over the place, down to the exact dollar, and occasionally the exact cent. Like young James, Fitzgerald would appear to have been a person of disciplined habit, at least in some facets of his life. Carefully hand-drawn columns of black ink dominate most of the two-hundred sheets. All of the pages, even those crammed from top to bottom, are tidy. In this *Ledger*, writing, as it has from time immemorial, serves primarily as a keeper of order, a fence raised to ward off chaos and loss. Writing like this also comes at a cost.

"Zelda's Earnings" and *This Side of Paradise*'s are treated with equal equipoise one year. *The Great Gatsby* checks in as nothing other than a tale slightly earlier than the short stories "John Jackson's Aready" and "Love in the Night." Income is very carefully tabulated in regular categories: "Stories," "Movies," "English Rights from Books," "Play advances," "Books," "Other Writings." *This Side of Paradise*, Caper judged, had to be one of Fitzgerald's favorite children, bringing in major and steady dough throughout the mid-'20's. *Collier's* and *Esquire*, too, were reliable cash sources, their "Articles" underwriting who knows how many bottles of gin. Sometime in 1925, a thousand bucks were "Advanced," recorded in cursive under the rubric "Misselaeneous" (handwriting experts might quibble over one or two of the vowels scribbled by Scott's unsteady hand, even as the novelist's well-known spelling struggles receive ample confirmation) for "Gatsby play." This dollar figure was hastily cut to 900.00, owing to something that looked like "Coll." followed by "%." Until he received this book as a gift, Caper had no idea that a dramatic adaptation of the classic novel had ever been in the works; learning of it, he developed no desire to investigate what may have happened to the prospective stage version.

But the text delivers far more than a cold accounting of Scott and Zelda's legal tender. Fitzgerald also provides, relatively late in the notebook, an "Outline Chart of my Life." The organizing principle shifts from headings by calendar year ("Record for 1923"; "Record for 1924") to headings by Fitzgerald year ("Twenty-two Years Old"; "Twenty-three Years Old"). The observations are often hilarious, sometimes sentimental, and occasionally revealing, in ways that must continue to surprise Fitzgerald specialists. The opening entry in this "Life" is one of the longest, and reads, "at 3-30PM a son Francis Scott Key FitzGerald to Edward and Mary FitzGerald. The day was Sunday. The weight was 10 lbs, 6 oz. The place was 481 Laurel Ave, St. Paul, Minn." Next to "Nov 1896," the second entry reads (in its entirety), "He had the colic." The third, under the year 1897 and next to "Feb," informs one that "the child laughed for the first time." No other context is provided.

What was Francis Scott Key up to? What a cool cat. He claims that his first word was "Up," uttered in July of 1897. He notes that in June of 1898 he "had a dutch haircut." All manner of "returned to St. Paul"s are recorded, lodged between trips to Buffalo, Orchard Park, and "Sarycuse."

Caper wouldn't be returning to St. Paul. It would be his first trip upstream. But Ricky had preceded him, a stern pilgrim reluctantly validating his own bitter suspicions, lending to Caper's journey at least the distant echo of a repetition. He had no idea what he would find.

* * *

"Avenue of the Saints," is it?

From Louis IX to Paul, he would be moving steadily back through the centuries, and steadily north, rarely seeing the storied stream shadowing him on his right arm all those hundreds of miles. But Caper didn't need to see the "Father of Waters" (one of those epithets that, purporting to be a translation of a Native American word or phrase, made his lower lip jut out skeptically every time) in order to be conscious of its ground-carving presence for the entire journey. If landscapes were capable of providing some sort of rough historical justice, the towns he passed in northern Missouri and then in Iowa and in southern Minnesota would provide an orderly supply of Hildegards, Bernards, and Basils, Anselms, Benedicts, and Cyrils. But there was no more order to be found here than anywhere else.

As is so often the case, Caper's long journey began with a series of short, maddening delays, each stoplight seeming to have conspired in extending the time he would spend trying to depart from the city. Naturally, he was eager to hit cruising speed on I 55, US 61, and about a dozen other highways heading relentlessly northward and, drifting left on a leisurely diagonal, westward. As is equally often the case, his opening gambit found him driving pretty much in the exact wrong direction, on a serpentine road hugging the city's primary sanitation and storm drain, the River des Peres. (Father and H^2O had decided to swap places, hadn't they?) Winding east and south, he aimed to minimize the time and space it would take to make that sharp left turn to St. Paul, seeking open highways that would shave off most of the kinks of the Mississippi. At present, however, Caper waited impatiently at the Gravois intersection idling in his Crown Vic. Directly in front of him, a compact Nissan pickup, elevated who knows how many feet above the smooth asphalt surface, also waited for green permission to continue east, its tailgate absent and its bed visibly quaking. The truck featured a host of sporting stickers and decals on the rear window of the cab: a muscular bass neck twisted in sharp, angular, angry protest; a buck neck supporting a rack whose score would be off the charts. One of the stickers on the passenger side unabashedly announced a momentous gender turnabout: "Silly Boys!" it gleefully scoffed. "Hunting is for Girls!" The license plate, an Illinois vanity truck tag, appeared to validate that sentiment foursquare: DEERGAL.

Of late, Caper had been feeling palpably older for reasons he couldn't even begin to enumerate. Sitting behind this Nissan, whose distended tires bulged outside and at a conspicuous distance beneath the comparatively modest wheel wells, did not serve to make him feel any younger. He would leave it to others, if they were so inclined, to detect in this alleged reversal in predatory prowess a "breath of fresh air," a healthy challenge to traditional gender expectations, bracing evidence of rugged, homespun female empowerment. Glancing at the distressed concrete banks of the French "river of fathers" on his left, he recalled with amusement that he had read or heard somewhere that Tennessee Williams had been known to refer to it as the "River Despair."

What would Caper find once he put some space between himself and the bellowing Huntress, elevated ever so high above the twisting sewer road? Could she see Illinois even now, he wondered, idling way up there, reverberating, still miles west of the "Father of Waters" she would eventually cross? And what visions awaited him when he—equal parts Marlow & Marlowe—took that sharp left turn, seeking the Twin Cities, up and up and up and back to the left a little? The "polis" of Minneapolis he knew well enough, and a few seconds of googling informed him that the rest was Dakota for "water." Poetic and gratifying, but was it true? Its "twin" had, like St. Louis, an official patron. Twain himself had always and everywhere stressed that going upstream and going downstream were two fundamentally different undertakings, that the "up" journey revealed the true river pilot, the one who had mastered the perilous business of finding and exploiting "slack" or "easy" water near the shore. The ones who hadn't were doomed. They would "knock the boat's brains out" one way or another, speared by a submerged tree trunk, ruined by a reef, sunk by their own slovenliness.

Would Caper be finding or exploiting anything? He expected to find some sort of wreck in the Golden Gophers practice room; he hoped not to be wrecked.

*   *   *

"You're the one I thought could make a difference." Ricky took a long draft on a rocks glass unlikely to yield much in the way of liquid refreshment, almond milk and vodka now in short supply amidst the glistening and dwindling cubes. "Maybe, just maybe, bring Peter and Max back down to the field. Off the juice. Removed from the cash-flow."

Ricky munched, steadily. "Back to band." He took in the wall-paintings, each scene testifying to Mississippi River exchanges either utterly forgotten or thoroughly sentimentalized. "Marching with purpose."

Caper stared at the shimmering remains of Ricky's vegan White Russian, now taking a well-earned breather on a besotted gray-felt coaster. The entire composition rested on a starched white cloth, carefully draped over a lightly-scored oak table. "Ricky," he started to ask—"and it's important to me for you to understand that the question I'm about to ask is in no way an attempt to change the topic of this conversation—"

"Got it, Dr. C."

"Ricky, I've got to know a couple things."

Pacchia nodded. "Shoot. Lemme have it. I'll answer the best I can."

"Ricky," Caper hesitantly repeated, "why the yellow...why the typewritten...?"

"I don't know, for sure," Ricky answered with steady assurance, clearly prepared for exactly this line of questioning. "I guess I thought that..." Quickly and improbably, Pacchia's practiced assurance seemed to melt away. "I guess the *means* of saying these things was just as important as what they—"

"What machine," Caper energetically interrupted, "have you been typing on, you staunch guardian of marching integrity?"

"Olivetti." Pacchia appeared to have regained his composure. "Sharp-looking Olivetti."

"Yellow Olivetti?"

"No." Pacchia shook his head. "Green. Sort of khaki. Looks like an olive." He smiled. "It's a 'Valentine.'"

"Everything doesn't always add up, does it?"

Ricky appeared to agree, in a vague sort of way. "Yeah—I mean no—I mean..." He angled his chin quizzically. "I don't know what you mean."

"You typed on yellow paper. Legal pad. I jus' thought the Olivetti might be yellow, too. Not a very rational expectation, I know. Still, I thought there might be some kind of pattern to the whole project."

"Sorry to disappoint. But it *is* olive. So that ought to count for something." Caper nodded in agreement. "The typewriter was a family thing. My mother's father gave it to her." Ricky paused, carrying out silent calculations of some sort. "She gave it to me. I'm pretty sure I was the first to use the machine in a long time."

"I don't doubt that." But Caper's expression remained a study of perplexity.

Ricky continued. "It wasn't in good working order. Needed a little bit of lubrication help, all along the keys. And a new ribbon."

"New ribbon? Ricky, do you even know what a...?" The older man's face suddenly registered the real possibility that *he* was the one not grasping the actualities of the matter.

"Yes, I *do*, Dr. C. I know more than you'd guess, probably."

"Yeah?"

"Yeah. Spools, for starters. Black over red."

"Good man." He dwelt upon the horizontal relationship. "Good man. Le rouge et le noir."

"What?'

"Nothing." Caper tried to return to matters he thought he understood. "I've got to ask. Why the yellow legal pad? Were you simply out of typing paper? Do you even know what typing pape—?" Again, he caught himself in mid-sentence.

"Yes, I do. And I happen to know that you can still acquire good multipurpose, quality onionskin, and even expensive linen pretty easily. Surprisingly easy. But none of it ever made much sense to me. Too much white space. Open white space," he repeated, each word separated by a brief pause. "No lines. Too much temptation to go off on a"—he paused, perhaps to make certain that his voice would be dripping with sufficient contempt—"a free-form jazz exploration."

"Got it, Ricky." Caper rapped the knuckles of his right hand sharply against the table's white cloth, looking up once again at the painted scenes of Mississippi wharf-life, circa 1858. One of the buildings had INTERNATIONAL FUR EXCHANGE in blue lettering along the top. "No lines, no direction. And before you know it, carefully chalked fields become devils' playgrounds. So sometimes, you gotta put the long arm of the law on the lawless. Jus' never occurred to me that legal paper would be tapped to do the job." Caper rapped his knuckles against the table's cloth once more. "But you've got other things to 'splain, Ricky. So get right to it. Wherefore Vineland?"

"Pynchon."

"Follow you so far. Sort of."

"*Lot 49. Gravity's Rainbow.* You used to mention them, more than the other stuff we couldn't read in high school." Caper nodded, chin cradled between thumb and index, waiting for more. "So I read them in college, and that led me to *Vineland.*"

"And?"

"And it's in New Jersey."

"And California. Sort of."

"So I thought a P. O. box with that kind of…" Ricky faltered.

"Pedigree?"

"Something like that. I thought it would make things more interesting."

"It does, Ricky."

"That was it. I was just going for a little echo. Reverb. Nothin' else."

"Got it," Caper responded reassuringly. "'Reverb.'" He appeared to be taking the measure of the word. "You musician-types sure do punch above your weight when it comes to peppy small talk."

*   *   *

On I-380, about thirty miles southeast of Waterloo, Iowa, Caper's hunger compelled him to look for some sort of convenient eats. Scouring the blue interstate markers for a likely stop, a lofty old sign (dating from the early 70's, he gauged) caught his eager eye. RESTAURANT, it announced generically and, for that very reason, intriguingly. From Caper's point of view, however, cruising north along the highway, the sign appeared to be rooted in the middle of an overgrown wooded area. Was it still a going concern? Or an abandoned, outdated, and now misleading artifact from an earlier interstate-era, when motorists' needs were met with curt assurances, not brand-offerings?

He took the next exit, on a whim. None of the directional arrows positioned on the off-ramp's shoulders offered any sort of specific (1.2 miles>; <.1 miles) or, for that matter, vague indications of RESTAURANT's location. His single advantage—a notable one—was the impressive altitude of the sign's ten upper-case letters. The thing looked like it might have been constructed to attract peckish airplane pilots who just might be in the mood for a piece of pie and a cup of coffee, and likely could have been spotted from the northern outskirts of Cedar Rapids, even if you were a munchkin squatting in the fields, the corn as high as an elephant's eye. Caper, as a consequence, had little difficulty in steering the Crown Vic ever closer to the astrally-demarcated RESTAURANT, its uniformly upper-case promise to "restore" hovering over the dark Iowa soil like an eternally faithful Huey.

He arrived at a blunt-cut clearing, backed by a dense wooded area forming a truncated horseshoe. Between the lot and the trees a large creek wound south, probably an offshoot of the Mississippi, perhaps soon to rejoin the source. Just to the north of what had to be the RESTAURANT building (Caper still couldn't say for certain whether or not the joint was open for business), a thin, creamy line roiled steadily and neatly across the creek's surface, an ivory echo of a sharp jut of rock invisible beneath. Most of the lot's surface was comprised of medium-grade gravel, gray-white in the late afternoon sun and shade, some light somehow managing to slant through the tree line. What caught Caper's eye immediately was the fact that the surface offered no suggestion of any sort of rutting, the first and surest sign of long-standing neglect. A roller had been on the premises, and recently.

The RESTAURANT building itself was located on the southern edge of the clearing. Trees on the western bank of the creek were still close enough and tall enough to enclose the structure in gloom. Surprisingly, no more precise identification of RESTAURANT was forthcoming at ground level. No "Pat's Bar & Grill" sign to greet the odd lonely motorist. No "Connolly's BBQ" neon script to lend a personal touch (even if a spurious one) to hurried, anonymous roadside meals. No lower-case identification of any sort. Just a building with one door and several uncurtained windows. Was it really still in business?

The crunching sound of the tires reminded Caper of the thousand unfinished roads and lots he had been driven over in the far back seat of the white Mercury station wagon, or the back seat of one of the Le Sabres, or the front seat of the LTD coupe, whose doors were as long as surfboards, but far heavier and dirtier. Several vehicles were lined behind the RESTAURANT building in a roughly formed row, maybe a sign of waitresses, cooks, and dishwashers, maybe also an indication that a few customers were already dining on hearty and wholesome Hawkeye fare. It seemed promising. But the dominating element of the whole composition, hands down, was a vintage Kenworth truck, abandoned and rusting on the northern edge of the lot. It had the long, low profile of road-haulers from the 40's or 50's, its front end suggesting to Caper the nose of those old Duesenbergs he had seen in photos and movies. A more than cursory survey would detect in the old rusting hulk evidence of a significant collision many decades before, its haunting scar scorched into the left front side of the cab.

Caper wheeled up close to the lone door. The interior was dark in a way that suggested inadequate lighting, rather than the complete absence of illumination. Sitting in his car, he could make out taupe-colored wood paneling high up on one of the walls, but as yet no people nor anything that would indicate a business devoted to serving food and drink. Perhaps when he approached the door a large Bunn coffee brewer would swing into view, or maybe side-by-side cold beverage dispensers, their orange and yellow contents tirelessly churning. "Curb appeal" was certainly not the building's strong suit; but it managed nonetheless to be inviting, in a quizzical sort of way.

Caper pushed open the door and immediately recognized that he was, in fact, inside a RESTAURANT of some description. A man and a woman moved behind a formica counter, each one sporting a damp white towel slouched over the left shoulder. They both nodded in greeting as Caper entered, neither one interrupting the conversations they were having with the only other customer in the place. The latter was seated and had already been served, though his meal didn't appear to have been disturbed in any way. Fork, knife, and spoon remained neatly swaddled inside a hand-folded napkin, just to the right of an ivory-tinted oval plate.

Caper grabbed one of the menus smartly stacked at one end of the single long counter, but found himself engrossed by the myriad burnt wood artifacts arranged high above the diner's stainless kitchen equipment. At least twenty-five chunks of wood, of a variety of sizes and shapes, served as irrefutable evidence that someone in the vicinity had contracted a virulent form of the rustics. Some of the signs were glossy; some were unabashedly not. But Caper had little difficulty in quickly determining that a single hand was responsible for all of the works, the blackened wood-script attesting to a needle-point as distinctive as Van Gogh's brushstroke, Rodin's chisel.

"How can we help you?" the man behind the counter asked.

"Thanks," Caper awkwardly replied, his attention still on the wall above the cook, and especially on a slab of wood hewn into a shape resembling the state of Tennessee. It was one of the shiny ones, and featured the single word "Believe," adroitly charcoaled in neat cursive. From the top to the bottom of the margins of the "rough" (east and west) borders of the varnished state, the artist had blackened in markings of an indecipherable sort, at least from where Caper stood. They looked like totem markings, or notches for a ruler whose metric he would never comprehend.

"Yes," Caper continued, with undiminished awkwardness. Still close to the lone entrance, he sat down on the circular red stool at the very end of the counter, next to the pile of menus. He opened one without really scrutinizing any of the offerings, gently hanging the curled grip of his cane on the outer lip of the diner's counter, the gold rubber bottom swaying softly for a few moments before coming to a rest just an inch or so above the polished pine floor. "Yes," he repeated, now just beginning to take in the enumerated victuals the RESTAURANT had on offer. At that very moment, however, an arrangement of objects neatly aligned in the center of the counter diverted his notice once again. He smiled. Not one but three cake stands stood at attention, each one properly bonneted in clear acrylic. The one in the middle was a few inches taller than its companions, cloaked—who knew this was possible?—in some sort of form-fitting gold and white cake-garment. Along the bottom edge of this hemispherical woollen robe, the word CAKE had been knitted three times, evenly spaced in golden yarn. Cake cosy! What mad Iowan had conceived of this ingenious stratagem? His admiration instantaneous and forever fixed, Caper also knew that Iris had her work cut out for her the moment he returned home. The concealed interior of the predominant cake stand, a *sanctum sanctorum* unavailable to the human eye, made evident, yet once more, the power of secrecy to furnish fertile ground for the human imagination. The only certainty was that the veiled mystery remained perpetually toasty.

By contrast, the two side stands were observably and amply stocked, each with a full loaf of white cake topped by pink and yellow and white icing. Caper relaxed just a little bit, now confident that his needs would be fully met. Furthermore, he could see that the other customer, seated at the opposite end of the counter, and at an equal distance from the two cakes and the three stands, was a fellow member of the Cane-Dependent Club. The markings of his crook were green and gold, or perhaps olive and mustard, or maybe some third observer would say avocado and yellow. It was hanging from the vertical back of his stool.

Caper's eyes returned to the menu. He began to home in on "Number Six: 'Meatloaf Special' (House-made Mashed Potatoes, Green Beans, and Applesauce inclu—"

"Yours looks like a Stink Flower."

"Excuse me?" Caper, and perhaps one or both of the RESTAURANT workers, replied.

"Stink Flower. It's the largest flower in the world."

"Yes," Caper answered the distant counter-companion, incoherently. With no benefit of warning, he felt he had been thrust into a cutting-edge, surreal re-enactment of one of the more famous scenes from *Citizen Kane*. "Largest fl—"

"*Very, very* stinky. Smells so bad that it's also called the—"

"Cadaver flower." Caper hoped to communicate the impression that he was listening attentively, and that he cared.

"No. No. Not as far as I know." The botany authority paused, even as everyone else in the RESTAURANT waited to be schooled on the alias of the "Stink Flower." "Corpse flower," he finally said, divulging the smelly plant's alternative moniker. "Stinks. Stinks, *very* badly. Indonesian plant. Grows on one of the islands. Flies love it. *Love* it."

"I'm afraid," Caper answered, this time more confidently, "that in spite of your plant know-how, I still don't know what you're talking about. Why," he asked, "are you talking about stinking flowers?"

"I'm not talking about stinking flowers, *per se*," he corrected Caper. "I'm talking"—he tapped the lip of the counter in front of him—"about your cane."

Caper darted a peep at his own walking-stick, hanging motionless on its perch. "What about it?"

"Reminds me of a Stink Flower. Burgundy and a few streaks of yellow."

The teacher shook his head. "It doesn't remind me of any such thing. I've never heard of a"—he paused and curled his index fingers—"'Stink Flower.'"

"This flower stinks, believe m—"

"Got it. Malodorous blossom. Biggest one to be found. But exactly why does my cane remind you of this unfortunate plant?"

"Burgundy and yellow. Same color combo."

"Others," Caper responded astutely, "have described it as maroon and gold, colors proudly worn at the University of Minnesota, where," he added, "I happen to be heading. And more specifically," now knowledgeable and smiling, "worn by the Golden Gopher Marching Band. The 'Pride of Minnesota'." Caper judged himself to have won the purple and yellow skirmish.

"Not gonna get in an argument," the other customer said brusquely.

"Not looking for one," Caper answered. "Yours," he added, "looks like an absinthe candy cane. I wouldn't lean on that too confidently, if I were you."

"Why not?"

"You just might fall over, my unsteady friend."

The end-to-end counter colloquy might well have stretched on for a long while had the woman behind the counter not intervened, ungrudgingly tendering Caper a small saucer, sparkling and white. Upon it, a loaf of white, pink, and yellow cake, topped by white and pink frosting, had been neatly displayed, together with a small fork placed at a rakish angle. The implement stood on its side, ready for duty. If the thing had descended from heaven with an escort of glimmering archangels, his delight would have increased not a whit.

"What have I done to deserve...? Wait a minute." Caper's face quickly assumed its best "I-smell-a-commie-rat" incarnation. "I haven't even placed an order for 'Number Six' yet. I haven't even *asked* about it. Have any idea how many probing questions about the mashed potatoes and applesauce and home-ma—?" Caper himself interrupted this litany of lost opportunities. "Kinda joint you runnin' here, lady?"

"A clean joint. With good cake." She thumbed the plate a few more inches in Caper's direction.

He looked down at the toothsome confection, white, yellow, and pink. He was not displeased. "Have a name?"

"Yeah," the woman answered, turning back to the middle of the counter.

"What is it?

"Ida."

"Ida cake?" He nodded his head approvingly. "First time I've ever tried it. Looks great."

"No. That's *my* name," she corrected, walking away.

"Oh." Warily, Caper sampled the maiden bite of the still nameless cake. "Sorry." A digital flip clock attached to the wall just beneath the epic wooden tapestry presented a time so wildly inaccurate that one could only surmise that it was broken. Far more irksome, it was just a hair from being perfectly level. "I was asking about the cake," he explained in a lower register.

Ida didn't hear, or didn't care to answer. She continued to walk away, white towel over her left shoulder, empty circular tray held waist-high, steadily.

"Pretty damn irrational, if you ask me," Caper said to the still receding Ida, his voice now assuming its normal volume. "Cake before meatloaf. Just what're you playin' at, Ida?"

She leaned her right shoulder into a shiny, swinging door, silently and speedily disappearing. Caper's overwhelming approval of the delicious cake could not readily dislodge his furrowed brow, which registered his disdain for such a wanton travesty of eating proprieties. He gazed up again at the wall of burnt-wood offerings. A different piece of lumber, this one almost perfectly square in shape and unvarnished, briefly held his attention. It, too, imperatively urged all who read it to "Believe."

Caper's eye returned to the fork, and to the white, yellow, and pink delicacy bestowed upon him by Ida, who ran a clean, perverse place, and served good cake.

*   *   *

Jack Nicholson, Caper could say with some confidence, was a devoted admirer of William-Adolphe Bouguereau. He had of course never met Jack, and almost certainly never would. Nor had he ever read anything relating to the celebrated actor's artistic tastes. Still and all, his wife (at one time the "Docent Program Coordinator" for the Carnegie Museum of Art) had once accompanied Nicholson and a flock of admiring docents on a tour of the museum's collection, during which the actor waxed eloquent whilst inspecting the institution's Bouguereau paintings, even making a point of noting that he had recently purchased one of the French painter's works for his then-girlfriend. He was in Pittsburgh for the filming of the Mamet-scripted *Hoffa*.

To anyone with a modest working knowledge of the visual arts of the past couple of centuries, Bouguereau's very name instantly conjures images of creamy, fleshy nymphs, twilight rosy hues, sumptuous sensory pleasure. Sweetly pastoral, mythological settings are the norm. Indeed, if the phrase "visual frosting" ever found itself in urgent need of a few palpable illustrations in order to establish its viability as a concept, William-Adolphe Bouguereau's paintings would quickly prove their utility.

In recent years, however, Caper associated the name of the artist not so much with the luscious stylistic elements that mark his work, nor even with the renowned movie star so openly appreciative of them, but with one particular 1850 painting. Not a single nymph is to be found in this picture. Not by a longshot. No shepherdesses. No Venus and no fawns. As a supplement to his class discussions of Dante, Caper liked to provide examples of visual interpretations of the *Divine Comedy*, and especially *The Inferno*, down through the centuries. Botticelli and Doré provide two of the more well-known resources for this sort of exercise, but Caper's flimsy online searches also led him to one William-Adolphe Bouguereau, who is alleged to have been inspired by a tercet from Canto VII, which has been translated into English thusly: "They smote each other not alone with hands/But with the head and with the breast and feet/Tearing each other piecemeal with their teeth." The painting is titled "Dante and Virgil in Hell," but very few viewers of the work would be likely to concern themselves with either the Florentine poet or the Roman literary predecessor who doubles as Dante's invaluable infernal guide, two pilgrims solemnly conferring in the shaded backdrop. Even the self-satisfied demon slicing through the orange-and-gray atmosphere of the fourth circle, a prototypical heavy-metal fiend *avant la lettre*, grinning ghoulishly as he strikes a sick-and-twisted Mr. Clean pose, could hardly hope to compete with the tableau in the foreground.

Gazing upon the two-and-a-half naked white guys bathed in bright hell-light front and center, most viewers would probably have a bit of difficulty squaring the activity of "smoting," of heads and breasts and feet and teeth being torn "piecemeal," with the balletically contorted exertions depicted in the painting. Perhaps this was simply attributable to the fact that Bouguereau had an imperfect grasp of Italian. But perhaps, the wounded Caper had good reason to conjecture in recent months, the painter was simply cutting to the crux of the matter, ignoring those regions of the body not germane to genuine torture. Please take note, dear reader, if you have occasion to view this diabolical image, that a certain hell-dweller's right knee connects sharply with the lower region of another unfortunate pit-occupant's spine. Leave it to others to interpret this savage act of aggression as they will. You will soon discover that they will be all too ready to discern the stirrings of other, only slightly less surface-level, activities. But that's their problem, not yours. They think of themselves as "intellectuals."

Caper well knew that Bouguereau knew *exactly* what he was about. It was the L3/L4 region all the way. Hell is lower-back pain. "Moderate to severe" herniated discs, authenticated by magnetic resonance imaging, and only partially alleviated (if you're lucky) by a steady diet of steroid injections. French guy was a genius.

He also decided pretty quickly that he would stick with Botticelli and Doré, with maybe a pinch of Hieronymus Bosch.

* * *

Adolphus Busch died in Germany. When Caper discovered this fact, he was genuinely surprised, well-nigh shocked. But why should he have been? Didn't a man with that name had every right to die in Germany, damn it?

Where, one wanted to know, did Andrew Carnegie die? Please don't say Edinburgh. Or Glasgow. Much better for "the Star-Spangled

Scotsman" to cross that last river in Carnegie, PA. Serenely saunter into one of your very own libraries. "Free to the People." Politely request that a volume of Robert Burns be made available for your delectation. Locate a quiet, comfortable chair. Sit in it. Open the book to one of your most cherished poems. Perish.

Thomas Mann couldn't concoct a better finale.

Busch suffered from dropsy. This was only one proof among a thousand that our ancestors died from maladies far more poetic than those likely to fell us. But let's get to the point. When Adolphus decided to move a bit west and south from his home abutting the Anheuser-Busch brewery on Pestalozzi Street (still one of the world's largest), he purchased a patch of land once owned by none other than Ulysses S. Grant. If one chooses to visit this location today, one will almost certainly hear from one of the fine, experienced, and friendly tour guides (unless she is derelict in her duties) that it would have taken Adolphus an entire day to make his way from the western banks of the Mississippi out to Grant's Farm in the 1850's, even drawn by the most stupendous draught-horses ever to grace the planet, and sitting comfortably in the finest carriage that lager-money could buy. One will also find oneself within the confines of the Lindbergh School District. Impressive numbers of bison, as well as a host of other species of mammals and birds not native to North America, currently roam the place. A strictly limited number of free beers (two, if you need to know) are available to the animal-lovers who visit the storied acres, the vast majority of whom are drawn there primarily by their passion for wildlife.

Caper had to give credit to the first king of the King of Beers. He purchased a farm once unsuccessfully farmed by the man who would become the great Union general, and even relocated a cabin Grant himself crafted long before the Civil War. (One can see it along the southern border of the National Park, facing the road that cuts a clean diagonal forming the southern edge of the grounds, and that heads straight into to the heart of the city.) Adolphus himself was said not to partake of the "slop" that his brewery workers produced. (The king was a wine-man). Carnegie did not drink at all, and urged others to follow his example. Grant drank. So, by all accounts, did William Tecumseh Sherman, the storied field commander buried just north of Busch, in north city.

A man named Dale Breckenridge Carnegey (who, inspired by the unparalleled steel magnate, would alter the spelling of his last name), would also emerge, like Grant, from the unforgiving Missouri soil. He would teach the world, in a host of languages, how to win friends and influence people. Caper did not know whether Dale partook of "slop" or wine or the harder spirits so prized by Sherman, but doubted that the Master would have advised anyone to embrace any one of the three as part of an influential or "winning" strategy. Charles Manson was alleged to have imbibed and admired Carnegey's philosophy, and would appear to have successfully implemented some of its core tenets.

Caper did know that the Sherman Antitrust Act (no relation, as far as he knew) was inspired by the activities of men like Carnegie and Busch, many of whom got their start under the administration of President Grant. He wondered now, on the trail of the Midwest's most prolific purveyor of illegal marching performance enhancement, whether or not Peter Kempf were forming some sort of PED Trust, systematically eliminating all real and potential competition, and, if so, whether some latter-day Teddy Roosevelt were already taking measures, soon to be about the business of busting it.

*   *   *

Determined, if also slow-paced, Caper made his way down a long, windowless hallway, a passage that would have effortlessly earned the designation "poorly lit," were it not for the rectangular glass display cases that receded brightly and regularly into the far distance. Each case illuminated its contents—trophies, ribbons, photographs, and occasionally even musical instruments—from above and below, long fluorescent tubes casting a rich diffuse glow upon Golden Gopher marching relics past and nearly present. The freshly painted cinderblock walls benefitted from the glister, as did the framed posters celebrating Minnesota marching bands of yore. Caper noted with approving surprise that none of the fluorescent tubes misbehaved, casting staticky, flickering light upon the meticulously arranged items. Walking down this corridor, one was pleasantly reminded that in some places the past still received due reverence, its icons attended to with hushed and reverent care.

Shelves upon shelves of band awards stood at attention, or perhaps knelt next to the largest trophy in the case, the latter placed on a conspicuously central pedestal. Marble, metal, and satin were in abundant supply, as were framed photographs of hundreds of Gophers from decades past. "Best Auxiliary" awards lined up sharply beneath a row of "Best Music" medals. "Outstanding Visual" trophies were arrayed in a neat diagonal to balance a knot of smaller "General Effect" cups. Caper half-expected the entire burnished collection to wake up *en masse*, only to launch into an intricately choreographed routine.

As his slow, regular footfalls echoed down the hall, the ghosts of departed Golden Gopher marchers were everywhere in evidence, lovingly realigned once more by a vigilant and deferential Minnesota band custodian, a person doubtless unknown to the outside world, mute and humble caretaker of Golden Gopher marching magnificence. All of the maroon-and-gold uniforms down through the years instantly met with Caper's enthusiastic approval. Spats! Spats! Rhymes with Gatz, don't it? And why shouldn't it? Spats to right of him,/ Spats to left of him,/ Spats very likely in front of him/ Gold and Maroon. The decorative gaiters made most of these musicians appear as if they were marching in the ranks of the AEF, thrilled by the prospect that they would soon be "over there," so please send the word, woncha? Who knows? Maybe they could have serenaded a few fellow Midwestern doughboys, one of them an honest young lad named Nick, the other a St. Olaf dropout, who would eventually make quite a name for himself before the two became West Egg neighbors, and before one would be shot in the back one cooling afternoon. In any case, the Gophers would make a gorgeous show in the Argonne, wouldn't they? Kaiser Wilhelm's weary troops wouldn't know what hit them. Fresh-faced Minnesota Lutherans recrossing the Atlantic clad in maroon and gold, twirling batons, blowing whistles, banging drums. What the hell were *die Amerikaner* doing to our *männliches Volk*?

Approaching the end of the corridor, Caper observed that "Best Drum" trophies had emerged as the dominant motif in the few remaining rectangular cases still lining both sides of the hall. Extra-large double doors marked the entrance to a farther room, by all indications an important one. Two students, one slim and one not, sat in metal folding chairs on either side of the two doors. Between them, they held four or five recorders in their hands, trading them back and forth, chuckling, happily inspecting the simple old instruments, exchanging amused remarks. As he walked closer to the guardians of the "Band Room" (as the bronze letters mounted to the wall above the double doors announced), even the pathetically unmusical Caper had a glimmer of recognition, an instant re-connection to the late-60's Tonette that had been firmly slapped into his tender second-grade palm by Sister Miriam Joseph. The black, bakelite baton was an offer he couldn't refuse, not without grievous consequences.

Neither of the two recorder-appreciators had looked up once to acknowledge the visitor slowly but steadily approaching them. When Caper had come within fifteen feet, the slim one arose from his chair and walked straight at the interloper, whose non-marching bearing would have been clear enough to any Gopher initiate even without the weakened posture his injured back had bestowed upon him, with or without cane assistance. One of the recorders continued to hold Slim's complete attention, it would appear, even though his path suggested a conscious determination to intercept the newcomer. The teacher, as a matter of fact, came to an awkward halt, fearing that the kid was going to walk straight into him, a collision he dearly wished to avoid. As if on cue, the student also abruptly checked his own advance, looking up inquisitively in Caper's direction. His get-up was standard-issue frat-boy, from sandled toe to madras shorts to backwards baseball cap. Around his neck was a sort of wooden kontiki choker, while each wrist and one ankle sported several rings of leather string that looked like truncated boot laces. A red, white, and blue tatt on his left shoulder served notice to the world that he was a true disciple of the Grateful Dead.

"How can I help you?"

"I'm trying to find out a few things about a former student of mine," Caper managed to answer calmly, still flustered by the collision that nearly happened. "He's a member of the marching band."

"Wonderful. Who is your former student?"

"Kempf. Peter Kempf. He plays drums." Caper paused a few moments to let the information sink in. "Loudly."

The thinner warden of the "Band Room" nodded stoically, now looking for the first time directly at Caper. "Kempf?"

"Yeah," Caper confirmed. "Kempf."

"He dropped." He placed the ivory-colored instrument he was holding into his mouth and blew, though he managed to produce little in the way of musical pleasure. He then rotated about without moving his feet, attempting to catch the attention of the huskier student. The latter, who was occupying himself by taking apart and putting back together again a few of the recorders, did not take note of the signal, whatever it was meant to be.

Caper's head jerked to the right, his eyes shrinking. "Dropped what?"

"Dropped out. Gone. Not here anymore. He and his crew have gone elsewhere." Slim swivelled again, this time to see that not-Slim was paying careful attention. The recorders were no longer the recipients of bemused attention.

Caper's chin jerked back. "His *crew?*"

The stouter, still-seated doorkeeper chimed in sternly, not bothering to look at Caper. "We've got a new drumline. All new. Cleaned house." He spun one of the recorders between his index fingers counter-clockwise, then back. "Taking things in a new direction."

Caper nodded appreciatively. "Know which direction," he asked, "Kempf took?"

"He's not here anymore," the seated student said flatly.

"No," the thinner standing man answered, tardily. "He's not here anymore," redundantly.

"I see." Caper stared at the double doors and at the large letters on the wall. "Any chance I could look around?

* * *

Ricky and Caper stood outside Alberi's Steakhouse awaiting the valet's retrieval of the Dino and Crown Vic, respectively. Softly scuffing the toe of his left shoe against one of the worn cobblestones of the bluff, Caper studied the brightly lit flat-top of the Eads Bridge, thin, dark, masonic scallops forming classical arcades above the riverbanks, three tireless steel spans supporting the deck above the legendary stream. The St. Louis Bridge Company, together with Carnegie's Keystone, had erected the steel wonder in the mid-1870's. Upon its completion, a circus elephant who just happened to be in the vicinity was invited out for a Sunday afternoon stroll across the river, a request designed to establish two very distinct things—namely, that an elephant, a creature renowned for its finicky reluctance to trust unworthy structures, felt perfectly at ease walking across the unprecedented bridge, the very first to connect the eastern and western edges of the Mississippi; and furthermore, that the unprecedented bridge, first to connect the eastern and western edges of the Mississippi, could support a fucking elephant. If only, Caper reflected, the entire engineering carnival had taken place just over a hundred miles upriver, in or around a town named Hannibal, the universe would have been for a brief moment in perfect tune. But even without this highly desirable coalescence, the only slightly less poetic reality majestically straddling the Mississippi right down there would hardly condone any extended period of complaint. It was beautiful. As it turned out, the elephantine guinea-pig walked all the way from Missouri to Illinois that summer afternoon, certainly the first of his species—and almost certainly the last—to accomplish such an astonishing feat.

Cool.

"That's the first bridge 'cross the river," Caper remarked, admiration evident in his tone. "Beautiful." Ricky's silence in the wake of this assessment might well have been taken as a mark of tacit agreement, were it not for the distracted cast of the young man's eyes. "Guess," Caper continued, his bland observation still encountering no opposition, "Mussolini's dragging down his allies once again." As he spoke, the Dino's front end purred leisurely into view, rolling to a stop at the street edge of the alley forming the western boundary of the restaurant. "But in a distinctly different fashion this time."

Ricky, whose eyes had lit up instantly upon the reappearance of his *fortissimo* yellow sled, now shifted his gaze quickly back to Caper, who was for one reason or another contemplating the word "fiat."

"What?"

"Nothing. I'm just trying to make a little bit of sense of things I don't fully understand."

Ricky looked back beseechingly to the vintage Fiat, whose temp driver was reluctantly stepping out onto the sidewalk, gaping over his left shoulder at an auto interior whose like he had never seen, and likely never would again. "I'm dragging them down, I guess," Ricky repeated. Then he turned back to look directly into Caper's eyes. "But so are you," he asserted with calm certainty.

"I suppose you're right," Caper agreed. "*If* I go up there."

"You're going," Ricky tartly retorted. "You'll see for yourself. You know you will. You need to hear about Peter's alteration, directly from the mouths of his bandmates. How he went from Band to Bad."

"Do I?"

"Yes," he continued boldly. "You do. In fact," Ricky's momentum slowed as he noted that the valet was standing in wait for him, holding the door and awaiting a tip. He reached into his right pocket and walked towards the car, motioning for Caper to follow. "In fact," he started again, when the latter interrupted him.

"I'll pick up the parking tab, signor. It's the least little thing I could do to pay you back for the Fitzgerald tour."

Ricky started to protest, then smiled. He slid into the Dino, waved his hand out the open window, and drove west very slowly over the punishing cobblestones.

*   *   *

Entering the practice room, one couldn't help but feel puny in the carpeted cavern. Maroon and gold were welded everywhere—floor, wall, even ceiling. It was a veritable Elysium, a radiant isle of Golden Gopher glee, absent splendid fields upon which worthy souls luxuriated in blessèd ease.

Caper gazed about in all directions, spinning slowly on the one leg he still possessed not wilted by L3/L4 insurgency, before turning his attention back to Slim, his nervous companion. He knitted his forehead, squinted his eyes softly, and cocked his head. "How many square f—"

"Forty-five thousand," Slim cut off Caper's inquiry. "At least. And that's not counting the property room."

"Okay," Caper nodded. "I see." The wispy manager blushed, embarrassed, perhaps, by his too-ready answer. "Where's the...?" He started over. "What's the 'property room'?"

"Nothing," the property manager uncomfortably replied. "I mean, it's a room. Nothing much to speak of. We keep the instruments there. And other useful stuff. It's secure."

"I get it." Caper strove to indicate he got the big picture—no big deal, I get where you're coming from, no worries—even as he knew that he had to have a look at the room where they kept "useful stuff."

At the far end of the largest of the rehearsal rooms, two velour drapes—one maroon, one gold—hung from an impressively high batten, also gold in color, the fabric so heavy as to seem to threaten the load-bearing capacity of the overhead pipe. The curtains met neatly at most points along the drop, though here and there a dark gap teasingly promised to render some of the dim background visible. The faintly lit ceiling behind the batten, extending far beyond what looked like a chain-link barrier erected ten yards or so behind the curtains, was enough to confirm that there was a room behind the maroon and gold draperies at least as large as the one Caper now stood in. His guide's skittishness was still very much in evidence.

Caper coolly pointed the tip of his cane at Slim's tattoo. "Deadhead, eh?"

With a sudden shift to deliberate and slow emphasis, Slim proudly nodded his affirmation. "Most *def*initely." Caper's crafty calming strategy appeared to be working.

"How many concerts?"

Slim's gaze fell to the maroon carpet.

"Sorry," Caper corrected himself. "I'm sorry. I never really thought about that. You were born—what?—'94 or so?"

"'93."

"Last Dead show couldn't have been later than—"

"July ninth." Slim twisted his decorated arm across his midsection, the better to see the gleaming bulbous cranium inked onto his shoulder. "Nineteen ninety-five."

"San Francisco?" The left side of the teacher's mouth tilted up knowingly. Slim wouldn't be freely handed the satisfaction of presuming that Caper knew nothing at all about Jerry and the boys.

"Chicago."

Undeterred, Caper absorbed the sanctified date and place. "Huh," he commiserated. "The Dead gods didn't give you much of a chance to…" His voice trailed off. "What's happening back there?" He now pointed and twirled his cane in the general direction of the gold and maroon curtains. "Hangar for the Golden Gopher G550's?" *Repetition accompl—*

Slim laughed, a little. "More space. Nothing much to see. Storage. Practice areas."

"Mind if I…?" Caper once again twirled the end of his cane, in pantomime inquiry.

"Yes, well, I'm afraid that we—"

"No. No. Not at all. Help yourself." The gruff rejoinder, uttered emphatically from behind by the far meatier of the two band room guardians, caught both Caper and Slim off-guard.

After a short pause, the teacher asked for a clarification. "You don't mind if I check out the property room?"

"No. Not at all. Knock yourself out."

Caper walked as steadily as he could toward the curtain seam, the Deadhead complying with the abrupt sanction given by his fellow guardian. He seemed a great deal more relaxed.

Reaching the opening between the two curtains, Caper used the rubber end of his cane to pry open the burgundy half, Slim doing the same to the gold fabric with his inked arm.

The first thing he noted was that the jumbo curtains were backed by another, more substantial barrier, a ceiling-to-floor chain-link scroll, padlocked at three points along the gleaming concrete floor. No maroon-and-gold cut pile in here. All business.

"Don't worry," Slim said to the not-worried Caper. "I've got keys."

"That's some property room you've got there."

"Yeah. Definitely. Might be the biggest in the Big Ten. My name's Russ. Russ Urberger."

Caught napping by this abrupt introduction, Caper still managed to reply, "Once had a student named Urberger." He paused. "If your last names are to be believed, both of you would be the earliest bergers, wouldn't you? The most primitive bergers." He paused again. "Wait. You can't both be that." He seemed mildly dismayed.

"What?"

"Nothing. My name's Mort Caper. Drove up here from St. Louis."

"*No* way! *I'm* from St. Louis." He fumbled with the keys. "Wait a minute. So was Pe..." The old, uneasy Russ made a quick comeback. "There was another guy up here from St. Louis looking for Peter a while ago." Russ' eyes swept in a slow arc across the high ceiling, evidently in an attempt to retrieve a name. "Robby or Willy or something like that. About our age. Big guy with a beard." Caper nodded politely. "Said he was a friend of his. Also played in a marching band somewhere."

"Yeah, well, I taught Peter for a couple years back in high school. Very good student. I'm really sorry to hear that he dropped out."

Russ softly echoed the final two words even as Caper spoke them. Then he added two hoarsely-whispered syllables: "Lindbergh."

Caper's measured nod confirmed the accuracy of slim Russ' high school recollection. He pivoted back to the padlocks on the floor, his gaze suggesting that perhaps they should continue into the property room. Slim took the hint.

With the metal scroll lifted just high enough for the two to enter, Caper could begin to roam through the neatly furnished chamber in the depths of which Band Peter had morphed into Bad Peter. The whole thing looked like a band equipment room ought to look, he supposed, though he had never before seen one. The ceiling had to be at least three stories from the polished concrete floor, whose gleaming expanse would have soothed the anxieties of even the most callow big-rig driver, an easy, unembarrassed turnabout guaranteed. The instruments themselves were tightly banded together into a neat, rough circle, defensive in appearance, and dominating the middle of the cool cavern. Big brass horns were carefully arranged in close proximity to smaller brass horns, and then still smaller ones. All of the winds had been similarly stationed and broken down into discrete, clearly identifiable groupings. It was like a strangely permanent and air-conditioned bivouac, each instrument leaning on others of its own rank, sleeping vigilantly through the night for the next practice. The general effect suggested a tightly knit Chain of Marching, every last Sousaphone in its allotted place. If this was the location where Peter unleashed his appetite for gonzo tub-tapping, you'd never know it from the props in the property room. The place was impressively policed-up, ready for duty.

In the center of all the instruments, standing on a rectangular stage elevated no more than six inches above the concrete floor, a life-size black-and-white cut-out of two unidentified Gopher marchers stood at permanent attention, Janus-style. It appeared to serve as a kind of all-seeing hub for the whole layout, holding all of the musical and marching elements together in harmony. Caper's gaze dropped to the two-tone shoes of the pictured marchers.

"Spat Camp," Russ said, noting Caper's attention to the freestanding photo. "Last summer."

"I'm sorry. What did you say?"

"Spat Camp. We have it every year."

"Cool name. 'Spat Camp'. Really cool. I like spats. Lament their demise, to be honest." Caper took a closer look. "But those uniforms look awfully warm. Weighty wool. Itchy." He gently shook his left (and far weaker) ankle as an act of empathy for the leg beneath the woolly pants, leaning heavily on his one strong gam.

"Old school. They *are* itchy, believe me. But we don't compromise. Same uniforms as they wore a hundred years ago."

Caper indicated that he approved. "But where are the drums? Percussion stuff. 'Snares,' I think. Also 'tenors' and 'bass' and—"

"Peter was a tenor."

"Was he?"

Russ looked off to one side. And to the other.

"Yes." Once again, nervous Russ Urberger returned, and once again, his thicker companion (who had somehow been monitoring the conversation from a discreet distance) intervened.

"Yes, Peter was a tenor drummer," the chunky man bellowed in an unshakable, stentorian voice. "He dressed a line as effectively as any drummer we've ever had. We always had him on the edge. His peripheral vision was phenomenal. No one was better."

"I'll bet," Caper concurred. His complete ignorance of marching band lingo might well turn out to be an effective weapon, he calculated, so long as he agreed with everything everyone else said. "I don't doubt that he came down hard on any slackers. On the line, I mean."

"You're quite right, Mr....?"

"Caper. Mort Caper." The teacher continued to cast about for any evidence of percussion equipment. "So where do the drummers arrange their equipment?"

For the first time, even the larger prop-room guardian betrayed signs of hesitance. He kept his gaze steadily upon the cane-toting intruder who had driven up—for reasons still unknown—from a long way down river. "We keep them in good order. Everything's in shipshape."

Caper's gaze was equally steady. "I can see that. Place is immaculate. Any chance I could borrow a few of these wizards of tidiness to come down to my classroom? Everything's tight as..." He spun about on his right heel, persistent in his questioning. "But where are the drums?"

No response was forthcoming from not-Russ. But the thinner man shot his eyes apprehensively to a spot to the right and just about a story above where Caper and the band duo were standing. The teacher followed the high-speed glance, to a prefab steel stairway climbing at a steep angle against one of the room's walls. A short catwalk at the top of the stairs led directly to a doorway, maroon in color, and illuminated by a single bulb, the latter housed in a protective wire cage.

"Up there?" Caper received no response from either party. "Can I have a look?"

Russ stared at the plumper property room manager. The latter stared at the elevated door. After a short, silent stretch, he seemed to relax. "Okay. Let's *all* go have a look."

Third in line as they walked up the metal stairs, Caper was a bit surprised when his property room guides leaned back against the wall after the maroon door had been unlocked and pushed slightly ajar, as if they wished to let him pass and enter first into the discreetly elevated inner sanctum of the prop room. "You first," the larger one said. Without entering, he slid his left hand inside and hit the lights, now looking directly at Caper. "You first," he repeated to the visitor, his eyes then shifting to Russ, as if to remind the latter that the visitor must have an unprejudiced view of the room's contents.

"Okay," Caper answered uneasily. He stepped cautiously against the rail and then above the Golden Gopher acolytes, his cane not particularly adapted to the open-air tread-work of the stairs. At the top, the sharp metal door edge remained just a few inches or so from the jamb. With the help of the steadily applied pressure of his own left hand, Caper began to take in an increasing swath of the room, which appeared to be unfurnished and, for that matter, drum-free. Only when the door had nearly completed its full 180^0 arc did he begin to distinguish the heap of amber-tinged, creamy-white material, an imposing pyramid piled densely against the far left wall.

Not saying anything nor turning about for any sort of explanation, he stood stationary in the doorway. If either of his two companions wished to provide any sort of commentary, he would allow it. Otherwise, Caper would try to make sense of the room's contents as best he could.

"What do you think?" asked not-Russ after an appreciable pause.

Caper didn't answer punctually, his eyes now attracted by a lone drum placed on the floor, at the epicenter of the pyramid, and very nearly touching it. Something propped beneath the drum kept it at a 45^0 angle, the better, it would appear, to appreciate its significance, whatever that turned out to be. From somewhere above, a lone, dim spotlight shone its light on the conspicuously foregrounded object. "What's that?" he finally asked not-Russ in response, pointing to the entire arrangement with his cane.

"Tenor drum," he replied rapidly and more specifically.

The teacher nodded his head uncertainly. "Tenor drum?"

"Yes." Caper remained motionless. "It's never been played." This latter assertion was uttered with conviction.

Caper's eyes slowly climbed once again up the pyramid of carefully piled but also unmistakably frayed objects. They had the look of tobacco-stained parchments, roughly circular in shape; most appeared to have been torn violently near the center, featuring telltale lesions one usually associates with exit wounds.

"Are those"—Caper paused, searching his threadbare musical lexicon for the right word—"'skins'?"

"Drum heads, actually. No one in band refers to any part of a drum as a 'skin.' That's civilian talk. Not band."

"I see." Caper communicated his gratitude for the band-vocab pointer. But before he moved on to the obvious next question ("Exactly who is the daring and brilliant artist responsible for this intriguing contemporary installation?"), he thought it wise to gratify not-Russ' musical acumen with another harmless drum inquiry. "So those are made out of...?"

"Polymer." Not-Russ was clearly eager to elaborate. "Polymer. 'Course, back in the day, they'd've been animal skins of one form or another. Hides. Goat-skin. Whatever. Not much anymore, though. Almost always polymer."

"Got it. Must be a big improvement. Lots more 'pop' when the drumsticks hit—"

"Exactly."

"What," Caper wished to specify once again, "kind of drum did Peter play?"

"Tenor."

Caper's gaze remained steady on the lone undefiled tenor drum. "That his?"

"No. Most definitely not. Peter Kempf has had nothing to do with *that* drum." Not-Russ was adamant. Caper had turned to catch the latter's facial expression, only to see that he, too, was staring fixedly at the haloed tenor drum.

"Got it," Caper repeated. "What, then," he asked, "is it?"

"Reminder." Not-Russ spoke this word softly and slowly, and now seemed to be looking not so much at the spotlit drum as through it.

"A reminder?"

"Yes. A pointed reminder. Of..."

"Earlier times," Caper completed the thought. "Simpler times. Times when skins"—he shot a quick look back at the immaculate drum reverently displayed at the base of the grisly pyramid—"sorry, when drum heads weren't ruptured by muscle-bound interlopers who had no regard for the drumming traditi—"

"Who," not-Russ interjected, "have no idea what *real* marching band commitment means. Who see it as nothing more than a step to something else. Who corrupt nearly everyone else in..." Not-Russ' passion ebbed as quickly as it had flamed, perhaps a sign that he had voiced his indignation a few too many times.

"*Who*," Russ now stepped in a bit gingerly, "are no longer here"—he paused in order to stare pointedly at Caper, evidently to ensure that the teacher absorbed this basic fact—"and no longer have any effect *at all* on our band." He darted a meaningful glance at not-Russ, his right index finger pressed over both the ring finger and the pinkie of his left hand, bending them back.

"On that note," Caper responded, not taking his eyes off the massive heap of diabolically breached drum heads, its meticulous arrangement only heightening its barbarous effect, "are you *sure* you don't know where Peter went when he left this hallowed campus?"

"No," the duo responded in something close to perfect unison. "He's got a friend who's a pilot," Russ added. "He can fly jets. Or he's learning to, or something like that." Not-Russ grinned at the Deadhead. He grinned the sort of grin some people grin when circumstances prevent them from saying aloud, "Shut your fucking mouth, asshole." Russ, alas, proved to be an ineffectual interpreter of grins. "Soon, Peter says, he and the pilot'll be in a good position to 'penetrate new markets.'" No question about it. This little scrap of business lingo tickled Russ.

"Know where?"

"Probably some sort of aviation school," Russ continued. "How would I know?"

"No. I mean the 'new markets.' Where might they...?"

"California." Not-Russ could hold off no longer. "They're definitely heading out to the coast. We don't know many more specifics." He glared at Russ. "We're washed of him and his whole line. Every one of them. That's the main thing. But Peter—"

"Is that what this sanctuary is about? To stay washed of him?"

Neither answered Caper's inquiry.

"Near the end," not-Russ picked up a thread of a conversation Caper hadn't previously been cognizant of, "Peter talked a lot about high school transcripts and transfer credits and which California colleges offered the best deals." All at once, the teacher rocketed straight back to a sunbesotted Lindbergh hallway, but remained resolutely silent. "Always going on about San Francisco and LA."

Transcripts. Guidance. Pulverizing handshake.

"A lot of schools out there," Caper mumbled lifelessly.

Law school. Stanford.

"A lot o' marching bands out there," not-Russ corrected, firmly. "LA alone's a turkey shoot."

City, Caper silently recited, *of pumped-up Angels. Drum-puncturing Dominions.*

"New markets," he repeated, though he wouldn't have been able to pinpoint the source of the phrase. His thoughts shot north.

'World's Largest Rock and Roll Band'?

Stanford, you have no idea.

Caper smiled confidentially. *Go right ahead, Cal Berkeley. Try that desperate last-second gimmicky kickoff return one more time. Make my day. Let's see who's standing at the final gun. And who's laid out on the California turf, looking up woozily through his helmet's ear hole at the Stanford thumper bangin' time on the tenor drum head.*

* * *

Caper eased down the core passage more slowly than he had once customarily done, the tenderness in his lower back and left leg enforcing a gait that wouldn't have vexed any of the overfed presidents who promenaded along the boulevards of the Gilded Age, the ones whose names he could never keep straight. Lessons were underway to left and to right of him, behind closed classroom doors. None of what he heard was clear or readily recognizable. No oft-celebrated phrase drifted into the dim air-conditioned tunnel; no clever banter brought to life a centuries-old star-crossed romance, doubly doomed by an even older centuries-old feud. Voices reached him all right, but only as barely recognizable, faceless rhythms, muted by dirty blonde-oak doors. On the other side of those doorways, those same voices surely carried some kind of meaning to the young people required to be there—bored young people, grade-savvy young people, or genuinely interested young people—but not to the teacher just back from Minnesota, treading slowly, cane held gingerly at its midpoint, not once touching the dully gleaming waxed tile. He placed Fitzgerald's *Ledger* back on top of one of his smaller piles of books, an apex from which it would soon begin its ineluctable descent.

Lunch tables had been cleaned and wiped and made ready for the next day's meal, but they bore no cakes, nor the remnants of cakes.

At the end of the passage, Caper turned softly left, leaning in to the entrance to Van Der Meyer's classroom. He placed his left ear to the door, hoping to discern what might or might not be underway on the other side. More voices, probably trading ideas about Macbeth (if, in fact, Caper remembered the tenth-grade reading schedule correctly) or King Duncan, or Banquo's ghost, rudely interrupting a banquet to which he hadn't been invited. Some laughter followed, then louder laughter, and then louder, and then, finally, trailing laughter. Maybe they were talking about the Porter doing his business right after the murder. Would strike a chord with the sophomoric crowd, wouldn't it?

Caper looked at his upturned wrist. Sixth hour would begin in only a few minutes.

He pressed against the belligerent door as stiffly as he dared with his shoulder, creating a two- or three-inch gap. *No reason whatsoever,* he reflected, *to worry about my defective memory.* It's in perfectly defective working order. Van Der Meyer & Co. weren't anywhere close to a Scottish-play discussion. Instead, a French-Algerian homicide was the focus of the day's lesson, a killing unencumbered by ghost or hag or roving woods. The laughter Caper had heard may have been in response to…he couldn't really guess what it may have been in response to. But then he had absolutely no idea what the tenth-graders were talking about a few moments before. Van Der Meyer might well have been getting off some uproarious stuff. Take the grins whenever you can. Ask questions later.

From his door-screened position, he couldn't quite make out the three-word phrase Van Der Meyer had scribbled in red caps high up on one of the whiteboards, now hovering steadily above the heads of heedful tenth-graders. No other words were in the vicinity. Somewhere to his left, unseen by Caper, Van Der Meyer was bringing to a close a discussion of the difference between active and passive voices. "The—"

Callously cutting in, the bell signaled that fifth hour was officially toast. Van Der Meyer would have to repeat this little morsel of rhetorical instruction at some later date.

After a few moments, Caper pressed against the door, the crowd of sophomores steadily diminishing as more of the classroom came into view. He walked directly over to Van Der Meyer's chair and, with a quick calculation that his own creaking condition granted him a due share of the deference owed to age, lowered himself into the younger man's chair.

The inevitable squeak immediately attracted Van Der Meyer's notice. Caper placed his cane horizontally atop the chair's arms, rolling it close to his stomach, as if in preparation for an impending rollercoaster ride.

"How was it," Van Der Meyer asked, pointing his remote at the projector, "up in the Twin Cities?" The beach passage from *The Stranger* faded to white.

"Quite a bit colder than Algiers, if you can believe it." He feigned a shiver. "Who knew?"

Van Der Meyer's expression indicated that he, too, would never have guessed at the stark temperature disparity between the two locales. "I'll keep that in mind should I ever have occasion to travel up there." He tossed a measured glimpse at the blank board. "And how 'bout those marching Gophers?"

"They're okay, I suppose. Turns out there's been a bit of a Stalinist purge of late. Comrade Kempf's being airbrushed out of the official Gopher history even as we speak. Things are headed in a 'new direction,' per the party line."

"Learn anything about the old direction?"

"I think so. I was granted an audience, you might say, with an imposing display of the collateral damage unleashed by the percussion renegades."

"Sorry I missed it."

"You oughta be. You'd've especially appreciated the potent mixture of the sacristy"—Caper paused to designate precisely the other element of the combination—"and the mausoleum. Percussion casualties piled just as high as Cheops would have arranged them. The entire heap, meanwhile, forming a formidable backdrop to—"

"An immaculately gleaming drum."

Caper beamed, the proud teacher. "Well done. I told you you'd have appreciated the mise en scène. Right up your street. And don't worry, my young friend. From here on out, Gopher drumlines will be dressed with due muscular modesty."

"Wouldn't expect anything less." His chair commandeered by the older man, Van Der Meyer had no alternative but to place the heels of both palms against the edge of the table nearest Caper, and to press himself up and back onto its surface. "And the Fitzgerald tour?"

"Most tragic part of the whole trip." Caper paused to collect himself. "I drove out to the Commodore Hotel, ready and willing to be guided through something—*any*thing—on the morning after the drum head exposition. Had my trusty *Ledger* safely in tow. All I wanted was for a cheerful and knowledgeable St. Paulean to assist me in my own private catharsis, to point out where the young novelist wrote *This Side of Paradise*, and where he first uttered the word 'up.' That's not so much to ask, is it?"

"And?"

"Fate had other ideas. My little cleansing operation was not to be."

"What other ideas?"

"Uncooperative taxi ideas."

"What?"

Caper shook his head painfully. "What's more, it was a Yellow cab. I'm not making this up." He took his right hand from the cane and struck it softly upon his heart.

"You were hit by a taxicab?"

"No." Caper shivered again, this time not shamming. His left hand tightened on the walking aid. "But our guide was."

Uneasy, Van Der Meyer awaited.

"She's gonna be okay; don't worry. The ambulance crew said as much right on the spot. Seems that the taxi in question had just made its way into the city from the airport. Driver zips up to the main entrance of the hotel just as our tour guide steps backward off the curb, ready to introduce herself to the ten or twelve of us gathered for a Fitzgerald fix." Van Der Meyer shook his head. "Said something like, 'Welcome to the Fit' when—Thump!—she's clipped in the calf by the careless cabbie."

Both teachers appeared to be absorbed in sober reflection.

"What happened after that?"

"Well, no Fitz tour, for starters. A little bit of blood on the back of the guide's pants. Ambulance. Cops. Porters yelling at one another. The cabbie was inconsolable. Through it all, the victim appeared to be utterly calm. She kept telling the driver not to worry about it. She'd be just fine in no time. Meanwhile, the guy just in from the airport asks to have the trunk popped, grabs his ritzy suitcases, and walks right into the lobby. He seemed to be a little miffed that none of the porters were paying him any attention."

"That was it?"

"Yep. I figured this was one of those rare times I ought to take an event as a sign of something else."

Van Der Meyer calmly absorbed the news. "What might that something be?"

"Not something in harmony with my desires, that's for sure. But more than that, I don't know. And I don't see the sense in trying to."

"So you came back."

"I came back down."

"No tour."

"Right."

"No regrets."

"None. I travelled to a place new to me, and I saw something I hadn't yet seen. I want to repeat that part of it. But I think I'll let the drum heads rest in peace for a while."

* * *

In the midst of a lively classroom appreciation of Bozo the screever, George Orwell's irrepressible London pavement artist, Caper's fifth-hour class was interrupted by an intercom message from one of the grade-level offices. Could he please call extension 934? Someone was on the line, someone who needed to speak to Dr. Caper quite urgently.

He complied with the unusual request, taking care to step out into the hallway, the better to shield the susceptible ears of his youthful pupils. Bringing his classroom door to rest against the stretched cord of his wall phone, Caper waited to be connected to the impatient caller.

"Dr. C?" the bearded voice resumed.

"Yes, Ricky."

"It's Ricky. You need to get out"—a noticeable catch in Ricky's throat— "to the Spirit of St. Louis"—prolonged pause, replete with more throat-catches—"Airport." Somehow, Ricky had managed to shepherd the distraught utterance all the way to its destination. It just took a while. "Right away."

"The band has its own airport?" *Cool.*

"No," Ricky impatiently responded. Another conspicuous pause. Caper speculated that this time Ricky may have been thinking, *That would be really cool.* "No. The County airport. It's in West County. They're about to take off."

"Still working, Ricky. It's fifth hour. In a few minutes I'm going to break for lunch. Gotta be on campus for another three hours. Plus—"

"They're taking off. I just found out."

"They who?"

"They Max and Peter. They're gonna get away with it."

"Who cares if they're taking off? Isn't that a good thing? And who cares if they get away with it?" Caper peeped back through the door's wire glass rectangle at his students, whose thumbs and fingers worked with frenzied agility upon the surfaces of a multitude of devices, some of which appeared to be custom-skinned. Only moments before, they had been discussing the enduring creativity of down and out scullions and tramps in Paris and London. In a flash, they had all mutated into suburban teenage iPhone zombies. After a short pause: "Exactly where," he asked, a note of complacency in his tone, "do you think they might be taking off"—his pinkie nail scratched his upper lip—"to?"

Ricky's voice sounded as if it had been completely drained of all vitality. "Tournament of Roses."

A weak blip sounded on Caper's *non sequitur* radar. But wait a sec. Maybe Ricky was offering a valid, if also unnecessarily cryptic, response. "Are you saying that they're headed to Pasadena?"

"No. I'm saying that the LHS band—the Spirit of St. Louis Marching Band—marched in the Rose Bowl parade. Twice in seven years. I was in the second band. Max was our leader, and Peter..." Ricky's exhausted voice couldn't finish the sentence.

"And now," Caper took up the baton, "they're flying back out there in their own private jet, purchased with steroid simoleons. And they're flying from the Spirit of St. Lou...Ricky, I'm telling you. They're stony-hearted hooligans."

No response from Ricky. Caper looked once again at his students, their greedy digits pecking and sliding, torsos flapped acutely forward over flat desk surfaces. In about thirty-five years, they would come to regret this posture.

Ricky rejoined the conversation. "They're going to San Francisco. And Los Angeles. I don't know in what order."

"A couple of tough-yet-noble detectives come to mind."

"Good for you," Ricky replied. "But two universities are in their sights." Something like vibrancy, probably born of indignation, had returned to his voice.

"Stanford," Caper said with assurance. "And Southern Cal, like enough. It'd be just the spot for Peter to set up shop as the LA regional sales manager."

"You're batting five hundred, Dr. C. Peter's gunnin' for UCLA."

Caper mulled.

"Dr. C?"

"Yeah."

"Anything wrong?"

"No. I'm just mulling. I'm thinking Max must have a thing for bears."

Completely ignoring the teacher's mascot speculation, Ricky returned to his urgent theme. "Gotta get out to the airport. Now. At least let 'em see that you tried to talk 'em out of it."

"Why? Do you think for a second that I'm gonna be able to stop them?"

Ricky hesitated. "No. Probably not. But it might haunt 'em, all their days out on the coast. And that's enough."

Caper nodded, looking back through the wire glass pane, not seeing anything this time. "Okay, Ricky. Okay. I'll put in an airport appearance. Pronto. And I'll do my best to plague their memories."

Later, he couldn't remember if he placed the receiver back on the hook inside the classroom. His eyes never straying from the core door, he managed to shift through his seated students, on the lookout for Van Der Meyer. Need a sub, stat.

* * *

Caper sped west on 40, through sprawling regions he rarely had cause to visit. "Chesterfield" and "Des Peres" were recognizable enough, as far as place names go, but held nothing in the way of association or experience. At the moment, they were nothing more than surface impediments, unfamiliar townships to be driven through as quickly as possible if he were to have any chance of intercepting Max and Peter before they took to the skies. Lucky Lindy himself could scarcely have condoned this wayward western flight, two young prospectors (Lindbergh Flyer alums, no less!) rushing to mine Golden State gridirons, to amass new fortunes built on booming, bruising halftime shows. Lindbergh, in sharp contrast (underwritten by a coterie of St. Louis money men), had been the first ever to cross the pond in a single go, equipped with a few sandwiches and probably too much fuel. The international community hailed the achievement. Max and Peter, in every sense, were headed in the opposite direction.

From the west, uneven, gusting downpours blew in at sharply raked angles, hammering the car's windshield like bursts of unwelcome applause. But every so often the roaring, blinding sheets gave way to relative calm, clear enough at least to see the low, mustard-gray clouds that surrounded him on every side. Intermittently, too, Jim Croce's cautionary voice managed to break through the buffeting, in those respites when the wipers weren't obliged to slap frantically port and starboard.

...stronger than a country hoss
And when the bad folks all get together at night
You know...

Crouching, the Spirit of St. Louis Airport was out there somewhere in front of him. Would it be the setting for a last-minute grounding? Or would it serve instead as the final midwestern launching point for a new growth industry out West? Bears and bespatted Golden Gophers unceremoniously thrown over for glitzy West Coast Bruins and non-St. Louis Cardinals? If so, the result would be no different: larger, louder percussion sections, courtesy of Peter's patented *Testost-O-Lozenges*, or whatever it was that those pills were bearding for.

He drivin' a drop-top Cadillac...

The rain began to ebb, incoming bursts reduced to impetuous showers, the gaps between each wave longer and more regular. On either side, glistening, storm-beaded structures formed an unbroken procession: hospital buildings; taupe churches boasting ample parking; more hospital buildings; unmarked corporate offices, clad in glossy, gunmetal glass; more large churches; private high schools that had orbited out from the city or from one of the inner suburbs; outlet malls; four-story offices capped with curious blazons ('Prolaxiance,' maybe, or 'Synzaleve'); acres and acres and acres of glowing, weedless sod, businesslike diamond patterns testifying to the diligent application of wide-deck mowers.

And everybody say, "Jack, don't you know..."

Gradually, the procession began to thin out, as did the slate-gray sound berms that stood like towering curbs, and very soon a smattering of road signs promised that he would arrive at the "General Aviation" airport in a matter of minutes. Caper's attention immediately turned to the next hurdle, one that could prove to be decisive. Exactly what did security look like at one of these places? Would even a short delay prevent the last-ditch rendezvous?

You don't pull the mask off the old Lone Ranger
And you don't mess around with Slim...

Once upon a time, the airport road heading south off the exit must have provided a smooth, comforting final approach to the busy regional air hub. But those days were long past. Although most of the clouds had lifted, the squeaky Vicky's springs now had to deal with aging concrete highway slabs, whose tined grooves had been worn threadbare, and whose achy joints were admirably suited to the task of rattling a car chassis, particularly one in its dotage. Scanning the bare, level landscape for some sort of ready parking (located, he hoped, smack next to the airport's main terminal), the persistent ka-thudding rhythm provided by surface gaps failed to soothe Caper's nerves. Worse yet, as he drove ever closer to the airfield, and at the very moment when the shrill whining of spoiled jets had just begun to drown out the road beating time on his ride, Caper perceived a problem he hadn't anticipated. Which one of the four or five medium-sized buildings coming into view was the main terminal? *Was* there a main terminal?

Suspiciously, parking was a breeze. No ticket; no gate; not even a meter to relieve you of a stray quarter. Towing trap? Caper didn't have time to dwell on these unpleasant possibilities. Standing on the puddled parking blacktop, he saw a St. Louis County Police SUV driving his way, slowly. On the side, "Spirit Airport" had been added to the usual decals and markings. Place's got its very own cop detail. *Nice.* Caper anxiously thought about security again. Why not wave down the officer for just a little bit of Spirit guidance? He spun as fast as he dared.

Too late. The lawman had passed him, and appeared to have been absorbed in an amusing radio conversation in any case. Caper turned around again and made a quick assessment of the nearby buildings. He chose the largest, marked "TAC Air." Advancing toward what looked like the main entrance, he saw further evidence of police presence. At least one helicopter and maybe a small plane as well were done up in the familiar County color scheme. A smaller sign reading *"TAC Unit"* was attached almost as high as the lip of the flat roof.

Caper opened one of two darkly tinted doors and wondered exactly when a uniformed airport official would demand that he produce some type of formal identification, or why don't you just turn around right now, pal? Would the LHS Faculty ID do the trick? Thus far, it didn't look like that that unlikely question would need to be asked. A couple pilots leaned against a floor-to-ceiling water-beaded window, their lax ties and unbuttoned jackets indicating they weren't flying anywhere soon. The few men sitting and slouching and reading in facing rows of terminal seating could only be passengers waiting for upcoming departures. In the back, close to a burnt-orange wall hanging, another cop was laughing, talking to someone Caper couldn't see in some farther room. No Max; no Peter; no security scanners.

To his left, working behind an official-looking counter, Caper saw three men wearing matching white polo shirts, complete with matching red and blue logos. He approached.

"Excuse me," he said, all three looking up at him in unison. Arbitrarily, Caper selected just one to be his talking buddy. "I'm looking for a flight," Caper began, then nimbly reconsidered. "I guess I'm looking for a plane. A Cessna," he added, reckoning that these two syllables just might earn him a little bit of Spirit cred. "Citation II." *Non-botched repetition.*

"What flight?" Evidently, the man Caper had chosen to talk to had also chosen to respond to only the first part of what he had said.

"Not sure, actually." Caper shook his head. "Like I said, these guys're flying a—"

"I got the Cessna part. Know where the aircraft is heading?"

"Los Angeles. San Francisco, too."

"Both?" He glanced meaningfully at the other fellas behind the counter and smiled, amused.

"Far away," Caper responded, his gaze now focused on some point above all three of their heads.

Voice #2 now entered the conversation. "Know which FBO they're using?"

Caper's eyes slowly returned to the present space and time. "What? No. I don't know which…What's an FBO?"

"Fixed-base operator. We've got five of them." He jerked his head to the right, in the direction of yet another TAC Air sign. "We're TAC Air."

"I noticed that as I walked through the…How can I find out which FBO they're using?"

All three heads spun in negative and synchronized disapproval. Voice #2 retained spokesman duties. "This is a General Aviation airport. You're supposed to know where you're going. Where and when other people are scheduled to depart or arrive is none of your business."

Caper absorbed well enough the overall tenor of what #2 was saying, even if he didn't fully grasp all of the weighty intricacies of Spirit of St. Louis etiquette. "Sorry" (pretending to be embarrassed by his own distracted state of mind). "I forgot."

After an indeterminate period during which no one said anything, #3 entered the fray. "What," he asked in an empathetic tone of voice, "d'they look like?"

"Asian kid," Caper replied appreciatively. "And a giant."

"Millionaire." #3 returned fire instantaneously, almost as if he had predicted the teacher's description. "I saw them about fifteen minutes ago. Outside Millionaire."

"Millionaire," Caper repeated, slowly. It was definitely a word he had heard before, and yet it had never served, as far as he could recollect, as a descriptor of a particular location. But he wasn't about to allow this linguistic enigma to prevent him from being relieved to learn that Max and Peter were still on the Spirit premises.

"Yep. About eight minutes from here. I saw both of them on my rounds."

"Where?"

"Millionaire. Both standing beside a Cessna."

Still pondering the precise significance of the m-word in this particular conversation (but also relishing the distinct possibility that something poetic was about to unfold), Caper asked, "Eight minutes which way?"

#3 began to extend his right arm over his shoulder, only to pull it back abruptly. "Follow me. It's the first FBO down the circle road."

"Check," Caper responded, beginning to suspect that the gods of aviation had already begun to fiddle with his vocabulary. Was he on the verge of uttering the word "Roger"? Walking as quickly as he could manage back to the sedan, he took comfort in the fact that he now knew what an "FBO" was, and that one of the "operators" in question bore the name "Millionaire." Now who's a life-long learner, C?

Presently driving south behind #3's "Spirit of St. Louis Personnel" SUV, Caper's sunny soul still had to brook the unsettling possibility that Peter and Max had taken to the air in the intervening minutes. Islands of roving, dense shadows rolled across the level landscape left to right, a stark reminder that the skies remained turbulent. Wind direction, on the other hand, appeared to have shifted dramatically; angry gusts, taking full advantage of the flat, wide airfield, were even stronger than before.

At Bell Avenue, the SUV made a right, and so did Caper. A short distance before them on the left, the "Millionaire" finally made its appearance. But there was a catch: the sign perched atop the structure informed visitors that they had arrived at the Million Air® FBO.

Will you never learn?

Caper had precious little time to devote to such cunning wordplay. He was already conducting a Cessna Citation II search even before he had parked his car, and in spite of the fact that he had no idea what a Cessna Citation II looked like. #3, who had parked ahead of him, was doing the same, and made an open-armed gesture indicating that the aircraft wasn't where it used to be. Both marched towards the main entrance, one faster than the other.

At the lone counter, a Million Air® official of some sort was holding court with three or four pilots. With his chair angled on its back legs, and both feet resting confidently on a well-worn stool, he was the very picture of the *raconteur* in his element. Everyone was already pretty well tickled pink; any second now they promised to be in stitches.

Breaking into the merry parley, #3 continued to assist Caper on his quest. "Hugh, has that Cessna taken off yet?"

Hugh brought himself up short, leaning forward so as to bring his chair back into regulation position. His smile remained etched on his face. "Which?"

"Huge guy and the Asian."

"They're goners."

Caper leapt in. "When goners?" he implored, incoherently.

"Just left. Cleared for takeoff." Hugh tossed his head casually to the right, in the direction of the airport's twin strips, neat concrete ribbons every now and again crossed by "H" bars. He had a killer punchline loaded in the chamber. Would anyone fiercely object if he delivered himself of it at this particular juncture in time—that is, if it wouldn't be too much trouble? In just this state of mind, or something quite like it, he turned his attention back to the flyboys. Facts related to actual take-offs and landings were of little consequence.

As quickly as he could, Caper pressed himself against the cloudy tinged glass of the Million Air® FBO, hands spread wide at eye-level. He could see no planes taking off or landing. The uproar behind him confirmed what everyone should have expected in any case: Hugh had just shot off a beaut. Caper turned to #3, said nothing, and mechanically proceeded to the lone door leading out to the strips.

Clouds had re-thickened almost back to their earlier texture, the wind loud and relentless. In the low distance, a single plane maintained a slow climb; Caper, leaning forward, paced in the same direction. From behind and to his right, he could tell that #3 shadowed. "That's them," the considerate TAC Air employee said in a soft shout.

Caper didn't turn around. "Don't think so. Plane's flying due east."

"They're flying into the wind," #3 corrected. "Have to. They'll start turnin' downwind any second."

Caper listened without responding or even nodding. Soon enough, the plane hooked south on a steady curve, tracing out a neat "J" as it sliced through the steadily gathering clouds. As if in synchronized sympathy, Caper rotated on his right heel. With his own eyes also held steady on the westbound plane, the TAC man thought he heard Caper mumble something that sounded like "truce."

The Cessna's black profile grew ever smaller; Caper tracked it until it had completely vanished.

He couldn't say how long he had been standing out on the edge of the strip, gazing vacantly at the western horizon. #3, his attentive guide, was nowhere in sight. The wind's roar had ebbed. From behind, a Spirit of St. Louis cruiser pulled up quietly only a few feet from his right hip and came to a noiseless stop, not a hint of a lurch.

"You're standing on an active aircraft apron." The cop voice floated out of a driver's side window lowered only a few inches. Nothing in it indicated rancor or aggression. "Any particular reason?"

"No," Caper said with a clarity that surprised even him. "I've got no reason."

The return trip wasn't as tempestuous as the rest of the Spirit safari seemed to have portended. Rain came pouring down once again, but in thick, slow, loud dollops, dropping at something like a vertical angle, and never in torrents. Had Caper's mind been of an entirely different stamp, he would have been sorely tempted to regard his radio an instrument of divine intercession. *All the sweet green icing*, Richard Harris wailed as only he could, *flowing down*. Travelling at ground level in a direction contrary to two airborne young men who had heeded the enduring call to go west, Caper thought about Ricky and his need for lines.

I recall the yellow cotton dress . . .

He headed straight towards the thickest part of the lemon, and tried to induce a catharsis. But he knew that giving the song's warbling complaint the shake was far beyond the reach of any act of self-will.

Someone left the cake out in the rain

I don't think that I can take it . . .

Exit signs soon alerted the eastbound driver that the St. Louis city limit was about to be broached, and that the Washington University/Danforth Campus could be found just a short distance to the north.

Caper got off the highway at Big Bend and headed south, back to Lindbergh's grounds.

* * *

Only moments before the final bell of the day would sound, Caper walked gingerly out of the Central Office building at the western edge of the sweeping campus, his cane a necessary crutch even on the wide concrete steps, modest as they were. When he reached level ground, half of his strides could do without the burgundy-and-gold stick, half could not. He hesitated briefly before turning left towards the rear parking lot blacktop, the added distance more than compensated for by the absence of stairs. He would loop back towards the playing fields, and then down into the lower building which housed the main office and, one floor lower still, the English department classrooms. This final descent would be effected via a soft, civilized concrete slope, gently declining to the bottom level.

Ascending the steady slant just as Caper threaded his way through the "Senior" section of the lot, Van Der Meyer walked deliberately past an outdoor tent set up by the Mother's Club, festooned in green and gold bunting. Nodding politely to the two mothers currently manning the booth, he appeared to be giving careful consideration to the scant remaining plants on offer, a few scattered bunches of golden dahlias punctuating shelves otherwise occupied by clumps of green zinnias. From the fields to the west, the beginnings of organized sound began to be heard, interrupted by distant and vaguely perturbed vocal commands. Still shambling through the parking lot, Caper soaked in the inimitable din of teenagers who had only seconds before been set free. Car engines came to life in waves, horns blared in mock-anger, and yet the simulated blasts somehow managed to be no less loud for that. With luck, perhaps he would be spared the sight of pair of Mustangs squaring off for a playful game of chicken.

He glanced to his left while waiting for a break in the first surge of departing cars. Activities underway on one of the fields told him that even this late in October, marching band season had not yet given over the baton to the sundry sit-down bands of winter. Turning his head to the right, he caught sight of Van Der Meyer parting company with the green-and-gold flora, perhaps with a promise that he would purchase an arrangement on the way back. Caper waved with his left hand, pointed to the fields with his cane, and walked over to the northern border of the student parking area, as soon as the stream of impatiently departing cars permitted his slow crossing.

Both teachers stood on the edge of the parking lot overlooking the newly renovated track and field, gazing through the shiny, high Cyclone fence. Intermittently, homeward-bound cars cruised behind them, many of them emitting a friendly shouted greeting. "Van Der Meyer!" "Doc C!" Caper had released the cane, setting it to rest at a soft angle against the lower links of the fence, glancing at it now and again. The teachers' arms, after acknowledging each verbal salute, slowly returned hands to pockets, or thoughtlessly resumed a folded posture. In front of them, more than half a dozen fields stretched far to the north and east. In the middle distance, the marching band was conducting drills. Fitfully, in between the sound of tires buzzing on the blacktop and steady student acknowledgement, Caper jerked his left ear up and center in puzzled recognition of the song the band was rehearsing. After some concentrated effort, his head tilting so as to maximize his hearing, he made out the hauntingly upbeat strains of the famous song, first introduced to the world when it swept the 1974 Eurovision Song Contest. *I was defeated, you won the war.* He allowed himself the shadow of a smile. *Napoleon did surrender.* Out of the corner of his eye, Caper observed that Van Der Meyer may have been moving his chin up and down in sync with the distant melody. *Always repeating itself.*

Shortly after, the band began to execute some sort of silent exercise beneath them at about the 50 of one of the fields. Marching without sound, not even spoken commands. Counter-clockwise. Low sunlight raked across the wide open spaces from the west, the tall, grand oaks creating dark nets of shadow on most of the fields. It was like those "dress" sessions a football team might go through the day before a game. You would put on the clean game uniform and walk or jog through the different formations. No hitting. Often no movement. Just a final check on formations. In this vast expanse, you could put a dozen or more teams through dress days. Or a dozen marching bands. Space to burn. *My, my.*

One lone drummer now tapped a soft regular pulse for the rest, a tentative signal, perhaps, that all should prepare to return to the world of sound. Caper watched and listened and tried to identify some of the sections. Color Guard. Used to be called the "Auxiliary," Linsenbardt once told him. The battery. Woodwinds. Brass. Two drum majors, standing atop mobile podiums stretched tall and green and gold, were carrying out instructions from the band director, whose stainless steel scissor lift remained immobile and collapsed, like a stretcher waiting for action. Caper and Van Der Meyer continued to stand elevated above the whole mobile composition, as each section and subsection strove for a pleasing or moving or just plain diverting general effect.

Presently the band shifted from their softly-timed choreography back into something resembling an actual performance. Motions were temporarily halted. Instruments were raised, arms rigidly angled. On the distant, low northern horizon, an airplane visible only as a brilliant gold dot left a vapor trail, clean and crisp at the one end. From the field, no sound as yet made its way back to the parking lot, though it appeared to be the case that at least some of the musicians had begun to play their instruments. Then, still standing at a remove and high above the green and gold and white lines, staring through the unbroken diamond patterns of the fence, Caper and Van Der Meyer simultaneously recognized the familiar strains of the exuberant 80's dance anthem, whose notes reached them, after this barely perceptible delay, undistorted by the journey. "What a Feeling." *Flashdance*. Laney. Welder and dancer. Fei and Kempf. Caper breathed in slowly and exhaled audibly. *I am rhythm now.*

"Forget about it, Cape," Van Der Meyer intoned without taking his eyes off the moving formations. "It's marching band."

More than ever, now at the worn end of a long search, Caper dwelt upon geography and location and formations, markings, structures, and lines constructed and enforced only to be destroyed, neglected. Dag Hammarskjöld, of all people, had hit upon this very nerve in a book that had been published several years after his sudden death, by plane crash, only a few months before Caper's birth. Exactly what caused the Congo-bound DC6 to plummet was a matter that continued to intrigue conspiracy seekers. Was the Swedish diplomat assassinated? A substantial number of people still wanted to make that the central question taken up by some sort of international variant of the Warren

Commission. A casualty in a battle over who would control the Congolese copper-mining industry? Caper supposed that the people who most fervently wished to pose that question would never be satisfied by any answer they would be likely to receive, and so would continue to demand that it be asked. He was certain, in any case, that even though he did not share a single shred of Hammarskjöld's spiritual inclinations, the diplomat's musings on permanence and impermanence resonated no less appreciably for that. After all, Caper had, in his own fashion, and in the words of the statesman, "followed the river/Towards its source."

As he drove into and out of the city on most days, Caper cruised past a church—or rather, a "worship center"—that bore more than a passing resemblance to a Holiday Inn Express. It had the trappings one routinely sees at Children's Hospitals nowadays—colorful, wackily-tilted lettering suggesting a gargantuan child using a giant neon crayon—together with the requisite electronic message board, more often than not programmed with a rolodex of evangelical puns ("Pre-Approved Master's Card: Apply Within"; "Enroll in our Prophet-Sharing Plan"). Exactly what goes on...? No doubt quite a few people could and would be eager to tell him if he bothered to investigate, given that the spacious parking lot was full on Sundays, as well as on one or two nights during the week. But Caper wouldn't.

Because their house stood at the intersection of three different streets (one a "Drive," the other two "Roads," an "East" and a "West"), the Capers had had far more than their share of mail mischief over the years. The original deed had them at one of the Roads, the county tax office on the other Road, and several of the utilities on the Drive. All sorts of miscommunication had ensued, and lasted to this very day. Caper smiled and shook his head as he recalled the most recent squabble: a curt, handwritten note on the electric bill, courtesy of one of the fastidious souls within the ranks of the postal service. The address had been circled by a lively hand, even as a phalanx of aggressive black-ink arrows positioned themselves like surrounding cannon, each one testifying to implacable postal impatience: "FIX THIS!!! NO SUCH ADDRESS!"

Strangers to the neighborhood were routinely confounded by a street-numbering system that suddenly and without warning, and in strict accordance with the county/city split, swapped odds for evens. A house ending in 33 inexplicably found itself smack next to a 34, in a single stroke condemning untold multitudes of address-seekers to flummoxing circuits round and round the divided ground, forever looking in exactly the wrong direction. In this neighborhood, playdate organizers, pizza delivery hopefuls, Tupperware home party hostesses— all would have to learn to wait at least a little while extra, as unsuspecting visitants attempted to negotiate the confounding lay of the land. Nor were modern navigational conveniences uniformly helpful. Software programs would begin to "complete" Caper's address just as soon as he had begun to make an online transaction, and would often doggedly resist any effort to change an East to a West, a Drive to a Road.

But what the hell, Caper thought, you never really know exactly where you are anyway. And that's probably mainly a good thing. Only four years earlier, having resided at their house for more than a dozen years, he and Iris had been abruptly informed that they were in fact part of a neighborhood "association." They had yearly dues to pay. There was even a legally-binding charter dating from 1950 or '51, one of whose stipulations contained very specific prohibitions regarding the residential presence of "colored people." Ghosts. The charter was promptly revised, against the wishes of how many of his neighbors Caper couldn't say. Seems a drunk driver had wrecked his car into the largest of the neighborhood traffic islands one dark night many years before. A legal settlement had been reached rewarding the association a substantial sum, a windfall that someone had arranged, in turn, to cover everyone's dues year by year. Four years previously the money had dried up. Now everyone had to pay what they should have been paying all along.

Climbing to the top step of his squat back stoop, Caper gripped the low railing separating the ascending concrete stairs from the motley collection of garbage containers below. In between the cans, wind-scuttled fast-food wrappers rasped along the red brick pad, mingling with restless, brittle oak leaves. He let the cane click softly on the metal rail, whose maroon paint had long ago made peace with numerous orange and brown rust blemishes pitting its surface. Facing east through a short alley of tall oaks, he could still make out, once again, the early evening stars. Out front, unseen, a slowly rolling car, quite possibly containing an aggrieved motorist, made its way from city to county, or from county to city. Caper listened attentively to the receding drone of the tires. Somewhere in the near distance, beneath the lights and under a canopy of branches only half burdened by their uniformly beige foliage, the invisible line marking the St. Louis City limit held steady. He knew it didn't matter where the line cut exactly. Diagonal. People would bother to find out when and if they needed to. They would choose sides, if they were looking to settle here, or they would seek other ground. Some would go on to sign their names on other lines, and thereby make commitments. The machinery of notarized deeds and official records, appropriate authorities and agents, functionaries and forms, would set about doing its imperfect work. People would go on living in one place or in another place, their whereabouts proximately known. They would be located.

Corrigenda, Errata and Other Stuff Like Thata

Max Fei graduated Magna Cum Laude from Washington University in May, 2013. He has never so much as cut a single class in his entire life. He is currently enrolled in Harvard University's School of Law (bummer!), where, undoubtedly, he will soon be elevated to the position of Dean. His high school English teacher thinks it highly unlikely that he has ever been a user of any tobacco products, let alone mentholated cigarettes. He thinks it even less likely that Max will ever become a gangster.

Peter Kempf is a tall, slim young man who would never dream of polluting his body with illegal substances. In addition to possessing major drumming chops, he plays the violin, viola, guitar, bass, ukulele, mandolin, trombone (!), and mellophone, not to mention various percussion instruments. He possesses a wide-ranging intellect, and is one of the most empathetic young men the author has ever had the privilege to know. He is not a bully.

Eric Pashia (not Pacchia) was in fact a good student, and has never answered to the name "Ricky." (One suspects that this may soon change.) His surname probably points to a Lebanese or Romanian, but not an Italian, lineage. He continues to play the 'bone in a couple of bands, one of them focusing on traditional eastern European music, the other a soundpainting group. The author does not know what kind of car Eric drives; nor does he have a solid grasp of what "soundpainting" is. He'll work on it.

The Lindbergh Mothers Club is, was, and always will be an irreproachable organization. All of its members are selflessly devoted to nurturing academic achievement in the Lindbergh School District, and (whether or not their modesty will permit them to acknowledge the fact) to maintaining Midwestern mostaccioli dominance in perpetuity.

The Spirit of St. Louis Marching Band is the crown jewel of the Lindbergh empire.

The staff at Washington University's Registrar are generous, knowledgeable, kind professionals, not Germanic robots. They are eager to help all who seek their services. Many thanks.

Jack Benning is a character born entirely of the author's imagination, fully warranting his identification with Athena, goddess of wisdom.

The author was motivated to compose these loosely joined vignettes early on the morning of May 23, 2013, at the very moment that he was made aware that a certain Miss Amelia Himebaugh had just published her *second* novel. Holding aloft a pristine copy of *See Clarence Fall*, he announced two things to the still-arriving throng of sleep-deprived juniors. "I'm going to purchase this novel," he enthused. Then, rashly: "And I'm gonna write one of my own." It was on that very morning, as Amy and her fellow students were sitting for their final exams, that a St. Louis City police lieutenant named John Gurney first knocked on Eric Van Der Meyer's door. The detective, after a protracted period of agonized soul-searching, would eventually opt for "Gus," deeming it the more suitable first name for a tough-talking homicide skipper. But never once in all that time did Van Der Meyer waver—not even ever so slightly—from his appointed teaching duties. He stood his post until the very end, without complaint.

Thank you for the inspiration, Amy.

This is a work of fiction.